D1407406

BRIGID KEMMERER started writing at school. Her first real 'novel' was about four brothers causing a ruckus in the suburbs. Those four brothers now live in the pages of the Elemental series, so Brigid likes to say she's had four teenage boys taking up space in her head for the last seventeen years. She lives near Annapolis, Maryland.

Brigid loves to hear from her fans and she has a smartphone surgically attached to her person. You can find out more about her and her books online at www.brigidkemmerer.com, on Facebook at Facebook.com/BrigidKemmererWrites or on Twitter @brigidkemmerer.

THE ELEMENTAL SERIES

STORM

THE ELEMENTAL SERIES

BRIGID KEMMERER

Much-in-Little

Constable & Robinson Ltd.
55–56 Russell Square
London WC1B 4HP
www.constablerobinson.com

First published in the US by K TEEN BOOKS,
an imprint of Kensington Publishing Corp., 2012

First published in the UK by Much-in-Little,
an imprint of Constable & Robinson Ltd., 2014

A copy of the British Library Cataloguing in
Publication Data is available from the British Library

ISBN: 978-1-47211-221-7 (paperback)
ISBN: 978-1-47211-340-5 (ebook)

Printed and bound by CPI Group (UK) Ltd, Croydon, CR0 4YY

1 3 5 7 9 10 8 6 4 2

For Michael:
Not every girl is lucky enough to marry her best friend.

ACKNOWLEDGMENTS

I originally wrote about these four brothers when I was in high school, and I'm in my thirties now, so thanking everyone along the way would be impossible.

That said, I'm going to try.

My mother has been a constant guide and inspiration in my life, and this book would never have been written without her unconditional love and support every step of the way—even if she hasn't read the whole thing. (Yet.) There's a good chance she still thinks it's about vampires.

Bobbie Goettler has been along for the ride since the beginning, since the Merrick brothers actually *were* vampires, since before I had kids and needed her advice practically every day, since before I knew what an amazing friend she would turn out to be. Bobbie, I never would have made it this far without you, and I can't thank you enough for everything you've done for me along the way.

Alison Kemper sent me a few chapters of her book for critique once, and I knew she had something special. We've been critique partners and friends ever since. She's read every word of this novel at least three times, and this book wouldn't be half as good without her input. Or her text messages.

Sarah J. Maas is my agency sister and friend, and it's been amazing going on this publication journey with you. I'll never forget holding my breath for days while I waited for you to get back to me on whether I could actually pull off writing a Young Adult novel.

Tamar Rydzinski is my brilliant agent. She's amazing and savvy and fabulous, and having her input during the development of this novel made all the difference in the world.

Alicia Condon and the entire team at K Teen have been wonderful since day one. I knew Alicia and I would get along right from the start, but she clinched the deal when we were supposed to be coming up with title ideas and we could only think of dirty ones. Thank you for everything.

Special thanks to Officer James Kalinosky of the Baltimore County Police Department for letting me know how much teenagers could get away with. If I bent the rules too far, it's my fault, not his.

Special thanks to Andrew McKay for helping me with trash talk when my husband turned out to be too nice a guy. (Oh, and for letting me borrow your name.)

Many, many people read this book and offered advice along the line. Special thanks to Kathy Fusto, Susan Gilmore, Thomas Berry, Jonathan Kemmerer, Sarah Fine, Gordon McKinney, Katrina Goettel, and Hannah Dwan. I know I'm leaving someone out, and if that person is you, thank you.

I never would have gotten this far without the unending support from my family. My husband, Michael, is my best friend, my support system, my confidant, and my inspiration. You've given me everything I've ever asked for and more, especially Jonathan, the best stepson in the whole entire world, and our two beautiful sons, Nicholas and Sam.

Extra special thanks to my sisters-in-law, Jenny Franklin and Tina Kasten, for reading everything I've written and offering support and suggestions.

And finally, many thanks to my in-laws, John and Dolly Kemmerer, for their love and support, especially for being willing to babysit at the drop of a hat.

CHAPTER 1

The self-defense class had been a waste of sixty bucks.

Becca hadn't felt like a victim going in, but she sure did now. When she'd seen the flyers around school advertising a three-hour session with a "women's defense specialist," she'd been eager to sign up. But the instructor—really just some college kid named Paul—had been texting half the time, happy enough to pocket their cash in exchange for halfhearted instructions about body blocks and eye gouges. She'd lose another Saturday scrubbing kennels to make this money back.

She'd left her cell phone in her locker, so after class she went to get it. Her best friend had left fourteen texts about some drama with her mom, so Becca stood in the shadowed corridor to write back. Quinn wasn't exactly patient.

The night air bit at her flushed skin when she slid out the side door, making her wish she'd brought a heavier jacket—but at least the promised rain had held off. Darkness cloaked the now empty parking lot, and her car sat alone near the security lamp in the middle of the cracked concrete.

This was exactly the kind of situation Paul had warned them about: secluded and solitary, offering little visibility. But Becca welcomed the darkness, the silence. She almost wished she smoked, so she could lie on the car's hood, flick a lighter, and make up names for the constellations while nicotine burned her lungs.

You should be so cool.

Her key found the lock, but the door handle to her aged Honda refused to release. She muttered the obligatory prayer, but nothing happened. Sometimes it took a curse.

Then she heard a muffled shout, a distant scuffle on pavement.

She froze, more curious than afraid. A fight? Here? She saw the combatants, just at the edge of the security light over by the east wing. Three guys fighting, two on one, it looked like. One caught another in a headlock, and the third swung a fist at the captive's midsection while he struggled.

They weren't saying anything, making the violence cartoonish and unreal, like watching an action movie on mute.

The kid in the headlock twisted free, his liberty quickly rewarded with a fist to the head, sending him into a stagger. Another punch brought him to the ground.

Then he didn't move. One of the other guys kicked him in the stomach.

She heard *that*. And the sound made her remember that she was just standing in the middle of a parking lot, watching.

Becca dropped beside her car. Breath whistled into her lungs. She didn't want to open the door and have the sound or the light draw their attention. She'd call the police. An ambulance. The whole frigging cavalry.

She thrust her hand into her bag for her cell phone.

Dead.

Damn Quinn and her fifty bazillion texts. Becca swore and punched the phone against the pavement. The cover snapped off, skittering away under her car.

Helpful, Bex.

She peeked around the front bumper. The fallen boy lay in a crumpled pile.

They kicked him again.

"Get up," she whispered.

He didn't.

She tried to make out who the kids were. Some senior boys got off on violence. She knew a few of them firsthand—some only by reputation. The Merrick twins, maybe?

They were circling now, like vultures. One nudged the fallen boy with his foot.

Then he kicked him. "Get up."

"Yeah," said the other one. "How'd you get rid of them?"

The voices were sharp, cruel. She held her breath, wishing she could help somehow. But what could she do? Run at them with her water bottle and the splintered plastic of her cell phone? Maybe she could practice that "confident woman's walk" Paul had demonstrated.

If only she had a weapon, something to level the playing field.

You idiot. You do have a weapon.

Her car.

Adrenaline made for a good ally. She'd barely thought it before she was crawling through the back door and climbing into the driver's seat, driving straight at them.

She had the satisfaction of watching her headlights illuminate their panic; then they were scrambling, diving to get out of the way. Not the Merrick twins, not anyone she could make out at all. Her foot punched the brakes at the last second, jerking the car to an abrupt stop.

"I called the cops!" she shouted out the window, feeling her heart kick against her ribs. "They're on their way!"

But the boys were already bolting into the darkness.

Her fingers refused to release the steering wheel for the longest moment. She finally pried them free, and, leaving the engine running, eased out of the car.

She wished she'd turned the car differently, because the boy was mostly in shadow, away from the headlights. He lay face-down, the thick dark hair on his head matted with blood at one temple. They'd done a number on his face: More blood glistened on his swollen brow. Abrasions scored his cheek in various directions, as though he'd met the pavement intimately, and more than once. His black hoodie had taken a beating, and his jeans weren't much better, sporting a tear down the side of one leg. He was breathing, a rattle of air pulling into his lungs, ending on a slight wheeze each time.

She'd never seen someone beaten so badly.

"Hey." She gave his shoulder a little shake. He didn't move.

Those boys had run off on foot. She had no idea if they'd stay gone.

Now what, genius?

She left her car engine running, its headlights cutting a path in the darkness. She reached inside the door and pulled out her half-empty water bottle. She crouched beside him, feeling the cold grit of the pavement through her jeans. Then, using her hand to slow the flow, she trickled water down the side of his face.

At first, nothing happened. She watched in macabre fascination as the water pulled blood across his jaw, trailing over his split lip.

Then he came to with a vengeance.

Becca wasn't ready for that, for him to explode off the ground in a fury, his fists swinging before his eyes were open.

She was lucky he was injured. She barely got out of his way.

His momentum didn't last long, however. He staggered to a knee, planting a hand against the pavement. He coughed and it shook his body; then he spit what looked like blood.

Now that he wasn't lying on the ground, she recognized him. Christopher Merrick. Chris. He was a junior, like she was, but she couldn't think of two words they'd ever exchanged. He was the Merrick twins' younger brother, the type of guy who'd slouch in the back of the classroom and stare at the teachers with disdain, daring them to call on him. People left him alone, but that's how he seemed to like it. An outsider by choice.

Unlike her.

"You gave me water," he rasped, his head down.

His voice startled her, made her realize she was just standing there, clutching her water bottle so hard it made the plastic crackle.

"Yeah," she said. "Those guys—they could come back—"

"Are you stupid?"

The derision in his voice was like a punch to the chest. "Funny. I was just asking myself that."

"No. I just—I could have hurt—" Chris coughed again, then pressed his forehead to the ground, making a low sound in his throat. He spit blood again. She felt like she was standing in the middle of one of those cable crime dramas—the kind where the violence is too much for network television.

"Do you have a cell phone?" She cast a quick look out into the darkness, but the night remained still. "You need an ambulance."

"I need a damn rainstorm." He seemed to laugh, but it choked him. "A drizzle. Fog even."

He was delirious. "Can you get into the car? I can drive you to the hospital."

"No. Home."

"*Whatever*. Climb in the car. Those guys could come back, and I'm not—"

A hand closed on her arm, hot and meaty and painful. A voice spoke from the darkness. "Did you think we wouldn't wait and see?"

"Big surprise." The other voice now. "No sirens."

That hand swung her around. This guy didn't go to her school. He looked older. College, maybe. Short blond hair framed a severe face, all angles and lines.

Something scraped on the pavement. "This is going to suck," said Chris.

The other one was dragging him to his feet.

Becca knew how to swallow pain and keep emotion off her face. "Let me go. I didn't call the cops, but he did."

Those sharp features cracked into a smile. "We took his phone."

"Good try," said Chris. He coughed again. The other guy punched him in the side, and he dropped to the pavement.

The one on her arm shoved her up against her car. It hurt. She squealed before she could help it.

"You should have driven away, sweetheart."

"Nah," said the other, his dark hair making him look sinister. "That right there is dessert."

Then she recognized his voice. Seth Ramsey. A senior. And part of the reason she'd been in that self-defense class.

His friend reached out to cup her chin. "Yeah. Dessert."

Maybe it was Seth's presence; maybe it was the implication in their words. Whatever, her mind didn't think, her body just moved. The water bottle went flying and her arm swung.

Eye gouge.

Something squished under her fingers. He dropped her arm like a hot potato, shoving her away, flying back to put a hand to his face. "Bitch! You bitch!"

Holy crap! It works! She was choking on her breath, but she was free.

"Shut *up*, Tyler," Seth hissed. "She might not have called the cops, but you're gonna—"

"Freeze. Right there."

At first she thought the cops *had* shown up. But it was Chris, her water bottle in his hand. He'd found his feet somehow, and though he looked a little unsteady, their assailants went still.

Chris drew a shaky breath. "Back off. Or I'll mean that literally."

Mean what literally?

"Yeah, right," said Seth. "It's one bottle."

Chris shook it. The water sloshed. "Try me."

He had to be out of his mind.

But they backed off. "Chill out, man," said Tyler. "We're just screwing around."

"Yeah." Chris gave that harsh laugh again, then swiped at his swollen lip. "Feels like it. Take another step back."

They did.

She stared at Chris, as if her water bottle had somehow morphed into a gun, or a switchblade, or anything more intimidating than a plastic cylinder that read *Aquafina*.

"Becky," he said. "Get in the car."

"Becca," she corrected automatically. Her voice was breathy, her hands still clenched in fists.

"For god's sake—" His eyes slid left. "Just get in the car."

She scrambled into the driver's seat, her hands fumbling for the seat belt. Just when she wondered if he was going to get in, he yanked the back door open and almost fell into the car.

"Drive."

Her foot smacked the accelerator and the car shot forward, swerving toward the building. Her heart beat on the back of her tongue, and she yanked the wheel. The car fishtailed before straightening out.

Chris swore. "Drive without killing me." He coughed. "I should have clarified."

She swung the car out of the parking lot and onto the main road, accelerating like a bank robber. Her breath was loud in the confines of the car. Houses whipped by, but she had yet to pass another vehicle.

She barely hesitated at the stop sign at the end of Old Mill Road, screeching through the turn.

"Hey." Chris's voice was quiet. "Take it easy. Their car was on the other side of the cafeteria. You can slow down."

She eased her foot off the pedal. "What did they want? That one guy doesn't go to our school."

"Not anymore." He paused. "Thanks."

She swallowed. What was the right response? *"You're welcome"* didn't quite seem to cover it. Then again, his *"thanks"* didn't, either. "Do you want me to take you to the hospital?"

"Nah. Home." His breath hitched, and she took a glance at him in the rearview mirror. His eyes were half closed, his voice ironic. "If you don't mind."

She didn't think that was a good idea, but what was she going to do, wrestle him into the ER? "Aren't your parents going to freak when they see you?"

That rough laugh again. "I'd probably freak if I saw *them*." A peal of thunder interrupted his words. Raindrops appeared on the windshield. "Figures," he muttered. "*Now* it rains."

Maybe he had a head injury. "Where do you live?"

"Just north of the fire station. On Chautauga. We're the blue house at the end of the court."

She nodded, her knuckles white on the steering wheel. He fell silent for a while, and she glanced in the rearview again to find his eyes on her. Blue eyes. Nice eyes, she noticed, sharp and intelligent under that fringe of dark hair.

Then he smirked. With the cuts and bruises on his face, it made him look a little scary. "You're probably thinking I owe you my life."

She jerked her eyes back to the road. "No," she snapped. "Just sixty bucks."

"You charge for the hero act?"

His voice sounded light, but she still heard the wheeze behind the words. Another quick glance in the mirror revealed his head had fallen back against the seat.

"I really think I should take you to the hospital. You probably have broken ribs." *And a concussion.* "They can call your parents from there."

"Why? You think they have a Ouija board?"

She glanced at him worriedly, and his eyes opened fully. "My parents are dead, *Becca*. Do you think you could open a window?"

Maybe the fresh air would help. She pushed the button to drop his window a few inches, not wanting to let the rain in.

He sighed. "Thanks."

He fell silent for a mile, and when they came to the red light by the community college, she turned in her seat. His eyes were closed.

"Chris?"

He didn't answer.

"Chris."

Nothing.

"Damn it," she whispered.

Chapter 2

The blue house at the end of Chautauga Court stood two stories high on half an acre of land. It was easily twice the size of her own, the kind of property better suited to Labrador retrievers and backyard barbecues than clotheslines and broken-down vehicles. Lights blazed in the windows of the main level, a clear sign someone was home.

He'd said his parents were dead. Did he and his brothers live with grandparents?

She parked behind a mini-SUV in the driveway, one of those newer hybrids. Dark red and gleaming in the light over the garage, the car didn't seem like a grandparent kind of vehicle. Vibrant landscaping enhanced the front of the house, the expensive kind, lush and modern. Thick, sculpted shrubs and greenery crawled along the walkway, giving way to rhododendron bushes and clusters of mums beside the porch steps.

Someone took good care of this yard. Maybe this wasn't the right house. But it was the only blue one. Could she really knock on the door and say some kid was bleeding and unconscious in her backseat?

Chris still sat upright, but his breathing sounded worse, a rush and whistle before the wheeze. She shoved on the driver's side door until it gave, jammed her hands into her sweatshirt pockets, and hunched her shoulders against the cool September rain.

As she approached the house, she prepared herself for either young, hip grandparents or maybe a middle-aged aunt and uncle. Instead, a rough-cut guy in his early twenties yanked open the door.

Becca stood there in shock for a moment, feeling rain drip from her hair down her collar.

He looked a little like Chris, she supposed, with dark hair and a strong jaw. But Chris's hair was short, his clothes fitted and current, while this guy looked like he woke up in the morning and didn't give a crap. His hair was longer, pulled into a haphazard ponytail, his tee shirt faded and worn. Calling his jeans threadbare would be a compliment. She wasn't surprised to see his feet were bare.

His eyes—brown, not blue—narrowed. "A little old to be selling cookies, aren't you?"

Jerk. "Does Chris Merrick live here?"

"Yeah." He gave her the up-and-down again, and she wasn't a fan of his expression. He looked like he wanted to say something else, but settled on, "He's not home."

"No kidding. He's unconscious in my backseat."

"He's *what?*" His eyes narrowed and finally seemed to focus on her. Without waiting for an answer, he leaned back to yell into the house. "Nick!"

Then he put a hand on her shoulder, moved her to the side—not gently, either—and strode off the porch. She was torn between following him and waiting, but the sky split and flashed with lightning, followed by a crack of thunder. She shivered and rubbed her arms, then backed up to stand closer to the house.

"Scared of storms?"

She jumped. The voice had come from behind her, and she forced her hands to her sides, ready to feign nonchalance. "No," she lied, starting to turn. "I'm just—"

Face-to-face with hotness.

Her tongue stumbled for a minute. She'd seen the Merrick twins around school, of course. But catching a glimpse down the hall wasn't the same as being six inches away from one of them, getting an eyeful of the way his long-sleeve tee clung to muscled shoulders, or of the faint shadow of stubble along his jaw, or the depth of blue in his eyes.

Eyes that studied her a little too closely just now, a spark of amusement there.

Nick Merrick knew exactly what he looked like, and he knew she was looking.

She squared her shoulders and pretended she couldn't feel the flare of heat on her cheeks. "Your brother got in a fight." She gestured to her car, to where the scruffy guy was half kneeling on the backseat, one leg braced on the driveway. "I brought him home."

Nick looked past her and sighed, almost with exasperation. "Damn it, Gabriel."

His twin. She shook her head. "Chris."

He'd been moving toward the steps, but stopped short and looked at her. "Chris?"

"Yeah. Your brother. Chris." Could she possibly stop sounding like an idiot? "He was in a fight behind the gym, and—"

Boom! Thunder shook the house. She flinched and lost her words.

Nick wasn't listening to her anyway. He jumped off the porch to sprint down the walk, and was now helping the other guy pull Chris out of the car. Somehow they got him supported between them, leaving her car door open to maneuver him onto the walkway. Chris seemed to be trying to help, his feet catching the pavement.

"Can I help?" she called.

The ponytailed guy glared up at her. "No. You've done enough."

Nick swore. "Leave her alone, Michael."

Like she'd been the one to beat Chris to pieces. "Look, I *wanted* to take him to the hospital—"

Thunder cracked. The sky opened up.

The rain fell loud and hard, a blanket of white noise that filled her ears and trapped her on the porch. The three on the walkway were drenched immediately. Rain caught the blood on Chris's face and pulled it down his chin. Lightning flashed, making his skin paler, his bruises darker. In the two minutes she'd been standing on the porch, she'd forgotten how bad it was. He'd taken a lot of damage.

They wrangled him up the steps. His knees buckled as soon as they were under cover.

Nick grunted and caught his weight. "Come on, Chris."

"Where was he tonight?" the other guy snapped. "I thought he was at school. If Gabriel got him into—"

"He was at school," she offered. "In the parking lot—"

"Yeah?" Now Michael turned that glare on her. "And what were *you* doing there?"

"Save it for later, Michael." Water was dripping from Nick's hair into his eyes. He wasn't looking at her, but at the other guy, and he jerked his head toward the doorway. "Let's just get him upstairs."

They mostly carried Chris through the doorway, leaving her fidgeting on the porch. She put a hand on the doorframe, wondering if they expected her to come in, to wait, to explain.

You've done enough.

Ingrate.

The back door to her car was open anyway, rain probably soaking the seat. She pulled her collar up against her neck and sprinted down the walkway, feeling rain beat against her hair and slap her cheeks.

Half her backseat was drenched. She swore and slammed the door, then fought with the handle of the driver's side door.

Lightning lit up the sky. "Hey."

The voice spoke out of the darkness, just beside her ear. She whirled, flattening against her car, thinking of Tyler and Seth and what they'd threatened to do.

But it was just Nick, his eyes dark this far from the lights on the porch. "You want to come in for a minute?"

He seemed to speak right through the rain, his voice intense, as if they weren't near strangers standing in the middle of a downpour.

His eyebrow raised, and he pushed wet hair off his forehead, making it spike a little from the rain. "How about it?"

Becca swung away to fight with her door handle. "Save it. The other guy didn't exactly roll out the welcome mat."

He reached out a hand and held the door closed—like it needed the help. "Michael's okay. Look—" He hesitated, and she watched the water sluice down his forearm. "Tell me what happened to Chris."

There. True concern. Enough to make her turn back around and swipe the rain out of her eyes. It made her think of Chris's half-lucid statements from the parking lot. *I need a frigging rainstorm.*

She stared up at his brother. "I'm getting soaked."

"So come in. Dry off." His expression darkened, along with his voice. "Tell me whose ass we need to kick."

Nick gave her a towel.

He flung it, really. She was dripping on his kitchen tiles, and he tossed it from the doorway.

"Let me change my shirt," he said. "You want me to get you something?"

She stared at him for a second, wondering whether he meant food or something to wear. When she realized her mouth was working but nothing was coming out, she quickly shook her head.

Then she was alone, long enough that she finally dropped into a chair and shivered. No woman lived in this house; she could tell that just from the kitchen. The paper towel holder sat empty and a stack of dishes hid in the sink. A pot of coffee had been made at some point, left to cool in the carafe long ago. But the counters appeared mostly clean, simple granite that still had a shine and didn't sport any spilled food. No curtains hung over the windows by the sink, no soft hand towels hung on the oven.

Becca's mom rarely had a chance to cook, but her kitchen was a place of warmth, with fresh fruit always spilling out of a bowl on the counter, a snack drawer that never went empty, and a feeling of welcome that never went cold.

This kitchen should have been nice, with a set of French doors leading out to a back porch and enough space for a large table and a cooking island. But the lack of family touches left it feeling institutional.

She gave her hair a cursory squeeze with the towel. She'd never been one of those girls who looked sexy with wet hair. Her dark strands weighed heavy on her neck, clumped and tangled from the water. She finger combed them away from her face, knowing it would leave her cheeks stark and pale, making her gray eyes appear huge. She zipped her damp sweatshirt all the way up, though it seemed to seal the cold to her body. Sitting in a house full of boys in a wet tee shirt didn't seem the best way to uphold her reputation.

Reputation. Ha.

The front door slammed, followed by heavy, clomping footsteps in the hallway. She sat up straighter, rolling the towel into a ball in her lap. Would this be a real adult, someone older and more authoritative than Michael? Nick wasn't back yet, and she had no idea how to explain her presence.

Those footsteps came all the way to the kitchen. No adult. Just a flash of déjà vu: Nick's twin.

Since they were identical, he was every inch the looker his brother was. But Gabriel was filthy, his hair wet and disheveled, a streak of dirt across one cheek. His wet hoodie had seen better days, and his shorts fared little better. Old Mill High's colors of bright red and blue tried to peek through grass stains and mud, but it was a losing battle. He wore shin guards and cleats, and he'd tracked dirt and bits of grass into the kitchen.

Her mother would have had a fit.

Becca opened her mouth to explain herself, expecting him to be surprised, to introduce himself, to ask what she was doing there.

She'd have settled for his acknowledging her presence.

He barely glanced at her on his way to the refrigerator. She watched him pull a jug of red Gatorade off the shelf and drink half of it while he surveyed the rest of the refrigerator contents.

"Hi," she said, just in case there was any way he'd missed the living, breathing female sitting in full view of the doorway.

He didn't turn. "'Sup." Then he swung the refrigerator door closed, slapping the Gatorade bottle on the counter while he riffled through cabinets. He must have been satisfied when he came up with a package of chocolate chip cookies, because he grabbed his drink and dropped into the chair across from her.

He smelled like grass and dirt and sweat, and he looked so much like Nick that she had to stop herself from staring.

He ripped open the package and pulled three out for himself, then shoved the cookies toward the middle of the table. "Want some?"

"I'm good. Thanks." She had to clear her throat to state the obvious. "You're . . . ah . . . probably wondering what I'm doing here."

"Nah." He took a swig of Gatorade, then wiped his mouth on his sleeve. "Finding a girl in the kitchen isn't exactly an oddity around here."

"Charming."

He glanced up at that, a glint of wicked humor in his eye. "I'm sure *you're* special, though."

It should have pissed her off, after Michael's brusque attitude and Nick's hey-baby-why-don't-you-come-inside. But Gabriel's teasing was straightforward, challenging, in a way. He expected her to girl it up, to huff and fold her arms. She could tell.

"Not special at all." She changed her mind and leaned in to take a cookie. "I just heard my number called and thought I'd better show up."

He grinned. "No way you're here for Nicky."

Was that an insult? She frowned. "No. I brought Chris home."

"Shouldn't that be the other way around?" He pulled a fourth cookie from the pack.

She shook her head and opened her mouth to explain, but his eyes narrowed, his gaze turning more appraising. "Wait. I know you from somewhere."

Probably, if he was on the soccer team. Drew McKay was the team captain, and thanks to Drew and his friends, she'd been the subject of locker room speculation since school started a few weeks ago.

She took another cookie. "Great detective work, Sherlock. We go to the same school."

He made a dismissive gesture. "That's not it. What's your name?"

Of course he wouldn't know. She got a quick flash of how this would go.

Becca, she'd say. *Becca Chandler.*

His sharp eyes would darken in recognition, and that smile would turn into a smirk, and she'd spend three minutes listening to idle commentary about her supposed talents.

Maybe not three minutes. She'd gotten better at walking away.

"Becca," she said. Then, knowing boys rarely gave up a chance to talk about themselves, she quickly added, "You play soccer?"

He nodded and took another swig of Gatorade. "Well, technically, Nick does. You're not allowed to play on more than two varsity teams per year."

She raised an eyebrow. "You pretend to be your brother? And no one has a problem with that?"

"Who would have a problem with it?"

The principal. The school board. The team. She stared at him. "Do people know you do it?"

"Maybe." He shrugged. "Who could prove it?"

"Me." Nick came through the doorway, wearing dry jeans and a black tee shirt. He pulled out the chair beside his twin and slid into it.

"You don't care." Gabriel didn't glance at him, just slid the cookies over. Nick pulled out three.

She wanted to ask how Chris was, but she didn't know him that well and asking felt awkward. She fidgeted with the wet sleeve of her sweatshirt.

Nick was watching her. "Chris is pretty banged up." He paused. "Thanks for bringing him home."

Gabriel turned. "What happened to Chris?"

Nick nodded her way. "Ask her."

Becca pushed wet hair behind her ear. "I only caught the tail end of it. Some guys were beating the crap out of him."

Gabriel's anger flared like a flame on a match. That easy smile vanished and he came halfway out of his chair. "Some guys were beating the crap out of *Chris?* Who? Where?"

His vehemence took her by surprise, and it took her a second to get it together. Becca was glad to have an answer to give him. "Ah . . . behind the gym. Seth Ramsey was one of them. The other one doesn't go to our school, but Chris said he used to. I think his name was Tyler."

"Tyler." Gabriel cracked his knuckles, then rolled his shoulders. "I swear to god, Michael should have killed that stupid prick when he had the chance—"

"Easy." Nick grabbed his brother's arm. "Chris was awake?"

"Yeah." They were both looking at her a little too intently, and she remembered why she'd first considered that they might be the aggressors in the parking lot. She wanted to push her chair back a few feet. "Well, he was unconscious when I chased the guys off, but I gave him some water—"

"You chased them off?" Gabriel's voice was incredulous. He gave her a once-over. "By yourself?"

"You gave him water?" said Nick.

"Yes." She wet her lips and glanced between them. "And yes." She hesitated, then explained what had happened.

When she got to the part where Chris confronted his attackers with the water bottle, she couldn't make it sound sensible. She must have remembered it wrong.

Freeze. Right there.

Or I'll mean that literally.

"Why'd you give him water?" Michael was leaning against the doorway molding now, his arms folded across his chest.

The question caught her off guard. "I don't know—he was unconscious, and my phone was dead—and—"

"But you knew."

Was she missing something? "I knew what?"

"Don't play with me. You knew the water would wake him up."

WTF? She glanced at the twins, but they were no help. "I hoped it would."

"Of course you did."

Nick sighed. "Jesus, Michael. Bring it down a notch. She goes to our school. She's in Chris's class."

Gabriel dropped back into his chair and flashed irritated eyes at the doorway. "Yeah, Birkenstock. If you want to get worked up about something, why don't you take a look in the empty fridge?"

Michael's eyes didn't leave hers. "You don't find this all a little convenient? Tyler's twice her size. Go take a look at what he did to Chris and tell me you believe he'd let her drive off."

Gabriel lost the sneer and turned to look at his twin. "He's that bad?"

Nick glanced at Michael, then nodded. "Pretty bad."

Now all three of them were looking at her, and she could feel the aggression in the air.

"Look, I was just trying to help Chris." She glanced at Nick and balled up the towel to set it on the table. "I told you who did this. I didn't mean to get in the middle of some . . . I don't know, turf war, or gang thing, or whatever you guys are—"

"Save it." Michael straightened until he filled the doorway, until she became very aware that he blocked the path out of the kitchen. "You expect me to believe you scared off Tyler all by yourself? And he just *let you* drive Chris home?"

"Tyler grabbed me." She swallowed, feeling guilty for absolutely no reason whatsoever. "I jabbed him in the eyes and we jumped in the car."

Gabriel smiled, and it stole some of the fury from his expression. "I like this girl."

"You jabbed him in the eyes," said Michael.

"Yeah."

"Tyler."

Her mouth was dry, and she had to wet her lips again. "What, you want a demonstration?"

He stepped into the kitchen. Instinct forced her out of the chair, and she backed away, toward the cooking island.

But he stopped, his eyes narrowed. "What are you afraid of?"

She was beginning to wish she'd just left Chris in the driveway. Her key ring was in her pocket, and she felt her fingers curl around the steel, her house key and car key poking through her knuckles. "You."

"But I thought you were just *trying to help*." The sarcasm came through loud and clear. Michael took another step toward her. "Why would you be *afraid* of me?"

She didn't understand his tone. Some of it felt like concern—but some of it felt like crazy-serial-killer. Becca took another step back, putting the cooking island between her and him, before realizing this felt very much like cat and mouse. "Stop it."

He stared back at her. "You're not going anywhere until you tell me the truth."

Gabriel pulled a cookie from the package and sat back in his chair. "My money's on the girl."

My money's not.

Michael took another step closer "How about it? You want to try another story?"

He stood in the gap between the island and the counter now, blocking her path to the doorway. He was close enough to touch, close enough to grab her. She kept hearing Paul's words in her head, bits and pieces from the class. *Eye contact. Target. Control. Balance.*

Then she was doing it. She swung her fist into his midsection, trying to scrape past him into the hallway. He caught her arms.

"Hey," he said. "Wait a second—"

She swung for his face with the keys, but missed and got his shoulder. She tried to kick him, to knee him in the groin, anything. She had no idea if her hits were successful. His fingers caught at her hoodie and she slid out of it. She felt her shirt ride up to her chest, but she didn't care. The wet fabric pulled free, and then she was loose, bolting for the doorway.

She felt him right behind her.

Her feet slapped the slate floor of the foyer; then her hand caught the doorknob. The door swung wide and she exploded into the darkness, slipping on the wet steps, skidding in the grass on the way to her car.

Thunder growled in the sky, and the grass gave way to mud, clutching her sneakers. Her knees hit the ground. Her hands squished into the dirt. She slipped and slid, struggling for purchase, but couldn't find her footing. Her fingers seemed to tangle in the grass, as if the roots grabbed her hands and held her down.

A hand seized her arm and hauled her to her feet. The landscape spun as her eyes tried to keep up. She saw the brightly lit front of the house, the twins on the porch, the frustration in Michael's face as he tried to get hold of her.

And behind him, on the second floor, Chris's face in a window, watching the whole thing.

Her breath caught. She pulled to get free, but Michael's grip was secure. "Just wait a minute," he said. "I'm not going to—"

Thunder broke again. Rain poured down, slicking her skin.

She felt stronger suddenly, invigorated by the chill in the rain. She fought Michael, wrestling against his hold. Her arm slid through his hand as if the water pried him loose. Her feet found traction as the mud thickened, and she was suddenly five feet away. Then ten, her feet on the pavement.

She flung the back door open and jumped into the backseat of her car, grabbing for the handle to lock herself in. Her hand jammed the lock down, and she scrambled over the center console to get into the driver's seat.

The key was firing the ignition when she realized Michael hadn't pursued her. He was already back on the porch, standing in the light of the doorway.

Chris was no longer in the window. Rain pounded on the windshield.

Her breath was shaking.

No one was coming after her.

He'd grabbed her, right? Come after her in the kitchen?

Or had she misread a situation again? She watched; they were ignoring her now, filing back through the front door of the house as if she'd left like a normal guest.

So she put the car in gear and backed down the driveway.

CHAPTER 3

Chris lay in the dark and listened to the rain strike the house. Breathing hurt. Everything hurt. He didn't bother to strip the wet clothes from his body, and he'd left his windows open so he could inhale the dampness in the air. The rain called to him, each drop begging him to join the downpour, whispering promises he didn't quite understand yet.

But the house was quiet. His brothers were quiet. Solitude and silence were precious things, and he'd cling to them as long as possible. Experience told him it wouldn't be long.

Rain came through the screen, droplets collecting on the wood surface of his desk.

An invitation.

"Later," he said.

God, was that his voice? He sounded like a ninety-year-old chain-smoker.

His doorknob turned slowly, and Chris sighed, listening to each click of the knob until the door swung open. A triangle of light from the hallway arced across the back wall of his bedroom, but he didn't bother to turn his head.

He knew it was Michael before his brother spoke. "I thought you might have fallen asleep."

Chris didn't say anything. He stared at the ceiling and waited for the reprimand that was sure to come. For the fight, for using his abilities, for helping Becky.

Becca. He smiled.

"What are you smiling at?"

That killed it. "Nothing." Chris lifted a hand. "Say your piece and get out."

Michael hesitated.

Chris hated this. This distance, this parental posturing. He could still remember the summer he'd turned nine, when Michael had just gotten his driver's license. His brother hadn't taken friends for his first drive, he hadn't taken the twins, who were older and sharper and got everything they wanted. He'd taken *Chris*. They'd driven fast, clinging to curves on the back roads all the way to Annapolis. Then they'd sat on the hood of Dad's truck and drunk sodas and watched boats on the Severn River.

He used to think Michael walked on water.

Now he mostly thought he was an asshole.

His brother stepped into the room. Chris felt him move close, but he kept his eyes fixed on the ceiling. When Michael wound up for a lecture, it was usually agonizing. Maybe he'd actually sit on the corner of the bed or something, just for effect.

But Michael remained standing, and his voice was low. "You want to sit out back for a while?"

Chris swung his head to the side and his vision swam for a moment. When his eyes decided to focus, they looked up at his brother. With the light at his back, Michael's face was in shadow, his brown eyes very dark, the way their mother's had been. The rest of them had blue eyes, like their father.

When their parents died, Chris hated waking in the middle of the night, wanting his mother, finding no comfort in his older brother. He'd resented seeing those eyes in Michael's face, and finding nothing he needed in them.

Michael was still waiting for an answer. "Come on," he said. "I'll sit with you."

The rain had formed a puddle along the edge of the desk. Pleading.

Chris nodded. "All right."

The twins sat in the kitchen, textbooks scattered across the table. Nick was working, while Gabriel rocked back in a chair, eating cookies and heckling his brother.

When they came through the kitchen doorway, Gabriel stopped short. The legs of his chair hit the ground.

"That son of a bitch," he said. Lightning flashed in the panels of sky visible through the window over the sink.

Chris gave him half a smile because a full one hurt. "You should see the other guy."

"Oh, I'm going to see him—in a pile of broken bones. Here. Have a cookie."

Chris shook his head, and his vision swam again.

Michael caught his arm. "You need to sit down."

Chris jerked away from him. It hurt more than it should have, and he had to grab the back of one of the kitchen chairs. "I've got it."

Nicholas had set his pencil down and was watching him. Chris didn't find any pity in his expression; Nick was good like that. "Where'd they find you?"

Chris looked out the window again. He'd stayed to watch Gabriel's practice, packing his things when the sky promised rain and the coach called for the players to take a long run. They lived three miles from school, but he'd never minded the walk.

Or he never had until tonight.

"Behind the school," he finally said.

"They come looking?"

Chris started to nod, then thought better of it when his vision swam. "Yeah. They said they're calling the Guides."

"They always say that," said Nick.

"I think this time they might mean it."

"They won't," said Michael. "They made a deal. We keep it, they keep it."

"They keep it, my ass." Gabriel rocked back in his chair

again. His eyes were on Michael, his voice acidic, full of judgment. "How long are you going to let them keep pulling this?"

"Don't start." Michael gave Gabriel's chair a good push, setting it straight. He pointed to the pile of notebooks. "Work."

Gabriel shoved back from the table, a motion full of promised violence. "What, you only have a pair when it comes to chasing a girl out of the house?"

Chris sighed and let go of the chair to turn for the back door. No one stopped him.

The air was cold, and the rain felt good on his bruised face. He gingerly pulled off his tee shirt and eased into one of the wooden Adirondack chairs. If he was patient, if he lay there long enough, the rain would offer to fix his injuries, would pull the bruises from his skin and feed him strength. He usually got sick of waiting and tried to force it. That just left him exhausted and pissed off, and he hurt too much to bother with it now. Michael said control would come, with time.

If Tyler and his buddies didn't kill him first.

Chris didn't hear the sliding door, but the rain told him when Michael stepped onto the porch.

He didn't bother to look over. "Fight over that fast?"

Michael dropped into the chair beside him. "We didn't fight."

Chris didn't buy that for a minute. "You got it all out of your system with Becca?"

"Who is she, Chris?"

Chris kept his eyes on the clouds overhead and replayed the events in the parking lot. Becca had been kneeling over him, pouring water across his face. He'd come up swinging, sure they were bringing him around to finish him off. Water was all too happy to lend itself to fury—she'd been lucky he didn't knock her flat. Or worse.

Chris shook his head slightly. "She's nobody. Just a girl."

"I think you should stay away from her."

"Looks like you already took care of that for me."

"You know what I mean." Michael paused. "I don't like her story."

"Well," said Chris, turning his head to the side. "*You* weren't there."

That one hit its target. Michael was silent for the longest moment. "What do you want me to do, Chris?"

Something. Anything. Chris looked back up at the clouds, keeping his eyes open to the rain. "Nothing, Michael."

His brother rolled back in the chair, staring up at the same dark sky, letting the downpour soak him, too. The rain didn't talk to him, but Chris knew Michael felt something when the drops struck the earth.

"I hate this," Chris finally said.

"I know."

"We're stronger than they are."

"That's the problem. You know that." Michael paused. "Don't let them bait you."

Chris pointed to his face. "Is that what this is? Baiting me?"

"Damn it, Chris. They want you to lose control. You know that, right?"

He did know that. Didn't Michael *know* he knew that?

"I want to leave," said Chris.

Michael sighed, a sound full of *oh-not-this-again.* "And go where? Just how long do you think we could stay hidden? We're not little kids anymore, Chris. If we move into another community, they'll report us for sure."

Chris scowled. "Then let's go somewhere there's no community."

"Oh. Great idea. Where's that?"

"Shut up. We don't need them. We don't need—"

"We don't need what? A house? School? You want to move to the middle of the woods somewhere and just live off the land?"

Yeah. He did. If that was the tradeoff, he'd take it.

Chris stared out at the darkness and didn't say anything.

Michael rolled his eyes. "Okay, Chris. Whatever."

Some of the tightness in his chest was loosening, making it hard to maintain his anger. He could feel it now, the rain tracing along his shoulders, feeding relief into his muscles.

"You want me to just leave you alone?" said Michael.

No. He didn't. He wanted Michael to sit here and tell him that *this* time they'd stand up to them, that they would show Tyler and all those freaks just who they were messing with.

But Michael would never do that.

"Yeah," Chris said. "I'm tired."

Chris heard him shift to stand, but he didn't look over. His brother was watching him; he could feel it.

But Michael just sighed and moved toward the door. "Me too, kid. Me too."

Her mom would flip out if she found mud tracked across the front hall, so Becca trudged through the grass to the back door and let herself in through the laundry room.

Her best friend was sitting at the kitchen table, pawing through a magazine. A half-empty dinner plate sat in front of her. Becca wasn't surprised to see her—any time Quinn had trouble with her mother, she ended up here. An untouched pile of stuffing and a small slice of turkey were left on the plate, but all the vegetables and most of the protein were gone.

"Hey." Becca struggled to kick off her shoes.

Quinn lifted her eyes from the magazine. "You walk home or something? Why do you look like that?"

Becca considered reviewing the course of the night's events. The fight. The drive to Chris's house. His weird brothers.

Too complicated. "Long story. Is that my dinner?"

Quinn speared the last piece of turkey and slid it into her mouth. "Your mom left two plates."

Of course she did. "She already leave for work?"

"Yep. Off to save lives, one dumbass at a time."

Quinn Briscoe had been Becca's friend since kindergarten. She was a middle kid, smashed between two brothers: Jake was on a basketball scholarship to Duke University, the kind of son who lived on a pedestal, his name trotted out any time the other—lesser—children didn't measure up. Quinn's younger brother, Will, rebelled by refusing to participate in any kind of physical activity—and he had the body to prove it.

Quinn could have been a female Jake. She'd inherited the same physical coordination as her brother, his same competitive drive. But Jake was tall and lean. Quinn came broad and stocky.

She'd never been fat—just built like an athlete. Becca used to joke that Quinn could do one push-up and end up with shoulders like a linebacker. Any sports team at the school would have been glad to have her—hell, the football team could probably *use* her.

But Quinn wanted to be a dancer.

She possessed the rhythm and the physical ability, sure. She just didn't have the grace or the elegance—or the money—to do it well. She was pretty enough. Long hair? Creamy skin? Big blue eyes? Quinn had those in spades. But skinny low-rise jeans never fit her right, and little baby-doll tees looked ridiculous with her biceps. She looked like she claimed she felt: as if she didn't fit anywhere, and what she wanted never wanted her back.

And Quinn had a temper. Fights with her mother were legendary. Frightening. The kind of knockdown, drag-out screaming matches that, once witnessed, made Becca want to run home and hug her mother.

Becca's mom had told Mrs. Briscoe that her daughter was welcome at their house anytime, no questions. Then she'd handed Quinn a key.

This year, more often than not, Becca came home to find Quinn in her kitchen. Usually, she was dumping her troubles on Becca's mom's shoulder first, then spending the night. It was like inheriting a sister.

Becca wasn't sure how she felt about that.

She padded across the linoleum to retrieve the second plate from the refrigerator. Her mom had used green beans to make a smiley face in her mashed potatoes.

Becca sighed and slid the plate into the microwave.

"I just took a message for you," said Quinn.

A message? The only person who ever called was sitting right here in the kitchen. "Who?"

Quinn slid a piece of notebook paper across the table. "Your dad."

Becca stared at her friend's loopy script. He called every six months, but every time still hit her like a sucker punch. "He called?"

"A man called and said to tell Becca that her father called. I said he had no right to call himself that, and he sighed and said to just give you the message. So I said it was my job to protect you from assholes—"

"Please tell me you're kidding."

Quinn licked gravy off her spoon. "You know I'm just looking out for you."

"Does Mom know?"

"Nope. She'd already left for the ER."

Becca stared at those numbers, as if they'd somehow shift into an essay on where he'd been this time.

Becca had been eleven when he'd left, in school and blissfully oblivious until she got off the bus that afternoon. Even then, her mom didn't drop the bomb until that weekend. Becca still felt like an idiot—believing some crap about a business trip. For *days,* she'd believed it.

But he was gone. He'd been gone. He'd woken up in the morning, gotten a phone call, and said he had to leave.

And then he didn't come back.

He pretended to give a crap, calling twice a year to ask about her life, but it wasn't like it made a difference. She used to make lists, so she could detail every accomplishment, tell him every way she'd be a perfect daughter when he came back. He made the right sounds, said the right words of encouragement, but then she'd beg him to come home, and he'd sigh and say he had things to take care of. When she'd been in middle school, it all sounded very exciting and mysterious. Like he was some kind of secret agent.

She knew now he'd played to that, strung her out on whispered conversations and empty promises.

What a dick.

She used to keep the ringer volume all the way up so there was no way she'd miss a call—because he never left a message, never left any way to get in touch with him.

Until now.

Staring down at his number, Becca wasn't quite sure how to react.

So she crumpled up the note, tossed it into the trash can, tied up the bag, and took it out to the curb. Her heart was pounding, but she told it to knock it off.

Then she walked back into the kitchen and grabbed her plate from the microwave.

Quinn was staring at her, waiting for Becca to talk. Waiting to follow some lead.

Becca dropped into her chair. "So." She picked up her fork. "What's this drama about your mom's candle party?"

CHAPTER 4

Chris couldn't breathe. A hand was clamped over his mouth, pressing his head to the pillow.

Darkness cloaked the room, but other than *night,* he had no concept of time. He thought of Tyler pinning his arms, holding him down while Seth threw punches. He came out of sleep with fists swinging.

He struck something. His assailant grunted. A hand caught his wrist and trapped it against the bed.

"Jesus Christ, Chris," a voice breathed into his ear. "It's just me, you idiot."

Chris stopped fighting, and the hand came off his mouth.

"Keep quiet," Gabriel said.

Chris stared up at him, trying to make out features in the darkness. The storm still raged outside, rain slamming against the siding, wanting to be part of his panic.

"What the hell are you doing?" he whispered, trying to convince his heart to slow.

Lightning flashed, lighting up Gabriel's expression and making his eyes glow for a moment. "I thought maybe we'd give Tyler a little warning of our own."

Chris felt his heart kick back into action. "You're crazy."

"Am I?"

Said by the brother who'd just woken him by suffocation. Chris glanced at the clock on his dresser. It was half past one. "Just—go back to bed."

Gabriel ruffled his hair. "Aw. Scared?"

Chris knocked his hand away. "No."

"Liar."

"Thanks for the offer, but I'm not in any rush to get my ass handed to me again." Chris gave him a shove. "Go ask Nick."

"Forget it." His brother backed off and stepped toward the door.

Chris sat up and rubbed at his eyes. He could count on one hand the number of times he'd been recruited for trouble. "Wait."

Gabriel waited.

"Why are you asking me?"

Gabriel smiled, sensing—correctly—that Chris was starting to waver. "Thought you might like a little vengeance."

"You mean Nick said no."

"Does it matter?"

Chris hesitated. *Did* it matter?

Thunder rolled outside, and Gabriel glanced at the window. "It seemed like your kind of night."

It *felt* like his kind of night. The rain liked this idea. Chris felt it pulling him, drawing his focus.

He hated Tyler. He hated them all.

But he hated his own fear more.

He nodded. "All right."

"Get dressed. Think you can rile the storm if I help?"

Chris threw back his blankets. Rain whipped against the screen, already willing. "Sure," he said, reaching for today's jeans from the pile in the corner. "Why?"

Lightning lit up the room. Gabriel smiled. "Because we need Mike's truck."

Michael's work truck sounded like an orchestra of chainsaws when Gabriel fired up the diesel engine. As soon as the rain touched his skin, Chris called to it, urging it faster, driving drops against the house until the rattle on the siding would be louder than the engine.

He kept the window of the cab open, his hand on the door. Storms liked adventure. Or maybe they liked panic. Whatever, he kept up a litany in his head, begging the rain to mask their departure.

Gabriel called lightning from the sky. Chris felt every surge, every strike, the electricity racing through his storm to find something to burn. It hit close now, as if the lightning sought his brother the way the rain looked for him.

A tree down the street took a bolt. Wood cracked and split, sounding like gunfire.

Chris glanced at the house, watching the dark upstairs windows for any sign of movement. They were rolling down the driveway in neutral, the headlights off, but any moment the porch lights could flare to life and Michael would come flying out of the house.

Chris swallowed.

Gabriel punched him in the shoulder. "Relax."

"Try not to strike the truck. We might not be able to explain that away."

Lightning struck the road at the base of the driveway, not five feet in front of them. Chris jumped a mile.

Gabriel laughed. "Now that was just lucky."

Chris scowled. "Do we have a plan or anything? Why did we need all the fertilizer?"

"Because it explodes when I hit it with lightning."

Chris wished he were driving, because he would have stopped the truck right then. "Run that by me again."

"What did you think we were going to do, toilet paper their house?"

"No—but—"

"It's just a little flash and bang, a warning not to screw with us. We're not bombing them. God, you are worse than Nicky."

Chris stared out the window, watching rain sluice through the darkness, making silver streamers in the path of the headlights. Gabriel drove fast, but Chris didn't worry about losing control. No matter how slick the roads got, the water would hold them.

"Hey."

Chris swung his head around. Gabriel was watching him, the humor gone from his expression now.

"Don't tell me," said Chris. "You changed your mind about the bomb thing."

"You know that chick's been around the block, right?"

Chris shrugged and looked out the window again. He hardly knew her.

She'd just saved his life.

He kept thinking of her eyes, dark and shining in the moonlight when she'd been kneeling in the parking lot.

"No, seriously," said Gabriel. "Like half the soccer team, some of the lacrosse guys—"

"I get it. Thanks." Rain beat at the truck, slapping at his hand where it hung outside the window. Feeding on his irritation.

Gabriel looked at the road again. "I just thought you should know."

Then something occurred to Chris. "You?"

"Please," Gabriel scoffed. Then he glanced over. "I mean, no offense—"

"It's fine."

"She's cute and all, but I like a little more to *grab,* if you get my—"

"It's *fine.*" But Chris smiled.

Gabriel killed the engine and the headlights when they pulled onto Tyler's street, letting the truck roll in neutral. Chris pulled his hand inside the cab despite the water's protest, worried the paleness of his skin would be a beacon in the darkness. He could hear his breathing again, louder than the rain outside, almost echoing inside the cab.

Gabriel was whistling through his teeth.

It sounded like an air horn to Chris.

"How do you know they'll explode?" he whispered, as though

his voice would carry. He didn't even care about the answer; he just wanted Gabriel to stop the damn whistling.

"You kidding? Nick and I blow stuff up all the time."

Chris stared at him, forgetting his tension for a moment. "Really?"

"Sure." Gabriel glanced over, then ruffled his hair again. "Feeling left out, Christopher?"

Yeah. He was. But Chris ducked and smacked his hand away. "You've never gotten caught?"

"Nah." His brother seemed to reconsider. "Okay, once, but we ran."

"Where do you do it?"

"Down the beach by Fort Armistead Park."

Chris wondered if Michael had any idea. He couldn't possibly.

Gabriel reached out and grabbed his arm, hard. "You'll keep your mouth shut, right?"

"Yeah." Chris kept his voice even, like it was no big deal. "Whatever."

Gabriel let him go. "Hey, is that Tyler's car?"

Ahead, parked on the street, sat a sleek black SUV, almost invisible in the darkness. Set back from the road was Tyler's house, a wide brick split-level with lazy landscaping.

Chris took a breath. He'd only been here once, but he wouldn't forget. "Yeah."

"Make it pour," said Gabriel. "Think you can do hail?"

Now that they were here, so close to the house, Chris wanted to cling to the truck, as if the cab was his only lifeline to safety. "Are you just going to put the bags in the front yard or something?"

"*We,* brother. We." Gabriel clicked his tongue against his teeth. "And I think I have a better idea."

You want to turn around and go home? Maybe they could go blow the bags up on the beach. No one would get pissed, no one would know.

No one would come out of the house and beat the shit out of them.

God, he was being such a wuss. "Yeah? What?"

"Help me put the bags around his car."

The rain welcomed him into the night air, soaking his clothes and feeding him strength. It felt better than adrenaline. Chris shook wet hair out of his eyes and grabbed a bag, heaving it onto his shoulder. He moved to throw it up against one of Tyler's tires, but Gabriel waved to him to stop.

His brother leaned close and spoke over the rain. "He might have an alarm. Don't touch it."

"Just how big do these explode?"

Gabriel had already moved away. "What?"

Chris sighed. "Forget it." He grabbed another bag from the pickup, setting it in front of the SUV.

Gabriel caught his arm. "Do you hear something?"

Chris only heard rain and his pulse. The darkness revealed nothing. He sought answers from the water in the air, but the rain was too focused on vengeance and danger.

"Come on," said Gabriel. "Hurry."

They stood in the middle of a paved road, surrounded by explosives—the worst place for a showdown with Tyler and his friends. But the only visible movement in the darkness was caused by the rain and the wind through the trees.

Chris swallowed his fear and grabbed another bag. This one went by the front quarter panel of the SUV. Gabriel placed one by the back tire, then straightened and rubbed his hands on the front of his jeans. He gave Chris a smile. "See?" he called. "Worried for nothing."

A car door slammed.

Gabriel whirled. The sound came from behind the truck, but there were no lights. They couldn't see anyone yet. Chris felt his hands curl into fists, ready to fight. When they'd attacked behind the school, he'd had nothing. Now, he had the power of the rain and a brother by his side.

Another car door slammed.

Gabriel glanced at him, and Chris could read the question in his expression. *Fight or run?*

A voice spoke from the darkness. "Aw. Look. The Merrick truck is sitting in front of my house."

Tyler. Fear grabbed Chris by the throat. The rain turned cold, biting his skin and urging him to fight.

He heard a rough scraping sound, thin and keening through the rain. Metal on metal. Then Tyler's face appeared from the darkness.

He was dragging his keys along the side of Michael's truck.

"Keys?" said Gabriel, stepping forward to shove Tyler away. His voice was easy, but the motion was full of threat. "What is this, middle school?"

Tyler glanced past him, clearly taking in the bags of fertilizer lined up alongside his truck. "Late night yard work?"

Thunder rolled through the sky. "Something like that," said Gabriel.

It was taking all of Chris's control to keep from choking Tyler with water, to keep it from freezing in the other boy's eyes, to keep himself from breaking the promise his parents had made.

Tyler cocked his head to the side, gave a twisted grin that looked maniacal in the moonlight. "You wouldn't be calling elements, would you?"

"Who needs elements?" said Gabriel.

Then he punched him.

Tyler staggered back into the truck, and Gabriel went after him, slamming the other boy against the quarter panel. "Don't you ever fucking touch my brother again."

Chris felt a surge of pride.

Then someone grabbed him from behind and shoved him into the front grille of the truck.

"What's wrong?" said Seth. "Don't have your girlfriend to protect you?"

God, he'd been stupid. This was Tyler's SUV. They'd heard the other car. Of course Tyler wouldn't have been alone.

Chris tried to round on Seth, but the other boy was standing on concrete, and that meant his grip was practically unbreakable.

The rain hardened into hail. With an edge.

Seth slammed him against the grille again. "Cut that shit out."

"What?" said Chris innocently, hating that his voice carried a wheeze. The rain had fixed his ribs before, but they still ached. "Don't like rainstorms?"

Seth spun him around and slammed him in the face.

Chris didn't know he was falling until the pavement whacked him in the back of the head. Jesus *Christ,* that guy could throw a punch. Chris had to remind his lungs to breathe.

The rain turned to sleet, whipping sideways, striking the truck and making a racket. Seth was going after Gabriel now, dragging him away from Tyler.

Then Seth had Gabriel up against the truck, choking him.

Chris flew off the ground. The rain fed him his brother's panic. He poured power into the sleet, trying to loosen Seth's grip.

It was like trying to fight a statue.

Tyler grabbed his arm to wrench him away. They grappled in the darkness. Lightning flared in the sky—bolts of power driving into the grass.

Tyler's eyes widened, then his grip turned hot, searing into Chris's forearm. Chris struck at him, but Tyler didn't let go.

Lightning hit the street, sizzling on the pavement, two feet from a fertilizer bag.

Freeze. Chris just thought it, and Tyler was screaming, his hands on his face.

But Seth still had hold of Gabriel. He made a sharp motion with his hands, like in the movies when someone wants to break a guy's neck.

Lightning shot through the sky.

Fertilizer exploded. The sound—the heat—was intense. Chris hit the pavement again, and lost sense of all direction. His eyes burned from the explosion, and he couldn't see yet. Seth couldn't have held on through *that.* Gabriel had to be around here somewhere.

His rain worked fast. The fire was already turning to nothing more threatening than billowing smoke.

A hand caught his arm, rolled him over. Chris fought, striking out before he knew who had hold of him.

"Hey! Kid!" A light was shining in his eyes. One guy, no, two, stood over him. "Take it easy."

Chris stared up, blinking stars out of his vision.

Not Tyler, not Seth.

Cops.

CHAPTER 5

The little green lines on the clock on the dash announced it was almost three in the morning. Chris was glad he sat in the back of the truck's cab, somewhat hidden in the shadowed corner behind his oldest brother.

"I don't get what you're so upset about." Gabriel was up front, slouched against the door, looking coiled and feral in the dim light.

Michael's fingers gripped the wheel. Headlights filtered through the back window of the pickup, and Chris could see the muscles of Michael's forearms stand out from the strain. Nick was following them in the SUV; he'd driven Michael to pick them up.

Chris had wanted to ride home with him, but Michael had practically dragged him to the truck by his ear.

"You don't get what I'm upset about?" Michael's voice was low and dangerous.

"It's not like they *charged* us with anything."

Chris looked out the tiny backseat window. The cops had threatened to—but thank god they'd bought some stupid story about a prank gone wrong. They'd searched them and hand-cuffed them, then made them sit on the wet pavement to wait while rain threaded through his hair and dripped into his eyes.

They'd done the same to Seth and Tyler.

Chris didn't regret a minute of it.

"You don't *get*," Michael said, his voice a bit louder, "what I'm *upset* about?"

Thunder cracked in the sky overhead. A bolt of lightning struck beyond the trees ahead of them, lighting Gabriel's eyes. "You mean, besides the fact that you're a big pussy?"

"Don't start with me."

Gabriel made a disgusted sound and looked out the window. "What are you going to do, ground me? Send me to my room without my frozen dinner?"

"You don't like it? *Leave*."

"Fine. Pull over."

Michael didn't.

Gabriel snorted. "See."

"Cut the crap. If I let you out, you'll just get in with Nick."

Chris almost wished they'd left him with the policemen. When his brothers got going, it was usually better to be somewhere else.

Michael glanced in the rearview mirror. "Care to weigh in?"

Chris kept his mouth shut and shook his head.

Michael turned his head to look at Gabriel. "The worst part is that you dragged Chris into this. It's bad enough the crap you pull with Nick—"

"He didn't *drag* me," Chris snapped. "I wanted to go." He hated the way Michael said that, as if Chris came along like a stray dog, coaxed by a piece of meat and a pat on the head.

Didn't you?

He shoved the thought away. Maybe Gabriel's plan had been over the top—Chris knew he should have been more suspicious that Nick wasn't in on it. But Chris didn't blame Gabriel. He was *grateful*. Christ, for the first time, he felt like one of his brothers *understood* him.

"It wasn't his fault," Chris said.

Gabriel glanced into the backseat, caught Chris's eye, and smiled.

Solidarity. Chris smiled back.

"You know I can lose custody, right?" Michael said. "You all start acting like a bunch of delinquents, and they'll yank the court order so quick—"

"Boo hoo," said Gabriel. That smile was gone.

Michael glanced over at him. "What were you thinking?" When he didn't get an answer, he reached over and smacked Gabriel on the back of the head. "Seriously. What the hell were you thinking?"

Gabriel drew back and practically snarled at him. "They beat the crap out of Chris. It's time for them to remember we can strike back."

"So wait." Michael raised his eyebrows, the sarcasm thick. "Getting arrested—that wasn't part of the plan?"

"Fuck you."

"Typical."

Gabriel leaned forward, those headlights catching his eyes and making them gleam. "I shouldn't have been the one taking him out anyway. Maybe if you gave a shit—"

"Maybe if I *gave a shit?*" Michael grabbed his arm. "Look, you little—"

Then Gabriel took a swing at him, and the car swerved.

"Hey!" Chris grabbed the handle over the door. They were grappling in the front seat, all barely contained rage.

He unclicked his seat belt and grabbed Gabriel's arm while Michael grasped the steering wheel again. Chris got an arm around Gabriel's neck and pinned him to the headrest.

"Lemme go," Gabriel ground out. "Damn it, Chris, lemme—"

"Chill out." Now Chris wished Gabriel had ridden in the SUV. Nick was better at countering his twin's rage. "Both of you. We're almost home."

But getting home solved nothing. Gabriel wrenched free and shoved out the door before the truck came to a full stop in the driveway.

"Wait a minute," Michael called. "Don't think this is over." He hustled to get the truck in park and slid out of the cab.

Chris swiped the water off his cheeks and followed his brothers.

Nick killed the SUV behind the truck. "What was that about back there?" he called, slamming his door.

"Just your brother having a tantrum," Michael yelled back. He'd almost caught up to Gabriel, and he reached out a hand to grab his arm. "Running? Who's the pussy now?"

Gabriel swung around and punched him.

Michael hit him back.

Chris didn't realize he'd stopped short until Nick appeared at his side. He could hear their breathing, too quick, a rush of air mixed with the rain and the thunder of his pulse. Chris shifted his weight, wanting to interfere, he just didn't know who to help.

Lightning hit a tree behind the house. Thunder cracked and branches fell.

Chris felt it through the rain. That lightning wanted a target.

Another bolt pierced the ground like a spear of light, hitting somewhere between them and Michael. Another struck the very edge of the porch railing. A small fire flared to life, crawling along the strip of wood.

Chris swore and begged the rain for help. It poured and doused the fire.

"It's too much," said Nick. "He can't control it." He started forward.

Lightning struck right in front of them. Chris grabbed Nick's arm and jerked him back. He suddenly felt like a sitting duck.

Michael had Gabriel pinned now, trapped against the ground. Lightning dove through the sky to strike three feet from Michael's shoulder. It sizzled into the grass and lit up the front yard for a moment.

Nick pulled free. "Damn it, Michael, let him up!"

Michael swore, staring down at Gabriel. "Try that again and see what I do to you."

"Fuck you," said Gabriel. His eyes lit with fury.

Nick grabbed Michael's arm and pulled. Chris helped. It must have given Gabriel the leverage he needed, because he shoved his brother off him and into the grass.

But Gabriel was still drawing power from the storm. Chris could feel it, the way rage coiled in the air, ready to pounce.

"Stop!" cried Nick. "Gabriel—"

They wouldn't be fast enough. Chris threw his weight against Michael and shoved, driving his brothers back a few feet through the mud.

Lightning sliced through the night to strike right where they'd been.

Right where *Michael* had been.

Gabriel had found his feet, and stood back from the paved walkway, his hands still in fists. His breathing was quick, his eyes dark. Michael stood beside Nick, closer to the porch, his stance tight, ready for Gabriel to make a move.

Chris clung to the darkness by the driveway, having no idea whose side he was on.

After a moment, Michael straightened. "Was that on purpose?"

Gabriel stared right back at him, baring his teeth a bit. "Does it matter?"

"Yeah," said Nick. He sounded pissed. "It does."

Some of the arrogance leaked out of Gabriel's expression. His shoulders dropped. He glanced at Nick, then at Chris, as if assessing damages.

Then his eyes swung back to Michael. "Not all of it."

Michael drew himself up, as if readying for another fight.

But Gabriel didn't move. "You're not our father." His voice was low, even, punctuated by the rain. Lightning flashed somewhere in the sky.

Michael flinched—almost imperceptibly, but Gabriel saw it and smiled.

Nick went to his twin's side. "Stop. Just—come inside."

Gabriel shrugged him off and started for Michael, stopping right in front of him. "You'd make a shitty father, anyway," he said. "But that's okay. That's not what you're supposed to be."

Michael held his ground. "Yeah? Just what am I supposed to be?"

Gabriel gave a humorless laugh and turned for the house. "Come on, guys."

"Hey!" Michael's tone was sharp. "Just what am I *supposed to be?*"

Gabriel turned in the doorway. "Our *brother,* asshole. Our brother."

He walked into the house, Nick right behind him.

Chris looked at Michael, standing there in the rain. Michael looked back.

Then Chris broke the eye contact, walked past him, and followed the twins.

CHAPTER 6

Chris wasn't in school on Thursday. He was noticeably absent from Becca's third-period English Lit class, and he wasn't in fourth-period World History, either. He wouldn't be missing much. Mr. Beamis looked like he could have been there when they commissioned the Model T, and his class usually gave her a chance to do a Wite-Out manicure.

But today brought a new student to the front of the room, and Becca raised her eyes from her nails. Old Man Beamis did a clear double take.

Make that a triple take. The teacher put a hand on the edge of his desk.

The new kid was a lot to look at. He'd certainly crossed that line from boy to young man, with a defined jaw, high cheekbones, lean, muscled arms, and not an ounce of baby fat—all pros. Sandy blond hair drifted across his forehead, broken by a clean streak of white, right in the center of his bangs.

Who dyes their hair white? she wondered.

But it didn't stop there: One ear had piercings all the way up. The other only sported two—the same number in his left eyebrow. Green eyes matched the tee shirt he wore, staring unflinchingly at the students watching him. His black jeans hung loose, suspended by a chafed leather belt. About fifteen bracelets encircled one arm, crude loops of twine that each held a small rock of a different color. He had a few small tattoos on his forearms, and one on the side of his neck. They looked like foreign symbols, the kind girls got on spring break, something that was supposed to be meaningful in one word, like *peace* or *wisdom* but really said *Do me*.

Beamis read the note the kid handed him, but didn't bother to introduce him to the class. God forbid someone should interrupt his lecture. He hurriedly shooed him to the empty chair in the middle of the room—Chris's usual seat. It was one row over and two desks down from Becca. The new kid dropped into the chair, and his backpack dropped to the floor beside him. She could see the marking on his neck now—not Asian, but no language she could identify. She could also see a black ring on one finger, a twine ring on another.

Tommy Dunleavy—who sat two rows over and liked to flick suggestive notes onto Becca's desk—coughed, "Fag!"

The boy didn't react, just pulled a blue spiral notebook out of his backpack. Then a pen.

Tommy tried again, his cough a little louder, his epithet a little meaner.

The boy clicked his pen. Beamis, oblivious, picked up his chalk.

Jeremy Blakehurst, Tommy's best friend, picked up the cough. "Fag!" He also flicked a paper clip. It struck the boy's shoulder and pinged off the edge of another desk.

Some people nearby snickered. A few girls near the back corner giggled and whispered.

The boy didn't turn around. But he did set his pen down.

Tommy bent a paper clip so the prongs stuck out, then used a rubber band to fashion a slingshot.

He didn't even bother with the cough this time. "Hey. Fag." Then he drew back the paper clip and let it fly.

The boy whipped around. His hand shot out to snatch the paper clip from the air.

There was a collective gasp from every student who'd been watching—Becca included. Beamis droned on.

The boy's hand had formed a fist around the paper clip, and

for a fractured moment, Becca thought he was going to take a swing, that they'd have a throwdown right here in the middle of World History.

But he half rose from his seat and reached across another student's desk to drop the mangled paper clip in front of Tommy.

"Look, dude," he said, his voice low and earnest. "You want to ask me out, you man up and do it proper."

Everybody laughed—including Jeremy. Tommy shoved the clip off his desk and fumed.

The new kid drew back to sit in his chair again. On his way there, he caught Becca watching him—and smiled.

She was so startled she didn't smile back.

Then Beamis asked a question and turned from the blackboard. The new kid was already facing forward, a pen on his notebook.

A tiny triangle of lined paper fell on her desk. Tommy Dunleavy was hiding a smirk.

Becca didn't want to unroll it, but somehow *not* knowing was always worse. So she did.

You give Happy Ending?

She crumpled it in her fist and wanted to punch Tommy. She wished she had a witty comeback, some shred of the new boy's easy charisma. Something that would make the rest of the class laugh and side with her.

But the new kid was just that—a clean slate.

Becca had no chance of that.

Since school started, she and Quinn had sat alone for lunch, at one of the shorter tables near the back stairwell. It was a lesser location, farthest from the main hallway and the line for food, somewhat hidden behind one of the support columns. Last year they'd spent every lunch with Drew and his jock buddies, and Becca would giggle and blush while Drew ate half her food. She and Quinn had never been popular before Drew showed interest in her. They had loved the attention.

What a waste.

The rain beat an incessant rhythm on the school windows, keeping everyone indoors, turning the cafeteria into a mob scene. Standing in line was just another opportunity to get hassled, so she and Quinn usually just nursed bottled waters. On a day like today, every seat was valuable, and two physics geeks were scribbling notes at the other end of their table.

Becca thought they were doing homework, until she realized they were plotting out some online role-playing game.

Quinn rolled her eyes at them. "Jesus, Bex, you think we can get them to go back to Mordor?"

One of the kids glared at her. "Shut it, Quinn. Why don't you go eat in the bathroom with the rest of the freaks?"

Becca sighed and twisted her water bottle in her hands. It had already gone lukewarm. She watched the rain coat the windows and started to peel the label off her bottle. Fourteen more minutes of "lunch."

As usual, she was starving.

"Sorry, precioussss," said Quinn. "Why don't you go eat in the lab with the rest of the losers?"

"Wow. This sounds like a friendly table."

Becca snapped her head up. Chris Merrick stood there, beside Quinn, holding a lunch tray. He wore an unbuttoned plaid shirt over a blue tee. The swelling around his eye had subsided, but the bruising along his cheekbone was downright spectacular. His hair barely covered the scabbing at his temple.

Actually, he looked surprisingly good, considering the damage he'd taken. The shirt made his eyes look bluer, sharp and intuitive and fixed on her face.

Her heart kicked. "Um," she said. "Hi?"

He dropped the loaded tray beside Quinn, then swung a leg over the bench to sit down.

Every person at the table stared at him.

He picked up a fry, glancing around. He offered the physics kids half a smile. "'Sup."

Quinn dragged her eyes back to Becca's. "Why is Chris Merrick sitting next to me?"

Chris popped the cap on his soda. "You know I can hear you, right?"

Becca couldn't stop staring at him. "What are you doing here?"

"And what the hell happened to your face?" said Quinn.

He raised an eyebrow and straightened. "I was mostly being sarcastic with that whole 'friendly table' comment, but I can take a hint. . . ."

Becca shook her head quickly. "I just—I meant—you weren't here this morning."

"It was a rough night." He shrugged and picked up another fry. "Michael let me sleep it off." He looked down at the table, apparently noticing for the first time that he was the only one eating. "You guys are already done? I barely made it through the line."

Quinn took a swig of her water.

Becca glanced away. "We didn't feel like braving it."

"Here." He held out his apple. "I can't eat while you're just watching me."

Quinn snorted. "The symbolism here might just kill me."

Chris grinned, withdrew his arm, and took a bite. "I'll eat it then." He pushed the fries off his tray and into the space between them. "You eat the fries."

Quinn gave him wide eyes. "But . . . whatever will *you* eat?"

A pear, two pieces of pizza, a cup of applesauce, and a Styrofoam bowl of macaroni and cheese still sat in front of him. He shrugged. "I'll make do."

Quinn took one, almost hesitantly. "Seriously. What are you doing here?"

"I came to apologize for my dickhead brother." He took another bite of his apple, his eyes intent on Becca. "And to thank Becky for last night."

"*Becca,*" she snapped.

He smiled. "I know."

Oh.

Oh.

Becca blushed and hated herself for it.

Then she realized Quinn was staring at her, a kind of shocked dismay on her face.

Crap.

"Quinn, look, it's not like you think—"

"Don't worry. I get it." Quinn was standing, slinging her backpack over her shoulder.

"Wait—Quinn—"

But her friend was already shoving past other students, making her way toward the common area.

Becca sighed. "Great."

"We're not gonna cry about it," said one of the physics kids.

"Shut up," she snapped.

Chris took another bite of his apple and set it on his tray. "Now she seemed nice."

Becca glared at him, irritated. Had he meant the double entendre about *last night?* God, for ten seconds, she'd entertained the thought that he was going to sit down and be a nice guy.

"So which one?" she said.

He frowned. "I'm sorry?"

"Which brother? I'm having a hard time differentiating on the dickhead scale."

"Oh." He looked startled. "Ah, Michael. But, all of them, I guess."

So Michael was a big brother. She should have seen that coming. "Great. Apology accepted. You're welcome." She started to rise.

"You're mad at me? Hey—wait a minute."

She waited.

"Look, I wasn't trying to mess with your friend." Chris looked away for a moment. "I wondered if you were doing anything after school. Gabriel's got a soccer match, if you want to come watch—"

"Are you *kidding?*" She could barely hear over the heartbeat in her ears. Gabriel must have figured out who she was, must have told Chris. If he hadn't known already.

"Ah . . . no." He scratched his head, pushing hair out of his eyes. "I'm actually pretty serious—"

"Look. Chris." She dropped onto the bench again and gripped the edge of the table. "I'm not going to sleep with you," she whispered fiercely, feeling her cheeks flush. "I'm not going to mess around with you under the bleachers. I don't give hand jobs in the men's room, or—"

"Wow. You like to get all this out of the way up front, huh?"

"Whatever you're playing, someone else has tried it, okay?" she said. "I wish you all would just stop screwing with me and leave me *alone*."

The table was dead silent for a moment.

Then he stood up. "Sure." He paused. "You can have the lunch."

She didn't look at him.

He hoisted his bag onto his shoulder, then tossed some paper onto the table in front of her. "I'll see you around, Becca."

When he was gone, she looked up. An envelope sat on the tray, the corner stuck in the greasy cheese of the pizza.

She picked it up and opened it. Three twenties.

You're probably thinking I owe you my life.

No. Just sixty bucks.

Becca stared at the money, feeling the crispness of the bills under her fingertips. She had no idea what it meant.

The physics kids stood up, taking their notebooks with them. "At least he didn't leave it on the dresser," one said.

Becca flinched, but they were gone, swallowed by the swarm of students. Typical. She was used to drive-by one-liners.

She reached out to seize her water bottle—then gasped and dropped it.

It was freezing. She could hear bits of ice swish inside the plastic. Cold crystals clung to her fingers before melting.

She stared at the bottle, now sweating on the table, droplets of water collecting below it.

Then she swiped her hand on her jeans and turned to lose herself in the crowd.

CHAPTER 7

Work sucked. But at least tonight she got to work the floor. You were supposed to be eighteen, but when people called in sick, Becca got a reprieve from cleaning kennels and scrubbing the pet baths, and instead put on a service smock and a name tag.

Working sales paid a full two dollars more per hour. Not like she needed the money this week, with Chris's sixty bucks securely stashed in the employee lockers.

She didn't want to keep it, but she sure as hell didn't want to have another conversation with him. Maybe she could just never spend it. She'd stick it in the domestic violence jar at the front of the store, or the homemade can for that kid with leukemia.

Then again, gas wasn't cheap. Or maybe she could replace her cell phone. Or save it for a Homecoming dress.

Homecoming. OMG, Bex. You're hilarious.

Becca stacked cans of cat food on the shelf, a practiced motion she could do blindfolded. A couple rows over, some guys were jostling each other in the dog food aisle, and Becca sighed. She'd been listening to their bullshitting for ten minutes, and she'd bet her paycheck they were counting on a five-finger discount.

Pets Plus wasn't exactly well patrolled. It was a PetSmart

wannabe, without the big-box budget or the floor space. The only other person working the floor was Jerry, the night manager, and he'd stepped out for a smoke.

When she heard at least a dozen cans rattle onto the tile, followed by a too-loud curse from one of the guys, she set the cat food aside and went to clean up the mess.

She fixed her expression into polite sternness. More cans hit the floor before she reached the aisle. What were they doing, sweeping them off the shelf?

"Ex*cuse* me," she said as she rounded the corner. "Maybe I could help you—"

She stopped short. At least fifteen cans of dog food lay scattered on the linoleum. A few were still rolling, and some bounced off her sneakers to career into the main aisle. But above it all stood Seth. And Tyler.

She almost couldn't breathe.

They looked just as sharp and frightening in the fluorescent store lighting as in the darkness of the parking lot. Tyler's face carried more shadows, his eyes almost electric. They both wore wolfish smiles, and she'd been right—Seth was clearly shoving a can into the black backpack that hung from his arm.

"Hey," he said, dragging the word into three syllables, a mockery of a catcall. "It's Chris's bodyguard."

Tyler had a can of dog food in his hand, and he tossed it into the air and caught it like a baseball, thoughtfully, as if he'd pitch it at her next. "You following us now?"

Following them? Couldn't he *see* the stupid smock and name tag?

She shook her head. "No. Let me just get—"

Tyler grabbed her arm. She hadn't even seen him move. "Maybe we didn't get our point across last night."

"Get your hands off me." She tried to jerk her wrist out of his grip, but he held fast. She fought him.

Tyler's free hand drew back with the can, as if ready to let fly at her face.

But Seth caught his arm. "Dude. Not here."

She stumbled over her words. She couldn't even get it to-gether to yell for help. Someone was whispering, "Holy crap," over and over again. It took a second to realize it was *her*.

"Yeah," said Tyler, jerking his arm free, the can still in his fist. "Try that kung fu shit again, and see what I do to you."

"The manager will be right back," she babbled. "He's . . . yeah. Take the dog food—whatever you want—I'm not going to kung fu—to—ah—"

Tyler pulled her closer. "What's yours?"

He still hadn't let go of the can, and she felt certain that he was going to slug her in the face with it. It took her a moment to respond, and even then, she had no idea what he was talking about. "What's . . . mine?"

He leaned in and inhaled, as if smelling the air around her. "Look, you want to play stupid in here, fine. Maybe we can send you home to Chris with a little message."

How frigging long did it take Jerry to smoke a cigarette? "I don't live with Chris—I mean, I barely know the guy—"

"Save it." He gave her a little shake. "That little stunt they pulled last night? The deal is done. Get it? *Done.*"

He was staring down at her as though his words should have made an impact. She shook her head. "I don't know what that means."

He shoved her up against the shelving, until metal dug into her shoulder and scraped her through the shirt. "If they pull this shit again, we're going to take care of it ourselves. Get it?"

She tried to squirm away from him, feeling her throat tighten.

His grip tightened, and her arm started to ache. No, it started to *burn*. She squealed, but that only made it worse.

He leaned in. *"Get it?"*

His hand felt hot through her sleeve, like a branding iron. She could swear her arm was on fire. Tears were in her eyes and she didn't care now. "But I don't—"

A dog growled to her left. A dark, menacing growl, the kind that prefaced an attack. She and Tyler both snapped their heads to the side.

Pets were allowed in the store, of course. Nice ones. But a massive German shepherd stood there, his lips pulled back, his black ears flat, a low round of bass rolling from his throat. His tail wagged slowly, a sure sign of aggression. A red leash hung from his collar, but there was no human attached to the other end of it.

Her head snapped back to Tyler. Her mind couldn't decide which to fear more.

"*Get.*" Tyler lashed a foot out at the dog. "Go on, *get.*"

The dog dropped a few inches and did that sharp snapping growl. Tyler lifted the can again, this time aiming for the dog.

"Casper." A male voice spoke from behind the guys. "*Hierr. Fuss.*"

Either that wasn't English, or her mental faculties had completely abandoned her.

The animal sprang over the spilled cans of dog food, dashed between the two guys who had her, and snapped to attention beside a man at the end of the aisle.

No, not a man, a teenager. Defined features, sandy blond hair with a streak of white, and small, odd tattoos—the new kid from World History.

Could her night get any *more* surreal?

Tyler and his friend were staring at him, too, sizing him up, their expressions locked in that panic between fight and flight. Tyler's fingers loosened on her arm. The burning stopped.

"Oh, good," said New Kid, his tone flat and ironic. "Here's the dog food."

"Get lost," said Tyler.

Becca forced her tongue to work. "Call the cops."

Tyler jerked her close and shook her hard. "Shut your mouth, you little—"

Then he screamed and she was free.

The dog was attached to his arm, snarling. She could see blood. Tyler scrabbled back, flailing into the shelves of dry dog chow, but the dog didn't let go. "Get him off me! Get him off! Get him—"

"*Platz,*" said the new guy. He stepped into the aisle. "Casper, *platz.*"

The dog released Tyler and returned to New Kid's side, dropping to the floor beside him. There was blood on his muzzle, but his tongue lolled out, as if it was all in a day's work.

Tyler clutched his forearm, glaring at New Kid as if he'd done more than just stand there. Blood stained his fingers and appeared in an artful splash across the front of his shirt. "I'm going to kill that dog. I swear. I'm going to rip his goddamn head off—"

"Really?" New Kid leaned back against the shelving and hooked his thumbs in his pockets. "Go ahead. Try it."

The dog shut his mouth and growled.

Seth grabbed Tyler by the shoulder. "Come on. Just—come on. Let's get the hell out of here."

Tyler let himself be dragged—for a moment. Then he turned back and looked at her. "You tell Chris. You hear me? You *tell him.*"

She wanted to tell Tyler to go to hell. But he was leaving, and she wanted that more. So she jerked her head up and down. "I'll tell him."

The door chimes rang at the front of the store, and she heard Jerry's voice as they shoved past him on his way in. "In a rush, aren't you, boys?"

A moment later, she heard her boss messing with the register.

She stared at New Kid, still leaning against the shelving, dressed exactly as he'd been that morning. The white streak hung over one eye, leaving the other to watch her.

She wiped sweaty palms on her jeans. Her arm felt stiff and sore where Tyler had grabbed her.

The dog pushed up and padded over to sniff her hand, then pressed his massive body against her legs. His tongue hung out the side of his mouth, his ears were cocked sideways, his demeanor as nonthreatening as the old Labrador that slept under Jerry's desk in the back room. She reached down absently to pet him, letting his wiry fur pull through her fingers.

"You're not afraid of him?" said New Kid.

"He took me by surprise before. I'm not afraid of dogs." She cleared her throat and glanced up at him. "You know, if an animal gets threatening, I'm supposed to make you leave the store."

"Yeah? What's your policy when people get threatening?"

Heat sat on her cheeks. She'd meant that as a joke. She ducked to start picking up the cans on the floor, setting them haphazardly on the shelves.

The dog was sniffing at her hair. She reached up a hand and rubbed him behind his ear, and he started doing that *rawr-rawr-rawr* the big dogs always did when you found their good spot.

Sure enough, in a moment he was on the floor, on his back, begging to have his belly rubbed.

"You're ruining his tough guy image," said New Kid.

It made her smile. She obliged the dog, giving his chest a good scratch. "Seriously, you should keep him on a leash. They're tough on dog laws around here."

"He is on a leash."

She gave him a wry look. "Then someone should be *holding it*."

He smiled, but it was brief, and his gaze was a little too intent. "Did they hurt you?"

Becca looked back at the dog. "Nah. They're just stupid punks."

"Who's Chris?"

She shrugged. "Guy from school. I don't really know him, but they . . . ah . . . saw me with him, and they think we're friends or something." She gave the dog a final pat and resumed picking up the cans.

New Kid dropped to a knee and started to help her. His arm brushed hers.

She told her cheeks to knock off the frigging blushing already. He'd made that comment to Tommy in class—he'd been kidding, right? Or was he gay? She couldn't get a read.

"You don't have to help," she began, but the dog picked up a can and set it on the shelf, then pushed it with his nose.

She stared. "What kind of dog *is* this?"

"A German shepherd." New Kid grabbed a few more cans. The dog grabbed another. "My uncle was a K-9 cop. Casper used to be a police dog."

"Used to be?"

There was a little flinching around his eyes. She'd said it before registering the importance of words like *was* and *used to be,* and now she wished she hadn't said anything at all. "God— that was stupid. I'm sorry—"

"Don't be. It's okay." He gave a little shrug, but he wasn't looking at her now. "My uncle died in a car wreck."

"So you got to keep his dog?"

"Sort of." His eyes were focused on the shelf, and his hands moved more slowly. "Casper was in the car with him." He paused, straightening the cans he'd just placed. "Me and my dad, too."

She studied his profile, the studs and rings along the outside of his ear, the markings on his neck. He didn't look like any teenager she knew, but was some hybrid of Goth and punk and new age. He rubbed at a can where the ruckus had torn a bit of the paper, and the light caught the stones on his twine bracelets.

"My mom thought it'd be a good idea for her and me to move back here," he said. "Stay with her folks for a while."

That had to mean his father had been killed, too. She started to say, "I'm sorry," but she'd just said that, and he'd brushed it off. It felt odd, kneeling here in the aisle talking about death with some guy whose name she didn't even know. She wanted to ask, but now, after such an intimate exchange, asking his name felt rude, like they were well past the basics. She fumbled to grab another can, but there weren't many left.

He reached for one as well, but Casper ducked under his arm and started licking his face. New Kid smiled and lightly pushed him away, scratching the scruff of his neck. "*Bravy,* Casper. *Bravy.*"

"Your dog speaks another language? Does he do your Calculus homework, too?"

"German. Just the commands." He placed the last can and straightened, looking slightly self-conscious for the first time. "Lots of police dogs do."

She scratched the dog on the top of his head again. "Well, I think he's pretty cool."

New Kid moved toward the end of the aisle and grabbed one of the forty-pound bags of dry dog food, and she took a moment to appreciate what that did for the muscles in his upper arms.

He gave her a shadow of a smile, and she realized she was staring. She jerked her eyes away, but he said, "I've never used him to meet girls, but this whole rescuing thing could work out for me."

Check. Not gay. "Well, I'm not sure the cheerleaders would go for someone whose dog weighed more than they do."

He reached up a hand and pushed his hair off his face. "Who would, you think?"

"Softball team," she said without missing a beat. "Those chicks are tough."

He grinned. "Thanks for the tip." He started to turn for the front of the store, then stopped. "You play softball?"

"Nope." Now she knew she was blushing. "Those bags are heavy. You should take that up front."

"Good call." He turned for the end of the aisle and Casper bounded up to walk beside him. She opened her mouth to stop him, to say something witty, to make conversation with someone who didn't expect her to do him a favor in the dark later.

Right. It's his first day. That'll last about five minutes.

Then New Kid stopped. He gave her a smile over his shoulder before looking at the dog. "Casper, she said someone has to hold your leash."

The dog barked.

Then he dipped his head, picked up the end of the leash in his mouth, and trotted after his master.

*   *   *

Her shift ended at nine-thirty. Becca made it to Chris's house before ten. Fury got her there, but fear trapped her in the car once she made it to the driveway.

She stared at the front porch for a long minute. If she sat here much longer, someone was sure to notice. She wondered if she should just pull out of the driveway and go home.

But she was supposed to work this weekend. What if Tyler and his friend came back?

She'd been lucky New Kid showed up with his police dog. Maybe she could ask to borrow Casper and just forget Chris Merrick existed.

Excuse me. Yeah, I don't know your name, but can I borrow your dog? I work three shifts per week. I'll give him a cut of my pay. Bonuses paid in rawhide.

Right.

The air sat thick and heavy with humidity when she climbed the porch steps to knock. Another storm was coming.

She remembered Gabriel's comment the night before, about girls not being an oddity around here. She wondered if she'd come across like that, knocking on their door at ten o'clock at night, like some desperate chick mooning after them all, especially after Chris had asked her—what? Out? What had happened at lunch?

The door swung wide. Michael stood in the light of the foyer. Same ponytail, same careless appearance. His jeans looked a little nicer, and he was wearing shoes tonight, but he still needed a shave. A cordless phone was held to his ear.

He wasn't a big guy, but he sure wasn't little. She remembered how he'd tried to grab her, and she took a step back. "I—ah—is Chris—"

He held up a finger, pointed to the phone, then took a step back and waved her inside.

She stepped across the threshold, trying to keep her shoulders square. She slid a hand into her jeans pocket and threaded her fingers through her keys again.

"No," he said, and it took her a second to realize he was

speaking into the phone, not to her. "You can buy it by the bag, but a sack of mulch will only cover about four square feet . . . mm-hmm . . ."

He headed for the kitchen, leaving her standing there by the door. She had no idea whether he expected her to follow.

When he reached the doorway, he glanced back and gave her an exasperated look. He put a hand over the bottom of the receiver and whispered, "You want to come sit down or what?"

She scurried after him, but he was already speaking into the phone again. "You're welcome to have your husband call me, but I feel fairly certain you'll need more than ten bags to go around your house." Becca could hear the sigh behind his voice.

He pulled out a chair for her without looking, and she perched on the edge. A laptop sat open on the kitchen table, next to a bottle of water and a three-inch white binder bursting with worn pages. A regular spiral notebook lay beside it, the page covered with chicken scratch.

"Yes, the bushes will take up some of the square footage— but still, I'm thinking truckloads, not bags. Would you like me to come out and—"

He sat across from her, put an elbow on the table, and pinched the bridge of his nose. "No, I fully understand. Have him call me. I'll come out and give an estimate . . . okay, then. Okay. Yes. *Okay*."

He pushed the button on the phone and set it on the table. Both hands came up to rub his eyes. "People give me a headache. Everybody wants to nickel-and-dime. Ten bags of mulch for, like, four thousand square feet. Jesus." His hands dropped and he looked at her. "You know that's crazy, right?"

How the hell would she know? Mom was lucky she could work the mower. Becca thought of the meticulous landscaping out front. "You . . . ah . . . you work for a landscaping company?"

"I *am* a landscaping company." He uncapped the water and took a swig. "You here for Chris?"

He didn't seem to be making any threatening moves, but she kept on the edge of the chair. "If I say yes, are you going to try to kill me?"

He sighed and glanced away. "Look, I didn't mean to frighten you last night. You ran out of here so quick—"

"You mean after you grabbed me?"

"You mean after you punched me with a fistful of keys?"

"Yeah, well, you were—" She broke off and flushed. He'd just been standing there, acting scary. Now that she thought about it, he'd never made a move toward her.

Then she remembered how she'd fought to evade him in the yard. "What about when I was trying to get to my car? I should have you arrested for assault."

He slid the phone across the table. "Go ahead."

Now she wanted to punch him with the keys and it had nothing to do with self-defense. "You're kind of a jerk, you know that?"

"Yeah, I'm such an asshole. Trying to keep an upset kid from flying out of here in the middle of a rainstorm." He rolled his eyes. "They'd better lock me up *for sure*."

Now *she* had to look away. She kind of felt like an idiot, but she hadn't imagined his aggression, his threatening tone.

Michael let the silence stretch out for a moment, until she wanted to squirm, and she had to focus to remember why she'd even come here.

She refused to look at him. "Is Chris home?"

"Yeah. Top of the stairs. Make a left."

He expected her to just go up to his *room?*

She remembered going to Drew's house once, last May. Drew's mom had made sure they stayed in plain sight in the den. The woman had seemed to know every time Drew's hands found Becca's knee or the curve of her waist. At the time, Becca had wanted the woman to go the hell away and mind her own business.

Now, in retrospect, she owed Mrs. McKay a hug.

"You want an escort or something?" said Michael. He was already looking at his laptop, his fingers striking the keys.

She shoved herself out of her chair and headed for the steps.

Five doors were on the second level, but she never got to make a left. A bathroom was just to her right, the door wide open. One of the twins stood in front of the mirror, brushing his teeth.

Shirtless.

Breath left her lungs in a rush and she almost stumbled on the last step. Loose button-fly jeans hung low at his hips, exposing just the edge of a pair of boxers. She could clearly see the clean muscled line of his back, the smooth tapering of his rib cage into a tight waist.

He caught her eye in the mirror and grinned around the toothbrush before ducking to spit. He turned off the faucet and wiped his mouth on a towel before turning to face her.

"You're back," he said.

She looked at him—a huge mistake, because it put her eyes right on his chest. The guy was no stranger to a bench press. "Ah . . . yeah. Are you Nick or Gabriel?"

He stepped close, until she could smell the spearmint in his toothpaste. "Does it matter?"

Her cheeks were burning. It was a lot harder to maintain independence and indifference when a hot guy was standing half-naked in front of her. She gulped and grasped at the banister. "I was looking for Chris's room—but, ah—you know, I'll just see him tomorrow—"

"No way." He grabbed her hand. "Come here."

He dragged her around the corner. His fingers were warm on hers. She stared at the beige walls, at the neutral carpeting, anything but the guy attached to her arm.

He knocked on a door. "Hey, Chris. There's a girl here for you."

Something heavy hit the door. "Shut up, Gabriel. I'm busy."

She stared at the doorknob, unsure whether to be dismayed or relieved. But at least she knew who had hold of her arm.

Gabriel knocked again. "Hurry. I'm not sure how much longer I can hold her."

Angry footsteps, then the door flew open. Chris glanced from her to his brother and back. "Oh."

She stared back at him, knowing her face was still flushed,

her eyes desperate for a fully clothed target. Luckily, Chris fit the bill with sweatpants and a tee shirt. She could see into the room behind him: nice, really. A double bed that hadn't been made that morning, with a navy comforter haphazardly thrown across the bottom. The floor was mostly clean, though his laundry sat in a pile in the corner, under a rather impressive fish tank. It had a fluorescent light and everything, and reminded her of something a little boy would have. Finding it in his room was somehow . . . charming. A desk sat by the open window, almost an afterthought. The tiny halogen light was on, books and notebooks strewn across the surface.

"See?" said Gabriel. "A real one. Breathing and everything."

Chris didn't look entirely happy about her presence. "What are you doing here?"

She dug her free hand into her pocket and pulled out the sixty dollars. "Here."

His face went stony. He made no move to take the money. "You came all the way over here for *this?*"

Becca wanted to throw the cash at him. She jerked her hand out of his brother's. "No. I came all the way over here to tell you Tyler and Seth showed up at the pet store where I work."

Gabriel got in front of her and crossed his arms. The smile was gone. "What are you talking about?"

She stared up and over his right shoulder and gritted her teeth. "Could you please put a shirt on?"

"Did they hurt you?" said Chris.

"No. Yes. It's fine. Tyler just—" Her throat suddenly got tight.

Stupid. Stupid, stupid, stupid.

They were both staring at her. Of course.

Chris shoved his brother in the shoulder. "Go. Put on a shirt." Then he took a step back. "Come in. Sit down a minute."

She deliberated in the doorway for a moment, then followed him in. She glanced dubiously at the bed. No *way* was she sitting next to him on it. So she edged around him and sat in the desk chair. She dropped the crumpled twenties next to his Physics textbook.

He settled on the corner of the bed and rested his forearms on his knees. "You want to tell me what happened?"

She fought for any emotion to replace the tears. Anger usually did the trick, and this time was no exception.

"Why'd you give me sixty dollars?" she demanded.

"You said I owed you." A dark smile, though there wasn't much humor to it. "Personally, I thought sixty bucks was pretty cheap."

"Whatever. You know I was kidding. Didn't you think what it would look like? You don't have to treat me like a—"

"Wait a minute." He came halfway off the bed. "I didn't treat you like *anything*. I asked you out, you said no."

"Asked me out. You asked me to a *soccer game*."

"So *what?*" He looked incredulous. "God, you are the most baffling girl—"

"Oh, okay. Your brothers didn't put you up to this? Maybe your friend Drew?"

He was standing now, his fists clenched, a little flare of color on his cheeks. "What do my brothers have to do with anything?"

"Hey, little brother." Gabriel came back through the door and flopped on the bed, drawing his legs up to sit against the wall. "Girls are more likely to stay if you don't fight with them."

Chris was still staring at her, his breathing a little quick.

She looked away from him. Gabriel had put a shirt on—a dark green one with a screen print of a truck. It said, *My other ride is your mom.*

Her eyebrows went up. "Hilarious."

He grinned. "I aim to please." He reached up over his head and knocked on the wall. "Nicky!"

She straightened. "Wait—look, I just came to—"

"Trust me. He won't want to miss this."

A door in the hallway opened; then his twin appeared in the doorway, wearing jeans and a Henley and an irritated expression. "If you want me to fix your homework, you need to leave me *alone*." Then he spotted her. "You're back."

"Yeah." She glanced between him and Gabriel. "You do his homework?"

"Just the math. It's a miracle he can count to ten."

"I can count to one." Gabriel gave him the finger.

Chris sighed. He'd settled onto the end of the bed again, his expression flat and dark and full of unidentifiable emotion. "Just tell us what happened with Seth and Tyler, Becca." His voice was low, intimate, almost too soft for company. He met her eyes and held them, making her pulse step up. "Then you can get out of here."

Becca couldn't sort out the sudden emotion—she felt as if her heart had started scattering butterflies through her abdomen, then he'd kicked her in the stomach and pissed them all off.

She swallowed. "They came by the pet store where I work. They were stealing dog food."

"Does Michael know that's why you're here?" said Nick.

She shook her head. "Does it matter?"

Gabriel snorted. "Doubt it."

A slow peal of thunder rolled in the distance. "They threatened you?" said Chris.

Her arm still throbbed. She had to make a conscious effort to keep from touching it. "Someone else came in, and they ran off. It's fine."

Chris was watching her a bit too intently. "They did hurt you."

"I'm fine."

A bolt of lightning split the sky, somewhere beyond the trees. This time, thunder cracked.

Becca shoved out of the chair and tucked her hair behind her ears. She should never have come here. "Forget it."

She felt Chris behind her when she made it to the stairs. "Wait a minute," he said.

She didn't. "Whatever your mess is with that guy Tyler, get me out of it, okay?"

"Stop. Wait. Just tell me—"

"You stop." She whirled on him at the door. "You, Chris. You stop. I get hassled enough. I need my job. I don't need to be in the middle of some version of *West Side Story* meets *High School Musical*."

"I'm not trying to hassle you." His voice was intense and quiet, the way you'd talk to a cornered animal.

"Yeah, well, then you're the only one." She seized the knob and gave it a firm yank. The humidity swirled through the doorway to grab her, latching onto her skin and refusing to let go. She stormed off his porch.

Chris kept up. "Wait."

She ignored him, shoving through the night air to get to her car.

"Wait. Please. Just tell me what happened."

Her key slid into the lock, but the door refused to give. She made a frustrated noise and slapped it with the heel of her hand.

Then it started to rain.

She swore. "Great."

Chris was still right behind her. She heard his breathing, could feel his presence like a weight at her back. Rain touched her cheek and rolled down her neck, finding a path under the neckline of her shirt to trail along her shoulder. The water felt warm, like a finger tracing the side of her face.

The thought made her shiver, and she swiped it away.

Chris reached out and took hold of the door handle. It lifted and opened without protest.

Figures. She turned to look at him. Her breathing felt a little quick. "Thanks."

His eyes were dark. He didn't seem to mind the rain on his face. "You're welcome."

Becca slid behind the wheel and pushed her key into the ignition. But she couldn't make herself start the car, and he was standing there with a hand on the door, holding it open.

She sighed. "Tyler said if you pulled this again, that they'd take care of it themselves. That the deal was done."

Chris didn't say anything for the longest moment. "That's it?"

"Yeah." She looked up at him, unable to figure out his expression. "What does that mean?"

Lightning flashed, illuminating his features for a moment. For an instant, he looked frightening.

Then the lightning was gone, and he smiled in the darkness. "I have absolutely no idea."

And with that, he swung her door shut and turned for the house.

CHAPTER 8

Chris wanted to sit on the porch and feel the rain. But Michael would eventually come out and ruin it, so he went back to his bedroom, where he could lock the door and sit by the window.

The heart of the storm was drawing closer, sending a strong breeze through the screen to ruffle pages of the notebook sitting there. Nick had claimed the desk chair to prop his feet on the bed. Gabriel was rolling a silver Zippo lighter across his knuckles, making it click every time it changed direction. Chris leaned against his dresser and looked out the window, watching the lightning flash in the distance.

Then he just waited.

"So she doesn't like rain," said Gabriel.

Nick smiled. "I kind of like the irony."

"Jesus, you are such a nerd." Gabriel flung the lighter at him. "Stop using big words."

"Five letters is a big word?"

Chris sighed. "No one likes rain."

"You do," said Nick. He flung the lighter back to his brother.

Gabriel caught it. "Maybe we should put some money on it, see how long it takes Chris to get her wet."

Chris ignored the double entendre and glanced at the pile of makeup work still sitting on his desk. "Could we maybe speed this up?" He could feel the rain pooling on his windowsill again. The red tail sharks in his tank circled and chased, slicing through the water until the less aggressive ones hid among the driftwood at the bottom.

Nick gave a low whistle. "Leave him alone, before the fish kill each other."

Chris gave a pointed look at the door. "Why don't you *both* leave me alone."

Gabriel laughed and made no move to leave. "You have got it *bad* for this girl."

Like that mattered. She'd been pretty clear where he stood. "Tyler shouldn't be hassling her."

"He'll back off," said Nick. "He'll realize she's got nothing to do with us."

"I don't know about that." Chris glanced at the fish. They helped him manage his temper—he didn't like riling them. But they seemed to be settling. "He threatened her. He told her the deal is off."

Nick pulled his feet off the bed to sit up straight. "He said that?"

Chris nodded. "Well. She said he did."

Gabriel rolled the lighter across his knuckles again, slowly now. "Because of last night?"

Chris met his eyes, then shrugged.

He still didn't regret it.

"The deal can't be *off,*" said Nicholas. "They can't just decide—"

"They can do whatever they want," said Chris, the words tasting bitter.

Nick stood. "We have to tell Michael. He'll—"

"He'll do nothing," said Gabriel. "Don't tell him."

His twin looked at him like he was nuts. "Are you crazy? We have to—"

"No." Gabriel sat up, any trace of humor gone from his expression. Thunder rolled in the air outside. "You saw him last night. He doesn't give a crap what they do. All he cares about is letting them have their way."

"So what do we do?" said Chris. He thought about the way he'd felt the water freeze into Tyler's skin. That had been a good storm. A powerful one. He wondered how much damage he could do if he practiced.

The thought scared him, a little. But it comforted him, too.

"Tyler says the deal is off." Gabriel flipped the lighter in the air and snapped it, lighting it as it spun. The flame danced between his fingers. "He's not going to hold to it. Right?"

"Don't be stupid," said Nick. He knew his twin.

Chris knew him, too. But he liked the note of danger in Gabriel's voice, the promise. It reminded him of that moment of solidarity last night. "Right . . . ?"

Gabriel smiled. "That means we aren't held to it, either."

Her mom was working the night shift again. The sheer irony was that any kid with a normal social life would envy Becca's freedom.

Quinn was sitting in the kitchen, but schoolbooks were spread across the table tonight. She looked up at Becca through a fall of blond hair. Her voice was small. "Hey. Your dad called again."

Swell. Becca hung her jacket in the hall. "What, you'll speak to me when you need a place to stay?"

"You're the one who didn't answer my texts."

"Maybe if you hadn't bolted from the lunch table, I could have mentioned that I broke my phone last night."

Quinn didn't say anything for a long moment. Becca grabbed a soda from the fridge and swung into a chair. She glanced down at the notebook on the table. Quinn was struggling with Trigonometry.

"So you want me to leave?" said Quinn.

Becca rolled her eyes and popped the can. The storm seemed to be sticking around—thunder still boomed every few minutes and lightning threw silhouettes against the glass. "You are *such* a drama queen."

Quinn flung her textbook closed. "Well, at least it's better than being a liar."

Becca sat up straight. "A *liar?* What the hell did I lie about?"

"Self-defense class? You could have just told me you were sleeping with Chris Merrick."

"Who said—wait—what the—are you *crazy?*" Becca couldn't string a sentence together. "You think I'm *sleeping* with him? Why on earth would you think that?"

"Gee, I don't know." Her voice dropped to a mocking baritone. *"I'm just here to thank Becca for last night."*

Becca stared at her, unsure whether to laugh or cry. "Quinn—"

"You could have told me, you know." Quinn doodled on the margin of her notebook. "I didn't even know you *liked* him, Bex. . . . I mean, after all the stuff with Drew—"

"I did go to self-defense class. And I didn't sleep with Chris." Becca paused, waiting for Quinn to look up. "When I came out, Seth Ramsey and some college guy were beating the crap out of him in the parking lot."

"Why?"

The question made her stop. It was a good one. "I don't know. But I chased them off with the car." She told Quinn everything, including what had happened in the pet store and her visit to the Merrick house.

"You should call the cops," Quinn said.

"And tell them what? I don't even know Tyler's last name."

"You know Seth's." Quinn's voice was careful.

"I'd rather not get involved, Quinn."

"Bex—"

"Leave it." Becca glared at her.

Quinn rocked back in her chair. "So you aren't interested in Chris?"

"Please. He doesn't really want to go out with me."

"I think the sixty-dollar thing is kind of adorable." Quinn chewed on the end of her pencil and glanced up.

Becca groaned. "You're not helping."

"I'm just saying—maybe people are over the Drew thing."

"Tommy Dunleavy's note today asked me if I give a happy ending."

Quinn winced. "Okay, maybe *some* people are over the Drew thing."

Becca replayed her comments to Chris, the way she'd lashed out at him over the lunch table. She frowned, but then scowled. "Still. A *soccer game?* That can't be a coincidence."

"Yeah, well." Quinn flipped the textbook open, her eyebrows raised. "Guess you'll never know *now.*"

"You suck." Becca grinned and shoved her notebook at her.

Then Quinn shoved it back, a little more pointedly. She tapped her pen where a number was scrawled. "You going to call your dad or what? I can only be a bitch for so long."

"You sure about that?"

Quinn made a face. "You know, that's a local number."

Becca stared. She hadn't noticed. Did that mean he was in town?

Did it matter?

Becca tore the piece of paper from the notebook.

Then, just like last night, she crumpled it up, shoved it in the trash, and carried it out to the curb.

CHAPTER 9

By Friday, Chris still looked like crap, and Becca wanted to call him on it. But in third-period English Lit, he sat across the room and didn't make eye contact once.

Fine.

She must have beaten Chris to World History, because New Kid was sitting in the same seat as the day before—Chris's usual spot. He'd paired a rust-colored tee shirt with dark jeans and black Vans today. Average, nothing-special clothes that looked striking and exotic just because he was wearing them.

Monica Lawrence was sitting at the desk next to him, leaning into him, giggling at something he'd said. She called Tommy Dunleavy her boyfriend, but you wouldn't know it from the way she was putting her assets front and center.

Not that New Kid seemed to mind.

Guess he doesn't need the dog to pick up chicks after all.

Becca swung her bag higher on her shoulder and moved down the aisle to her seat, carefully avoiding Monica's eyes.

New Kid looked up when she passed. "Hey—"

"Ohmigod, no," said Monica. Her manicured hand latched onto his arm and a spill of blond hair pooled on his desk. Her boobs were going to explode from the neckline of her shirt in a minute.

Then she leaned in close and whispered into his ear, breaking off to glance at Becca more than once.

Yup, that had lasted about five minutes.

"Grow up," Becca muttered. She dropped into her chair, busying herself with pulling a textbook from her backpack, finding a pen, and establishing the mental fortitude for the abuse that would start when Tommy sat down.

"Hey."

It was Chris Merrick's voice, his tone almost aggressive—and so startling that she jerked her head up, sure he was talking to her.

But he was standing next to New Kid, a hand braced on the nylon strap of his backpack. "You're in my seat."

New Kid lifted his head, a slow, deliberate movement. Becca watched him size up Chris—but his eyes widened fractionally when they got to Chris's face. The bruising along his cheekbone and jaw had lightened, turning a mottled yellowish blue. His lip was healing, but you could still see a split.

Monica was staring, her lips slightly parted. "What happened?" she said, her voice soft with awe.

"Wow. Yeah." New Kid settled back in his chair—a clear refusal to move. One eyebrow lifted, and his voice was dry. "Someone sit in your seat?"

Monica snorted with laughter and giggled behind her hand.

Chris leaned down, his blue eyes dark, like the ocean at night. The bag slipped off his shoulder to hit the floor.

Mr. Beamis chose that moment to step into the classroom. He cleared his throat. "Mr. Merrick. I presume you're welcoming our new student?"

Chris put a hand on New Kid's desk. "Welcome. Move."

"Keep moving, Mr. Merrick," said Beamis. His tone drew the attention of the rest of the class, and conversation died. "There's a seat farther down. I suggest you find it."

Chris didn't move. Neither did New Kid.

Beamis dropped his briefcase on the top of his desk and snapped the latches. "Or would you prefer to find a seat in the office?"

Half the class did that stupid "Oooh" thing. Then laughed.

Chris grabbed his bag and sighed, then walked six feet to drop into the next empty seat in the row.

Right next to Becca.

He didn't even glance at her, just pulled a textbook from his bag.

"That's Jocelyn Kanter's seat," she said under her breath. "You gonna make her fight you for it later?"

He stopped, turned his head, and looked at her from under his bangs. "You too?"

"I'm not the one who picked a fight over a chair."

He looked away, so she did, too, staring down at the glossy pages of her textbook. From the corner of her eye, she saw New Kid glance her way, but she kept her gaze down and flipped a page, not wanting to make eye contact.

Furniture scraped along the tile floor. Students were moving desks, shifting the writing surfaces together. Becca threw her head up. What had she missed?

They seemed to be turning six rows of desks into three. She started pushing her desk to the right, watching the others to make sure she was following instructions she hadn't heard.

"What are we doing?" she whispered to Chris.

"Succumbing to the whims of a bitter old man." He shoved his desk the rest of the way, until it was up against hers.

She sighed. "I meant—"

"Rewriting a peace treaty," he said. "Semester project."

Talk about a thrill-a-minute. "Why are we moving the desks?"

He snorted. "Who the hell knows. He probably read about this in a teachers' magazine."

"Quickly, everyone," said Beamis. "Quickly. Now that you're partnered, you will work together over the next six weeks—"

The class erupted in groans, and several girls scrambled to change seats so they could be together.

She and Chris didn't move for the longest moment.

"Great," said Chris, his tone flat.

"Sorry," she snapped. "I'm sure you'd rather be with Monica."

But Monica looked all too pleased to be partnered with New

Kid. Two rows over, Tommy was fuming, sprawled in his chair, completely ignoring his partner Anthony Denton, the scrawny boy who was two years younger than everyone else because he'd skipped a couple grades in elementary school.

"Do you know the new guy?" said Chris. "He keeps looking at you."

She glanced up in surprise. New Kid was writing in his notebook, not looking anywhere near her.

Chris leaned in. "Earlier."

Becca looked down and doodled on the corner of her paper, feeling warm. Chris was so close, his voice dark and intimate like it had been in his bedroom the night before.

Her tongue felt tied in knots, so she just shrugged. "Not really."

He went silent for a while, every now and again copying instructions from the assignment as Beamis outlined the structure of the grading.

He kept his eyes on his paper and said, "Look. If you want to partner with someone else, I get it."

Did he not want to be with her? "It's fine," she said quickly. Then she added, "It's only six weeks."

He gave a short, humorless laugh. "I'll try to suffer through it, too."

She had no idea what that meant.

A folded piece of paper flew through the air and landed on the center of her book. She jumped.

Tommy Dunleavy was hiding a smirk. Her throat felt tight. *Now? Really?*

Chris reached out and grabbed it.

"No!" she hissed, trying to take it back. "Give that to—"

Then he had it open in front of him. With their seats so close together, she could read it over his arm.

$5 Sucky sucky?

Gross. She snatched it out of his hands and crumpled it up. Her cheeks burned. Her eyes weren't far behind. Seeing the notes privately was bad enough. Having a guy like Chris Merrick read them—right in front of her—was a million times worse.

"Hey. Dunleavy." Chris's voice carried a shred of wicked humor.

Tommy looked over his shoulder. His eyes were amused, and a dark smile still hung on the edge of his lips. He sat ready for his efforts to be appreciated. "Yeah?"

Chris took the crumpled ball of paper out of her hands and flung it. "Fuck off."

Tommy came halfway out of his seat, his hands balled into fists.

Chris came halfway out of his.

"Gentlemen!" Beamis was knocking on his desk, though Becca couldn't imagine what he expected that to do. Chris hadn't moved farther; his glare locked on Tommy now.

The class sat frozen, Becca included.

"Christopher," said Mr. Beamis. "Take a visit to the office."

And though she was staring at him, Chris didn't look at her. He just shoved his books into his bag, slung it over his shoulder, and strode out of the classroom.

"So let me get this straight," said Quinn, spinning her water bottle in her hands. The rain seemed to be holding off, so they had the lunch table to themselves again. "He threw the note at Tommy and *then* told him to fuck off? Or do I have it backwards?"

"I'm detecting some sarcasm."

"And *then* got himself sent to the principal's office because he was ready to defend your honor?"

"Quinn."

Her friend waved a hand. "No, I think you might be on to something. This is clearly an elaborate plot to screw with you. He asks you out, he defends you from that meathead—what next?" Quinn's eyes flashed wide in mock surprise. "Crap, Bex, do you think he'll do something truly horrible like buy you flowers?"

Becca gave her a look. "So you think I should apologize."

"No. I think you should give him a shot." Quinn rolled her eyes and dropped her voice. "I think you should give *someone* a shot."

Becca chewed on her lip and peeled at the label of her water bottle.

A shadow fell across the table and a lunch tray slapped down next to Quinn.

Becca jerked her head up, surprised by the quick flutter in her chest.

But it wasn't Chris—it was New Kid.

She stared up at him. It took her brain a second to get it together.

"Hey," he said, dropping onto the bench beside Quinn. "Why do you sit all the way back here?"

Quinn looked at him for a moment, then back at Becca. Her expression was some combination of bemused and incredulous. "Did you save his life, too?"

New Kid picked up his fork and looked over. "Whose life did you save?"

Becca opened her mouth, then closed it. Her brain was refusing to engage. She couldn't figure out how to play this without knowing what his motives were. The quick and easy intimacy of discussing death in the aisle of Pets Plus didn't exist here—especially since she'd seen him sit head-to-head with Monica for fifty minutes.

"Quinn's just being silly." She kept her voice disinterested. "You . . . ah, you're eating with us?"

His whole tray was full of healthy food—grilled chicken, steamed vegetables, brown rice. No wonder he'd gotten through the line so quickly. He went for the stuff most kids wouldn't touch.

He peeled the lid off something that looked like sliced fruit. "That all right?"

Quinn put an elbow on the table and gave him a level look. "She wants to know why."

He raised an eyebrow. "I'm hungry and I don't know anyone else?"

Becca wasn't going to buy any poor-little-new-kid crap now. "You seemed to be getting to know Monica Lawrence pretty well."

He met her gaze head on, a spark of boldness in his green eyes. "Oh," he said, his voice flat. "You mean instead of sitting here, I could hear all about Monica's badass cheer routine and where she gets her highlights done and how some girl named Claire, who's a total whore by the way—"

"Okay, okay." Becca couldn't help the smile.

"No, wait. I'm just getting going." He sliced into his chicken.

"Claire *is* a total whore," said Quinn. "She and Monica sit behind me in Trig."

Becca watched New Kid work the cutlery. "Bet you wish you'd given up your seat now, huh?"

"Oh." Quinn settled back on the bench and gave him a more appraising look. "This is *that* guy."

He looked thrown for a second. "*That* guy?"

Quinn nodded. "Pet store hero, ex-police-dog owner, seat stealer."

Trust her best friend to be absolutely direct. Becca glanced away and tucked her hair behind her ear. "I might have mentioned you."

"She spilled all your secrets," said Quinn.

"Yeah?" He sliced off a piece of chicken and glanced across the table. "What's my name, Becca?"

Busted. Becca wanted to melt into a puddle.

Quinn grinned. "You mean it's not really New Kid?"

Becca kicked her under the table. "That's not fair. I was wearing a name tag."

"It's Hunter." His fork went still as he held her eyes. "Want me to write it down?"

Yeah, with your number. Talking to him felt entirely different from sitting with Chris, exhilarating and challenging and breathless all at once—like running a race.

"Nah, I've got it," she said.

He picked up a forkful of broccoli. "Was Chris the same one those guys were looking for last night?"

She lost the smile. "Yeah."

"I shouldn't have been a dick about the seat. I didn't realize you'd get stuck with him."

There was a thread of disdain woven through his voice. She frowned. "He's okay."

"He looks like a thug."

"Those guys did that to him."

Hunter must have heard the tone in her voice, but he didn't back off. "Somehow I get the impression it might have been deserved."

Becca stared at him for a moment, torn over whether to defend Chris. Hunter didn't help, either, just looking at her across the table as if he could hear her thoughts fighting it out.

"What's with the white hair?" said Quinn.

He broke the eye contact with Becca and smiled at her friend. "I thought you knew all my secrets."

Now Quinn blushed.

His smile turned into a grin. He looked down at his tray and shoveled rice onto his fork. "You guys hitting that party tonight?"

"Which one?" Becca said drily. "We try to make the circuit."

He smiled in a way that said he saw right through her. "Well—and I want to make sure I get this straight—Monica said Claire said her boyfriend's best friend's brother was home from college with that skank Melissa—"

"No," said Becca sharply. "We're not."

His eyebrows went up.

"Jesus," said Quinn. "You followed that?"

Becca faltered, knowing she sounded like a freak. But Claire's boyfriend was Matt Carpenter. The goalie of the soccer team.

And Drew McKay's best friend.

"I might have to work," she said lamely. Her heart was kicking.

"I hear you," he said.

"You said you weren't working tonight," said Quinn. "Free and clear, you said."

Becca slapped her water bottle on the table. "Damn it, Quinn."

"Free and clear, huh?" Hunter said.

"Look," she said, hearing her voice come out choked. She had to clear her throat. "That party is going to be at Drew McKay's house. . . ."

"Old boyfriend?"

"*No.*"

"Yes," said Quinn. When Becca glared at her, she shrugged. "It's true."

His pierced eyebrow lifted. "Still carry a torch?"

"No," she snapped.

Hunter was just looking at her, his eyes bright and challenging again. Her breath caught. Forget running a race—this felt like dancing.

"In or out?" he said.

All that air left her lungs in a rush. She stared right back at him.

"*In.*"

Chris counted the rust-colored cinderblocks of the detention room. Twice.

When the bell rang, he scowled through the lecture about a *next time* and hustled up the stairs to the front hall. Gabriel and Nick weren't exactly patient.

They weren't exactly *there*, either. The bench by the double doors sat empty.

Chris swore.

It was only three miles. He'd walked it before.

The last time sucked.

But Michael's work truck sat idling in the fire lane, a massive red pile of steel with their last name on the door. The diesel engine roared over the extracurricular students spilling through the double doors, a low thrum that moved the pavement.

Michael was working on something, his head bent over a notebook.

Chris was halfway through the crosswalk when Michael's voice caught him. "Don't screw with me, Chris."

Whatever. Chris climbed into the cab and flung his backpack on the floorboards. The truck perpetually smelled like mulch and grass clippings and always reminded him of his father.

He didn't look at his brother. "What are you doing here?"

Michael flipped the notebook closed and shoved it into the center console. "It seemed as good a place as any to catch up on paperwork."

This would go on forever and a day if Chris let it. "Would you just say whatever you came to say?"

Michael waited for students to clear the road before pulling the truck away from the curb. "I think you're the one who needs to do some talking."

Chris had no idea what that meant. Did Michael know about what Tyler had said? About the deal? He kept his mouth shut.

Michael glanced over. "You picked a fight in class?"

Christ, this was *worse*. "The school *called* you?"

"No. I'm psychic. What the hell is wrong with you? First that crap with Seth and Tyler, and now this?"

Chris felt his hands curl into fists. It wasn't like he'd laid a hand on Dunleavy—and that was the rule. No contact, no parents. Now he wished he'd just slammed that stupid prick in the face. "I didn't pick a fight."

"Chris—"

"I *didn't*."

Michael said nothing for the longest time, and Chris felt his hands start to unknot. He leaned back against the headrest and stared out the window as the trees raced past.

"Then tell me," Michael said finally.

"They shouldn't have called you." Chris picked at the upholstery on the door. "I didn't even touch him."

"Why don't you tell me what you *did* do?"

"I told him to fuck off." Chris sighed. "That's *it*."

"Wow, just like that. Middle of class. No provocation at all—"

"God, would you shut up? He was hassling someone, okay?"

Chris expected that to launch a new round of interrogation, but Michael looked back at the road and didn't say anything.

He was thinking, though. Chris could practically *feel* that.

Finally, he couldn't take it anymore. "All right, *what?*"

"Was this 'someone' a girl?"

This felt like a trap. Chris hesitated and decided not to say anything.

Michael glanced over. "Could it be the girl who dragged you home? The one who conveniently showed up last night?"

Maybe his brother *was* psychic. "How the hell do you know that?"

"Because I'm not an idiot. I know you helped her get away from me that night."

Chris scowled and looked at the trees again.

"Stay away from her, Chris."

"Jesus, could you sound more dramatic? I already told you, she's got nothing to do with Tyler. She's just a girl in my class."

"Average girls don't jump into the middle of a fight between three guys. Stay away from her."

Like it mattered. "Fine."

They drove in silence for a mile, both staring through the windshield at nothing.

"Look," said Michael, and his voice was low, quiet. "Even if she's an average girl—you don't have the control for a relationship, Chris."

"I'm not in a relationship!" God, he should be so lucky. He'd give his left arm for *someone* outside this family to talk to. Chris rounded on him. "Besides, don't you think maybe you should be having this talk with Gabriel, who might actually be screwing half the cheer squad right now, or Nick, who has to beat girls off with a stick?"

Michael hit the turn signal to pull into the driveway. The twins were tossing a basketball at the hoop over the garage. "They don't worry me."

"Oh, but I do."

"Yeah." Michael glanced over. "You do. Emotion and elements—they're too closely tied, Chris. Control—it can snap like *that*."

Chris sighed.

"Trust me," said Michael. "What if you hurt that girl? What if you—"

"What if I *hurt* her?" Chris swung his head around. "You're one to talk."

For an instant, he thought he'd pushed too far, that Michael would come after him the way he'd gone after Gabriel.

But Michael just pulled the truck beside the garage and shifted into park, his jaw set, his hands tight on the wheel.

Chris knew he should apologize. He didn't want to.

"Look," said Michael, his voice rough. "Just let this mess with Tyler and Seth blow over, and they'll leave you alone again—"

"Are you *crazy?*" Chris glared at him, the rage so pure he could barely speak around it. "Do you know they tried to kill Gabriel? Seth had—he had his hands—he was going to—"

The cab door swung open. Gabriel stood there, a basketball under his arm.

He met Chris's eye, then glanced past him at Michael. "Still being a dick?"

"Shut up," said Michael. "Close the door."

"Chris—want to play?"

"We're talking," said Michael.

Chris grabbed his backpack and swung out of the cab. "No, we're not."

Then he slammed the door, flung his bag by the corner of the garage, and caught the ball Gabriel passed him.

CHAPTER 10

Becca was standing in the kitchen when her mom came down at seven, wearing an old tee shirt and threadbare sweatpants instead of her nursing scrubs.

Becca stared at her. "What are you doing?"

Her mom yawned and headed for the refrigerator. "There were too many nurses on, so they canceled me. Did you already eat?"

"I found something." Becca dug her nails into her palms. Her "dinner" had consisted of a glass of chocolate milk—she was so nervous the thought of eating made her want to puke.

Her mom started pulling food out of the refrigerator. "Isn't this nice? Maybe we can rent some pay-per-view or something."

"Um, Quinn and I were going to catch a movie, actually," she said. "I'm supposed to pick her up—"

"What are you seeing?"

What is this, the Spanish Inquisition? Becca took a gulp of her chocolate milk. "I forget. Quinn picked."

"Well, let me put some jeans on. I haven't been to a movie in *ages*."

Becca almost dropped her glass. "You want to *go*? Mom—it's kind of a girls' night out. . . ."

Her mom rolled her eyes. "I'm a girl, Becca. I haven't seen you all week—"

"And whose fault is that?"

Crap. Becca winced, wishing she could suck the words back into her mouth.

"Becca, you know I started working nights so I could be home during the day." The refrigerator door swung closed, and her mother came to lean on the cooking island, a stern expression on her face. Becca couldn't remember seeing gray hair threaded along her mother's temples before, but it was sure there now.

She wondered if her mom knew her father had called. Twice.

"Look, Mom, I know—"

But her mom was already off and running with the lecture. Becca resisted the impulse to keep glancing at the clock.

When it seemed like she was winding down, Becca sighed and played the guilt card and glanced up at her through her lashes. "Mom, it's really about Quinn," she said in a hushed voice. "I think she wants to get away from parents for a while."

That was probably true. Quinn was more than likely sitting in her living room, staring out the front picture window, desperate for Becca to pick her up.

So they could drive to Drew McKay's house.

Maybe a movie with Mom wouldn't be *such* a bad idea.

Her mom studied her. "Just you and Quinn?"

Becca averted her eyes and downed the last of her milk. "Yeah, Mom, who else?"

"Well, you look very pretty."

"It's just an old pullover." Thank god the house had been chilly. Otherwise her mom might have seen her in that silk top that exposed half an inch of midriff and made it look like she had a chest to write home about.

Monica can kiss my ass.

"I meant your hair. The makeup."

That had taken forty-five minutes. She'd actually had to hunt for the curling iron.

Becca started to put her glass in the sink, then thought better of it and rinsed it for the dishwasher since her mom was standing right there. "It's a Friday night. You know."

"I know." Her mom was leaning against the refrigerator now. Becca bit the inside of her cheek, sure she was blushing.

"Wow," she said, looking in the general direction of the clock, though her brain was too addled to register the time. She grabbed her bag and her car keys. "I'd better get going if we're going to get popcorn and stuff."

Her mom was still watching her just a little too carefully. "Be careful, Bex. Not too late, okay?"

"Sure, Mom." She'd almost made it to the front door.

"I'll be up when you get home."

Can't wait.

Then Becca was out the door and into her car, well aware her mom watched her pull down the driveway, roll down the street, and waited at the window until she made the turn toward Quinn's house.

Quinn wore a beaded tank, Capri pants, and strappy sandals, an outfit that demanded nicer weather. Her blond hair hung straight and shiny down her back, swinging when she jumped into the car.

Quinn was fishing through the glove box for gum. "Why didn't you let Hunter pick you up?"

Because that meant it was a date. This wasn't a date. This was a dare. Becca started to bite at her cuticles, then told herself to knock it off. "I wanted a getaway car."

Quinn laughed—but when Becca didn't join her, she stared. "Seriously?"

"Yep."

"What do you think Drew's going to do, throw you down and rape you right in front of the soccer team?"

That was probably number five on her list of worries. "I'm hoping Drew doesn't notice I'm there."

"I'm proud of you."

"Thanks, Mom."

"Seriously." Quinn sounded hurt.

"Thanks. Seriously." But Becca didn't feel like she'd done anything to be proud of.

Drew lived down off River Bay Road, in an old shore house that could fit two of hers inside it. The house backed up to one of the many tributaries of the Chesapeake Bay, and sported a thirty-foot span of beach beyond his backyard. The water was nothing you'd want to swim in, but the beach was nice in the summer; just enough sand to make you feel like you were vacationing all the time.

She remembered it well.

She had to park down the road a ways, and they could hear the music from here. Some kids already had fires going in a couple of drums down on the beach. Smoke and charcoal wrapped around her and flavored the air.

Quinn reached over and turned off the ignition, then put the keys in her pocket. "I'm taking your keys."

Becca snapped to. "What? Quinn—I never drink—"

"I don't give a crap if you drink. I don't want you bolting without consulting me." She smiled and it looked a little vicious. "Now get your ass out of the car."

When they started walking toward Drew's house, Becca focused on the narrow strip of asphalt in front of her until it started to feel like a gangplank.

One wrong step and she'd fall.

What the hell am I doing here?

"You came."

The voice spoke out of the shadows to her left. Becca jumped and swore and almost took her friend down.

Quinn grabbed her arm to steady her. "Damn it, Bex! God, I should have snuck you one of Mom's valiums. It's only New Kid."

"Hunter," he said, but his voice was amused. He was leaning against a late model Jeep Wrangler with the top off, partially cloaked by the shadow of a cherry tree. He'd worn cargo pants and a charcoal long-sleeved tee, and his thumbs were hooked in his pockets.

Casper's head hung over his shoulder, his tongue hanging out. Becca widened her eyes, delighted. "You brought your dog!"

Quinn was just as wide-eyed. "He . . . brought his dog."

He reached up and rubbed the dog's ears. "I never really *bring* Casper anywhere. He gets out of the yard and finds me all the time. I'm always worried he'll end up under some guy's tires." He grimaced. "It's easier to let him hop in the car."

This was awesome. The dog could be her bodyguard. She imagined Casper tearing into Drew the way he'd done to Tyler.

But then Hunter said, "He'll just sleep in the back of the jeep." As if on cue, the dog lay down and rested his head on the tailgate.

Damn it.

Hunter pushed off the car and stepped closer, and suddenly she remembered this wasn't a chance meeting on the side of the road. "You didn't want me to drive."

She looked up at him, tightening her grip on the strap of her purse. He smelled good, like woods and fresh air and confidence. "Is that a problem?"

"I thought you might be planning to stand me up." His eyes were bright, his voice gently chiding. He glanced at Quinn. "Make New Kid walk in alone."

Quinn rolled her eyes. "She just wanted a getaway—"

Becca elbowed her in the side. "Have you been waiting long?"

He shook his head. "Shall we?"

The music pouring from the house seemed to move the sidewalk, and the front door stood wide open. It wasn't like those high school parties in the movies, where everyone was hot and well dressed and straight sober despite having a drink in hand. In front of Drew McKay's house, three guys were sitting on the front step, smoking. A girl wearing a fleece tracksuit was already puking in the front shrubbery. The word *Juicy* was plastered across her ass, and most of the vomit ended up in her hair. She staggered like she might pass out.

One of the smokers jeered and flicked ash her way.

Becca hesitated on the front walk.

"Leave it," hissed Quinn. "Come on."

Maybe she had too much of her mother in her, but Becca couldn't just blow right past that kind of train wreck.

"Hey. Are you okay?" she asked.

The girl looked up, rings of mascara under her eyes. Taylor Morrissey, varsity cheerleader. She swiped at her mouth with the end of her sleeve.

"Becca Chandler?" she whispered.

"Yeah." Becca tucked her hair behind her ear, very aware of the weight of Hunter's presence at her side. "You want me to get you a towel—or a washcloth—"

"Why are you here? Did someone pay you to strip on tables or something?"

One of the guys on the stoop snorted with laughter, blowing smoke through his nose.

Becca jerked back. Despite hearing comments like that on a daily basis, it was still a surprise.

"Drunk bitch," muttered Quinn.

Then Taylor was laughing, almost hysterically, until she fell on her side in the grass. She narrowly missed rolling in her own vomit. "Or—wait—you just do it for free, right?"

"Ignore her," said Hunter, his voice low and close to her ear. "She's hammered."

But Taylor's words had punched her in the gut, and now Becca couldn't get enough air. She shook off Quinn's arm and spun for the sidewalk.

Two of Drew's soccer team buddies were coming up the walk. One had a case of beer under his arm. She couldn't remember his name, but his eyes didn't get as far as her face—he was staring at her chest. "Hey, baby, where you going?"

The smoke, the laughter, the sheer number of people surrounding her—it was all suffocating. She needed to get away. Quinn had her keys, so she bolted through the open door, into the foyer.

Music slapped her in the face, something with a loud, driving beat pounding from the bass speakers in the living room. Some guy she didn't recognize had shot glasses lined up on the hall table, and he held one out to her.

"A drink for every lady," he said with a wink.

Liquid courage. Just what she needed. She took the glass from his fingers.

It was like swallowing fire.

It felt fantastic.

He whistled and held out another. "Let me see you do that again."

Her limbs felt hot and heavy already, as if the alcohol were traveling through her veins to her fingertips. She reached out and took the second glass.

This burn was twice as nice.

Some people from the living room were whistling now. She shut her eyes and felt her body waver, as if a wind had whipped through the hallway.

When she opened them, he'd come around the table and was holding another shot in front of her. She could smell him now, liquor and smoke and male sweat. His voice turned low and taunting. "Let's see you get that down your throat."

A hand reached out and took it before she could. "Let's not."

Hunter.

She meant to turn, to confront him. Her legs had a different idea. She stumbled and the room tilted sideways. She knew she was falling, but her brain couldn't get it together to do anything about it. She probably should have eaten dinner.

Hunter caught her. She heard the shot glass rattle on the hardwood of the foyer.

Her veins were still burning. Her knees wouldn't lock to hold her upright.

Hunter glared over her shoulder. "What is that, tequila?"

"Dude, it's not like I held her down—"

"Stop it," she said, not wanting to hear any more talk of being held down. She tried to shrug out of Hunter's hands. The music was still slamming into her body with every beat. "Lemme go. I just want—I need my keys—"

"Here." He backed her up until she was leaning against the molding between the hallway and the living room, then let her go. He looked at the guy with the shot glasses. "Get her a cup of water or something."

She braced her hands behind her on the wall and stared up at Hunter. She couldn't figure out his expression, whether he was disgusted, or disappointed, or exasperated.

Maybe Quinn was right. Maybe she was going about this all wrong.

"Where's Quinn?" she said.

"I told her to give me a second."

Traitor.

"Isn't this what you wanted?" At least her voice wasn't slurring yet, but everything felt warm. "Now I'm all liquored up. You didn't even have to work for it."

His eyes narrowed. "Why would I want you trashed?"

"You're a guy, right? Isn't that why you asked me here?"

He glanced away and sighed.

"See." She reached out and poked him in the chest. Hard. "Monica told you about me. About Drew. That's why you brought me here."

"Damn. You're on to me." He was untying one of the twine bracelets from his wrist.

His words drew her up short. "Wait. What?"

He got one bracelet free and held it between his fingers as he untied another. He shook his head. "I have no idea what you're talking about."

The movement of his fingers had her spellbound. What was he *doing?*

"Monica talks too much," he said. "I stopped listening." He was on to a third bracelet, and he didn't look at her. "Besides, I prefer to figure things out for myself."

Shot Glass Kid showed up with a plastic cup. "Here. Drew will shit if she pukes in the hallway."

That made her want to stick her finger down her throat right there.

Hunter took the cup and held it out to her. His eyes leveled with hers. "Drink."

She took the cup and sipped. Water did nothing to tame the inferno in her stomach.

He reached out and started tying one of the bracelets around her wrist.

She was so startled that she let him. "What are you doing?"

The silvery black stone strung on the twine fell against her skin, smooth and cool. It cut through the fire better than the water had. "This is hematite. For anxiety." His voice turned wry. "And clarity of thought."

"It's a rock." But the tequila did seem to be having less effect.

The corner of his mouth quirked, and he started tying another one. His fingers were gentle and warm against her wrist. "Amethyst. It does a lot of things, but really, I'm just trying to take the edge off so you can walk."

He was walking around with a hunk of amethyst on a piece of twine? "You're giving me a bunch of rocks?"

"Not giving." He glanced up. "Loaning."

"What, are you afraid you'll be off balance?"

"Something like that." He tied the third bracelet. "Quartz. To help the other two."

She looked down at the three stones on her wrist and wasn't quite sure what to say. She sure didn't feel drunk now. Just a buzz.

She touched her finger to the stones, and new awareness was bringing heat to her cheeks. She felt like a freak. It was probably a miracle he was still standing in front of her.

Then again, he was the one tying on rock bracelets. She glanced up at him from under her lashes. "Don't tell me. You read Tarot cards, too?"

"Mock all you want. You feel better, right?"

She did. Standing in the hallway in this house full of people, with R&B music so loud it seemed part of her body, he somehow made her feel like they stood alone in the middle of a field. At night, under a silent moon.

Becca had to take a deep breath.

"I didn't realize coming here would upset you," he said.

She shrugged and looked down into the cup of water. "It's all right."

"My father used to tell me something, when people would screw with me," he said. His voice got kind of quiet, and she had to lean in to hear him.

People used to screw with him? He seemed so . . . untouchable. Above it.

She didn't want to hear some sentimental pep talk, either. But his father had died, and whatever the words were, they were important to Hunter.

"What?" she said.

"Fuck 'em."

Her head shot up. The edge of a smile played on his lips, but she could read the emotion in his eyes.

"It helps," he said.

Fuck 'em. She smiled. It did help.

She looked up at him, standing so close. Her pulse picked up. She licked her lips. "I think I'm going to go . . . ah . . . straighten up."

He took a step back and grinned. "You all right to walk?"

Becca straightened and pushed off the wall. Her head still swam, but her legs felt steady. Mostly.

"Yeah." She took a step into the hallway. Then another. The water in her cup didn't even slosh.

"Thanks for the magic rocks," she called over her shoulder.

As she turned the corner, she banged into something hard. Her eyes saw the blue shirt first, then the spread of water across a male chest. He swore.

She recognized the voice and jerked her eyes up.

She'd just soaked Chris Merrick.

CHAPTER 11

Chris looked pissed.

"Holy crap," Becca whispered. The entire front of his shirt was wet.

"Pretty much." He pulled the fabric away from his chest and sighed. "At least it's water."

She felt a little light-headed. She wrapped her hands around the cup, like it could somehow keep her upright. "What's wrong—you can't freeze it in midair?"

His eyes snapped to hers, suddenly fierce and intimidating. "What did you just say?"

She sucked in a breath. Her voice wouldn't work.

Then she started giggling. It was somehow hilarious in the way things only are when you're drunk. She thought of Taylor out front. At least she wasn't rolling in the grass. "You're lucky I'm not shorter," she said. "It could have been a whole different look for you."

He backed off a little. "Glad to amuse you."

She couldn't stop laughing. She had to put a hand on the wall. "You should thank me for my aim."

He looked at her like she was crazy. "Are you drunk?"

"I'm not supposed to be. I have magic rocks." She held up her hand, still giggling.

"What are you even talking about?"

The tone of his voice threw her again, and she stopped laughing. She fought for true mental clarity, finding herself focusing on the cool dark stone on her wrist.

"Becca." Hunter appeared at her side. "You all right?"

Chris glanced at him, and his expression wasn't friendly. "Does this look like it's any of your business?"

"Since she's here with me, yeah, it does."

Chris looked startled, then glanced at her. His blue eyes turned hard and flat like slate.

Why the hell was she standing here feeling guilty about it?

Becca shook off the weight of his eyes, and touched Hunter's arm. "Look. It's my fault. I ran into him with the water."

Chris didn't say anything, but she saw him glance at her hand.

She pulled it back and stood there helplessly for a moment, feeling tension thicken the air.

Hunter's eyes narrowed just a bit. "I'm sure he'll get over it."

Chris set his jaw. His shoulders tightened.

She couldn't move. The whole moment had a surreal quality to it, Chris and Hunter glowering at each other over her head. Over *her*.

A voice called from down the hallway. "Hey. Chris."

One of the twins. She didn't know which. Of course they'd all be here—Gabriel played on the soccer team.

Chris didn't turn his head. "Yeah?"

"We're going out back to shoot hoops with Mark and Drew. You coming?"

Her breath caught, just for a second, as if the mere mention of Drew's name held power over her.

For a long moment, Chris didn't move. But then he glanced over his shoulder at his brother. "Yeah. Sure." He took a step back and started to turn.

She let out a breath she didn't remember holding. "I'm really sorry about your shirt," she called.

He didn't even look back. His voice was mild. "Already over it, Becky."

The way he said it was like a pinch in the arm.

Bastard. She scowled.

Hunter was watching Chris walk away. She touched his arm. "Come on. Let's find Quinn."

Her friend was dancing in the living room, her eyes closed, her arms over her head, moving as though the music were making love to her.

Apparently, Becca wasn't the only one who thought so, because two guys were dancing alongside her. Becca didn't recognize either one of them.

The trio wasn't lacking for an audience, either.

"Quinn seems lonely," said Hunter. He'd grabbed some sodas from somewhere and was holding out a sweating can. She took it.

Quinn thrust her hips with the beat, then smacked the insides of her thighs.

Becca winced. "I've never seen her do *that* before—"

"You sure?" Hunter's voice at her shoulder was dry. "That looks kind of practiced."

"Hey." She glared at him.

He shrugged and took a draw from his can. "Just saying."

The guy behind Quinn moved closer. He stood a head taller than she did, with dark skin, maybe Middle Eastern or Hispanic—it was too dark for Becca to tell for sure. He put strong hands on Quinn's hips and pulled her back.

Becca stiffened. She'd punch a guy for grabbing her like that. But her friend smacked his hands playfully and spun away from him, giving him a pouty look and shaking her head.

Becca caught her eye. *You okay?* she mouthed.

Quinn nodded, making it work with the beat. *He's hot,* she mouthed, fanning herself while her back was to the guy.

The song changed. Quinn held out a hand, a clear invitation.

Hunter leaned in to speak over the bass line. "You want to dance?"

Becca drew back and rubbed her neck, his closeness making her flush. "Not now. It's kind of hot in here."

"Let's go for a walk then."

The outside air felt ten degrees colder than it really was.

Wind blew across the water to ruffle her hair and whisper across her skin. The entire back patio was surrounded by white holiday lights, opening to a path illuminated by tiki torches, just like she remembered it. Some guys were grilling burgers, though they seemed more interested in turning the tongs into a branding iron—then chasing each other with it. At the far end of the patio, there was a short break of grass before the landscaping revealed the end of the driveway—where eight or nine guys were doing more roughhousing than playing basketball.

It was too dark to make out Drew, and she didn't look too hard.

Becca gestured in the opposite direction. "Let's walk down by the water."

"Sure." He hung close. "You won't be too cold?"

She'd probably be freezing, but she didn't want to stand here in the patio lights, waiting for Drew to notice her. "I'm good."

They walked toward the water. The sand was tight and hard beneath her feet, reluctantly giving way to her heels. She wrapped her arms across her stomach, regretting the inch of flesh that the cropped top revealed.

Hunter steered her to the far side of one of the fire drums where some folding chairs sat empty. There were other kids there, too, mostly seniors, no one she knew. Voices were hushed, beer bottles pushed into the sand haphazardly. At the fire drum a bit farther down, some kid had a guitar.

Hunter pulled two chairs together, and she sat, grateful for the fire licking heat across her cheeks. "Thanks," she said.

Water lapped at the sand ten feet away. She fingered the rocks strung along her wrist, running her thumb over the sharp edge of one, the rough side of another. She couldn't tell which was which from the feel, except the hematite, which was smooth and round. Her fingers kept seeking that one, rolling the slick stone between her knuckles.

Becca fixed her eyes on the fire, suddenly aware he was looking at her. "So—are you into a lot of . . . ah, new age stuff?"

"Not really." He sounded amused.

"How do you know so much about the rocks?"

"I grew up with it." He paused, as if he planned to say more, then thought better of it.

She glanced over at him, studying his profile. His lips were parted slightly, and the fire had turned his green eyes almost golden, sparking light from the rings in his brow.

"You don't have to tell me," she said.

"No, I don't mind. I just want to explain it the right way." He fingered one of the rocks on his own arm, the way she'd been doing with hers. She wondered if he sought a particular one.

When he spoke again, his voice was quiet. "You have a favorite color, right?"

"Blue," she said without thinking.

"Always, right?" he said. "You just like it. No one ever *made* you like blue."

"Sure." She thought about it for a moment. "A favorite color is a hard thing to screw with."

"All right then." He glanced over. "You ever walk through a jewelry store and find you're really drawn to something? Like maybe you're into platinum, where someone else likes gold, or you like emeralds, while someone else might prefer sapphires?"

Becca nodded. She was personally drawn to amethyst, but since it was one of the stones he'd strung on her wrist, she didn't want to volunteer that.

"My mother believes everything in existence has a consciousness," he said. "An awareness. As in, maybe it's not what *you* like." He reached out and touched her finger, which was still resting on the hematite. "Maybe it's what favors you."

His touch stole her voice. She watched the fire flicker across his cheeks.

A smile found his lips, and he drew back. "When I was little," he said, "my mother had a box of stones like these. All different kinds. She'd let me play with them."

He was playing with them now, absently lining the remaining stones up along his wrist.

"When I turned six," he said, "she told me to pick the ones I needed, because she was putting the rest away forever. I told her I wanted them all, but she told me that would make me sick."

He laughed a little and looked away, almost sheepishly. "Like too much candy, right?"

"Sure." She had no idea what he was talking about.

Hunter smiled and leaned close, over the arm of his chair. "Don't patronize me."

She blushed and fumbled for words. "So these are the ones you chose?"

"Nah." He rolled back in the chair and held his arm up to the light. "These, I picked up at Hot Topic when I got the piercings done—" He noticed her look and grinned. "I'm screwing with you. Yeah. I picked these." He sobered. "Or Mom likes to say they picked me."

It should have sounded ridiculous. It didn't.

"What do the other stones mean?"

Firelight caught his eyes and made them flash gold. "You'll have to do more than down a few shots to find out."

Her heart kicked against her ribs until she was sure it wanted her to jump into his lap. Wind peeled off the water to bite across her skin. She felt herself leaning, resting her weight on the arm of the chair.

He was drifting, too, and she found her eyes tracing his lips, the line of his jaw, the odd markings along his neck.

A dog jumped in between them. And barked.

She almost came out of her skin. Her foot sent the can of soda shooting across the sand. Gooseflesh sprang to life on her arms.

Casper. He barked again. Then spun in a circle.

"What?" she said. "What's wrong with him?"

"*Platz*, Casper," said Hunter. The dog just barked and backed up.

"What's wrong?" She couldn't tell her body to turn off the adrenaline, and she gave a nervous giggle. "Is Timmy down the well again?"

"I don't know." Hunter stood and put a hand on the dog's head, but Casper just backed away and turned to face down the darkened part of the beach. Then growled.

She stood to look, but couldn't see anything in the darkness.

She edged closer to Hunter. "Do you think—"

"Shh." He was staring, too. Casper kept growling.

Then she saw it, tall figures walking down the beach, coming their way, still well beyond the next fire drum. Men. She saw the glow of a cigarette.

They were talking, their voices carrying, though she couldn't get any words yet.

She stood frozen, feeling danger though she couldn't identify why. Casper ran in circles around them, stopping every lap to growl.

Then the men drew close enough to the fire drum for her to begin to make out features.

Tyler. Seth.

And five other guys.

CHAPTER 12

Becca grabbed Hunter's hand and spun him around. His back was to the fire now, and he was tall enough to block her from view.

Her palm was sweating, but she didn't let go.

Hunter didn't, either.

He leaned in close, keeping his voice low. It probably looked like they were about to make out. "Those are the guys from the pet store?"

She swallowed and nodded, ducking her head a bit to make sure she was hidden.

"Did they see you?" he asked.

"I don't think so."

Casper growled again.

"Casper!" Hunter hissed. *"Platz!"*

The dog whined and dropped to the ground beside them.

"Are they coming toward us?" asked Hunter. "Can you see?"

Fear had her stomach in a vise grip. Her tongue felt like rubber. "I can't see." She didn't *want* to see.

Hunter pulled her closer, then slipped that hand behind her back. His fingers splayed along the bare inch of skin, and she sucked in a breath. Her eyes flashed up to his.

"Shh." He dropped his head and pressed his cheek against hers.

For an instant, she completely forgot about Tyler. Her entire awareness centered on the inch of space between their bodies, the warmth of their shared breath, the strength in that hand on her back. His free hand found her neck, his fingertips threading through the loose hair there.

She should pull away. She would. In a second.

Make that a minute.

But then he turned her, so quickly that she almost stumbled. His hand held her upright. She felt the warmth of the fire at her back.

He spoke against her cheek. "They're heading toward the house. They didn't see us."

He slid his hand from her neck and straightened. His eyes were following Tyler and his crew, not looking at her at all.

That was all some kind of . . . *espionage?* Her brain couldn't do a 180 that quickly. She stared up at him, feeling her mouth working, though no sound was coming out.

But his hand was still on her back, his fingers five points of warmth against her skin. She didn't want to move.

"I don't think they were looking for you," he said.

"There are a bunch of college guys here," she said, finally finding her voice. "Maybe they're just here for the party. Chris said Tyler used to go to our school—"

Chris!

She pulled away from Hunter and whirled to look up at the house. The group had made it to the back patio, where they appeared to be talking to the guys by the grill. She glanced right. The basketball game was still going on.

Becca grabbed Hunter's hand. "Come on."

She sprinted across the sand as well as she was able, heading diagonally toward the driveway. Hunter kept up with her easily, Casper bounding at his side.

"What are we doing?" he said.

"Warning Chris."

Hunter caught her arm and hauled her to a stop. "You can't be serious."

She stared up at him, surprised by his tone. "Yeah—actually, I am. They almost killed him—"

"Yeah, so I heard. I also saw the way they treated you at the pet store. Those guys aren't screwing around, Becca."

"No kidding." She craned her neck to see if Tyler was still on the patio. He was. "You weren't there when they were beating him up—"

"You *were?*"

They were wasting time. She shook free of his hand. "Look—just—if you don't want to be involved, it's fine. But I have to warn him." She took a step back, then turned toward the driveway again.

The air felt colder with his absence. For two steps, she felt the wind lift her hair and taunt her for being alone.

Then Hunter was beside her. "Fine. We'll find him. But don't be surprised if he's an ass about it."

They clung to the darkness and approached the driveway from the opposite side. The scent of beer hung thick in the air, and half the guys were playing with bottles in their hands.

Becca spotted Drew right off, so she sucked back into the shadows behind Hunter.

She didn't see Chris at all. Or his brothers.

"Becca?"

She froze. Drew had stopped at the edge of the makeshift court and was peering into the darkness. The ball hung under one arm. Light from over the garage caught his gelled hair and made it shine, leaving his face in shadow.

It didn't matter. She remembered the angles of his cheekbones, the depth of his brown eyes, the line of his jaw. He looked good. It pissed her off.

He'd already seen her. What was she going to do—run? "Hey, Drew," she said.

"What're you doing here?"

He looked honestly perplexed. Like maybe he'd put her out of her misery five weeks ago, and couldn't imagine she'd show her face now.

"I slipped the bouncer a twenty," she said. "He let me jump the line."

He frowned, then his expression turned furious. He'd always been the type to get mad when confused. "What the hell are you talking about?"

"It was a joke," she muttered, knowing her voice was too low for him to hear.

"He's trashed," said Hunter. His voice wasn't low at all.

His presence at her side gave her courage. "Want me to give him your rocks?"

"Definitely not."

"Dude, are you talking about me?" said Drew. He came a few steps closer. "Who the hell are you?"

One of the guys on the court swore. "Christ, Drew. Let's just play ball."

Hunter didn't move. "I moved down here last weekend. This your house?"

Drew's eyes narrowed, as if he sensed a trap in the question. "Yeah." But then he snorted. "Lemme guess, Bex. You rolling out the, uh, welcome mat?"

Some of the other guys snickered and catcalled, but two stepped off the driveway to flank Drew. Greg Connolly and Mark Durant, both boasting more testosterone than brains. Wind blew in off the water again, carrying some sand with it to sting her ankles.

She watched Hunter size up the competition. He did it slowly, deliberately, as if memorizing each guy on the court. "Chill out." His voice was careful. "We were just looking for some-one."

Oh. Right. They had a purpose here.

"Have you seen Chris Merrick?" she said quickly. "Or his brothers?"

"I forgot you were into that." Drew smiled wolfishly, then glanced at Hunter. "Well, send her back here when you all are done."

High fives all around.

"Hey." Hunter took a step forward. "Lay off."

"Hunter." A gust of wind caught her hair and kissed her neck, making her shiver. "Forget him. He's not worth it."

She turned on her heel and started toward the house, not even waiting to see if he'd follow. She didn't want to see them fight; she didn't want to hear any more comments. She'd rather face Tyler than Drew.

But she felt Hunter behind her, and her shoulders tightened. It was one thing to shrug off some girl's bitchy comments—entirely another to hear a guy's trash talk.

Especially when Drew called after them, "Wear a rubber, dude."

She was practically running when she made it to the side door.

"Becca," said Hunter. "Becca. Wait."

She stopped in front of the door and didn't turn. Something cold thrust under her hand.

Casper's nose. He was licking her fingers.

She couldn't resist a dog. She half turned and rubbed him behind the ears. Hunter's gaze felt like a lead weight on her back, but she couldn't look at him yet.

"Fuck 'em, right?" she said flatly. She buried her fingers in Casper's fur.

"The hell with that," Hunter said, heat in his voice. "I wanted to punch him in the face."

She glanced up, then. His jaw was set, and a bit of color heated his cheeks.

"Thanks," she said. He was still staring at the court, as if considering going back to lay into Drew.

She held out her wrist. "Here. You want the calming one back?"

He faltered for a second. Then his eyes warmed as he smiled back at her. "You hold on to it."

Behind him, one of the basketball guys stepped to the edge of the court, staring out at the patio. She recognized him after a moment—Drew's older brother. "Tyler! Hey, man. Come play."

Becca felt the blood drain from her face.

Hunter reached around her and turned the knob. "Come on. We'll find Quinn and go catch a movie or something."

She sucked in a breath to protest. "But we have to—"

He rolled his eyes and cut her off. "All right, all right, you get Quinn. I'll take a walk through and 'warn' Chris if I see him." He sounded as though he were volunteering to change the litter box. "Meet me at the car."

Quinn was making out with the Latino guy in the corner of the living room. They weren't being subtle about it, either—his hand was up her shirt.

Becca jerked her eyes away. What the hell was she supposed to do with *that*?

Then again, they were in the middle of the living room. Not like she couldn't walk right up to them. Becca edged closer. Hopefully, Quinn would feel the heat radiating from her cheeks and look up.

No such luck.

Once she was close enough to yell over the music, Becca said, "Hey. Quinn. I think we need to leave."

Quinn didn't even break the liplock. She just reached into her pocket, pulled out Becca's keys, and held them out.

Wow.

Becca took her keys, but fidgeted. She cleared her throat. "Aren't you . . . ah . . . supposed to be staying at my house?"

"Don't worry about it." Quinn broke free. Her cheeks were flushed, leaving her eyes bright and her voice breathy. "Rafe will drive me home."

Rafe. Seriously?

He mumbled something against Quinn's neck that sounded like, "Yeah, later." But at least his hands had found their way to the outside of her clothes.

"Quinn . . ." Becca hesitated, not wanting to mortify her friend, but not wanting to leave her with some guy who seemed determined to get into her pants right here in the middle of the McKay living room. "Do you even know this guy's last name?"

Quinn's eyes lit with irritation—and maybe a little embarrassment. "Gee, Bex, do you know Hunter's?"

Oops. Touché. Becca looked away. "That's a *little* different."

Rafe lifted his head and grinned. "It's Gutierrez."

Quinn clapped him on the shoulder. "There you go." She flashed annoyed eyes at Becca. "I'm good."

Becca stared at her for a long moment, then opened her mouth to protest again. "I'm just trying to make sure you're okay—"

"Jesus, Becca," said Quinn. "I have a mother."

Rafe turned his head and looked at Becca. "She's all right," he said. "I'll get her home."

To his credit, he appeared straight sober. He was one of the first guys she hadn't smelled alcohol on all night. He had a sexy smile, too, and his tongue did nice things to his R's.

"I'll talk to you tomorrow," said Quinn. She traced a finger down the side of Rafe's cheek. He obligingly leaned in to kiss her again.

Becca shoved the keys into her pocket. "Whatever. Have fun."

She wove through the dancers crowding the living room floor, replaying the exchange with Quinn. Her friend seemed pissed—had Becca missed something? Or had Quinn just been lost in a lustful moment, resenting interruption?

Becca was so wrapped up in her thoughts, she nearly missed one of the twins standing in the archway to the foyer, leaning against the molding with a bottle of water hanging from his hand. He looked almost bored, so she felt certain he didn't know Tyler and his buddies were around.

"Hey." She hesitated. "Gabriel?"

He offered half a smile and straightened, then leaned close to speak over the music without yelling. "Nicholas." He smelled good, warm, like a lazy breeze in summertime. His breath traced the line of her jaw. "Having a good time?"

"Is Chris around?" she asked.

He nodded. "He and Gabriel are hunting down some food."

Did that mean they'd gone out back? "That guy Tyler is here. With friends."

Nick lost the easy smile. "Where?"

"Playing ball now, I think."

He swore and set the bottle of water on the hall table, then turned for the hallway that led to the back door.

She watched him take a few steps, curiosity telling her to follow him, common sense telling her to get the hell out of the house.

"Shouldn't you take that with you?" she called.

He stopped short. His head whipped around.

She picked up the bottle of water. "For Chris."

Nick's eyes narrowed, and he smiled a little, but it was a calculating look. "I'm going to pretend you didn't say that." His eyes flicked to the foyer. "You should, too. Go home."

Then he turned on his heel and walked away.

Oh, she was *so* following him.

But she wasn't an idiot about it. She held back for a minute so he wouldn't see, peeking into the nearby rooms to see if she could spot Hunter. Guilt flickered in her mind—he was probably heading back to his car now.

Unless he was out back, too. He'd also gone to look for Chris.

She slid past some couples who were making out in the hallway, then eased through the sliding glass door onto the darkened patio. It was easy to hide—someone had killed the light over the door, and the only illumination came from the tiki torches and the slight glow from the grill.

The wind had kicked up, pulling at her hair and stinging her eyes with charcoal smoke. It battered the bamboo wind chimes hanging by the door, sending them spinning and knocking against the siding.

She spotted the brothers right off, standing in a tense cluster by the grill, flanked by two torches. She couldn't hear a word of their conversation. No sign of Hunter or his dog.

Some guys from her class shoved through the door, jostling each other onto the patio. She flinched and shuffled to the side, retreating more deeply into the shadows.

Tyler wasn't on the basketball court, and she couldn't see him anywhere else, either.

A few more guys came through the door, trailing some giggling girls. It was too dark for her to make out any of them clearly, but one of the girls saw her and stopped. She was pretty, but in a rough, used way. Becca didn't recognize her, but she looked older than the others. Maybe another college student.

Alcohol hung on her breath, and a cigarette rested between two fingers. "Hey. You got a light?"

Becca shook her head quickly. "No, I don't."

One of the guys doubled back. "Damn, Lilah. Can't you wait a frigging second? Just light it on the drums."

Lilah rolled her eyes at Becca and muttered, "He's such an asshole." She tossed a look over her shoulder. "Shut it, Seth. I'm not putting my face up to one of those things."

Seth came up beside her. Becca froze.

But he was still looking at Lilah. He gestured. "Light it on the grill, then."

Becca wanted to run—but where? Seth was blocking her path to the door. It wasn't like she could take off across the sand and hope for any speed.

Maybe it was too dark for him to recognize her. She ducked her head and let her hair fall across the side of her face.

Lilah shoved him lightly, then leaned in toward Becca again. "Thanks, anyway."

Becca studied the darkened bricks of the patio. "Sure."

Lilah turned away.

Seth didn't.

Becca didn't want to breathe. He smelled like cigarettes and beer, and she could feel the weight of his gaze. The moment hung on the air like that eternal instant before a car crash, when you know it's coming but there's no time to stop the collision.

He was going to recognize her.

Becca shoved him and ran.

It was stupid. She knew it was stupid as she was doing it. But panic tightened her throat and made it hard to breathe, and all she wanted to do was get the hell off that patio.

No chance. He caught her before she made it ten feet. His

hand was tight and hard on her arm, and he swung her around. Becca balled her hand into a fist, but then she got a look at his face, and her determination wilted.

He'd hurt her if he could. Like in the store, when Tyler had been ready to punch her with a can of dog food. No pranks, no taunts. Genuine harm.

She remembered what Chris had looked like when she'd found him.

Becca forced herself to stare up at Seth. Flinching now would be a mistake. "Let me go."

Lilah was yelling, smacking at his arm. "What the *hell*, Seth!"

But he was staring down at Becca. "I remember you now," he said. "You're that little tease from Drew's party last month. I didn't know you were one of *them*. We could have had a lot more fun."

One of them. What did that *mean?*

"Get your hands off me," she said, hating how her voice turned breathy at the end.

He tightened his grip and gave her a little shake. "Lilah. Get Tyler."

"Get him yourself, you idiot! You can't just—"

"Lilah." He silenced her with a look. "She's one of them. Get him."

The girl took a staggering step back, then fled through the door into the house. There were a few kids at the edge of the patio, staring now, drawn by the commotion. No one made a move to help her.

Then Chris appeared out of the darkness. "She's not one of us, Seth. Let her go."

Seth glanced at him. "No way, man." He looked down at Becca, his eyes pools of darkness. "We're sick of playing around— maybe you just need a little more convincing."

Chris started forward like he wanted to take a swing at him, but Seth's grip tightened on her arm, pinching into the ligaments beside her elbow.

Holy *crap*, it hurt. She cried out and struck at him wildly.

Seth jerked her close. The pain was making her see stars. "I'll break her arm."

The words made her freeze. Chris, too, his hands in fists at his sides. One of the twins stepped up beside him. Different clothes from before—it had to be Gabriel. "Jesus, Seth. Just let her go. She's got nothing to do with this."

Becca stood on her toes to take some of the pressure off her arm, whimpers creeping out under her breath. Seth glanced between Gabriel and Chris. "Tyler can decide."

The torches along the patio blazed brighter for an instant, whipped into a frenzy by the wind coming in off the water.

Seth flinched, and Gabriel smiled. "Scared you the other night, didn't I?"

Seth took a step toward him. His fingers loosened fractionally. "Fuck you, Merrick."

Becca held her breath. Sand beat at her legs.

"Nah." Gabriel's eyes glittered in the firelight. He grinned, baring his teeth. "Nothing personal. I just don't take Tyler's leftovers."

Chris's foot shifted on the patio, and Gabriel grabbed his arm. He stepped forward, almost pushing his younger brother out of the way. He moved closer, into Seth's space.

Becca could feel the ready aggression in Seth's grip. His voice came as a lethal hiss—but Gabriel was right. Fear hid behind his words. "We're not even going to wait for the Guides, asshole. We're just going to take care of you ourselves."

The guides?

The torches cracked and spit flame, fighting the wind.

"Yeah, I heard the deal was off." Gabriel shoved Seth. Not hard, but enough that the other boy fell back half a step. "Works for me."

Seth glared at him, but he didn't react. "I'm not screwing with you, man. When Tyler gets here—"

"Yeah, yeah, you'll cry to Mommy." Gabriel shoved him again. Harder.

Every time Gabriel provoked him, that grip on her arm got a

bit looser. Could she help this along? Becca did her best to make her voice nonchalant. "Aw. You're afraid to fight him. That's really . . . sweet."

Mistake. His grip tightened right up, and he glared down at her. "Shut up, you stupid—"

Chris stepped up and punched him square in the face.

Seth rocked back and almost fell. She almost went with him. Her knees hit the brick walkway.

Then her arm slid out of his hand, and she was free.

Seth recovered quickly, and she scrambled to get away from him. He was going after Chris, renewed fury in his face. He moved like a bull facing a flag, his shoulders down, his fists clenched.

Chris dodged one swing, and narrowly missed another.

"Damn it, Chris!" Gabriel had drawn back, away from Seth, moving closer to the grill. "Are you an idiot?"

Chris drove a fist into Seth's midsection.

Seth recovered and clipped him on the jaw. It didn't look hard, but Chris went down.

Then the grill seemed to burst, spraying flaming charcoal into the air, and for a terrifying moment, fire rained from the night sky. The wind caught the fiery debris and sent it spinning across the patio.

She was frozen by the surreal beauty of it, nightmarish fire-flies that stung her skin and sizzled on the bricks. Fire was suddenly everywhere, more fire than the grill could have possibly produced. The torches grew, shooting sparks into the sky.

Bigger pieces of flaming debris started to fall. Clothing caught fire. Kids were screaming, running, bolting from the narrow area.

A hand grabbed hers and gave a fierce tug. "Run."

CHAPTER 13

Becca dug her feet into the sand, scrambling after Chris, abandoning her sandals when they made it impossible to keep up. She'd had no sense of direction when he seized her hand, and it wasn't until the glow from the fire drums hung in the air above them that she realized he hadn't dragged her to the cars and the parking lot.

He'd dragged her to the water.

All the way to the water, too. He towed her past the fire drums until a frigid wave crept over her toes, and she squealed and pulled away from him.

"Wait," Chris said, his voice low and rough. His eyes were focused forward, on the house.

She wanted to jerk her hand out of his, to run for the road. But then she spotted Tyler cresting the slight hill that led down to the beach, Seth hot on his heels.

She held her breath.

Chris pulled at her hand and she followed, moving more deeply into the water until it swelled over her ankles and then to her knees. It was low tide, and this far from the fires the darkness over the water seemed to work as a cloak. Seth and Tyler were scanning the groups of kids clustered around the drums, most of whom were talking excitedly. Girls who'd bolted from the patio were displaying their wounds to people who had no idea what was going on; guys were talking about the grill's badass explosion.

Becca thought of Quinn, safe in the house, clueless. She thought of Hunter, who was probably leaning on his car, looking at his watch. Worrying? Or getting irritated?

His rocks hung cool and comforting against her wrist.

Wind whipped across the water, covering the sound of her shaking breath. Another wave pulled up the shore to sweep over her knees. Her jeans clung to her skin. She shivered and tried not to think what was *in* this water.

"We should have run for the cars," she whispered, though there was no way Tyler or Seth could have picked up her voice from so far away.

"We're safer here. They won't come in the water." Chris glanced at her. "And we had to get Seth away from the patio."

What did that have to do with anything? "I don't see your brothers."

"They're there." His eyes were trained on the beach again.

Wind caught her hair and traced an icy finger along the inch of skin exposed by her shirt. She shivered again, bracing an arm against her stomach. The gust caught the flames in the drums, whipping them higher, making the girls on the beach giggle and scatter a bit.

Tyler and Seth flinched away from the drums, as if the fire reached for them.

Seth strode between the fires, spinning full circle to scan the beach. "Cut it out!"

Something cracked and split in one of the drums, shooting sparks and flaming bits into the wind.

A piece must have caught Seth on the arm, because he swore and smacked at his bicep.

Chris smiled, his eyes bright in the distant firelight. "See?"

She didn't *see* anything. Another wave brought the water almost to her thighs. Had they moved? The water felt deeper suddenly, as if they'd drifted out another ten feet. She watched the wave roll up the shore, carrying foam and debris far higher than the last one had.

Seth began to pace the shoreline while Tyler hung back be-hind the drums, looking infinitely more frightening with the glow of the fires on his face.

Her teeth were starting to chatter, some mixture of cold and adrenaline. Chris's hand was still wrapped around hers, strong and warm. She focused on that feeling. "How long do you think they're going to wait?"

"They want to kill us." His voice was dry. "It might be a few minutes."

The wind kept up, pulling sand and debris into the air, toss-ing it into the fire to sizzle and spark. Girls fought to keep sand out of their clothes, tucking themselves against guys and gestur-ing toward the house.

"They're clearing the beach," said Chris.

Tyler and Seth? Or the twins? No one seemed to be doing anything except the people streaming toward the house.

Chris glanced down at her. He stood close, and his voice was rich in the night air. "Nick said you warned him. About Tyler being here."

"It seemed like a good idea at the time." Gusts were spraying water now, sending the flames sideways from the drums. An-other wave soaked her jeans above the knees and she shivered violently. She'd never seen the tide roll in this quickly.

All of the party kids had abandoned the beach. Seth and Tyler were standing at the edge of the water now, staring out into the darkness. Tyler seemed to be staring straight at them, but the wind had to be stinging his eyes.

"I know you're out there!" he called.

She shifted closer to Chris, as if that would help. She wanted to duck behind him, to hide, to bolt for the shore. She couldn't stand immobile in the frigid water much longer. She started to pull free of Chris's hand.

He held fast, and his voice came low and ironic. "So. You're here with the new guy."

Becca whipped her head around, feeling the choppy water swirl around her thighs. "You want to talk about this *now?*"

"Shh." He gave a warning glance at the shoreline.

She froze, but Tyler didn't seem to have heard.

"As I was saying." Chris gave a low whistle. "Dude works fast."

"Shut up."

"Would you rather talk about our History project?"

He was so infuriating. She wanted to punch him—but then she realized she wasn't shivering. The water actually felt . . . *warm*.

She trailed her fingers through the waves licking at her waist. "I think I'm getting hypothermia," she said. "I'm not cold anymore."

"Yeah, it takes me a while."

Infuriating and cryptic. She glared up at him. "Why don't you tell me what's really going on with you, Chris?"

That derailed his amusement. His expression went dark.

She shoved him with the hand he was holding. "Come on!" she whisper-shouted. "I'm standing in water up to my ass because of you."

He looked away, out across the water, then inhaled to speak.

But a gunshot split the air.

Her body reacted before her brain could. She'd dropped to her knees in the water, her breath shaking in the wind. The water swelled around her neck now, but she didn't care. Her fingers were crushing his and she couldn't convince her body to stop shaking.

That shot was the loudest thing she'd ever heard.

Then she heard it again. A bullet hit the water three feet to her left. She'd never seen a gun fired; she'd never touched a bullet. But the sound of the lead round entering the water was unmistakable.

As was the sight of Tyler, his feet in the surf now, firing in their direction.

"A gun. Tyler has a gun," she babbled. "He has a gun. Chris. He—he has—he has—"

The fire drums exploded.

It was nothing like the grill. This was a full burst of flame, as if someone had poured gasoline on the drums. Wind grabbed fistfuls of fire, sending it dancing down the beach. The entire stretch of sand burned. She lost sight of Tyler and Seth.

"Hey." Chris squeezed her hand so hard it hurt.

She was hyperventilating, choking on her own oxygen. Smoke, thick and sudden, clogged the air. She couldn't look away from the flames. Had any kids been left on the beach?

"Hey!" Chris jerked her around. She stared up into his eyes, seeing the reflection of the inferno behind her.

He still had a death grip on her hand. "Take a deep breath."

She inhaled and tasted fire. The water pulled back, sucking away from them the way it did on the beach at high tide, the kind of undertow that led to the big waves.

Wicked danger sparked in his eyes. "Now hold it."

Water crashed around them, pulling her under, dragging her body beneath the waves. Chris still had her hand, but she spun in the darkness, losing sense of time, of location, of which direction was *up*.

Her lungs weren't burning, but it felt like they'd been underwater for hours. Chris was pulling at her hand, dragging her deeper, towing her through the murky water.

How long could she hold her breath?

Everything was so black.

Did he still have her hand?

Her body felt foreign, heavy, a dead weight in a weightless atmosphere. How long since that last breath? Hours. Days.

Her body took over and she fought him, struggling for the surface, for oxygen, for freedom. She struck wildly, her limbs moving slowly underwater. She made contact and dug with her nails, flailing at him until he finally let her go.

She inhaled. Her lungs filled with water.

And the world went flat.

Chris Merrick was kissing her. His hands were buried in her hair, his palms burning against her cheeks. Sand shifted below her body and the stars danced above, bright like his eyes when he drew back to look at her.

Then he was kissing her again, his face descending to press to hers.

But his mouth was rough, aggressive. She wanted to whimper, but his breath rushed across her tongue. She couldn't move.

He drew back, and then his hands were on her chest, a heavy weight over her heart. "Goddamn it, Becca." He pushed. *"Breathe."*

She did one better. She coughed and spit water all over herself.

He swore again and rolled her to her side, and she coughed up what felt like a gallon of the Chesapeake Bay. By the time she was done, she'd made it to her knees, her forearms pressed into the sand, hair pooled around her, her forehead braced on her knuckles.

Chris was kneeling beside her, the sand beneath his knees gray in the moonlight. He didn't say anything, but she could hear his breathing, rough and almost shaking.

Inhaling hurt, but her lungs grabbed the oxygen and wouldn't let her stop. Her voice came out as a croak. "So I should have just met Hunter at the car."

"You were out for a long time." Chris sounded frightened.

"Feels like it." Then she paused. "How long really?"

"Maybe five minutes." He ran a hand through wet hair. "God. You let go of my hand and—"

"Oh. Okay. This is my fault. Got it."

He didn't say anything for a long moment, and she listened to their breathing. The wind had gone, leaving the air soft against her skin. Her feet were still in the water.

"I'm sorry," he said softly.

She rolled over and sat in the sand. The closest light came from a streetlamp about twenty feet behind them. Thank god, since her shirt was completely sealed to her chest. "Where are we?"

"About half a mile south of the party." He pointed. She could see the glow of fire on the beach. "Do you want to start walking?"

Becca shivered. She wasn't ready to go back to that house. Not yet. She shook her head, then had to hug her arms across her chest. "He had a gun."

"He was firing blindly. He couldn't see us."

"He had a *gun*."

He nodded, looking at the water again. "I know."

She'd seen that bullet pierce the water, close enough to touch. Tyler hated Chris and his brothers enough to kill them. She shivered again.

The water rolled up the sand to drift over her bare feet. It felt warm again, tropical almost.

In September.

Her head snapped sideways, but she couldn't see Chris clearly in the darkness. He was looking out at the water, his expression resigned.

I need a frigging rainstorm. A drizzle. Fog, even.

"Do that again," she said.

He didn't look at her, but the water pulled higher along the sand, hanging for a moment to warm her, then receding with the tide.

She licked her lips, unsure how to proceed. Another swirl of warm water wrapped around her legs to drift down the beach again.

Chris scooped a handful of water out of the surf, letting it pool in his palm. He held it there for a moment, then spread his fingers to let the water trickle between them.

It never reached the wave below. The water dripped from his fingers to turn into steam in midair, where the wind caught it and pulled it into nothing.

She was just staring, when she really wanted to grab his hand and look for a hidden heater or something.

So she did that. His hand felt normal, warm and steady. Not even waterlogged, like hers felt.

"Show me again."

He moved closer, scooping the water while her hand was attached to his. Water trickled between their joined fingers, turning to steam that wrapped around her wrist before drifting into the night.

She lifted her gaze and met his eyes. "So . . . did you do the fire, too?"

"No." He paused. "That was Gabriel."

Her breathing caught, just for a moment. "And the wind was Nick?"

He didn't volunteer anything further, just nodded and glanced over as if unsure what he'd find on her face.

"How?" she said.

He had to think about that for a while. Then he rolled forward onto his knees and drew a circle in the sand with his finger.

"Imagine everyone in the world lives inside this circle," he said.

When she nodded, he drew a five-pointed star inside the circle. "Think of each of these points as one of the elements."

"I'm assuming you're not talking about the periodic table?"

He smiled, and there was a shred of relief to it. "No."

"So fire, water, air, earth—" She thought of the landscaping business, the way she'd run from the house that first night and the grass had grabbed her sneakers. "Michael, right?"

"Yeah."

She pointed at the star he'd drawn. "But there are five points."

"The fifth element represents the spirit." He glanced up, wet hair drifting across his forehead. She must have been frowning, because he tapped his chest and said, "Spirit. Chi. Life."

She got it. "Feel the force, Luke."

"Exactly. The Fifth is almost like a . . . a jack-of-all-trades. There's a connection to everything—or so they say."

"So they say?" she echoed.

"We've never met one." He grimaced. "Which is kind of a good thing." Before she could question that, he looked down and moved his hand over the entire circle. "If everyone on earth falls somewhere in this circle, you can see that some people would fall close to the points, while some people would be way off. You might get someone between air and water who grows up to have some skill with sailboats. Or someone between fire and earth who might . . . hell, I don't know, study volcanoes or something."

She thought of Hunter's story of his mom, of being drawn to his stones. Did that mean he fell close to Chris's "earth" point?

"Tyler and Seth are like you, too?" she said.

"Yes. Not as strong, but—yes." He pointed. "Seth falls along the earth branch, close to a point, but not quite there. He can pull strength from the ground he's standing on, which is why we needed to get him off the brick patio."

She remembered the damage Chris had taken that night behind the school.

When she'd found them fighting in the middle of a concrete parking lot.

"And Tyler?"

"He falls somewhere near fire." Chris gave a short laugh that didn't have any humor to it. "Which is probably why he's walking around with a gun."

"Are there—are there a lot of people like you?"

"Everyone's like us, Becca. We're human. We're all inside the circle. My brothers and I—we just fall on a point."

She scooped up a handful of water, letting it trail through her fingers. It dropped into the wave below, nothing supernatural at all. Then she gave him a wry glance. "Not everyone's like you, Chris."

He sighed. "Yes. There are a lot of people like us. Communities in every town—if you listen to Michael."

"Every *town*? Whole communities of people who can control the elements? But that's—"

"Not everyone can control the elements," he said, and his voice sounded bitter, plus a little self-deprecating. "Like I said, some people are just born with an affinity. Only those of us with the strongest connection can actually *control*—god, I'm boring myself." He swiped the pattern out of the sand.

She caught his arm. "No! I knew—"

He looked up, his face close. "You knew what?"

"Something," she said. "I knew . . . something."

He held there, unmoving, until she became aware of her heartbeat, of the scent of sand and fire on his skin.

Then a wet tongue was on her cheek, a cold nose in her ear, and a ruff of fur pressed into her hands. She recoiled, pushing the dog's muzzle away from her cheek.

"Casper!" she cried.

"You know this dog?" said Chris.

Becca rubbed Casper behind the ears until he started his *rawr-rawr-rawr.* "Yeah, he's—"

"Mine."

She whirled.

Hunter stood ten feet back, near where the wild grass met the sand.

CHAPTER 14

God, an hour ago she'd felt guilty for being at the party with Hunter. Now she felt guilty for sitting here with Chris.

You weren't sitting on the beach, idiot. He just pulled you out of the water and performed mouth-to-mouth.

Becca brushed sand off her cheek and looked up at Hunter. She could hear his breathing from here—just a little hard, like he'd been running or he was angry—but she couldn't make out the expression on his face.

She had no idea what to say. "Hey," she offered.

"Are you all right?"

"Ah . . . mostly." That was a loaded question. She pointed to the guy sitting next to her. "Found Chris."

Chris snorted, but if it made Hunter smile, she didn't see. Casper was sniffing at her hands, and she petted him again, glad for an excuse to look down. After Chris's revelations, this whole moment felt surreal.

No, this whole moment felt awkward.

"How'd you find us?" said Chris.

His voice wasn't friendly, and shadows cloaked his eyes. He still sat halfway in the water beside her, and she felt the tide crawl over her fingers again.

She snatched her hand out of the water. Chris smiled.

"Oh, I'm sorry." Hunter was glaring back at him. "Was I interrupting?"

"Yeah." The water climbed farther up the shore this time, warmth seeping into the space behind her knees.

For god's sake. "Don't be a jerk," she muttered, then struggled to find her footing in the wet sand. Her head swam a little, like her ears were full of seawater. Hunter stepped forward to help—right when Chris found his feet to do the same thing.

They both held on to her for a long second, aggression flickering like lightning between them.

Then Chris let go and stepped back as if it was nothing.

Hunter's hand remained on her forearm, steady and secure. His fingers were warm, and now that she wasn't sitting in the water, she realized how cold the night air was.

But he was still staring at Chris.

She felt like she should send them to opposing corners or something. "How *did* you find us?" she said.

Hunter took a breath—then shook his head. "You're soaked and it's cold. Let's walk."

She started to follow him toward the grass, but Chris hung back. "We should stick to the beach," he said.

Did he think they were still in danger? Her eyes flashed to his.

Chris pointed to her feet. "You don't have shoes."

Oh.

So they walked. Hunter hung near, his arm still supporting her, though she stayed close for warmth now rather than any need for assistance. Chris walked in the surf, splashing with every step. Casper bounded ahead of them, jumping in and out of the water, circling back every few feet.

"You didn't meet me at the car," said Hunter. "Yours was still there, so I knew you weren't blowing me off. I came inside to find you—"

"You didn't come in his car?" said Chris, and there was no ignoring the sudden interest in his voice.

Hunter ignored him. "I found Quinn. She said you'd taken your keys. Someone else said they'd seen you go out back. By the time I got there, I saw the wind knock the fire drums over—" He stopped short and glared out at Chris, who was walking in deeper water, splashing hard with each step. "For god's sake, what are you, six? Could you walk on the beach?"

"Suck it, punk. It's cold."

It was cold. She hugged her elbows to her body and tried not to shiver.

Hunter just sighed, but he moved fractionally closer. "I saw that Tyler guy. I heard the gunfire. I saw him shooting into the water, and I knew it had to be you."

"How?"

The moonlight caught the rings in his eyebrow and made them shine. His voice was low, too low to carry past her ears. "Because I saw the way he went after you at the pet store."

She said nothing, chilled now by more than just the air.

"So," he said, facing forward again. "I followed the direction of the tide and told Casper to find you." He paused, and she heard an odd note in his voice. She wondered if he'd been expecting to find a body. "We should probably call the cops."

"Narc," said Chris.

Hunter threw a glance his way. "Suck it, punk," he mocked.

"Whatever." Chris bent and pulled a stick out of the surf. Becca had no idea how he'd even seen it in the dark. But he whistled, caught Casper's attention, and threw it down the beach.

The dog galloped away, his paws making wet sounds in the sand.

"You don't think we should call the police?" she asked Chris.

"And tell them what?" Darkness hid his expression, but the derision in his tone was clear.

She could see the fires on the beach behind Drew's house now. The flames had fallen to small piles of burning debris, barely flickering in the breeze off the water. The stretch of sand was empty of the kids that had been there before.

She looked up at Hunter. "Do you think it's safe to go back?"

"Tyler and his friends are gone. They headed north, the way they came."

When Casper brought the stick back, Chris flung it hard, sending it spinning into the darkness.

Hunter said, "Casper. *Hier. Fuss.*"

The dog abandoned the pursuit and bolted to his side.

Chris gave Hunter a dark look. "Killjoy."

Hunter looked right back at him. His voice was level. "What do these guys want with you?"

"What the hell do you care?"

"They've clearly got an issue with you and they're taking it out on Becca. For god's sake, he brought a loaded firearm to the party."

"A *loaded firearm?*" said Chris, his tone incredulous. "Jesus. You're not *really* a narc, are you?"

Hunter flinched a little bit. "No."

Becca thought of his dead uncle, the K-9 police officer. She wondered if his dad had been a cop, too. "Could we report Tyler for having a gun?" she said.

"He's over eighteen," said Chris. "It's probably legal."

"It's not legal for him to be *shooting at me,*" she snapped.

Chris shook his head, and now his voice sounded tired. "You don't want them after you, Becca. You don't want their *attention.* Just stay away from them and you'll be fine."

"Like you're fine?" said Hunter.

Chris rounded on him, splashing to a stop in the water. A hard wave rolled up the sand, reaching almost to where she walked. "What the hell is that supposed to mean?"

"Look in a mirror and I'm sure you'll figure it out."

Chris started to slosh his way out of the surf.

She got between them and threw up a hand. "Stop."

They stopped. Becca could still taste the seawater on the back of her tongue. "Both of you. Just stop." She looked up the stretch of sand. They were one house down from the party. Music still poured from Drew's place, and she could just make out kids fooling around on the back patio.

No danger. No drama. It almost made the entire night feel as if she'd imagined it.

But her throat burned and felt raw, and seawater sealed her

clothes to damp skin. That trip underwater was no fantasy. No way was she going back through Drew's. They could cut between houses and make it to her car from here.

Or *she* could. She pulled her arm free from Hunter. "I'm going home."

He followed her. "Let me drive you."

The grass felt soft under her feet, but the gravel by the road was going to be a bitch. She shook her head. "So I can explain to my mother why I'm soaked *and* my car is gone?"

"You can clean up at my house," Chris said from behind them.

"Yeah, right," scoffed Hunter. He was already leading her away.

"I'm serious," Chris called. "There's no one home to give a crap if I bring her around. Can you say the same thing?"

That made her stop and turn.

Hunter set his jaw and looked at Chris—but said nothing. He lived with his mother and his grandparents. That felt like a double whammy. She turned back to Chris.

His eyes were dark and intent on hers. "You can. If you want."

Becca faltered a bit. "Won't your brothers be home?"

"Michael will. I have no idea if the twins have headed back yet."

She'd be lying if she said curiosity wasn't spurring her to agree—if for no other reason than to spend fifteen minutes alone with him, to let the questions in her mind spill off her tongue.

"You're considering this?" said Hunter.

She looked at him, feeling a spot of warmth on her cheeks. She was glad for the shadows to hide it. "It doesn't mean anything. I just—my mother—"

"Wow, thanks," said Chris.

"That's not what I meant." She fingered the stones along her wrist, then glanced up at Hunter through her lashes. "Do you want these back?"

Now Chris went still. She felt his eyes on the bracelets on her wrist, the bracelets that obviously had come from Hunter. That blush flared a little hotter.

Hunter was looking down at her, and he offered a small smile—a private smile. "When you're ready."

She smiled back. She couldn't help it.

Then he swung around to glare at Chris. "Look. If you drag her into danger again—"

"What? You'll come after me with a loaded firearm?"

"Damn it, you are one pain in the ass—"

She didn't stay to listen to the rest. She rolled her eyes, turned on her heel, and stomped across the grass, heading for her car.

CHAPTER 15

Chris watched Becca waver a bit while she slid her key into the lock. She'd been drunk at the party—right? And she'd practically drowned.

He reached out and took her keys.

"I'm okay," she said.

Like he wanted to find out the hard way. "Humor me."

That new kid was still standing nearby, watching their exchange. "I still think I should take you home," he said. "Or at least follow you."

The only way this guy was coming along was unconscious in the trunk. Chris gritted his teeth and focused on getting her door open.

Becca left him with the keys and headed for the passenger side. "I'm fine, Hunter." She hesitated. "Chris is all right."

Yeah. Bite me, dog-boy. Chris gave a firm yank to the door, and it swung open.

But Becca paused before getting in the car, pushing her hair behind one ear. "Thanks for inviting me," she said to Hunter. "I had fun. I mean, before the whole gun thing."

Chris dropped into the driver's seat and pulled the door closed. He sure didn't have to sit here and listen while they exchanged digits.

But she slid into the car almost immediately, pulling the door shut behind her.

When he started the ignition, Becca twisted the dials to blast the heater. Her car protested and blew cold air, but she slapped her hand on the dash until it finally gave in. She pressed her hands against the vents and shivered, a rush of breath through her teeth.

Chris glanced at the clock on the dash. Barely ten. The water on her skin was talking to him, coaxing him to reach out and run a finger along her wrist.

Where those stupid rock bracelets were hanging.

Chris kept both hands locked on the wheel.

"What's wrong?" she said. "You run out of one-liners?"

He kept silent for a long moment, then glanced over. "I didn't mean to get in the middle of your *date*."

She didn't look at him, but she mimicked his tone. "It wasn't a *date*."

"Oh. Okay."

"Look, if you're just going to be a jerk—"

"I'm not." He paused. Maybe he was. "Forget it."

She seemed to edge away from him somehow. He heard her sigh, a soft breath of air. Her shoulders looked tight, hunched against the cold.

Or hunched against him?

"Thanks," he said. His voice sounded rough. "For not telling him what I said."

She looked up. "Did you think I would?"

He had no idea. He'd never told anyone before. That moment when they'd knelt in the surf and the water flowed between their fingers—it felt intimate, powerful. The water liked her. He wanted to drag her back to the beach and do it again.

That frightened him, a bit. It felt as if he'd turned something loose that he'd never be able to catch. If he made this a big deal, would she?

He just shrugged and brushed wet hair out of his eyes.

"Thanks," she said. "For pulling me out of the water. For what you did."

A smile pulled at his lips. "I owed you."

"I probably should have just taken the cash."

He laughed softly, but then silence fell between them again. He glanced over.

That was a mistake. Her shirt was slicked to her skin, catching the light from oncoming cars to accent the soft curves of her body.

He jerked his eyes back to the road. "If you don't mind . . . it's probably better if Michael doesn't hear about the gun." Michael would shit a brick if he knew about that—especially if he found out Becca was there.

"Sure," she said.

He hesitated. "It's probably better if Michael doesn't hear about any of it, really."

Now he could feel the weight of her eyes, and he did his best to keep his own on the stretch of dark pavement. She wanted answers. He didn't blame her. If a dick like Tyler had been shooting at him on *her* account, he probably wouldn't be sitting there as patiently as she was.

Then again, she was still shivering. Was it all cold? Should he reach out and touch her?

He remembered the way she'd snapped at him in the cafeteria, like the words had etched themselves into his brain. But he kept thinking of the feel of her hand in his, how she'd hung close to him in the water.

Or how soft her lips had been.

When you were performing mouth-to-mouth? You are one sick bastard.

"Look." Chris cleared his throat and rested his arm on the door. His fingers found a loose piece of upholstery there, and he picked at it. "This thing with Tyler—it goes back a ways."

"How far back?"

He shouldn't be telling her this. Despite Tyler, despite the fights—there was safety in this community. Risking discovery—

and telling an outsider was definitely risking discovery—was a mistake.

Then he remembered Tyler's warnings, about the Guides. Maybe they weren't safe here at all.

Stop thinking. She's going to think you're a freak.

"Pretty far," he said. "My parents moved here when I was four. Michael was eleven—he started middle school as the new kid." He paused and glanced over. "That's a tough age for . . . ah, people like us. Things are starting to happen—you know."

"So you get your powers at puberty?"

"*Powers.*" God, this felt ridiculous, like she expected him to reveal that he secretly wore green spandex and could talk to marine life. "It's not like in movies. He didn't dream about earthquakes and wake up to find the house split in two or anything. It's more like your element calls you *to* it—speaks to you, I guess—" He broke off and glanced at her.

Again, a mistake. They were rolling past evenly spaced streetlights, turning the lines of her body into a neon sign.

On.

Off.

He swallowed and looked back at the road. "Michael hated school. Too many walls—he wanted to be outside *all* the time. He'd sneak out of the house and sleep in the yard at night. Things like that." These memories were hard to piece together sometimes—his four-year-old self hadn't understood, though he did now.

"My parents knew what he was going through, of course," he continued. "Especially my father. Dad was an *Earth*—it was his idea to start the landscaping company. But it was a new town, they'd just started the business, the twins and I were still little kids—they didn't exactly have a lot of time on their hands. And they didn't know Michael was a pure Elemental. Not then."

They'd come to a traffic light on Ritchie Highway, and he looked over. She was watching him, her expression patient. "Is that what you call yourselves? Elementals?"

"We don't really *call ourselves* anything—" He shrugged and looked back at the road. She'd said it like it was something impressive. His cheeks felt hot. "But yeah."

She was frowning a little, but that was ten times better than laughing at him. "Your dad was an Earth . . . so it's not hereditary?"

Wait. She sounded intrigued. He glanced over. "It is. It's kind of like how brown-eyed parents can have a blue-eyed kid—just, there are five different . . . what's the word?" He should have paid more attention in biology. "Alleles," he finished. "So even though Mom and Dad were an Earth and an Air, we're all different."

"So the twins aren't really identical."

Chris shot her a smile. "That's a point of family debate." She started frowning again, so he lost the smile. "Whether you think what we are is natural or . . . or not."

Her eyes were big in the darkness of the car. "Or supernatural."

Chris looked back at the road. She was staring at him again, and her scrutiny sat heavy on his shoulders. He wanted to shrug it off.

She cleared her throat, and he wondered if she was going to ask him to pull over so she could get out.

But then she said, "You were telling me about Tyler."

Chris nodded. "My parents moved here to be closer to a community of people like us. Their parents had been farmers, so they'd been raised out in the boonies, and they wanted us to be around our own kind. But they didn't realize how strong Michael would turn out to be. And before they could hide it, the whole community knew."

"But—I thought it was a good thing to fall on a point."

She'd paid attention. "It's a powerful thing. Too powerful." He paused, wondering how she would take this next part. "What we are—it can be very dangerous."

"I got that."

He drew a breath, thinking of Gabriel's lightning last night.

He could still smell the scorched earth, feel the heat on his skin from the explosion. "More than you saw."

She was silent for a moment. He could practically feel her thinking. "Just . . . how dangerous?"

"The elements don't always want to obey. It's easy to start something you can't finish." His free hand tightened into a fist. He'd lost her in that wave, when the water had been focused on nothing but destruction.

He'd almost drowned her.

"I don't understand."

He needed to stop beating around the bush. "We could kill people, Becca. Without meaning to. It's not as simple as just controlling water or air or whatever. Gabriel can pull power from sunlight to burn someone in the middle of the day. Nick could get pissed and suffocate someone by accident. Michael could have a bad day and trees could rip out of the—"

He stopped. She was looking panicked again.

"Control comes with age," he said, his voice more even. "Age and practice. I don't have a lot of either, but I seem to be getting a crash course lately." He took a breath and blew it out through his teeth. "I was eleven when my parents died, and they were the closest thing to a teacher that we had."

"But Tyler and Seth—they're like you," she said.

He shook his head. "They're not like us. They aren't the risk. We are."

"Like . . . when I gave you water. When you were unconscious in the parking lot, and you came up fighting."

At that, he did look over, meeting her gaze. "Yeah." His voice was rough. "Or when we're being shot at."

She looked away, out the windshield, and now he knew she was putting two and two together.

Stupid. He shouldn't have said anything.

"Am I in danger?" she said. "Right now?"

Chris shook his head. He didn't hear fear in her voice, but he felt like a freak anyway.

Now she cleared her throat. "So with Michael—why did the others care that he was a . . . a pure Elemental?"

"Because we're not supposed to be allowed to live."

She didn't say anything, so he kept talking, just so he wouldn't have to sit there with that sentence hanging out in the silence. "According to legend, pure Elementals used to control the others. Apparently it wasn't pretty. There were battles for territory, uprisings, rebellions, you name it. If you look back through history for natural disasters, I can almost guarantee each one fell around the time of an Elemental war."

"Like . . . tsunamis and—"

"Think broader. How about the great Chicago fire?" He glanced over. "Or the Spanish Flu?"

"You can spread *sickness?*"

"Nick can control air. That includes things *in it.*"

"Holy crap." She was staring out the windshield again.

"It was getting out of control. So about a hundred years ago, a bunch of the strongest got together and started a sort of law enforcement to take down pure Elementals. It's not like the cops. We all stay the hell away from them."

"Is that what the Guides are?"

He swung his head around. "Where'd you hear that?"

"From Tyler. He said he'd called them. And then Seth said it on the patio."

"The Guides are people who were born on the fifth point. They can control all the elements. They're rare—it's like hitting the genetic lottery. Just like people are supposed to report a child who shows the potential to be a full Elemental, they're also supposed to report a child who shows the potential to be a Fifth."

Her eyes were wide again. "That's a lot of dead kids."

"They don't kill the Fifths. They track them to see if they come into their full power, and then they train them."

"To do what?"

"To kill the full Elementals."

She whistled softly through her teeth. "Holy crap."

Chris looked back at the road. "When Michael hit thirteen or so, Tyler's parents told our parents they were going to call the Guides, that Michael had to be turned in."

Her breathing sounded shallow. Was he frightening her?

"So . . ." She sounded like she was reasoning this out. "Why didn't they?"

"At first, because my parents were well liked. Mom and Dad were good people. But not everyone felt the same. The kids started hassling us. Some of the adults started threatening our parents."

Chris stared out the windshield again, hearing resentment in his own voice. Michael had gotten the worst of it, back then. He'd wanted to fight back—their parents wouldn't hear of it.

"Give it time," Dad had said. "Arrogance and aggression come from insecurity."

Michael hadn't liked that. Talk about aggression—Chris could still remember the fights his oldest brother had had with their father.

Not unlike, Chris realized with a start, the ones Michael had with Gabriel now.

"My parents put up with it. I mean, they were caught between a rock and a hard place—as long as it was threats and stuff, no one was killing Michael. I think they wanted to leave, but they were scared, you know? If we left, would our former neighbors send the Guides after us? This went on for months." He shook his head. "Years."

"But why *didn't* they just call the Guides? Why do all the threats?"

"You know how when someone's hassling you at school, and you tell the teacher, and the teacher yells at the person causing the problem?"

She hesitated, staring out the window. "Sure."

Something in her voice caught him. He'd forgotten about that note from Dunleavy. That guy was a complete tool—had she taken it personally?

"What are you *looking* at?" She hunched down in the seat and crossed her arms over her chest.

He snapped his eyes to the road. Christ, now she probably thought he was a complete lech. "Well—when the Guides come, they don't just look at the accused. They look at the accusers, too."

"They were afraid to turn you in."

"Yeah. And when we started school, Tyler and Seth and the rest of them started ragging on us." He glanced over. "It *sucked*. So then we started fighting back, and then we got in *trouble* for fighting back, and we hated them more—"

"I get it."

She didn't get it. Not really. She'd seen one fight. What did she know about feeling powerless?

She saved your ass.

He ran a hand through his hair, pushing the wet strands out of his eyes again. "My parents offered them a deal. The others would swear to never call the Guides. And my parents would swear to keep us from causing harm."

"They agreed."

He nodded. "My parents were smart. Because once the others made that bargain, it gave my parents leverage. The others could get in just as much trouble for keeping us hidden so long."

She shivered again, then twisted in the seat and began fishing in the back for something. It put her shoulder against his, just for an instant, then the curve of her side. He could feel every drop of water on her skin.

His breath almost caught, but he shifted away.

"I just want my pullover," she said.

He nodded.

She pulled a fleece over her head and dropped back into the bucket seat. "So everyone was happy."

Chris shrugged, resisting the urge to clear his throat again. "You'd think so. But no. The parents were fine—it was the kids. They treated us like shit."

"All of them?"

He thought back, remembering. "No. Not all of them. Tyler's older sister, Emily, was in Michael's class."

"Yeah?"

There was hope in her voice. He should shut up, before he

crushed it. "She was nice, I guess. She didn't hassle him—any of us, really. I think he liked her, but they were juniors in high school, and basically on opposing sides of a long-standing fight. I mean, it's not like he asked her out or anything."

"Kind of the start of a whole Romeo and Juliet thing?"

"Maybe." Chris shrugged. "She drowned in that old rock quarry just south of Severna Park."

The atmosphere in the car seemed to flicker. He'd shocked her. "Wait. So—she—she—"

"She died." His voice was flat. He didn't know any other way to say it. "It was the summer before their senior year. Lots of kids used to sneak in to swim there—they still do. There'd been a lot of rain. One of the rock walls was loose, and started to slide. People were diving, goofing off, the same stupid crap kids do every day. A large rock fell and hit Emily. She went under and drowned." He paused. "Michael was there."

Becca didn't say anything to that, and Chris wondered what she thought. They were close to his road, so he hit the turn signal.

"They all thought Michael had something to do with it," he said, his voice a bit softer now. "He was fighting with Tyler. I don't even remember why. But it got out of hand. And it made people start to wonder if he'd started the rock slide."

Chris had only been eleven. He distinctly remembered Tyler's parents coming to the door. He'd never seen his father argue like that with anybody. Mom had sent him and his brothers upstairs, telling them to lock the door. Funny how his mind latched onto every detail of that moment, the gray yoga pants she'd worn, the soft tank top with stains from working in the yard. The way her hair had been tied into a ponytail, bangs dusting across her forehead. The way she'd stared hard at Michael. *Lock the door. Do you understand me? Lock it.*

They had, all of them bunched into their parents' bedroom because it had the biggest bed. They'd tried to listen. Michael had been shaking.

He'd never forget that, either.

Chris pulled into his driveway and killed the engine. The SUV wasn't back—but the porch lights were on. Becca made no move to get out of the car.

Chris didn't, either. He was in no rush to see Michael. "You want me to keep going? Or are you too cold?"

She nodded quickly, then must have realized he'd asked two questions. "Keep going."

"You ever see those old movies, where a mob goes through the village with torches and pitchforks, looking for the monster?"

"Yeah?"

"That's what it was like, when they came after Michael. First it was Tyler's parents. That was just an argument, but I get it. Their daughter was dead. They wanted someone to blame." Chris gave a humorless laugh. "By midnight, we had twenty people in the living room, demanding that my parents turn Michael over. It stopped being an argument, and it started to get physical. We could hear every word—then furniture was breaking, glass, you name it—"

Chris stopped. This was over five years ago, but the memory still had the power to grab his throat and hold on.

"We were hiding upstairs," he continued softly, as if he could sneak the story in before the panic caught up with him. "We had the door locked. Someone started pounding on the door. There's still a crack in the wood. Mom started screaming—I don't know if they were doing something to her, or if she just panicked to get to us. But every lightbulb in the house exploded, and half the lamps caught on fire."

"Gabriel," she murmured. "He would have been twelve or thirteen?"

He nodded. "I don't think he even knew he was a *Fire* until that day. It cleared the house. The adults didn't know who it was, but they knew it was one of us, and they were afraid. You saw what he did on the beach. Our level of power—it's not subtle.

"Everything was worse after that. The adults started hassling my parents—saying they hadn't kept up their end of the deal. My folks threatened right back. So the others started spreading rumors, destroying equipment from the company. We used to have a storefront in Annapolis, but they set it on fire—"

"They were never *caught?*"

Chris gave a short laugh. "Becca, everything is natural. With what we are—it's easy to commit a crime without any evidence. Very easy." He paused, thinking of the wave he'd called from the water. He'd wanted to drag Tyler and Seth under, to convince the water to hold them until they stopped fighting.

Water clung to his skin, to hers, reminding him it was still willing. He stared out at the night. "Too easy."

Becca looked away from him.

Chris wondered if he'd frightened her again. His voice came out tight. "Right after Michael started his senior year, Tyler and a bunch of his friends ambushed him when he was out working a job for Dad. They tied him up, drove him to the quarry, and threw him in."

Chris had been with him. He'd just started middle school, and he loved going along on jobs, having a purpose, feeling useful. The windows had been down, their skin full of sweat and sunshine, and Michael had just asked if he wanted to hit the batting cages before sundown.

Then Tyler had tried to run them off the road.

They were driving Dad's truck—Michael wasn't going to wreck it. They'd pulled over. Michael had gotten out. Chris remembered thinking his brother wasn't afraid of anything.

He stared out the window again, running a finger along the weather strip.

"How did Michael get free?" she asked, her voice rough in the silence.

"He wasn't alone."

It took her a minute to piece it together. "They dumped you in the quarry, too?"

Chris didn't say anything for a moment, then turned to look at her. He banished the emotion from his voice, and now he gave her half a smile. "You don't think you're the only person I've ever dragged out of the water, do you?"

"Did they know? About your . . . powers?"

He shook his head. "They learned real quick." Some of them had still been in the water—making sure he and Michael didn't escape, probably. But Chris remembered drawing power from the water, dragging their attackers to the center of the quarry, begging his element to pull them under and steal their breath.

The power had been terrifying. Addictive.

Michael had stopped him.

Chris ran a hand through his hair, pushing the damp strands off his face. "Mom and Dad had been willing to deal. They'd put up with a lot. But after those guys threw us in the quarry, after they tried to *kill* us, Mom decided to go talk to the others. She brought us with her. Dad didn't want her to go, but she got her way. I don't think she meant to start a fight—I think she wanted to remind them that we were just kids, you know? She just wanted to work it out. They didn't."

It was getting tough to keep his voice level. He stopped talking, picking at the upholstery again.

Becca swallowed. "So what happ—"

"I'm cold."

His tone must have startled her. But he couldn't help it—and she nodded anyway. "Okay."

"Let's go inside."

With that, he didn't glance at her, just threw open the door and stepped into the brisk night air.

CHAPTER 16

Becca followed Chris into the house, keeping her footsteps light. Michael was asleep on the living room sofa, the television throwing flashes of red and blue across his face and tee shirt. One arm hung off the side of the sofa, resting on that beat-up spiral notebook.

Becca hung close to Chris, afraid to breathe, worried about waking his brother.

Chris wasn't. "Hey. Mike. Wake up. I'm home."

Michael stirred, running a hand across his face before sitting up to face the doorway. He rubbed at his eyes, then stopped short when he saw her. "And you brought a friend."

He said it in the same voice her mother had used when Becca was seven and took to "rescuing" stray cats in the neighborhood—by luring them into the house and attempting to hide them in her closet.

"Be nice," said Chris.

Becca shoved her hands into the pockets of the pullover. "I'm not staying long."

"Why are you staying at all?"

Chris gave a disgusted sigh and turned away from the doorway. "Ignore him. Come on."

"Why are you all wet?" Michael called.

Chris didn't answer, just started up the steps. Becca followed him—only hesitating for a moment. "Does he hate me or something?"

The upstairs hallway was a well of silence, their footsteps muffled by carpeting. "It's not personal. He's a dick to every girl who comes around here."

Bizarre. "Just *girls?*"

"Yeah." Chris reached out and turned the knob to his bedroom. He didn't elaborate, just pointed at the half-made bed. "Sit down. I'll give you some sweats so we can throw your clothes in the dryer."

She dropped onto the edge of the mattress. Chris pulled open some dresser drawers, rooting through them. A new bruise was forming on his jaw from where Seth had hit him. His tee shirt was still damp, clinging to the muscles across his back.

Becca realized she was staring and jerked her eyes away.

He'd jumped out of the front seat so quickly that she didn't want to press for painful memories about his parents—but she couldn't sit silent, doing nothing but inhaling the September night air that poured through his window. "So . . . why is your brother mean to girls?"

"Because," said Michael from the doorway, "I have three younger brothers who think it's hilarious to parade jailbait through here on a daily basis."

His tone was enough to make her glad she'd worn the pullover into the house. "No one told me there was a *parade,*" she said acidly. "And here I forgot my banner."

Michael leaned against the doorjamb to study his brother. "What happened to your face?"

Chris busied himself with digging through the clothes again. "Nothing. Go back downstairs so she can change."

Michael stepped into the room and stopped beside the dresser. He reached out a hand to lift Chris's chin.

Chris smacked his hand away. "Jesus. Stop."

"You want some ice?"

"No." The dresser drawer slammed, and Chris turned to her with a gray tee shirt and a pair of cutoff sweatpants. "Here."

She reached out to take them, feeling like an intruder. "Thanks."

Michael watched this exchange. "I thought you'd still be at that party."

Chris wasn't looking at him. "We were. Nick and Gabriel might still be there."

"Nick sent me a text. They wanted to make sure you got home before they came back with the car."

Becca definitely wanted to be changed before the twins got here—and she didn't want to sit through an argument between Chris and his big brother. She hugged the sweats to her chest and half rose from the bed. "I'll just—ah, go in the bathroom—"

Michael swung his head around to look at her. "You involved with Tyler somehow?"

The expression on his face made her mouth go dry, and she remembered Chris's comments from the car, that Michael had a temper. She shook her head quickly.

"She's not," said Chris.

"Because," Michael continued without looking at him, "when Chris comes home from two fights in one week, and you're with him both times, it starts to look—"

"Damn it, Michael." Chris shoved him toward the door. The move was a little too aggressive to look brotherly. So was the glare. "Just—go downstairs."

For an instant, she thought Michael would shove him back. That kind of tension hung between them, as if some pendulum would shift and they'd fight. But Michael drew back to hang by the door. He gave Becca another long look, and she fought not to squirm, but then he just turned and stepped into the hallway.

Chris was leaning against the dresser, his jaw set, his arms tight at his sides. He watched his brother leave.

Becca wet her lips. "Sorry," she said softly.

"It's not your fault."

That wasn't what she'd meant at all. "I just—I'm sorry."

Chris glanced at her with eyes shadowed with anger and tension, making her wonder at his relationship with Michael.

But Chris gave her a dark smile and pushed the hair off his forehead. "Don't sweat it. He likes being angry. Go change."

The bathroom smelled like boys, from spicy sticks of uncapped deodorant and a large bottle of body wash that looked like it could climb a mountain on its own. Nothing floral here. At least the towels looked clean.

Becca locked herself in and peeled the filthy clothes away from her body. Thank god her mother had seen her leave the house in a pullover, because the silk cropped shirt was nearly ruined. She rinsed out her jeans in the bathtub, but kept her underwear. Damp or not, she wasn't handing over a bra to Chris Merrick. She held her hair under the bathtub faucet, squeezing it into a towel before finger combing it away from her face. One of them had a bottle of some guy-brand face lotion sitting on the counter, and she used a dab under her eyes to wipe away the running mascara.

Another look in the mirror convinced her that she'd made the right decision in coming here—once her hair dried and she had her jeans back, her mom probably wouldn't notice that her daughter had taken a swim. The borrowed clothes felt soft on her skin, worn and almost threadbare. She wondered if Chris wore them to sleep, and the thought felt too personal, so she blushed, even there in the privacy of the bathroom.

Becca pulled the fleece back on, balled her soaked clothes into the towel, and unlocked the door.

She heard the twins before she saw them, and she stopped short in the hallway, scowling. They were talking to Chris from the sound of it. She wanted to just walk down the steps and out the front door. Maybe she could hang her jeans out the car window and dry them that way.

But one of the twins—Nick, if she remembered the clothes correctly—was closest to the door, and he spotted her first. "Hey, Becca."

She put the ball of damp clothes under an arm and squared her shoulders. His dark hair was a little windblown, but he clearly hadn't taken a swim. It seemed unfair—he looked even *better* than he had at the party, while she knew from the mirror that she looked like a drowned cocker spaniel.

She looked right into his eyes, determined to show him she

wouldn't get all flustered like she had in Drew's hallway. "Hey," she said flatly. "Nick."

His smile warmed a little, as if she'd amused him. He stepped forward and held out his hands, gesturing to her bundle of clothes. "Here. I'll throw those in the dryer."

She faltered, not expecting kindness from him. Uncertainty almost made her clutch the ball of fabric to her chest, as if this was some kind of trap.

Idiot. Just give him the clothes.

She thrust the bundle forward. "Thanks."

When he jogged down the stairs, she shoved her hands into the pullover pockets again and edged toward the doorway. Chris was sitting backwards on the desk chair, leaning his forearms on the back. He'd changed into a gray tee shirt and jeans that weren't wet, and now his hair was drying with a slight wave to it.

"Find everything you need?" he asked.

"Yeah." She paused. "Thanks."

Gabriel was sprawled on the bed, leaning up against the wall the way he had last night. He glanced up at her, a spark of humor in his eye. "Want to sit on the bed?"

She gave him a dark look. "No."

Chris sighed and uncurled from the chair. "Here. Sit." He stepped away to lean against the wall between the window and the aquarium.

She did, drawing her knees into the chair to sit cross-legged. She bit her tongue, unsure if Chris had told his brothers what he'd told her.

Chris shrugged, his gaze on the window. "The jig is up." Then he glanced at the door, and she read the unease in his eyes. "Not with Michael, though. So keep your voice down."

Gabriel smiled, and there was an edge of challenge to it. "You want me to set something on fire or what?"

"Subtle," said Chris.

"Can you do that?" she said, pleased that her voice was even, almost skeptical. She wouldn't let Gabriel intimidate her, either.

He glanced at his brother. "Chris. Give me your Trig book."

Chris did no such thing. "Michael will go ballistic if you start a fire up here again."

"Michael needs to switch to decaf." Gabriel dug in his pocket and fished out a lighter.

Becca straightened, feeling her eyes grow wide. Was he really going to start a fire right here in the bedroom?

Way to be nonchalant. She forced her voice to sound bored. "A lighter? Isn't that cheating?"

"Fire needs something to burn, sugar." Gabriel flipped the lighter between his fingers, somehow lighting it while it spun.

"Frat boy tricks," she said.

"Don't encourage him," said Chris.

Gabriel grinned and did it again, faster, rolling the lighter through his knuckles until the silver was a blur, the red gold of the flame a near constant arc.

She stared despite herself, leaning forward, mesmerized by the motion.

Then he snapped his other hand forward, pinched out the flame, and flicked the lighter into the air to snap it closed.

She lifted her eyes to meet his. Impressive, but nothing supernatural. "Should I applaud or something?"

He turned his closed hand over and uncurled his fingers. "You tell me."

She froze. Fire sat on his palm. Not like his hand was burning, but a suspended flame, as if his hand had lifted the plume of fire off a candlewick. A blue base climbed to orange and red as it flickered there.

"Let's see a frat boy do *that*," said Gabriel. The flame was big enough that it threw light on his face.

She uncurled from the chair and moved closer to the bed, unable to help herself. She reached out a hand to touch it. Her fingers brushed across the tip of the flame, feeling it nip at her fingertips.

"Careful," said Chris. "Sometimes it looks for something real to burn."

She couldn't tear her eyes away. "What's it burning now?"

"Energy," said Gabriel.

"What energy?"

"Mine."

Did that mean he was . . . *feeding* the fire somehow? She swallowed, almost compelled to touch it again. A breeze whispered through the open window, lifting the ends of her hair. The flame flickered and jumped, biting at her outstretched hand.

She thought of the drums on the beach, the way they'd snapped fire at Tyler and Seth. She pulled her hand back. The fire began to swirl in the breeze, a tiny whirlwind of flame stretching higher in his palm.

Then it lifted clean off his hand, spinning wider and faster until it burned out into nothing. She couldn't even smell smoke.

"I'd say you're playing with fire," said Nick from the doorway, "but it kind of loses effect when you really *are*."

"You didn't have to do that." Gabriel rolled the closed lighter across his knuckles again. "I had it."

"You had it *this time*," said Chris. He paused, and there was a thread of envy in his voice. "Your control's gotten better."

"*My* control?" Gabriel grinned. "I'm not the one who brought down a tsunami on Sillery Bay."

"Yeah, well." Chris glanced at Becca, and he looked a bit sheepish. "That didn't quite work out like I'd hoped."

Becca had thought it was downright amazing, but she didn't say that. "Are you worried about Tyler and Seth coming after you?"

"After that?" said Nick. "They ran."

He sounded pleased. She'd wondered earlier what kind of parents Tyler would have, allowing him to run around with a gun. But Nick's tone reminded her of something she'd read once in a textbook, about how guns were invented so man could level the playing field.

"They're afraid of you," she said softly. After watching the demonstration on the beach, she almost couldn't blame them.

"Of course they're afraid of us," said Nick, his voice a bit dark. "That's why they're breaking the deal."

"They'll try to prove that we're a danger to the community," said Chris. He folded his arms and looked at Gabriel. "Some of us try a little harder to stay out of trouble at school."

Gabriel sat up straight. "I haven't gotten in a fight yet this year!"

Despite everything, that made her smile. "It's September."

He waved a hand. "Details."

"So why do they care about *me?*" she asked. "I'm not involved in any of this."

"They're really after *us,* not you," said Chris. "We scared them off tonight. That will buy us some time."

"You have any classes with Seth?" said Nick.

She shook her head. "He's a senior."

"He's also an idiot." Then Nick glanced at Gabriel, and he raised an eyebrow. "That's right—don't you have, like, two classes with him?"

Chris ignored them, watching her. "Has Seth ever hassled you at school?"

Becca froze, then tucked a piece of hair behind her ear. She had to clear her throat. "Not since the fight in the parking lot."

Chris frowned. "But before?"

"It's nothing." She shook her head quickly. "What are you guys going to do?"

"What are they going to do about what?" Michael said from the hallway. He put his hands on either side of the door and leaned in.

"Nothing," Nick and Chris said at once.

Gabriel flung the lighter at him, hard, with true aggression. "Why don't you quit acting like you give a shit?"

Michael caught it and flung it back. Harder. "Why don't you quit acting like a smartass kid?"

Gabriel moved to throw it back, and Becca heard him flick the lid, then saw the flare as it spun free of his hand. She sucked in a breath.

Nicholas stepped into the line of fire and snatched the lighter out of the air. He snapped it closed. "Come on. Not tonight."

Michael was already backing out of the doorway. "Whatever." His voice was tired. "I'm going to bed."

Silence hung over the room for a moment as he moved down the hallway.

Then he called from somewhere farther in the house. "Send her home by midnight, Chris."

Becca flinched.

Gabriel rolled his eyes. "Stay as long as you want. He'll turn on SportsCenter and be asleep in ten minutes."

"I'm only here until my clothes are dry," she said quickly.

Chris shifted against the wall. His eyes were flat now, emotionless. "Don't worry. We won't keep you any longer than necessary."

That wasn't what she'd meant—or was it? Did he think she was insulting him?

Something in the tenor of the room had changed. While her brain was stumbling over something appropriate to say, Chris pushed away from the wall and headed for the door. "Come on. I'll turn on a movie or something for you downstairs."

From the sudden shift in his demeanor, she half expected him to leave her alone in their living room, but he sat on the couch—at the opposite end—while one of the Shrek sequels played on cable. The twins had remained upstairs.

She studied Chris, the way the light from the television played off his features.

"You and the twins don't get along with Michael?" she said.

Chris half shrugged, keeping his eyes on the television. "Gabriel fights with him the most. Mom used to say they'd eventually grow up and be best friends, but it sounds like a load of wishful parenting crap to me."

"The twins get in a lot of fights at school, too." She paused. "Actually, that night I helped you—I thought it might have been them causing trouble."

Chris smiled, but it was grim. "Nick's not the fighter. He just takes the fall. It's almost always Gabriel. Part of it's his element. They're all difficult to control, but fire—fire is pretty awesomely destructive. It feeds his temper. I think the only reason he hasn't picked a fight is because the coach told him he'd be benched all year if he caught him fighting again."

She wondered what it would be like to live with someone whose temper could start fires. Gabriel had flicked that lighter at Michael—what would have happened if Nick hadn't grabbed it out of the air?

"So Nick's the peacekeeper," she said.

Chris snorted. "He always has been. Our parents died when Michael was eighteen. The courts weren't going to give him custody. It was spring, and he hadn't even graduated yet. He fought like hell to get it. They still send a social worker around every year to check up on us, but it used to be every frigging month. He's a freak about making sure we don't get in too much trouble or draw any attention."

Becca tried to think back to middle school. She remembered Chris, of course; had written him off as just another surly preteen floating somewhere in the rotation of classes. Her father had left then, and she'd been so wrapped up in her own family drama that she hadn't had time for anyone else's. She'd spent her middle school years rescuing hurt animals so she could prove to her father that she wanted to be just like him.

What a joke.

"At least he cares," she said.

Chris's eyes narrowed. "Is that what it looks like? Caring?"

She narrowed her eyes back at him. "At least he's *here*."

"Ah." He settled back against the cushion and gave her a knowing look. "Divorce?"

Startled, she flushed, like it was something to be ashamed of. She brushed hair off her cheek, tucking it behind her ear. "Does it make a difference?"

"Yes," he said evenly, holding her gaze. "It makes a difference."

She had to look away, wanting to apologize but unsure whether he deserved it.

Chris was quiet for a long while, but then he sighed. "I'm sorry," he said. "That was a shitty thing to say."

His voice was disarming, rough and guarded and just a little bit vulnerable, his eyes wary the way they'd been in her rearview the night she rescued him.

"Me too," she said. "I didn't mean—your parents—"

"I know what you meant." He looked away. "But Michael doesn't give a crap what they do to us. Like the other night. I got a lecture that I shouldn't provoke Tyler and Seth. I shouldn't provoke *them*. Now they're breaking the deal, and they're threatening to call the Guides, and—" He broke off and ran his hands through his hair, the movement tense and agitated. "Do you have any idea what it's like, to have someone treat you like shit, and then feel like it's your own fault?"

His eyes were midnight-blue pools in the dim room, and she felt her heart speed up. She rubbed at her neck, feeling a flush crawl up her cheeks. "Yeah. I do."

Chris drew back, watching her. He must have picked up on something in her voice. "You want to tell me the real deal with Drew? Or Seth?"

She froze, unable to speak.

"I heard a little of what went on in the driveway." Chris picked at the hem of his jeans. "And . . . what you said at lunch—"

"It's nothing." She swallowed hard. "It's not a big deal."

His eyes flicked up. He said nothing, but she heard his response all the same.

I told you our secret.

Not like hers was a secret at all. "Didn't Gabriel already tell you?" she snapped.

He hesitated—and that was answer enough.

She couldn't face him now. Becca shoved herself off the couch, hating that her throat felt tight. "I'm going to check on my jeans."

For an instant there was nothing but silence.

"Becca. Wait."

She stopped short, afraid to look at him, terrified of what he might say.

"I'll get them." Then he was on his feet, stepping around her, his movement brisk. "Don't want to trap you here too long."

And before she could think of a retort, he was through the doorway, leaving her in silence, with nothing but second thoughts for company.

CHAPTER 17

Becca woke to the smell of coffee and the sound of pots clang-
ing. Dishes clinking. Then water running, followed by more
pots.

Her mother was scrubbing the kitchen.

That meant something had happened. Maybe the car broke
down, or an unexpected bill had appeared in the mailbox, or
maybe they were cutting her hours at the hospital again.

Becca rubbed at her eyes and wished she had to work today.
She knew from experience that she'd be better served to just go
downstairs and deal with her mother's manic behavior right up
front.

"Such a freak," Becca muttered. She dragged herself out of
bed, wondering if this was her penance for getting away with
last night's adventure.

She discovered her mom surrounded by a dozen boxes of
cupcake mix and Shake 'n Bake, scrubbing the shelf liner with a
rasp-back sponge.

Becca sighed and grabbed a mug from the cabinet. "Really,
Mom? The shelf liner?"

"This is filthy. It's crazy."

Becca spooned three heaping tablespoons of sugar into her
mug. "Right. That's what's crazy."

"Did you know your dad was in town?"

Becca almost spilled creamer all over the counter, but she saved it at the last second. "Oh?"

Her mother was scrubbing with a vengeance. "He said he left a message for you."

Busted. "Maybe Quinn took it. You know how she is. You talked to him?"

Her mother glanced up. "Obviously, Becca."

Becca poured coffee into the remaining two inches of space. "And you . . . aren't surprised he's in town?"

"Well, I suppose I should have figured he'd show up eventually." Her mother started slamming the boxes back onto the pristine shelf, punctuating every other word of her sentence. "I just would have appreciated a little forewarning that he'd called *you,* you know, so when he confronted me and asked if I've, you know, *poisoned* your opinion of him—"

"Mom." Normally her mother wasn't quite this keyed up. "Are you all right?"

"No, I'm not all right." Her mom flung pasta boxes into the cabinet. "First, a man I haven't seen in years shows up on the doorstep, and then I discover that kids spray painted all over the front of the house."

The coffee was burning her hands through the sides of the mug, but Becca kept a death grip on the ceramic. She'd been stuck on her mom's comment about her father showing up, but now her thoughts went in a new direction. Was this retaliation for showing up at Drew's party?

Her mom was still ranting, snapping yellow vinyl gloves onto her hands before grabbing a can of EASY-OFF. "I don't know why these people think I have time to deal with the front of the house being treated like a highway overpass."

Becca carefully set her coffee on the counter and turned for the kitchen doorway. She would just go see for herself.

She was almost running by the time her hand seized on the doorknob. She yanked at the door, ready to throw herself onto the porch to see the damage.

So she almost fell on top of her father, kneeling there with a paintbrush in his hand.

He looked the same, but sort of different, which was surprising enough. It was like looking at her mom's old yearbook photos—still clearly the same person, just . . . not. He was a good-looking guy, she guessed, with sandy brown hair that had yet to turn gray, though a few gray whiskers had crept into his goatee. His eyes were a steely gray she'd inherited, though his were deep-set over solid cheekbones. He was wearing some kind of uniform, khaki pants and a button-down shirt with patches on the sleeves, alternately reading *Department of Natural Resources* and *Wildlife Control Division*. A green truck sat in the driveway, a matching logo on the door.

"Easy," he said. "The door's wet."

She jerked her hand away, though she hadn't touched anything but the interior knob. A fresh coat of paint made the door shine in the early light. He'd gotten three-quarters of the way down, and she could just see the edge of a line of red spray paint near the base.

She stared at the door, as if she could somehow read what had been written through the beige layer of Duron.

Her father put the paintbrush in his left hand, then held out his right. "Bill Chandler. Nice to meet you."

Becca scowled. "Hilarious."

He pulled his hand back, then gestured for her to step onto the porch. "Pull that shut so I can finish."

She was tempted to close herself on the inside. But she stepped onto the porch, careful of splinters, and pulled the door shut. Now, facing the house, she couldn't see any graffiti, except the stripe at the bottom of the door.

She had no idea what to say to her father, so she stuck with the mundane, as if she saw him every morning. "Mom said it was all over the front of the house."

"It was just the door. Your mom tends to exaggerate."

That pissed her off. Her back straightened. "How would you know?"

He nodded, then dipped the brush into the paint can by his right knee. "You're right." He paused and glanced up. "She *used* to exaggerate. Does she still?"

Becca didn't want to nod. But he was right. She stared out into the yard instead.

He brushed a stroke up the front of the door. "I left a message for you to call me."

"I don't return calls from complete strangers. You never know what they might be selling."

"That's true. Why take a chance, right?"

An insult was hidden there, she was sure of it. She frowned. "What do you want?"

"Right this second, I want to finish painting this door."

"You think slapping some paint on the door is going to put you back in Mom's good graces? Where'd you even get that paint, anyway?"

"Your mother had it in the shed. And I have no idea about her graces, good or otherwise. I just thought I'd help out while I waited for you to wake up."

"Why?"

He looked up. "Because I'm your father, Becca."

She stared at him. "Wow, and you said that with a straight face and everything."

He looked back at the door and slid another line of paint up the side. "Be as nasty as you want. I know you're curious."

She wanted to punch him. Or kick him; the angle was better. "So?"

"I am, too. I have an assignment in town, so I'll be here for a while." He paused. "I thought maybe we could catch up."

"An *assignment*." She rolled her eyes. "How exciting."

"Not at all. I'm investigating crabbing violations in Annapolis. Couldn't be more boring."

She leaned against the siding next to the door and looked out at the street. "You want to just roll in here after years of nothing but random phone calls, and act like suddenly we can be—"

"Becca." He looked up at her. "I don't want to act like anything."

And then she was hit with a memory. She must have been four years old. Her father had been holding some kind of animal, a ferret, maybe, or a guinea pig—the memory was fuzzy around the edges. Show and tell? She couldn't remember. But she remembered the feel of his hands around hers, helping her cradle the animal, letting her show it to the other kids.

Jesus Christ, her throat felt tight.

He was still looking up at her. "Becca?"

"I'm busy today," she said.

"Doing what?"

"I need to go to the mall. My cell phone broke, so I need a new one."

He was looking at the door again, brushing slowly. The door had been green, but he must not have had enough paint. Now it was going to be beige like the back door. It looked unnaturally bright against the brown siding.

"Well, why don't you go get dressed." He glanced up. "Maybe I could go with you. We could get lunch."

She snorted. "Yeah. Okay, *Dad*. Like Mom is going to let me go off with you."

"I already talked to her." When Becca couldn't think of anything to say to that, he glanced up. "I've been here for two hours. We had coffee."

Becca fidgeted with the edge of her pajamas. Her mom was okay with this? "I was kidding about the cell phone. I don't have money for a new one. Yet."

"I can take care of it," he said.

"Oh, you're going to buy me off?"

"Is that possible?"

She took a breath and fidgeted again. He sure had a cache of retorts. "I don't want you to," she said after a moment.

"Sometimes it's not about what you want, Becca."

"Clearly."

He swung his head around, and she saw the first flash of irritation in his eyes. "All right, maybe we can cut the attitude."

"Sometimes it's not about what you want, *Dad*."

He stared right at her. "Clearly."

That made her flinch.

He didn't hold her there too long. He looked back at the door, and his voice dropped. "I'm serious. Go get dressed. I'm not on the clock until one."

Great.

But now he was looking at her again, and she felt his uncertainty. That meant he cared. She could refuse right now, and there really wasn't a whole lot he could do about it. But she got the distinct impression it would hurt him if she did.

She shouldn't care. He didn't deserve it.

But she did care. "All right." She paused. "I have to take a shower first."

"Take your time. I still have to do the molding." He shifted so she could get back through the door.

But halfway through, she paused. "What did it say, anyway?"

He was already reloading his brush. "What did what say?"

"The door."

"It didn't say anything. Just some stupid kid's idea of art."

It didn't say anything. Relief shoved some of the guilt out of the way. Regardless of how she felt about her dad, she didn't want him reading that some "stupid kid" thought his little girl was a whore.

He ran the brush against the side of the can, scraping off the excess. "Seems a little early for Halloween, though."

She didn't follow. "Halloween?"

He glanced up at her. "Didn't your mom tell you?"

When she shook her head, he reached up to take hold of the door handle, obviously wanting to get back to painting before it dripped off his brush. "Yeah, they drew a pentagram."

Then he pulled the door shut, leaving her standing in the hallway, staring gape-mouthed at nothing.

Becca wanted to storm over to Chris's house and demand answers.

Instead, she had to suffer through a phone demo at the Verizon store in the middle of the mall, given by a guy not much older than she was. Christ, she knew how to send a text message. Couldn't they just swipe her dad's card so they could get out of there already?

When the salesman finally went into the back to program the phone, her dad leaned on the counter and looked at her. "You all right?"

She couldn't stop thinking of the pentagram on her front door. Had Tyler done it? Seth?

They had a gun and they knew where she *lived?*

She shrugged and picked at her nails.

"Do you like the phone?" he asked.

"It's fine." It was great. Better than her last one, with Internet access and a keyboard instead of just ten digits on the face.

"You want to tell me what's bothering you?"

Yes. She did. She didn't care who listened, but she needed to spill her guts and ask someone what to do. If he asked twice, she might actually do it.

She hunched her shoulders and stared at the wall of protective cases. "No."

"Fair enough."

Well, that solved that. She shifted to trace her finger along the peeling edge of the service agreement taped to the counter until the man came back.

"Becca, this thing between me and your mom—I think you might have the wrong—"

"God, *Dad*." Of course he thought this was all about him. She spun to look at him. "Here? Really?"

"Easy," he said softly, making her realize her voice had risen in pitch. "I'm just trying to talk to you."

She scowled. "I'm not going to listen to some story about why you screwed over my mother. And me, for that matter. In the middle of the mall or otherwise."

He drew back, putting distance between them. "Loud and clear, Becca."

She'd pushed too far. She could read it on his face, the steady tension that made his eyes hard while he studied the wall behind the cash registers. He didn't say anything further, and her comment hung in the air between them.

Not like she'd take it back.

But now she squirmed while he stood like a statue, waiting for the guy to return to the counter. When her dad ran his card through the machine, she swallowed, watching the triple-digit number flash on the register.

She jerked her eyes away and took the phone from the salesman, burying it in her sweatshirt pocket, running her thumb over the smooth newness of the keys.

They made it all the way out of the store before she chanced a look up at her father.

"Thanks," she said, and her voice was soft in the general cacophony of the crowded mall aisle.

"You're welcome." He didn't look at her, but some of that tension seemed to have dissipated. "Rocky Run for lunch?"

His voice seemed uncertain again, like maybe he suspected she'd bail on his earlier lunch invitation.

Becca tucked her hair behind her ear and nodded. "Okay."

There was a wait, of course. But it wasn't too long, and she sat next to him on the vinyl bench outside the restaurant while some grade school kids roughhoused across the aisle.

Her dad didn't offer any conversation, and she wondered if he felt as awkward about this as she did.

She let her mind wander, running her eyes along the storefronts down the way. The jewelry store made her think of Hunter, and she absently ran her fingers over the stones still strapped to her wrist, hidden under the sleeve of her hoodie. The music store near the corner was almost empty, since no one bothered to buy CDs anymore. Forever 21 was blasting some R&B song with a heavy beat. Girls were streaming out the door, laden with bags, laughing and giggling and heading this way.

Then she recognized one of them. Lilah.

Seth's girlfriend.

Her brain kicked into high gear, trying to keep up with the sudden spike in her heart rate. She felt hot, panicked. Was Seth with her? No, it was just girls. But Lilah would recognize her, right? Were Seth and Tyler *here,* in the mall?

"Becca?"

Her dad's voice, and it sounded like he'd called her name more than once. She had to pry her gaze off the girls to look back at him.

He glanced down at the bench, then back at her face. "You okay?"

She followed his gaze. She'd grabbed his hand without realizing it.

Don't be such a baby. She snatched it out of his grip and swiped her palm on her jeans.

The girls were almost beside them, and she looked down at her knees, letting her hair fall across her face. Her shoulders tightened. They'd see her. They'd have to see her.

They didn't see her.

But they walked up to the hostess to ask for a table in the restaurant.

Her dad leaned in. "Becca?"

"Yeah." She swallowed. "I don't want to have lunch here."

He wasn't an idiot. "What just happened?"

Tension almost made her bite his head off. She glared at him from under the spill of her hair. "I just don't want to eat here, okay?"

"Got it." He stood up. "Let's go."

She sat hunched in the passenger seat of his truck, leaning against the door, knowing he wanted to interrogate her.

Sure enough, they'd barely made it to the main road before he said, "You know those girls?"

Becca looked out the window. "Not really."

"Seemed like you did."

She shrugged.

He let a moment pass. "Is this about a boy?"

"No!" She made a frustrated noise and shifted in the seat to face him. "*Now* you want to have the *boy* conversation? Are you *kidding?*"

He sighed. "I'd settle for any conversation."

Becca straightened. *Where've you been all this time?*

The words were practically burning her lips. She just wasn't ready for the answer.

"What about lunch?" she said when he turned onto her street.

Her dad kept his eyes on the road. "You didn't seem like you were into it."

Did he want an apology? One almost fell out of her mouth anyway. She bit at her lip as he pulled into the driveway. She was still struggling to think of what to say when he killed the engine.

She started to climb down from the cab and was surprised when he did the same.

"You're coming in?" she said.

"I want to talk to your mother."

Those words had weight to them, and she knew—she *knew*—they were going to talk about her. Probably thinking up some way to manipulate her into spending more time with him.

She rolled her eyes. "Whatever."

"I'm not your enemy, Becca."

She didn't have an answer for that, so she bolted up the stairs as soon as they were through the door. He could talk to her mom all he wanted; she didn't have to be a part of it.

Her mom would probably scrub the gutters with a toothbrush after this.

But maybe Becca could use this distraction to her advantage.

She pocketed her keys and crept down the stairs. Sure enough, they were talking in muted tones in the kitchen.

She could hear her mother's voice. "Bill, you can't show up and expect me to force her to—"

Then her dad's whisper. "I don't want you to force her to do *anything*. But something obviously happened, and I warned you—"

"Bye!" Becca yelled, opening the door wide. She could still smell paint. "Going to Quinn's!"

"Becca," her mother called. "Wait just a min—"

Becca slammed the door.

Then she hopped down the steps, jumped into her car, and started the ignition.

But at the end of her block, she didn't turn right, and she didn't head for Quinn's house.

She turned left and drove straight to Chris's.

CHAPTER 18

When she pulled into the driveway, the garage door stood open. The Merrick brothers were outside, hauling bags out of the garage to load them on a flatbed trailer. It was hitched to a red pickup with their name and a landscaping logo on the side.

She tightened her grip on the steering wheel. This gave her absolutely no chance to reconsider what the hell she was doing here. She'd planned to talk to Chris privately, to mention what had happened to her house, to demand answers.

Confronting him in front of his entire family was not part of the plan.

Sunlight warmed the air as she climbed out of the car, though she was glad for her jacket when a breeze raced through the trees to whisper down her neck. The scents coming from the garage made her think of the garden center at Home Depot, something damp and woodsy and not entirely natural, like mulch and topsoil overlaid with a hint of Miracle-Gro. The open garage revealed a huge space that clearly doubled as storage for Michael's landscaping business. Pallets were stacked along the walls, with bags of things like soil and white sand and red cedar chips. Tools hung everywhere, crammed into every space imaginable, though there had to be a method to the madness.

Michael was closest to her. He dropped a bag labeled LIME-STONE SCREENINGS on the pile at the front of the flatbed. He wore a red tee shirt and jeans and his arms already sported a fine layer of dust. As usual, his voice wasn't friendly. "You know it's the twenty-first century?"

She had no idea what he was talking about. "What?"

He swiped his hands on his jeans and turned back to the garage. He called over his shoulder, "Ever hear of a phone?"

She straightened her back and stared after him. "Ever hear of manners?"

He was already heaving another bag onto his shoulder, his expression lost in the shadows. "You mean like driving up to someone's house uninvited?"

What an asshole. "Maybe if you weren't—"

"Becca." Chris was carrying a bag of the same stuff out of the garage. "Just ignore him."

He flung the bag on top of the pile, then jumped off the trailer to come over to her. His tee shirt was black, and dust streaked across the front of his chest. Sweat had collected on his forehead, and he ducked his head to wipe it on his sleeve.

He seemed wary; that vague tension they'd shared last night still hung between them. "What's up?"

"I just—" She faltered. One of the twins was carrying another bag to the flatbed. He barely gave her a nod. They looked tired—and those bags looked heavy.

They were busy.

All at once, she wanted to slink back to her car. Someone had just painted a star in a circle on her door. Tyler had a gun, and had demonstrated he wasn't afraid to use it—would he really stoop to something like teenage pranks to intimidate her? Maybe it was just like her dad said, some stupid kid being stupid. It wasn't as if pentagrams were unique to Elementals.

"You're busy," she backpedaled. "I shouldn't have just shown up like this—"

"It's all right." Chris moved closer, until she caught his scent, like sunshine and limestone.

"Chris." Michael had another bag, and he added it to the stack. "Less talk. More work."

A spark of irritation lit Chris's features, but he turned toward the garage. "Come on. Talk to me while I load. He's just pissed because he's already late."

Becca followed him into the cool cavern of the garage. He picked up a bag from the stack and heaved it onto his shoulder.

This felt awkward. "Can I help you? Or—"

"Go ahead." He flashed a smile. "Bring one out."

She bent and slid her hands under the slick edges of the sack. It felt like a bag of sand, and it was marked 35KG. She could never remember if kilograms were more than pounds or the other way around, but she crouched and heaved and attempted to lift the sack of limestone.

Christ. It's more. Kilograms are more. The bag had to weigh at least eighty pounds. She couldn't even get it off the pallet.

"Excuse me."

One of the twins, his voice threaded with humor. She stepped back, already sensing sweat on her back, just from that moment of effort. She felt like an idiot.

Especially when he hooked his hands under *two* bags and lifted them against his chest.

"Showoff," she said.

He shook the hair off his forehead. "Maybe you could go in the kitchen and bake us some cookies or something."

"Shut up."

He gave her a wicked grin over his shoulder. "Just saying."

Then Chris was back, grabbing another bag for himself. "Come on. Gabriel will rag on you all day if you let him."

How does he tell them apart?

He let her walk in silence until he dumped his bag. Then he stood on the side of the flatbed and looked down at her. "Becca?"

She had to give him some reason for being here. "I . . . ah . . . thought we should talk about the project."

His brow furrowed. "For History?"

Yeah, it sounded lame to her, too. "I didn't have your number, so I thought maybe—"

He pointed at the side of the truck. "It's the same as the business number. I'll write it down for you, or you can just Google it—"

"Chris!" Michael had a clipboard in one hand now.

Chris swore under his breath and gave his brother a scathing look. "Would you give it a rest—"

"I'm supposed to lay a flagstone patio by sundown. Move."

"I'll go." Becca tucked her hair behind her ear and glanced quickly at Michael. "We can talk on Monday."

Chris shifted closer to her. "He can wait one minute." He studied her face, and his voice dropped. "Tell me what you really came to say."

This close, she could hear his breathing, just a little quick from the exertion. He looked good, all dirty and rugged and streaked with dust. She felt like she should move away.

Michael came around to their side of the trailer, and she felt Chris stiffen. Becca almost wanted to duck behind him. But his brother held the clipboard out to her. "Here. You want to stay? Keep count."

She opened her mouth. Closed it. "Ah . . . okay. Sure."

He didn't even stay to explain what she was counting, just handed her the pen and walked off to grab a bag for himself. Chris followed him. The clipboard held a carbon form, with scrawled handwriting listing different products she'd never heard of. But she made out *Limestone Screenings,* followed by the number 18.

She hustled to count. "You need three more," she called.

The other twin—had to be Nick—lifted his shirt to wipe his face. "How many bags of pavestone?"

And just like that, she found herself playing foreman.

They worked fast once they found a rhythm, and she did her best to keep track of what was what, especially when each brother started loading a different product. She called quantities when they asked for them, making tiny marks to keep herself straight. The labeled bags were easy, but who the hell knew the difference between flagstone and granite pavers? Or arctic slate and pavestone dividers? At first she felt awkward, especially when they were clearly looking to her for direction on what to put on the trailer.

But it felt good to have a task to occupy her mind, to do something *normal*.

Less than an hour later, the trailer was packed with bags and equipment, and Michael stopped in front of her, his hand out for the clipboard.

She gave it to him, ready for a snide remark.

He didn't give her one. He just read down the list—checking her numbers, she guessed—then glanced up. "Nice work."

Becca waited for the other shoe to drop. "Thanks?"

He reached into his back pocket for his wallet. Then he pulled a twenty out of the fold and held it out to her. "No, thank *you*."

She shook her head quickly. "I didn't—you don't have to *pay* me."

"Sure I do. You worked, you get paid."

"Take the cash!" called Gabriel. He'd found a basketball somewhere, and despite the fact that he'd been hauling eighty-pound bags for the better part of an hour, he was tossing it at the basket above the open garage door. "We'll get a pizza."

She blushed and faltered, surprised at the sudden cama-raderie. "But—"

"Would you take the money?" Michael thrust it forward. "I'm late."

"Fine." She snatched it out of his fist.

He turned away to slide the clipboard onto the dash of the truck. "Come on, Nick."

Nick was already climbing into the cab. He'd pulled a base-ball hat onto his head, a red one with a logo that matched the one on the truck. "See you, Becca."

Michael leaned out the window and looked at his brothers. "Stay out of trouble."

Gabriel bounced the basketball off the side of the truck. Hard. "No promises."

Michael actually looked like he was going to get out of the cab and go after him, but Nick grabbed his arm. "I have his keys. Let's just go."

Now Gabriel flung the ball at the truck. "Nicky, you suck." But Michael was starting the diesel engine, and then they were pulling down the driveway.

She stood there for a moment, feeling awkward. She'd flown over here, ready for everything to fall apart at the seams. Finding them doing normal Saturday things left her thrown.

Chris was watching her; she could feel it. Just when she'd worked out how to get back in her car and pull down the driveway without looking like too much of an idiot, he said, "You hungry?"

She hesitated—and it was long enough for him to turn away, for her to realize he expected her to refuse.

"I am," said Gabriel. He'd reclaimed the ball, and threw from halfway down the driveway for an easy three-pointer.

"Come on," said Chris, and she wasn't entirely certain he was talking to her. "Pizza sounds good. Let's go inside and call." He reached up and grabbed the garage door, giving it a yank to start it rolling.

Becca was still deliberating whether Chris had issued a real invitation—or whether he was just waiting for her to leave. So she didn't pay attention to the stripes of red spray paint on the light blue of the wooden panels as they rolled, and she didn't make out the pattern until the whole thing had slammed to the ground.

But there in the middle of the garage door, as tall as she was, sat a red pentagram.

CHAPTER 19

Becca couldn't stop staring. "A pentagram."

Gabriel whistled through his teeth. "Wow, brother, you do pick the Mensa candidates."

Chris shot him a glare. "Shut up."

Becca couldn't even get offended—she was still staring at the garage door. This couldn't be a coincidence. "But . . . what does it mean?"

"It's a warning," said Chris.

"Wrong," said Gabriel. "It's a target."

A target. She glanced between them. "I don't understand."

Chris came to stand beside her, staring at the door. He lifted a hand to rub at the back of his neck. "It means they've called the Guides." He hesitated. "Nick found it this morning. Michael doesn't know."

Gabriel snorted and flung the ball at the center of the pentagram. "Like it would matter."

She bit at her lip. "But that doesn't make any sense."

"They've been threatening this for a while."

"No," she said, rotating to face them both. Her fists clenched at her sides. "It doesn't make any sense because there's one on *my door.*"

They both stared at her for the longest moment.

Becca didn't like the way they were looking at her—a little too intensely. "My dad painted over it this morning. Aren't the Guides the ones who kill people? Who take out the accused and the accusers?"

Gabriel shoved Chris on the shoulder. "I see you held nothing back."

Chris ignored him. "When did you find it? This morning?"

She nodded. "So . . . does that mean Tyler put it there?" That would make sense, since Tyler clearly thought she was involved. It would make her feel better somehow, as if she could extricate herself from this mess with a simple explanation or a written note.

To whom it may concern: I'm not involved. Honest. Hugs, Becca

"It doesn't have to be Tyler. It could be any one of them." Chris shrugged. "The Guides come to town in secret, just to observe."

"Then," said Gabriel, emphasizing his words with another three-pointer, "they judge."

"How are you so *calm* about this?" she demanded. "They're going to *kill* me, and you're—"

"Shh." Gabriel put a finger over her lips. Her eyes widened.

"First," he said quietly, "anger is not our friend right now. You get me?"

His hand was warm against her face. She stared up into his eyes and remembered the coil of flame on his palm last night.

Or Tyler's grip on her arm in the pet store.

She swallowed and nodded.

"They're not going to kill you," he said. "Because you don't *matter*."

He didn't mean it the way it sounded. She knew that. But the words still made her flinch, just a little.

Chris grabbed his brother's hand and shoved him away. "Leave her alone. She doesn't know."

"You should have kept it that way," said Gabriel. "The more naïve she is, the better off she'd be."

"*She* is standing right here," said Becca.

"The Guides won't bother you," said Chris. "Sure, they might be watching you—"

"*Watching* me?"

"—but you *aren't* one of us. They'll realize that you aren't an Elemental." Chris leaned in, and she heard the strain behind his voice. "When I said they're judge, jury, and executioner, I meant they don't fuck around. But they aren't *stupid*."

Her breathing felt too quick, matching his.

"What about you?" she finally said.

His blue eyes hardened, and his voice was flat. "If they're watching *you*, you should probably stay away from me."

A phone started ringing, and it took Becca a minute to realize it was in her pocket. She looked at the display of her new phone and recognized Quinn's number.

She pushed the button to answer and skipped the greeting. "How did you know I have a new phone?"

"Called your house. Your mom's pissed." Quinn sounded pissed herself.

"Why?"

"Because you told her you were with *me*."

Crap. "What'd you say?"

"That she shouldn't worry; I'd only seen you drunk behind the wheel a handful of times. Where are you that you need a cover?"

Becca glanced up and swallowed. Chris hadn't moved. He still stood in her personal space, very close. He could probably hear Quinn.

She turned to face the front walkway and had to clear her throat. "Chris Merrick's house."

There was a very obvious pause. "Uh huh," said Quinn.

"Is that a girl?" Gabriel bounced the ball across the driveway. "Invite her over."

"Is that Chris?" said Quinn. "Did he just invite me over?"

Were they crazy?

"His brother," Becca ground out. "And he's kidding—"

"Listen," said Quinn, "if you're busy and all, I get it, but I was wondering if you'd go to the mall with me for a few hours."

"Now?" Becca felt heat crawling up her neck. Chris had to have moved close—she could feel the warmth from his body again, could smell the limestone dust on his skin.

"Well, you're working tomorrow," Quinn prattled on, "and I need a dress—"

"Go," said Chris.

He spoke right at her shoulder. She couldn't focus on both of them at once. "A—a dress? For—"

"Homecoming," said Quinn. "See, after last night, I thought Rafe might ask me, and I wanted to have some ideas—"

"Go," said Chris. There was no give in his expression.

"Hey, Quinn. You know what?" she said into the phone. "I think shopping sounds like a great idea."

CHAPTER 20

Sunday. Work.

Becca's nerves were shot. Thank god she could work in the back today, where no one would see her. Scrubbing the kennels wasn't glamorous, but it was in a locked room with no windows. She'd trolled the mall with Quinn for almost three hours yesterday, nodding and murmuring through dress after dress for some date Quinn didn't even have lined up yet. The whole time, she'd felt like she was traveling in the sights of a sniper rifle.

Becca couldn't stop thinking of Chris and his brothers, of these Guides who'd been sent to kill them. Would they run? Lie low? Michael had been heading off to a job yesterday afternoon, but they'd all seemed tense. Were they just going to go about life as usual?

But maybe that was the point. To prove they were harmless.

I think you should stay away from me.

By four, she was glad to lose her smock and grab her purse.

When she was winding through the displays of cat gyms, someone stepped in her way.

Becca's hand was fumbling through her purse for her keys, and her head was down. She just sidestepped without looking.

But a slim hand caught her arm—not hard, but firmly enough that she had to stop.

Becca threw her head up. "Lilah."

Lilah didn't look like the kind of girl you'd want to screw with. She had a few inches on Becca, and her smoking habit had drawn premature lines around her mouth, leaving her cheeks drawn and her eyes hard. Her hair was curly, and long, but the edges frizzed along her shoulders. Combined with the tight black tank top and low-slung jeans she wore, it made her look like a biker chick.

Maybe she was.

Becca drew back. "Leave me alone. I'll call the manager."

"And tell him what? That I'm standing here?"

Flustered, Becca glanced around. She wasn't afraid of Lilah—yet—but Tyler could be here. Or Seth. She didn't see anyone, but that didn't mean anything. "Look. I don't know why you guys keep hassling me—"

"Hassling *you*." Lilah's eyes narrowed.

"Just what do you think you're doing right now?" Becca hissed.

Lilah leaned against one of the shelving units, her expression almost incredulous. "Look, chick, I just came here to *warn* you."

Becca pushed past her. "I think I got enough warning on my front door. Thanks."

"Tyler told me about you," Lilah called. "That you said you weren't one of them."

Becca stopped and turned. "I'm not."

"He doesn't believe you," Lilah continued. "But I think I do."

Becca studied her. Had she misinterpreted this whole interaction? Was Lilah truly offering a warning, instead of threats? "This thing between you guys and the Merrick brothers—I don't want to be a part of it. I'm not what . . . what you are."

Lilah shrugged. "If you're not, then you'll be fine." She stepped closer, and her voice dropped. "If you are, you'll be killed, too."

Oh, so they were back to threats. Becca shrugged her bag onto her shoulder and turned away. "Fine. Then leave me alone, and let the Guides do their job."

"See," said Lilah, "that's what makes me believe you. You honestly don't have any idea what you're talking about."

Becca spun, hearing the disdain in the other girl's voice. "I know that you guys all keep talking about Chris and his brothers like they're dangerous. But I saw what Tyler and Seth did to Chris. Then they came after me here, at my *job,* and they would have hurt *me* if another customer hadn't come along. Tyler was *shooting* at me Friday night. With a *gun.* That's attempted murder. What's the worst thing Chris and his brothers have ever done to *you?*"

"You know they killed Tyler's sister?"

Hearing it from Lilah gave it a distinctly different spin from the way Chris had said it. But still, despite Michael's temper, she couldn't imagine him killing someone. "I know she drowned, in the quarry."

Lilah stepped close again, and now her eyes were angry. It made her look fierce. "She was my friend. You know she drowned right after that oldest one started hassling her at her summer job? Who do you think chased her into the quarry in the first place?"

Enough pain crept into her voice that Becca had to swallow. "It was an accident," she said.

"You sure?"

No. She wasn't. And Becca couldn't lie to Lilah, especially in the face of such honest pain.

She remembered holding Chris's hand, feeling the water pull her down, turning her world into nothing but darkness and suffocation.

Lilah moved even closer. "Let's give them the benefit of the doubt on that one—even though they don't deserve it. Did you know their parents killed Seth's parents?"

Becca shook her head.

"Yeah," said Lilah. "After Michael killed Emily. We just wanted them to *leave.*" She kept going. "Did they tell you this isn't the first time we've called the Guides to take care of them?"

Becca had to clear her throat. "Chris said you threatened to. Back then. That his parents made a deal—"

"No." Lilah shook her head. "A few *months* ago."

Becca was having a hard time figuring out how to play this. Tyler and Seth were cruel, true bullies. But was she in a position to defend Chris and his brothers? "And?"

"They sent two. The Merricks killed them."

"I don't believe you."

With what we are, it's easy to commit a crime without evidence. Very easy.

Too easy.

Dismay must have been written on her face. Lilah nodded. "You believe me."

Becca couldn't think over the rush of her heartbeat.

"You need more?" said Lilah. "Chris and Gabriel tried to blow up Tyler's truck Wednesday night. Sure, the cops caught them before they could do anything—but who knows what more would have happened?"

That had been the same night she'd driven Chris home. She remembered the way Chris had slouched into school Thursday. He'd looked like crap, but she'd attributed that to the fight she'd rescued him from. Had he gone out and picked another? "They tried to—blow up—"

"His truck. By lighting bags of fertilizer on fire. Do you know how big those things explode? Do you know they could have *killed* people? *Innocent* people."

Becca stared at her.

"Look it up," said Lilah. "There's a police blotter in the Sunday paper."

She would. When she got home, she would.

He'd fed her that song and dance about how they were being persecuted, when two nights earlier he'd been bombing Tyler's truck?

"Tyler and Seth—they're cruel," Lilah said. "But it's not because they want to be. It's because we have to be."

She took a step back. Becca just stared at her.

"Yeah," said Lilah, "I don't think you have to worry about the Guides. I don't think you have to worry about them at all." She turned and started to walk away.

Then she paused and called over her shoulder. "I just think you need to worry about the Merricks."

Becca tried to get it together before leaving the store. Her feelings kept jerking her around. She was afraid of these mysterious Guides—but pissed at Chris for feeding her a line of crap. She hated Tyler and Seth—but if they were just defending themselves, were they really the bullies?

It reminded her of Quinn's question, about the night she'd saved Chris. Had she helped the right guy? Or had she just followed the natural instinct to help the victim?

When the electronic doors opened, she stepped into the blinding sunlight. She wanted to call Quinn, to tell her everything.

But Quinn was such a drama queen, she'd probably drive straight to the Merricks' house to start rolling heads.

Anger is not our friend right now.

Had that been a warning? Or a threat?

Not like there was really a difference.

"Becca."

Her name hit her like a gunshot. She almost stumbled.

Hunter sat on the long iron bench in front of the store. He wore a green long-sleeved shirt with a pattern of thorns over the heart and down one arm, paired with worn jeans and Doc Martens. Casper lay on the concrete in front of him, ears at half-mast, his tongue hanging out.

Hunter looked good. Normal. Safe.

"Hey," she said.

"Sorry I scared you. I just wanted to make sure you were okay."

It took her a second to realize he was still talking about the party. It felt like a month ago.

Hunter stood, looking a bit uncertain. "I don't want to seem like a stalker or anything, but you said your phone was broken. I stopped by yesterday, and the manager said you got off at four today."

"Oh." She nodded. *Get it together, genius.* "Yeah."

An awkward moment passed between them.

"Wait. I'm a jackass." His expression changed, and he took a step back. He looked away. "When you said it was *broken,* you were just being—"

"No! It is. My phone. Broken." Now she sounded like Yoda on crack. "I mean, it was. I got a new one. Yesterday."

He still seemed unsure. "All right." He hesitated. "Well, I guess I'll see you at school then."

"Wait!" She surged forward and put a hand on his arm. "You just came by to check on me?"

Hunter glanced down at her hand, and half a smile found its way onto his face. "It seemed like the right thing to do."

He'd just come by to check on her. Not to drop nasty comments about her sexual prowess like Tommy Dunleavy or Drew McKay. Not to threaten her life like Tyler and Seth.

Not to mislead her like Chris.

The sunlight caught the white streak in his hair and made it shine silver. His eyes were bright, open, no hint of cunning or guile.

"You're still wearing the stones," he said softly.

Becca pulled her hand back, self-conscious now. She'd only taken them off to shower. She tucked a piece of hair behind her ear and felt heat creep up her cheeks. "Yeah, well, I didn't want to *lose* them. . . ."

Lame.

"I'm glad."

And now she was replaying the feel of his fingers along her wrist, the night he'd tied them on. She had to look away from his eyes, studying the pattern of thorns across his chest and shoulder.

Mistake. The shirt was thin and didn't leave a lot to the imagination. She wondered if Hunter played any sports.

She jerked her eyes away. "I'm sorry—you probably want them back—"

"Not yet." Now his voice was amused.

Oh. She looked back up at him, very aware of his closeness, of the way the sun skimmed his cheekbones, of the warmth of his body.

Casper pushed up from the concrete and started sniffing at her hands. She patted him absently, rubbing behind his ears. He pressed his body against her legs, and she wondered if the dog knew she needed a distraction.

Hunter lost the smile, and she felt him studying her face. "You hungry?"

Her head was nodding before her brain could get into gear.

"I mean no." She glanced down at her old jeans, the ones that had a tear in the knee. The tee shirt from eighth-grade graduation that had everyone's signature on the back, and a small rip near the hem from an overaggressive Airedale. God only knew what her hair looked like. "I'm filthy."

"So we'll have to go somewhere dirt won't matter. Come on."

And then he had her hand.

Becca had never ridden in an open-top jeep, but she loved the feel of the wind through her hair and the sun on her face. Hunter took her through the drive-thru at KFC, where he bought a bucket of chicken and potato wedges, then proceeded to drive while blindly tossing french fries to Casper in the back.

Becca giggled as the dog snatched another out of the air. "Don't you worry that one will go over the side?"

"I like to think Casper has some sense of self-preservation."

"Where are you taking me?"

He glanced over, and his voice was low. "Somewhere dirt won't matter."

She had to look down in the bag, blushing, as if it were hard to find another fry to toss into the back.

"I just thought we'd head over to Quiet Waters," he said. "I heard it was nice."

Quiet Waters was a beautiful park, probably one of the best in the county. She used to love the gardens, how there were dozens of gazebos where you could hide for hours with a book.

Or a boy.

Drew had taken her there. Once.

She must have been quiet too long. Hunter glanced over. "Lame?"

She heard the smile in his voice—and the self-deprecating tone beneath it. Some of the tension slipped from her shoulders, but she still felt off balance and uncertain. At times like this, she wanted to kill Drew. "No, no—it's a beautiful place."

"All right." He paused, and she wondered if he was going to poke at her wounds, the way Chris had. But there was no curiosity in Hunter's tone—just challenge. "In or out, Becca?"

She straightened in her seat and smiled back at him. "In."

Chapter 21

Hunter kept an old blanket in the back of his jeep. They sat at the base of a hill on the east side of the park and picked at the bucket of chicken. A playground sat out of sight, and Becca occasionally heard the shrieks of overexcited children, but mostly, a peaceful stillness hung over the grass. She forgot about killers and elements and relaxed into Hunter's quiet presence.

He was good company, too, talking about stupid things to amuse her. How he'd moved just two hours away from home, but it felt like too far to visit friends. He talked about the friends he'd left behind, who Facebooked him every night asking for pictures of girls. He mocked the movies he hated because the actors were idiots. He talked about books he'd read—and ones he'd pretended to read, just to get through a class. There were a lot of those.

"Even *Pride and Prejudice*?" she said.

"Please." He gave her a crooked smile. "Wikipedia." He stripped the skin off his chicken and fed it to Casper.

"Don't you feel like you're cheating?"

"I like to think of it as challenging myself *more*."

That made her smile. "Do you still pass?"

"Of course." He flung another fry for Casper. "If I failed a class because I didn't read the book, my dad would kill me."

His words were like a stone thrown into a pond, in flight for a moment, then sinking fast. Hunter lost the smile, as if he realized what he'd said.

Becca wanted to reach out and touch him—then wondered if that would be appropriate. The moment felt precarious, as if one small movement in any direction might throw everything off balance. He tossed another fry to the dog, not looking at her now.

"So he was strict?" she asked quietly. "Your dad?"

He looked up, and she found emotion trapped in his eyes. "No. Not really."

"You must have been very close."

He shrugged.

She waited, but he didn't offer anything further. "So . . . were you and he—"

"Can we talk about something else?"

She flushed. "Of course."

Becca busied herself with cleaning up their plates, though there was barely enough to warrant a clean-up effort.

"Hey." Hunter caught her wrist and stilled her movement.

She held her breath.

"Thanks," he said softly. "I—can't. It's just—"

His voice stopped, and she chanced a look up. His expression was frozen, his breathing quick and shallow.

"I can't," he finally said.

She nodded, then bit her lip. "I'm sorry, Hunter," she whispered.

"Don't be sorry." Now she earned a shadow of a smile—but it looked like it might shatter. "Just—talk about something else."

She struggled for something to say that wouldn't completely derail him. "Well . . . I went shopping with Quinn yesterday, and I think she could wear a bathing suit to Homecoming and cover more skin than the dress she bought."

His smile widened—just a bit, but enough. "Quinn likes attention."

He'd sure read her friend fast. "Yeah." She glanced away and gave a light laugh. "Who doesn't, right?"

"You."

Becca swung her head back around. He'd sure read *her* fast.

He settled back on the blanket and rubbed Casper's fur. "When's Homecoming?"

"Two weeks." Why had she brought up the dance? Now he'd think she was fishing for an invite. She kept talking, hoping she could turn his focus elsewhere. "It's usually on a Saturday, but it's a Friday this year, because of the budget. It was cheaper for a DJ or something. They're doing the game on Thursday night. A lot of people are pissed."

"Are you going?"

"To the game?" She shrugged like it didn't matter. "Probably not. I might have to work."

"No." He smiled, his eyes bright. "Are you going to the dance?"

She rubbed at her neck, very aware of her pulse, of the weight of his gaze. She shrugged again and plucked some clover to start a chain. "I don't know. Depends whether Quinn gets 'Rafe' to ask her."

"You're not going with that Chris guy?"

"No! Chris and I—we're just—" She stopped herself. They were just what? Friends? Were they even that?

"We're not going," she said. "We're not even—I mean, I never really spoke to Chris until last week."

Hunter was watching her now. "So how'd you get mixed up in his mess?"

God, she wished she knew. If she could go back to Wednesday night, the night Tyler and Seth had been kicking his ass, she'd—

She'd do the exact same thing. Even knowing what she knew now.

"Quinn said you saved his life," Hunter said.

Had Quinn said that? She couldn't remember. "I was leaving school late one night. Those guys, Tyler and Seth, the ones with the gun?" When he nodded, she continued, "They were beating

Chris up in the parking lot. There was no one else around, and my cell phone was dead."

"Did they come after you?"

"No." She hesitated. "I chased them off."

"How?" His voice was even.

"First with my car. I just kind of . . . um, drove at them." She had to be blushing. Her face felt like it was on fire. "But then they came back, and one of them grabbed me, so I did some self-defense stuff, and they bolted."

Now he smiled. "Some 'self-defense stuff'?"

"Don't tease me! It's true."

"Okay." He sobered. "Show me."

Like she needed to make a bigger fool of herself. "No. It's silly."

"Silly? You chased off two big guys. I'd like to see this 'self-defense stuff.' Maybe I could use your techniques."

"I'd just taken a class the school offered," she said. "It was fresh in my mind. I couldn't do it again."

He raised an eyebrow.

Ugh. She folded her fingers the way Paul had told her, and did a halfhearted swing.

Hunter caught her wrist. "Stand up. Show me. For real."

His eyes held that challenge again, like they had in the car. She pushed to her feet and stepped off the blanket, feeling the sun on her face. When Hunter joined her, Casper shifted forward to nose at the abandoned box of potato wedges.

"I don't want to hurt you," she said.

Hunter grinned. "Now *that's* funny."

Oh, he wanted to get cocky about it? She didn't even warn him, just folded her fingers and swung.

He caught her hand. He was quicker than she'd expected. Stronger.

It stole her breath for a second.

"Not like that," he said. He gently pried her fingers loose and refolded them, making her thumb more prominent. "Like this. Do it again."

Holy crap. "You know about this stuff?"

"Oh yeah. I'm a 'self-defense stuff' expert." His tone was wry, but it didn't sound like he was kidding.

"Really?"

"Nah." He shrugged. "I know a little. You're stalling."

She swung. He caught. His hand was warm, wrapping around her knuckles.

"Try again," he said.

She remembered the way he'd grabbed the paper clip out of the air, that first day. "I'll never be faster than you."

"The point isn't to be *faster* than me. The point is to mean what you're doing." He took a step closer to her, until there wasn't room for her to take a swing at him. "Try again."

She backed away and started to swing, but he caught her wrist and took another step. "Try again."

She took another step back. He came after her.

And then, just for an instant, she felt a flicker of fear. She didn't even think. Her hand shot out, aiming for his eyes.

Thank god he was quick. She almost got him. But he ducked to the side and deflected her blow with his forearm.

Then his face broke into a smile. "Hey. Nice."

She flushed, pleased despite herself.

"What else you got?" he said.

Becca had a pretty strong feeling she should quit while she was ahead. She could barely remember half the stuff Paul had shown them in class. But Hunter's closeness left her a little breathless, a little euphoric. Her heart was still kicking like they'd been running.

She shook her hair back from her face and looked up at him. "What else *you* got?"

His eyes widened—just for an instant. Then they filled with resolve. He looked fierce and gentle, if such a combination was possible. He moved until he stood close enough to share secrets, to dance. To kiss.

"Choke me," he said.

She jerked back. God, she'd been staring at his mouth.

She coughed to cover her nerves. "I'm sorry—what?"

He smiled, not fooled for a second, then reached out to take her hands and place them on his neck.

The warmth of his body reached across the space between them. She could smell whatever detergent his mom used, something fresh and soft, like baby powder and lavender. With her hands against his skin, she felt the beginnings of stubble under his jaw, the muscles in his neck flexing under her fingers.

The position reminded her of those silly dances in middle school, the way girls would hook their hands behind a guy's neck and kind of sway to the music.

"Now what?" Her voice almost cracked.

Breathe.

"I'm going to make hooks with my hands—" He demonstrated. "—and catch your wrists to spring your hands free. Don't let go."

Becca nodded, gazing up at him, thinking his eyes were exactly the color of the grass here.

Now they flickered with challenge. "Don't. Let. Go."

She tightened her grip, but he reached into the gap between her wrists and snapped her hands free.

Hey! Her eyes narrowed. "Do that again."

He did it again. And a third time.

She felt warm, her breaths coming quickly again.

"There's no counter leverage," he said. "I'm just using your strength against you. Want to try?"

She nodded before thinking of how his hands would be around her neck, strong and secure, his thumbs brushing her chin, reminding her too much of the way a guy would pull you close to kiss you.

Touch was funny like that. How one movement could choke you and kill you, but another meant nothing more than a caress and an invitation. How sex and rape were just a few motions apart.

"What are you thinking?" He'd stopped moving, his hands loose now, almost on her shoulders instead of her neck. She couldn't figure out his expression, but she didn't want to try too hard.

Becca shook her head and looked right back at him. "Nothing. Do it. I want to try."

He did. She broke his hold on the first try.

She grinned, pleased. This was a bazillion times better than learning from Paul. "I did it."

He smiled back, but his eyes were serious. "Don't let go this time. Break free, but hold on to me."

"Why?"

"Keep me close so you can hurt me. So you can knee me in the stomach." Now he gave her a rakish smile. "Or lower."

They practiced breaking choke holds until she mastered that. Then he showed her how to pin an attacker's forearms to her chest, to control his movement so she could be the aggressor. He showed her the strength in her joints, how an elbow or a knee in the right place could cause more damage than she'd ever thought possible.

Sweat collected under the spill of her hair. At first she'd thought Hunter was going easy, but then she saw the sheen of sweat on his forehead as they moved faster. This was nothing like the self-defense class—she felt sharper, fierce in a way she'd never anticipated.

For the first time in a long while, she felt powerful.

Darkness crept up on them, sneaking over the hill to throw Hunter's features into shadow. She couldn't hear children on the playground anymore. Casper had long since fallen asleep on the blanket.

"It's late," said Hunter.

"What, did you run out of things to show me?"

He grimaced and bent to shake out the blanket. "I might have to show you how to walk back to the pet store. Do they gate the entrances to parks around here?"

Becca gathered their trash. "I think we'll be okay. It's not full dark yet. They usually drive around and warn people."

She was right. The gates were still open, but they got a stern glare and a warning from the gate attendant. "Sundown means sundown, kids."

"It's her fault," said Hunter, pointing at the passenger seat. "She had me in a choke hold."

Becca laughed as he drove off, loving the feel of the wind in her hair, the sudden chill in the air cooling her cheeks. Loving the easy company by her side.

This is what it's supposed to be like.

She turned her head to look at Hunter. "Thanks."

He glanced away from the road long enough to meet her eyes. "You're welcome."

"You know more than just 'a little,'" she said. "Are you, like . . . a black belt in karate or—"

He snorted, and it sounded like he was trying not to laugh. "No."

"Then how do you know all that stuff?"

He was silent for a moment, air whistling through the open cab of his jeep.

"People used to screw with me," he finally said. "When I was younger, I got a lot of crap. My father—he told me there were two options: I could learn to defend myself, or I could suck it up."

Harsh, she thought.

Hunter must have seen the look on her face. "No, Dad was right." He hesitated. "He taught me."

Becca held her breath, unsure how to proceed. His words didn't seem broken as they had a few hours ago. Maybe doing something physical had loosened something in him, too.

"Is it martial arts?" she said.

"Not really." He glanced over. "It's called Krav Maga. Heard of it?"

She shook her head and whispered the phrase. *Krav Maga.* It sounded exotic and violent and lethal.

"It's for self-defense," Hunter said. "With the purpose of taking your enemy down instead of running away."

"I love it."

He looked over. "Me too."

The pet store wasn't far enough away. He was pulling beside her car well before she was ready to get out of his jeep.

Hunter didn't turn off his engine, but he unclicked his seat belt to turn and face her. He brushed some hair off her cheek and tucked it behind her ear. "Thanks for going with me."

She flushed and looked down, wishing time would slow so she could memorize the passage of his fingers along her jaw. They'd grappled in a field for hours, but this tiny stroke of his hand on her face felt like the most intimate thing she'd ever done.

The thought made her freeze.

Would he kiss her now? Would that change everything, turn this . . . this *courtship* into a chase? She'd always hated how guys measured goals with a girl like bases in baseball. First base, second base—but when you hit a home run, you go back to the dugout and wait for your next chance. She liked *this,* when there was no game, no ball in play.

"I've kept you out too late," he murmured, and she could tell he'd moved closer. His breath brushed her temple.

Her lips parted. She wondered what his mouth would feel like, what he would taste like.

She wondered if she'd let it get that far. Her hands were sweating again.

Keep me close so you can hurt me.

Hunter stroked her hair back again. She leaned in to his touch.

"Do you have your keys?" he said.

Her keys? She nodded.

His thumb brushed along her cheekbone, but he didn't move closer. His voice was rich and warm and gentle. "It's late."

She nodded again, feeling her heartbeat, her breathing. She held still, her face against his palm. He didn't move.

Then she figured it out.

Do you have your keys? It's late.

She drew back, unable to look at him now. She thrust her hand into her purse, praying the keys would find her shaking fingers. "Thanks for dinner, Hunter."

"Hey. Easy." He caught her wrist and pulled her back. This

time when his fingers found her chin, they lifted her face so she could meet his eyes. "Look at me."

What was this going to be, some ease-his-conscience let-down?

"Becca," he said. She loved the sound of her name on his lips—and she hated herself for it.

His eyes were wide. She looked right back at him and willed her voice to be steady and quiet. "What?"

He moved closer, until a breath would bring their lips together. "You deserve better than a first kiss in a deserted parking lot."

She couldn't breathe. She almost kissed him anyway.

But then he was shifting away, making sure she found her keys, waiting to be sure her car started and she got out of the lot safely.

She wasn't sure how she drove. Maybe the car propelled itself, fueled by her euphoria. This was how it could be: no games, just simple chivalry and kindness. Gentle strength, the way a man *should* come to a woman.

Giddiness got her home. She hadn't forgotten Chris and his brothers, but their troubles had drifted to some distant part of her brain.

But they snapped to the forefront when she pulled into her driveway.

There on the door, shining in the beams of her headlights, was a shiny brand-new pentagram.

CHAPTER 22

Chris slouched in the back of the classroom, drawing a pattern along the margin in his notebook.

He'd forgotten she was supposed to be his History partner.

Maybe he should ditch. He still had time before the bell. He'd seen her in English Lit, the way she sat across the room and avoided his eyes. Her shoulders had been hunched, her torso twisted deliberately away from him.

Good.

The thought made him wince. She'd looked exposed, moving like someone had a sniper rifle trained on the center of her back. His fault—all of it. It made him want to take her by the hand, lead her into a corner, and offer reassurance. But keeping his distance was better. She'd be safer. The last thing she needed was to be seen whispering with him.

But maybe he could talk to her now. She'd be close, a captive audience for an hour. He remembered the way she'd smelled on Friday, like almonds and vanilla, from lotion or shampoo or something.

Yeah, on second thought, he should definitely ditch.

But she appeared in the doorway of the classroom, dark hair pouring across one shoulder. Her movements were still tight and controlled, but some of the tension had leaked away.

That Hunter guy was walking behind her.

No, wait. *With* her.

Whatever. Chris dropped his head and sighed, sketching a cube on the lined paper. He'd just started a pyramid when he felt someone watching him.

He looked up. Becca was headed his way, her jaw tight, looking anywhere but at him. Chris shifted his gaze. Hunter was glaring at him, his eyes dark.

Chris could read that look like a book. The guy's posture had a whole monologue going. *Don't screw with her. Don't talk to her. Don't even breathe in her direction. Get me?*

Chris gave him the finger.

"Mature." Becca dropped into the seat next to him and flung her backpack to the ground.

A lot of force hid behind that movement. It made him pause. "You all right?"

"I'm great." She yanked a notebook out of her backpack. Then a pen. All this aggression was throwing spots of pink on her cheeks.

She didn't turn her head. "Stop looking at me."

He jerked his eyes away. Now *his* cheeks felt hot.

Beamis swept into the room. "Good afternoon, class. Thank you for your patience. Today we'll be comparing the Treaty of Versailles with the Treaty of Paris, and how they immortalized the fall of two of the greatest powers in Europe's . . ."

Chris felt his attention drift. He couldn't look right, because Becca was sitting there.

To his left, Tommy Dunleavy was sneaking glances at Becca, a smirk on his lips. A piece of paper was folded between his fingers. He glanced furtively at Beamis, clearly waiting for his chance.

Chris gave him a wordy glare of his own. *Try it, dickhead.*

Tommy glared back—but he backed down and crumpled the piece of paper when Chris didn't look away.

Typical.

A pen knocked against his knuckles, and Chris swung his head around. Becca was staring straight ahead, at the board, but she tapped her pen on her notebook.

He looked down.

There's another pentagram on my door.

He didn't doubt it. She could paint over it twenty times and they'd put another one up there. He wrote the only thing he could think of.

Sorry.

She stared at that word for a long time. What was she thinking about?

Then she put her pen to the paper again.

Lilah came to the pet store.

Chris froze. He'd thought for sure that Tyler and the others would leave everything to the Guides. That's how these things worked.

Are you OK?

She very deliberately rolled her eyes.

What do you care? You lied to me.

Then she went back and underlined *lied* again.

He studied the words on the page, feeling his chest tighten. He almost spoke out loud, but then took a quick glance at Beamis, who was scrawling all over the board.

Chris drew a question mark, then circled the word *lied*.

Becca turned her head to look at him. Her eyes always reminded him of the ocean after a storm, a gray so dark you just knew there were secrets in there. Just now they hid some kind of pain that he didn't understand.

She dropped her gaze, letting her hair fall across her face

while she wrote. The scent of almonds and vanilla was making him crazy.

Then he saw the words across her notebook.

You killed Seth's parents?

Chris stopped breathing, staring as if just looking at them would rearrange the letters into another sentence.

Her breathing was quickening, and he knew she was assuming the worst since he hadn't denied it.

Chris lifted his pen and forced himself to write.

Not what you think.

She practically knocked his hand out of the way to write more.

Did you try to kill Tyler last week?
After I saved you?

What? He started shaking his head. She wrote furiously.

Arrested?

Then she underlined that three times.

Damn.

Chris drew a long breath. How could he explain that he'd needed to feel powerful for a night, for an hour, for a *minute?* How could she understand what it felt like to have this strength inside you, but to always have others knock you down?

He tapped his pen on the words he'd already written. *Not what you think.*

She picked up the notebook and flipped to a clean piece of paper.

I'm going to ask for a new partner.

Chris looked at those words for a long moment. It felt like she'd stabbed him with the pen. He leaned over and wrote the only thing he could.

OK.

Becca waited after class to talk to Beamis. "I don't think I can work with him."

Something softened and hardened simultaneously in Mr. Beamis's expression. "He's threatened you?"

Becca thought of the way Chris had yelled at Tommy last Friday. Beamis had thrown him out of class. Did he think Chris would hurt her?

"No! He—he just—I don't think I can see him outside of school."

"This project will be mostly completed during class. Any additional work can be done here, in the library. You aren't required to see him off school property."

This wasn't going the way she'd hoped. Sitting next to Chris had been an experience. She'd come to school ready to lay into him. But he'd frightened her from the doorway, looking dark and saturnine with his hair falling into his eyes.

Then she'd sat next to him, leaving her aware of every movement he made, every breath he took. Despite everything Lilah had said, Becca kept remembering Chris's hand on hers in the water Friday night. The way he'd sat with her on the beach in the moonlight, almost embarrassed as he talked about what he could do.

His affinity to water made sense. He reminded her of the sea, alluring and mysterious, calm on the surface, with who-knew-what brewing underneath. They'd read about the Sirens of Greek mythology in English last year, mermaids who coaxed sailors into the water to drown. Maybe she only felt it because she knew of his abilities, but when she was near him, she longed to find water, to stand in it with him and let it slick her skin.

You need to stay away from me.

"Miss Chandler?"

Becca jumped. "Sorry."

"So you will try to work out your differences with Mr. Merrick?"

"Yes." She nodded. "I'll try."

She found Hunter waiting for her in the hallway. Becca hadn't expected that.

She tucked her hair behind her ear. "You didn't have to wait."

"I didn't mind."

She hesitated, then headed for the cafeteria. "I wanted to ask about switching partners."

"I figured." Hunter fell into step beside her. He was quiet for a moment, a weighted pause like last night. "Rough class?"

She shrugged. The class hadn't been rough at all. Chris had left her alone, once she'd told him to. He'd stuck to his side of the desk, huddled over his notebook, and he hadn't looked her way once.

Really, this was one of the most peaceful History classes she'd had in a long time.

It took her all the way to the cafeteria to figure out what had changed.

For the first time since school started, Tommy Dunleavy hadn't dared to throw a note on her desk.

CHAPTER 23

After school, Becca was starting the engine when Quinn said she wanted to spend the night again.

Quinn had stayed over after dress shopping, of course. And last night, Becca had found her friend in the kitchen, cramming for a Trig test and eating sugar cookies. That had been okay—Becca had giggled over Hunter and made popcorn, glad to have something to keep her attention off the "graffiti" on the front door.

But now she kind of wanted to throw on sweats and hole up in her room, to have a few minutes of peace where no one could find her, where the only problems she had to worry about were which iTunes playlist would best suit her mood or whether to paint her toenails purple or fuchsia.

Becca didn't respond to Quinn's announcement, just put the car in gear.

Quinn was digging through her purse. "You know, if you don't want me to stay—"

"I always want you to stay," Becca snapped. "Don't be stupid."

The second that tone escaped her mouth, she regretted it.

Quinn started gathering her bags into her lap. "Wow, Bex, with an engraved invitation like that, it'll be hard to give up my dream of sleeping on the park bench—"

"Ugh. Stop." Becca scrunched her eyes shut and threw the car back into park. "I'm sorry. It's been a crappy few days."

"Yeah?" Quinn fumbled for the door handle and shoved the door open. "Funny how you haven't *mentioned* anything crappy happening. I mean, maybe almost making out with New Kid was *kind of*—"

"Quinn! Shut *up* a second." Becca stared at the steering wheel. The big silver H was the only shiny thing left on the vehicle. "I'm just under a lot of stress, okay?"

"Got it." Quinn swung her legs out of the car. "Wouldn't want to add any more with my problems."

Damn it. "Quinn, wait—"

Her friend slammed the door.

Becca glared after her, debating whether to climb out of the car and chase her across the school parking lot. Hunter sure had nailed it: *Quinn seems to like attention.*

And who was Quinn to get all huffy? She was practically living with Becca lately. Becca's mom was making an extra plate of dinner every night and routinely washed Quinn's clothes. Becca figured she should count her lucky stars that she and Quinn didn't wear the same size or her closet might be empty.

But half a mile down the road, she felt like a total bitch. She rolled to a stop at the turn to Old Mill Road. Should she go back for Quinn? Would her friend have time to catch the bus?

Becca fished her cell phone out of her purse. She kept her foot on the brake and started a new text.

A gust of wind hit the car hard enough to make it rock.

Becca grabbed the steering wheel. The intersection looked clear and still, but trees set back from the road were swaying in the sudden wind. Clouds seemed to be rolling in from the south.

She thought of the mysterious Guides. She'd never bothered to ask Chris how they'd come after her. Would it be some kind of Elemental attack?

Then she told herself to knock it off. It was September. Maryland got the remnants of every hurricane in the Gulf of Mexico. It rained every other day all month. They always had a tornado drill the first week of school.

But maybe she should forget about texting Quinn and just get home. She shoved her phone into her pocket.

Wind buffeted her car as she pulled into the intersection. A few raindrops smacked her windshield. Then a lot more.

This wind was crazy. Her car didn't want to stay on the road. She had a hard time holding the vehicle on the right side of the yellow lines.

Rain began to pour. An SUV swerved and honked as a strong blast of wind almost propelled her straight into oncoming traffic.

Becca screamed and yanked the wheel. The car fishtailed but leapt into the correct lane.

Slow down. Maybe she was going too fast. Her car was small, no match for this sudden storm.

Her foot pressed on the brake, but rain was coating the road now, and her car started to skid. The wind slammed her sideways.

Other cars were having trouble. Old Mill Road was turning into an obstacle course. She yanked the wheel again, hoping to straighten out. Should she stop? Keep going? Rain poured out of the sky to pound her windshield.

Didn't Chris say water talked to him? Did he talk to it, too?

Please stop, she thought. *Stop raining.*

For a breath of time, she almost thought it worked. The rain whipping her car hesitated, a break in the noise like driving under an overpass in a storm.

Then a gust swept against her car, stronger rain beating the glass.

People bolted from the sidewalk, running for houses, for shops, for cover. Probably running from the swerving vehicles. Becca said a quick prayer that she wouldn't end up on the sidewalk. She could see the creek ahead, usually a calm flow of water eight feet below the roadway bridge. But now the water was high, raging, passing only a few feet below the bottom of the bridge supports. That she could see water from a block away was terrifying.

Flash flood? Could that water swell over the bridge? She'd heard stories of people swept away in floodwater.

Then something caught her eye.

Some*one*.

A lone figure stood at the crest of the hill, just before the woods that backed the road. The storm and the rain kept her from making out any features. Just dark clothes, some sense of focus in his stance.

Was he *watching* her?

Tyler? Chris?

One of the Guides? Was there only one?

A blast of wind shook her car, and she fought to keep hold of the wheel. The bridge loomed close, and the guardrail at the corner seemed small and flimsy. That man remained still.

He *was* watching her. She could feel it.

Ridiculous. He stood over a hundred feet away. She could barely see him—no way he could see her through the windshield.

But that focus was there. Something about him seemed familiar.

What did he expect her to do, stop the storm? Prove she was one of them?

"I can't do anything," she whispered. "Please. Stop."

Crash! The sound came from behind her. Becca flinched and almost lost the wheel. A Dodge SUV and a Toyota sedan had collided. The SUV pushed the smaller vehicle into the ditch on the west side of the street. The earth gave way, spraying mud and grass chunks into the road.

Brake lights lit up her windshield, and she realized she'd been staring in her rearview mirror too long.

A black station wagon had sideswiped the side of the bridge and stalled in the road.

Becca punched the brakes.

Too late. She ran right into it.

"He wants to kill us." Nick was in the passenger seat, his fingers wrapped around the door handle, his knuckles white.

"No shit," said Gabriel. "Keep it together."

Chris sat in the back, clutching his own door handle. He could feel the rain striking the car. This rain meant harm with every drop—the kind of storm that sought to form tornadoes, to destroy.

The storm itself didn't scare him. He wanted to be part of it. *That* scared him.

Chris pressed his forehead against the window and shut his eyes. Wind rocked the car. He heard Nick suck a breath through his teeth.

"I'm just going to drive us through it," said Gabriel. "Okay? I'll get us past this."

He didn't sound frightened—he sounded determined. And this storm carried no lightning. No fire, no natural burst of energy to draw Gabriel's own abilities.

Maybe he *could* drive them through it. Chris lifted his head.

Bad idea. Rain sheeted across the roadway, every drop an invitation. The creek sat ahead, swollen with rainwater, raging with the strength of the storm. Chris could stand in that water, let it wrap around his body until he was drunk on power.

"Hey." Gabriel smacked him in the forehead.

Chris jerked back—and almost fell down.

He didn't remember unbuckling his seat belt, but he must have. He'd been leaning between the two front seats, kneeling on the floor there.

Nick had his hands over the vents.

"Stop it." Gabriel turned dials until the vents were closed, blocking the moisture of the storm. The air in the car almost immediately went stale. Brake lights winked ahead of them. Gabriel punched the steering wheel. "Jesus Christ, could these people *drive?*"

A gust shook the car again. Nick shut his eyes. "There's going to be a tornado."

"Yeah, well, you're not going to be a part of it. Think of something else."

"Yeah, right," Chris muttered.

Nick gave his twin a look. "Like what?"

"First-round draft picks. Holly Sater's ass. I don't know." Gabriel ran a hand through his hair, then grabbed the wheel as an oncoming vehicle swerved toward them. *"Something."*

Becca, thought Chris.

"Hey," said Gabriel, pointing. "Isn't that your girlfriend's car?"

There, a few cars ahead, just moving onto the bridge, was Becca's little brown Honda. Chris recognized the small dent in the frame.

Her car shuddered in the wind. She must have been struggling to keep it straight.

"Get your hand off the door!" Gabriel snapped.

Chris let go of the handle. He'd been ready to go out in the rain, to pull her out of this downpour, to let his power protect her.

You're crazy. Now he felt like a stalker.

"Look," said Nick. "On the hill."

"Fucker," said Gabriel.

Chris could see the dark figure, but he couldn't make out features. The swell of power from that direction was unmistakable.

Gabriel punched the brakes and Chris stumbled and grabbed for something to keep him upright. But he'd been half kneeling in the space between the seats, and he crashed into the center console, killing the radio and almost throwing the car out of gear.

Nick caught his shoulder and kept his face from meeting the center vents.

Then Chris heard a crash ahead, and he shoved himself upright.

One of those new jeeps was creaming a tiny hatchback, plowing the smaller car across the road and into the side of the bridge.

Both vehicles missed them by inches.

"Holy shit," breathed Gabriel. His knuckles were white on the steering wheel.

"Nice driving, bro," said Nick.

Gabriel shifted in the seat and began to turn the wheel to get them around the crash. "I'll get us home. Just keep it together."

Then Chris saw the curl of flame race along the edge of the jeep's hood.

Gabriel hit the brakes.

"Drive," said Chris. He knew he sounded panicked and he didn't care. "Drive, Gabriel."

Nick punched his twin in the shoulder. "Go!"

The fire grew despite the rain. Gabriel's nostrils flared as if he could smell the smoke, even with the windows and the vents closed. "He's going to blow up the cars."

Nick punched him again. "Then get us the fuck off the bridge."

Horns started blaring. They were only half a mile from school—students sat in the cars around them. People would die.

They would die, if they didn't move.

Then Chris heard the second crash.

They all watched. A car up ahead skidded along the guardrail and stalled on the bridge.

Tires screamed into the storm. Becca's car crashed right into it.

And caught on fire.

CHAPTER 24

Becca couldn't breathe around the crushing pain in her chest. She wanted to cough, but she couldn't seem to get enough air for that, either.

Or maybe that was the smoke.

Red glowed through her windshield. Was there a fire out there?

She couldn't seem to find her seat belt. First she needed to find her hands.

Her head hurt.

Everything hurt.

The rocks on her wrist felt warm, twisted around to fall against the pad of her thumb. She wondered if they were keeping her calm.

Good thing Quinn had stayed at school. Becca probably should have taken the bus, too.

Phone. Where was her phone?

Something pounded against the car. She wished it would stop. Didn't they know how tired she was?

Oh, good. The steering wheel was right here. She'd just put her head down.

For a second.

* * *

Chris didn't remember bolting from the car. He was just suddenly aware of the rain pouring down the neck of his shirt, soaking through his hair to welcome him into the storm. He ran through standing water, splashing hard with each step.

Why wasn't she getting out?

Fire licked through the gap around the hood of Becca's Honda. Billowing smoke ignored the rain and made paths to the sky.

From five feet away, he couldn't see through her windows. The car was full of smoke.

Chris stretched an arm out to grab her door handle, ready to yank her free.

The door wouldn't open.

He fought with the steel, swearing when the door wouldn't give.

"Unlock it!" he yelled, pounding on the glass. "Becca! You have to—"

"Chris." Nick caught his arm. "We have to run. He's stronger. He'll kill us."

Gabriel was beside him, his eyes trained on the fire. "Now, Chris. The car's on fire."

"She's trapped." Chris could feel the heat coming from the hood now. The strength in the storm soaked into his skin with every drop.

He could seize this power. Use it.

Chris looked over the roof of her car. There, by the edge of the woods, the Guide remained.

Chris wanted to freeze the rain, to turn each drop into a tiny dagger, to attack this man and let him feel what true power could do. He'd never felt this clarity before, this surety in his own ability.

"Get her out." Gabriel swiped a hand across the narrow gap along her hood, pulling the fire into his fist, then shaking it loose to hiss and die in the rain.

More fire immediately replaced it.

Gabriel swiped it clean again. "But hurry."

Chris pounded on the window again. "Becca! Open the door!" Wind sent the rain sheeting sideways, stinging his cheeks and promising revenge if he'd just respond.

The water fed his strength without his even asking. Chris slammed the side of his fist into the window. A crack formed. Nick slammed a fist right beside his. The crack widened.

Sirens sang somewhere in the distance.

Water rushed over his feet. He punched her window again. Another crack. *Damned safety glass.*

More fire shot from around her hood, but Chris didn't spare a thought for whether Gabriel could control it all. People were starting to get out of their cars, jackets hunched over their heads.

"You kids get away!" some lady shouted from far back. "That car's on fire!"

Fist. Glass. *Crack.*

"Becca!" Jesus Christ, why wouldn't she open the door?

The ground shook. Hard. Chris caught at the side mirror to keep his footing.

Nick caught his arm to keep from falling. "He's flooding the bridge."

"No," Gabriel yelled. "He's taking out the bridge."

The ground shook again. Cars were sliding, shifting along the concrete surface. The water was halfway up Chris's calves now. People were screaming, running for solid ground.

If the bridge collapsed, they'd go down with at least six cars.

For the first time in a long while, Chris wished Michael was with them.

He punched the window again. His knuckles split and left a wash of blood across the glass, gone in an instant from the downpour.

But the instant the water got inside his skin, Chris couldn't refuse the element. This time his fist went right through the glass.

Smoke poured through the hole, blasting around his arm and almost forcing him out. He felt the wind whip around him. Nick was forcing clean air into the car.

"Chris," said Nick, his voice low, yet carrying over the storm. "She's not breathing."

Chris ignored him and fumbled to find the door lock. Blood streaked down his arm, but he didn't care.

The bridge dropped a few inches. Nick grabbed his arm and kept Chris on his feet. Becca's car started to slide. They were going into the water in a second.

Gabriel jumped on the hood. "Chris, get her out!"

Glass ground into Chris's skin, feeling like it might take his arm off.

There. He found the latch and jerked. The door gave.

Her body weighed nothing. Chris dragged her out of the car and into his arms. Blood was everywhere, in her hair, on her clothes, down the side of her face. His own joined it, soaking into her sweater.

Rain poured down her cheeks, taking the blood with it.

"Breathe," he whispered.

She didn't.

"Nick!" Was his voice shaking? "Nick! Make her breathe. Please—"

"I can't." Nick pressed a hand to her cheek. "Chris, I can't."

"Chris!" Gabriel was still on the hood of her car. The flames were huge, lighting his eyes. "We have to get off the bridge!"

The concrete fell another few inches. Chris almost dropped her.

She'd saved his life, and now she was losing her own.

Because of him.

The rain was in his blood. In hers.

Save her, he thought.

The bridge groaned and dropped again. Metal shrieked as cars slid and collided.

Save her.

Rain poured down on her cheeks, into her mouth, over her eyes. Chris watched it streak down her skin.

He'd never done this before, fed power into someone else. He didn't even know if it would *work.* The water swirled around his legs, begging for direction—for *his* direction, not the man's on the hill.

"Save her," he said.

"Holy crap." Nick's voice was breathy. "Do you feel that?"

"What are you guys *doing?*" Gabriel called.

Then Chris could feel it, through the rain. Gabriel's wonder, that the fire suddenly belonged to him. Nick's awe in the air, that he'd harnessed the wind, that it bowed to his will.

Chris pressed his bleeding hand to the side of her face. Blood to blood. *Save her,* he thought.

Becca opened her eyes.

And inhaled.

Chris gave a choked sob. "Becca."

"Chris—" Her voice was raw. "Wait—there's an accident—"

The bridge dropped again. She screamed and clutched at him.

Nick grabbed his arm, hauling him back. They dodged between two cars and made it to the walkway of the bridge. Water was pouring over the side.

"Is it the Guides?" Becca said.

"Yeah." Her voice was steady, and the rain was rinsing the blood from her face. He saw no injuries—had the power healed her? "Just one."

"Just *one?*"

"I told you they don't fuck around." Chris glanced back. Gabriel was still on the hood of her car, surrounded by flames.

"Come on!" Nick yelled to his twin.

"Run!" called Gabriel. "I'll hold off the fire—"

Lightning hit her car. The front end exploded.

The force knocked them back. Chris saw nothing but sky and fire for a moment. He couldn't breathe.

Then he could.

Gabriel. Chris couldn't see him. He couldn't *feel* him. Nick lay beside him, his presence a cool breeze inside his mind, like always. Water rushed over his legs. He sent power across the bridge, seeking his brother, seeking information.

Nothing.

Chris couldn't think. Becca shook against him. "Where did he go?" she whispered. "Is he—"

"No," Chris said. But he'd seen that explosion.

Nick was white, his eyes wide. "Chris," he said. "I can't—I don't—he's not—"

"I can't, either." He sent another surge of power into the water, begging, praying.

Nothing. He punched a fist into the water. "Damn it, where is he?"

Wind whipped across the bridge, blowing water and stinging Chris's eyes.

Nick found his knees, supporting himself against the crumpled guardrail of the bridge. His eyes were dark, his jaw set. Wind blew faster, harder. Large trees in the distance started to bend.

Smaller trees started to snap.

"What's happening?" said Becca. "Chris, is the Guide doing this—"

"I am," said Nick. "I'm going to kill him."

Chris felt his brother's fury. His own responded, sending the rain on a path of destruction he'd never attempted before. He didn't care if he lost control; he didn't care if his power brought every Guide to their door.

Wind spun, dragging the rain and the clouds into a spiral. Roof tiles began to tear loose and fly.

"Oh my god," said Becca. "You're making a tornado."

He was. They were. He'd never felt this strength, but it was all funneled in one direction.

Lightning struck the bridge, ten feet in front of them. They jerked back.

Chris poured more power into the rain. He urged every drop to find the Guide, to destroy. Becca's hand was clenched on his.

Their enemy was having trouble keeping his feet. Chris could see it.

"More," he called to Nick. "Stronger."

"Can you control it?" said Becca. "You told me—"

"I don't care," he said.

She grabbed Nick's hand, too. "Please—this will kill people—"

"He killed my brother." Nick's voice was strong, emotionless. But his hand didn't let go of hers.

Maybe it was because she clutched both their hands, or maybe it was because she sat in water up to her waist. But Chris felt a sudden connection, a link to Nick's power he'd never felt before. Like the moment he'd fed power into Becca, he felt every drop of water, every particle of his element. He felt the water and the wind, and fed strength into the space around them.

The wind howled, beating at their clothes. The Guide made it to the other side of the bridge, grabbing his end of the guardrail. Chris still couldn't make out any features in this storm—just focus and control.

Lightning struck five feet away.

Becca screamed.

Then lightning hit the other end of the bridge, almost directly hitting the Guide.

Chris froze.

Another bolt, five feet off. The man darted back, away from the bridge, fighting to keep his footing in the wind.

Another bolt. And another. Lightning rained from the sky, targeting their enemy.

The Guide ran.

"Yeah," growled a voice from behind them. "Watch that fucker run now."

Chris whirled. Gabriel was on his hands and knees, holding on to the bumper of a Chevy Tahoe. His clothes were scorched and his face nearly blackened from smoke, and blood marked his skin, but he was alive.

Nick grabbed him before Chris even realized he was moving.

"Easy, Nicky." Gabriel coughed. "I mean—me too—but explosion—hurt—"

But Chris didn't hear what else he said.

Because he was hugging him, too.

CHAPTER 25

Becca ended up in the ER.

The Merrick brothers didn't.

She'd lost track of them somehow, when emergency personnel stormed onto the bridge and separated them all. Four different men had stood in the rain shouting questions at her, shining lights in her eyes, taking her pulse. Did she know her name? The date? Did she know she'd been in an accident?

She'd been freezing. A fireman had wrapped her in a Mylar blanket and carried her to the ambulance. She'd been so shaken that she let him. The rain refused to stop, streaking into her eyes and creeping under her clothes, as much a stranger to her as it had been before the accident.

Had she imagined that connection?

Was that what Chris felt, that link with the elements?

He'd held her so close—had she been feeling his power?

Now, in the hospital, she huddled on her stretcher, pulling the thin hospital blanket more tightly around her shoulders.

Her mom stuck her head through the curtain. "You all right, Bex?"

One of the best parts of her mom working the ER was that Becca didn't have to wait long for anything.

One of the worst parts was that her mom was actually *working* the ER tonight. When Becca proved to be shaken but unharmed, her mom left her to sit alone in an eight-by-eight cubicle.

Someone moaned nearby. A baby screamed somewhere down the hall. The place was packed with victims from the storm. Becca kept hearing nurses speak in low voices about things like crushed femurs and compound fractures. Becca didn't even have a concussion. She just wanted someone to hold her hand.

God, could she be more selfish? Becca sniffed back waiting tears and nodded. "I'm fine. Can we go home?"

"Your dad's on his way, sweetie." Her mom's voice trailed after her as she rushed down the hall.

"What?"

"I can't leave," her mom called back, "and Quinn's mom wasn't home."

Ugh. Her *dad*. Now Becca wished she did have a concussion. Especially when he showed up in work clothes, his boots caked with mud. Dirt streaked across the khaki shirt he wore, and it looked like he'd been in a fight with a wild animal—his pants were torn, and dried blood trailed out of his shirtsleeve and across the back of his hand.

He came rushing into her cubicle, flinging the curtain to the side. He seemed to draw up short when his daughter obviously wasn't dying. Just wet.

"Hi," she said without enthusiasm. "What happened to you?"

"Becca." He studied her, as if he must have missed some life-threatening injury. "Are you all right?"

Just great. They got me out of the car before it blew up.

She wanted to say it, to roll her eyes and push past him. But his eyes were dark with concern, his hands hovering halfway between his body and her own, as if he wanted to hug her but he just wasn't sure how she'd take it.

Becca swallowed. She wished he'd jingle his keys and act like this was a hassle. It was hard to keep walls up against someone who truly gave a crap.

But maybe it was just the shock. Had Mom made it sound bad so he'd rush?

"I'm fine," she said. Her voice sounded like she'd been swallowing gravel. "I just . . . I want to go home."

"We can go back to my place—"

"No!"

He flinched, and she shut her eyes. "No—just—I don't have any clothes there. I want to go home."

"You have keys?"

Her keys were in her car—and probably melted into a ball of steel by now. She shook her head. "Mom will give me hers."

But her mom didn't like that idea. "Becca, go home with your father. You've had a rough day, and you shouldn't be alone—"

"I just want to get into some dry clothes and go to bed." She shoved herself off the stretcher. A patient down the hallway started screaming, and Becca clamped her hands over her ears. "Please, just take me home. Please—"

Arms wrapped around her, stroking the hair back from her face. For a bare instant she thought it was her mom—but then she felt the strength in those arms, the solid wall of her dad's chest.

"Calm down," he said, his voice a gentle rasp. "I'll take you home."

His voice sparked another memory, of an eight-year-old Becca who'd found a half-dead bird in the backyard. She'd been near hysterical, sure her father was going to have to kill it—so she hid with it in her bedroom, trying to feed it sliced Velveeta and bits of hot dog.

Her mom had been furious when she found out. A bird! In her house!

But her dad had talked Becca out of her closet, then taught her how to set the bird's wing and nurse it back to health.

"Becca?"

His breath touched her hair. Becca realized she'd been leaning on him for what felt like a while.

"Okay," she whispered. "Let's go."

Becca couldn't make herself look out the windshield. Rain freckled the glass, stealing any visibility. Cars seemed to be moving too quickly, every oncoming pair of headlights a collision waiting to happen.

She stared down at her dad's hand, resting on the center console.

"What happened to your wrist?" she asked, just to make her brain focus on something other than the sound of tires on wet roadway.

He cleared his throat. "Tree came down in the storm. Trapped a buck up against one of those electric fences. I was the closest one, so I took the call. Poor thing was fighting like hell."

Now she regretted asking. "So you killed it."

He hesitated. "No."

Now she swung her eyes up. "Are you lying?"

"No. I'm not. We hit him with a tranquilizer, patched him up, and let him go." He glanced away from the road. "Just what do you think I *do*, Becca?"

She had no idea—all she had were old memories and the patch on his sleeve. She hunched her shoulders and looked at the glove compartment.

"Wild animals can be dangerous," he said. "Sometimes they're too dangerous to treat and rehabilitate." He paused. "And sometimes they're not a threat at all."

"I bet you kill more than you save."

He stared out the windshield. "What do you want me to say, Becca?"

"Nothing."

Silence filled up the car until there wasn't room for anything else. He'd gone to vet school, she knew.

"I don't always like what I have to do," he said finally. "But that doesn't mean it isn't necessary."

"For the greater good?" she mocked.

"Exactly."

Becca leaned back against the door and gripped her elbows against her chest. This felt like being chastised. Not quite, but almost. Whatever, she didn't like it.

"Are you worried about your car situation?" he asked.

She was. Becca didn't want to consider how many hours she

was going to have to work to save up enough money to buy a new car. She had no idea how insurance worked. Didn't a deductible come into play somewhere? That old Honda had barely cost more than a thousand dollars.

"I'll talk to your mom," he said when she didn't answer. "We'll figure something out."

"I don't need your money."

"I'm not quite sure that's true."

She swung her head around to glare at him. "Look, you can't come swooping in here with a MasterCard and pretend to know everything I need."

He sighed, loudly. The exasperation was clear. "All *right*, Becca."

She pressed her forehead against the window. "All *right*, Dad."

Irritation thickened the air in the cab of his truck, heavier than the silence had been. He flung the truck in park roughly when he pulled into her driveway and saw the pentagram on the door. "What the hell is with this kid?" he demanded.

For an instant, she entertained telling him.

So, Dad, about the accident. Really, there's a guy who wants to kill me.

"Who knows." Her voice sounded tired.

"I'll have to come back to paint tomorrow," he said. "It's too wet now."

He trailed her onto the porch, and she shoved her mom's key into the lock. "Leave it. They'll just put it back up."

His attention shifted, focusing on her. She felt the change in his demeanor. "Becca." He caught her wrist, keeping her from opening the door. "Do you know who's doing this?"

She wriggled her hand free. "No—god, Dad, I'm *tired*."

He let her go, then stood in the foyer and watched her flick lights on. The house stood empty—no Quinn. Becca felt a flash of guilt for their fight outside the school, but then caught a glimpse of herself in the hall mirror. She looked like—well, like she'd been in a car accident and a flood. Her hair straggled over her shoulders, and her clothes were ruined. Her makeup formed dark circles around her eyes, making her look almost macabre.

Quinn was on her own tonight.

"I'm going to take a shower," she said.

He glanced around, like a wannabe police officer checking the place for criminals. "I can make a pot of coffee and stay for a while."

"Or you could remember that I'm almost seventeen years old, and I stay by myself almost every night."

He stared down at her. She stared back.

"I'm fine," she said.

His eyes narrowed a bit—but not in anger. More like assessment. "What's going on with you, Becca?"

"My car was just totaled. Sorry I'm not at my best."

He kept studying her. She kept looking back at him.

Just when she thought this was going to end up being some immature staring match, he said, "You need a ride to school in the morning?"

She shook her head. "I'll ride with Quinn."

Thank god he didn't know that Quinn had no car.

He nodded. "All right." He started to take a step toward the living room. "Maybe I should stay for a—"

"Just go," she said. "I have your phone number. I'll be *fine*."

"All right, Becca. All *right*." He turned for the door.

Then he paused. "Here, I want you to take this."

He was holding out a credit card.

Her own mother had never handed her a credit card. She stared at him. "I just told you—"

"I'm not swooping in, and I'm not solving anything. It doesn't even have a high limit, so don't go try to put down a deposit on a Porsche. But this might help you get started until the insurance mess is straightened out."

The plastic sat between his fingers, but she didn't reach to take it.

It was hard. Was he buying her off?

She was too tired for this.

"It's not even a MasterCard," he whispered. "Totally Visa."

That made her smile.

He smiled back and set the card on the hall table. "Lock up behind me."

And then he was gone.

She regretted his absence almost immediately.

Every creak had her imagining the Guide coming after her. The brothers had frightened him off—but how long would that last? Did the Guide still think she was a part of it? She took the fastest shower in history and reconsidered calling Quinn.

No answer.

So Becca turned on all the lights and inspected every closet.

She wished her mom would come home.

Her phone chimed from her bedroom. It was the only thing to have survived the crash and the flood.

She'd used it to call her mom from the ambulance.

1 New Text Message

Had to be Quinn. Becca scrolled through the menu. She didn't recognize the number, but the message was loud and clear.

What RU Up to? Practicing Krav Maga? :-)

Hunter had no idea about the accident. Just a normal boy sending a girl a text. Becca grinned. She couldn't help it. She texted back.

Did you just text a smiley?

His return message was lightning quick.

Don't girls love smileys?

She was blushing. At a text message. She whipped her thumbs across the keys.

Girls love the real thing.

This time there was a pause.
Or maybe he was typing something long.
Then her phone flashed. New message.

Is that an invitation?

Her heart kicked against her ribs as if the adrenaline on the bridge had been a warm-up. She remembered the challenge in his voice at the park. *In or out, Becca?*
Her fingers flew across the keys, typing quickly before she chickened out.

Sure is.

Still, her heart continued to pound. He could say no. He could say he was kidding. He could say something like, "Guess you'll have to wait 'til tomorrow."
Then her phone flashed.

See you in ten.

CHAPTER 26

Becca changed clothes three times. She'd pulled on pajamas after her shower, but she sure wasn't greeting Hunter at the door in the threadbare cami set she'd had since eighth grade. Jeans and a sweater seemed too stiff, considering it was nine o'clock at night and she'd just climbed out of the shower.

She finally settled on black yoga pants and an electric-blue tank top, twisting her half dried hair into a loose knot at the back of her head and securing it with a set of hair sticks. She barely had enough time for blush and mascara before Hunter was knocking on her door.

He'd changed clothes since school—or at least his shirt was different. A long-sleeved tee shirt clung to his chest and shoulders, red with some black silkscreening across the front in a design she couldn't make sense of.

Stop staring at his chest.

She jerked her gaze up and found his eyes close. "Hey."

Holy crap, her voice sounded breathy.

He smiled, and goose bumps flared on her arms. "Hey." His eyes flicked down her form, and for an instant, she wished she'd worn something completely different. More clothes. Less. Hair down, maybe. Something.

Then his eyes returned to hers, a spark of appreciation there. "Can I come in?"

"Yeah. Sure. I mean—sorry." She stepped back and held the door wide. "Come in."

Hunter stepped into her foyer, and Becca watched him look around for a minute, taking in the couch and TV in the living room, the photographs cataloguing her childhood that plastered the wall by the staircase, the stretch of hardwood leading back to the kitchen. Her mom kept the house neat as a pin, so at least Becca didn't have to worry about anything embarrassing lying around.

Then he said, "So what's with the pentagram?"

Yeah, nothing embarrassing—except maybe that. "Ah—long story," she said, almost stammering. "Stupid kids—er, vandals."

He winced. "That sucks."

She stood there beside him and told herself not to fidget. She knew she should invite him past the front foyer, but where? The kitchen? The living room? She couldn't figure out which room gave the wrong idea—or the right one.

It hadn't even occurred to her until now: She'd never had a boy over—not even Drew.

Hunter was looking at her again. "Smells nice," he offered.

"Cinnamon." Like he couldn't figure that out. "I lit a candle."

He smiled and glanced past her. "Your mom's in bed already?"

"Oh. No." That brought her up short. "Mom works nights."

His eyebrows went up, just enough. "So . . . there's no one else here?"

He seemed closer suddenly, warming the space between them. She shook her head and tucked a loose strand of hair behind her ear. "Just us."

"Interesting." The word lingered in the air.

Then she realized what this looked like. She snapped her head up, folding her arms in front of her stomach. Now she wished for a sweater. "I didn't mean—it's not like that."

His expression didn't flicker. "Like what?"

Her cheeks felt hot. "This is *not* a booty call."

He smiled and put his hands on her elbows, leaning in to

speak along her jawline. His fingers were warm on her skin, and his breath brushed her neck. "Relax."

She inhaled, wondering if cinnamon was an aphrodisiac. Part of her wanted to pull away—and a bigger part wanted to lean into him.

But he let her go and stepped into the hallway, leaving her swaying in the foyer. "Mind if I have something to drink?"

Becca hustled to beat him to the cabinet. She grabbed two glasses and poured lemonade, then watched him take a sip. The flame in the jar candle on the counter fluttered and jumped, keeping time with her heart.

She had to stop staring at him.

"Want to . . . ah . . . watch a movie or something?" she asked, then wanted to kick herself. What, was she six years old?

But he lowered the glass from his lips. "Sure, Becca."

She folded herself into the corner of the couch and prayed for something decent on cable. Apparently, Comcast wasn't on her side. She settled on some adventure flick she didn't recognize and glued her eyes to the screen.

Hunter dropped into the dead center of the sofa. He watched the movie for five seconds, then glanced at her. "Are you actually watching this?"

"I'm actually looking in that direction." She tossed the remote at him. "*Watching* might be a little strong."

He caught it without looking and muted the television. "Talk to me."

She smiled and glanced up at him through her lashes. "About what?"

"Anything." He set his glass on the coffee table, then leaned back into the cushions and hooked his thumbs in his pockets. It pulled his jeans down, just a little, but enough to show a millimeter of tanned skin at his waist, just the barest edge of his boxers.

Becca reminded herself to breathe.

"What'd you do tonight?" he said. "Did you have to work?"

That snapped her back to reality. She shook her head quickly, but her eyes kept flicking back to that strip of skin. "No—I was driving home from school, and there was a storm, and I—I to-taled my car."

Hunter sat up straight, and his tone was almost angry. "You what?" He looked her over, his eyes intense. "Jesus—are you okay?"

"No—yeah, I'm fine." She remembered that his father and his uncle had been killed in a car wreck, and her tone softened. "I'm okay. Really. My dad would never have left me alone other-wise."

He probably wouldn't have left her alone if he'd known she was going to invite a boy over, either. Too bad for the absent parent.

Hunter looked distraught. "But—totaled? Where?"

"The bridge on Old Mill." She'd heard the paramedics recite the events so many times that it was easy to forget that super-natural happenings had almost led to her death.

"The creek overflowed." Becca hunched her shoulders. This was the last thing she wanted to relive. "It must have buckled the bridge supports or something—"

"I heard about it. A lot of people were hurt." He ran a hand through his hair. Multicolored lights from the television danced across his features, making him look vaguely frightening—or frightened. "Becca, I had no idea."

She stared at her hands in her lap. Hunter was so earnest, of-fering anything less than truth felt shady. "I didn't want to be alone."

When he didn't say anything, she glanced up. He was study-ing her, his eyes shadowed.

That was too much. "I'm fine." She stretched out her bare arms. "Look. No bruises even."

He took her wrists in his hands, running his thumbs lightly along the inside of her forearms. "Hmm. No bruises."

His touch was making her shiver, but she couldn't pull away. This was the exact opposite of grappling in a field—but some-how she wanted to tackle him all the same. "Yeah. Chris and his brothers pulled me out of the car."

His fingers stilled, and his voice went hard again. "Really."

She nodded. "They were a few cars behind me."

"Convenient," he scoffed. His jaw was set, and he looked away, at the television. "Why am I not surprised?"

Becca snatched her hands out of his. "What does that mean?"

Hunter wasn't easily intimidated—he held her eyes and matched her tone. "It means the guy seems to be a magnet for trouble. For *you*."

She opened her mouth to protest, but she really didn't have a leg to stand on.

"Look," said Hunter. "I don't even *know* him. But every time I see him near you, you end up getting hurt."

Becca took a breath. "It's . . . complicated."

Hunter leaned in, his voice low and sharp. "I don't know what's going on between you and Chris, but that guy on the beach had a gun, Becca. He was firing *at you*. People shoot guns when they want to *kill someone*. And now you tell me your car is totaled and Chris was there?"

"It was an accident," she whispered. Her throat felt tight.

His green eyes were hard. "I don't believe in accidents."

She didn't realize she was crying until tears rolled off her chin.

He swore, then shifted forward to brush the tears away with his thumb. "I'm sorry. God—I'm a jackass. Becca, I'm sorry."

This couldn't be more horrifying. She shook her head and swiped at her eyes. "I can't believe I'm crying."

"I think you're allowed." He stroked a finger across her cheekbone, brushing a stray hair behind her ear. His voice dropped. "If I offer to hold you, are you going to think I'm making a move?"

Was he teasing? She couldn't tell. She blinked tears off her lashes and looked up at him. "I'm not worried. I know Krav Maga."

He grinned, and she loved how it stole the tension from his features. But then he was pulling her to him, shifting until they were in the corner of the sofa and her face was against his shoulder. His arm fell around her waist, holding her close. She had no idea where her free hand should go—there were so many *wrong* places—and finally settled on resting it across his chest, until his heart beat under her palm.

Becca held her breath, afraid to move.

"You okay?" His voice was closer. His breath touched her forehead.

She nodded.

He reached up and pulled the sticks out of her hair, and she felt the semi-damp strands drop onto her neck. "I don't want to put an eye out," he said.

She giggled. "Sorry."

He said nothing for the longest time, and she relaxed into the feel of his body, allowing the rhythm of his breathing to settle her own.

She'd forgotten what this felt like, to rest against a boy, to share the weight on her shoulders with someone else.

"Do you have a curfew?" she asked.

"Not really." He paused. "Mom's not . . . she's been kind of distracted since Dad died. She might not even know I'm gone."

His voice wasn't empty, but carried a note that warned her to tread carefully. "What about your grandparents?"

"I don't think they remember that teenagers are supposed to *have* a curfew." Another pause, and she heard a smile in his voice. "Why? Want to go out?"

She shook her head, glad he couldn't see the blush on her cheeks. His hand came up to rest over her own, his thumb sliding along her wrist until he found the twine bracelets. He slid them until the knots were aligned.

"Why don't you believe in accidents?" she said.

Hunter was silent for so long that she thought he might not have heard the question—or he might not want to answer. But he ducked his head and spoke low, as if the words were too much for the living room to hear.

"My father and uncle used to go on these . . . trips," he said. "I always thought it was adventure-type stuff. Male bonding, sleep in the woods and skip shaving, you know."

She could imagine. Her dad would probably love it. "Was your dad a cop, too?"

"No." Hunter paused. "He worked for the government. Ex-Marine—Special Ops. That's where he learned the self-defense stuff. When he got out of the Corps, he took a job in the private sector. I still don't know everything he did, but Mom used to worry that he'd die on some top-secret mission and we'd never know what really happened. I don't know if he was aware of the car crash—like, I don't know if it was instantaneous or whatever—but I know he'd be pissed to go out that way."

A lot of pride hung in his voice—and grief, too, though that was better hidden.

"When he and my uncle got together—they never let me come," Hunter said. "The last time, I'd been bitching about it for days. I always thought they just went fishing and told bullshit stories, and it used to drive me crazy that they wouldn't let me go. We had a big fight the morning they left."

Tension crawled across his shoulders, and she lifted her head to look at him. Hunter's face was close, his eyes dark in the shadowed room.

"They left," he said. "I was pissed, but they were gone."

He held his breath, looking at her. The look in his eyes was almost fragile.

"You don't have to tell me," she said.

He glanced away. "I just—I've never told anyone," he said, and his voice was nearly steady. He paused again. "They came back."

She nodded.

"My uncle—he'd told my dad that if I was old enough to put up a fight like that, I was old enough to come along. So . . . I went along. But it wasn't a guys' weekend at all. My dad was taking private security jobs. Like, on the side. Mom had no idea."

Hunter's eyes flashed to hers. "She still doesn't."

Becca nodded, and he continued.

"It was supposed to be something simple," he said. "I never

learned all the details. I kept some of his things after the crash, but most of it was lost. Just some surveillance or something— Dad was careful about what he told me, but they didn't think it was a big risk for me to come along. I'm not stupid, and I can take care of myself. He made sure of that."

His voice started to sound fractured.

"He did a good job," Becca said softly. If anyone could take care of himself, Hunter could.

Then she wondered if he'd agree with that.

Becca thought of her father's hand on her back in the hospital, the gentle support he'd offered. She'd run him out of the house without even a thank you. She'd been pretty clear that she didn't need him.

But was that true?

"We were driving fast to make up time," said Hunter. "When we drove through western Maryland, where you're practically climbing the Appalachians? There was a thunderstorm, and a rockslide, and the car was crushed."

The last sentence fell out of his mouth as if he lost control of it. Hunter was staring at her like her gaze was a lifeline—if she looked away, he'd be lost.

But she swallowed. "Were you . . . hurt?"

He nodded, and his eyes flicked up. "Dislocated shoulder. Concussion. I had a pretty bad cut across my hairline. Thirty-six stitches. The white streak—it's a scar. They said it would probably go away, but it hasn't."

She wondered why he didn't dye it—why he'd want a reminder in the mirror every morning.

"That's why I don't believe in accidents," he said. "The timing was too perfect. Coming back for me, the fight that made them late in the first place—the storm, the rockslide. All of it."

"It wasn't your fault," she whispered.

"I know." His voice hardened. "But it wasn't an accident, either."

She held still, feeling his breathing slow under her palm. He seemed to sandbag all that emotion, and he reached up to push her hair over her shoulder.

"I didn't mean to get so heavy," he said. "I don't want you to think I'm a psycho."

Hardly. She wanted to hold *him*. "I don't think that."

"I get protective."

Her eyebrow went up. "I noticed."

That made him smile. "Sorry."

"What a crazy thing to apologize for." She wished she'd met Hunter six months ago. Hell, six weeks ago.

He shifted his weight until he was sitting straighter, looking down into her eyes. "Thanks, then, for listening."

Becca could feel him distancing himself, as if he regretted saying so much. She reached up and traced her finger over the piercings along his brow, and he went still. "I never would have figured you for a military brat," she said.

"My parents were *definitely* an unlikely pair."

The metal studs felt warm from his skin. "Did these hurt?"

He shook his head.

"Liar." She poked at one.

He smiled and caught her wrist. "Are you going to tell me your story?"

Her heart stepped up. Was he talking about Chris? Had he guessed about the Elemental stuff somehow, in their talk about accidents and car crashes?

Hunter reached out to rest his palm against her face, his thumb sliding along her cheekbone until his fingers trailed in her hair. "You know there's . . . talk. About you." He paused. "Around school."

Oh. That.

She ducked away. "Yeah, well—"

Hunter caught her chin. "I don't believe it."

She almost pushed free of him. "Well, don't do me any favors."

"Hey." One hand secured her wrist, the other holding her face, reminding her how strong he was. "That right there is why I don't believe it. Any girl who wanted to sleep with half the school wouldn't pull away when I touch her."

She couldn't look at him. "Leave it. It doesn't matter."

He didn't move, but his voice became very careful. "Does it bother you when I touch you?"

"Stop it." She glared at him, knowing exactly where this conversation was going. "I'm not a *victim*."

"Does it?" He didn't look away.

Her breathing felt too quick, and she didn't like the way all that heavy emotion had somehow shifted into her. "Do what you want, Hunter."

He shook his head, very slightly. "What do *you* want, Becca?"

She wished everything could stand still, that everything could be as simple as his fingers on her wrist, his palm against her cheek.

Hunter shifted on the couch until he had to duck his head to speak to her. She heard her breath tremble in the space between their bodies.

"Do you want me to let you go?" he said.

She shook her head and had to shut her eyes.

He did anyway, releasing her wrist so his hands could touch her face. He traced the shape of her eyes, the arch of her cheekbone, the line of her jaw. His touch was light, reverent almost.

"Is this okay?" he said.

Her traitorous body warmed to his voice, seeking his touch. She opened her eyes. "I'm not broken."

"Liar."

"I'm not." But it sounded halfhearted, even to her.

"I'd be more inclined to believe you"—Hunter's head moved close, until his lips brushed her cheek while he spoke—"if you'd give me a straight answer."

"It's okay." She wet her lips, feeling lightheaded. "It's okay—you touching me."

He traced a thumb across the edge of her mouth, and she felt him smile against her cheek. "Just okay?"

"Why?" she said carefully, because teasing felt precarious. "You think you can do better?"

He leaned down and brushed his lips against hers, just for a heartbeat, maybe a moment more. His mouth felt warm and dry, very sure. He only drew back an inch, weighing her reaction.

Becca held still, not trusting herself.

Hunter kissed her again, this time lingering just a bit, giving her a chance to respond. Her lips parted, but he kept the kiss chaste, butterfly touches of his mouth against hers.

Her hands wanted to find his chest, to slide beneath his tee shirt and see if his skin felt as warm as she did. These kisses were addictive, simple promises of more with each press of his lips. And she found freedom here, in his restraint. She didn't have to struggle to find her own boundaries.

He pulled away, but not far, kissing along her jaw. "Better?"

She nodded, pressing her forehead into his neck. He smelled good, like woods and shaving cream and lemonade.

She lifted her head and smiled. "But I think there's still room for improvement."

This time when her lips parted, he responded, sliding his hands to her waist to pull her close. Her body softened into his, her breasts pressed against his chest as his fingers teased at the tiny edge of skin revealed by her tank top. His tongue brushed hers, quick, then slower, drawing a low sound from her throat.

Her hands pulled at his tee shirt, her fingers finding the smooth stretch of skin across his stomach, the muscles that defined his waist.

"Easy, Becca," he whispered against her lips.

She froze.

"Easy," he said again. He kissed her cheek, her mouth, her eyes. "There's plenty of time."

He kept her so off balance. "For what?"

"For you to trust me." He caught her hands, kissed her fingertips. "I'm not going anywhere."

Then he drew back on the couch and pulled her up against him.

And did nothing more than stroke her hair until she fell asleep.

Hunter spent the night.

She fell asleep curled against his chest, warm and secure between his body and the sofa cushions.

And that's exactly where she woke up, seven hours later.

Hunter's eyes were still closed, his breathing slow.

Becca started to push herself away, shoving her hair behind her ears. It felt like a tangled mess. She blinked her eyes a few times to orient her contacts. Hunter shifted slightly, his arm tightening to hold her in place. His eyes cracked open. "Hey."

She froze. "Hey."

His hand came up to brush hair out of her eyes. "Don't run."

Becca flushed. He was too perceptive. "I'm not. I'm gross." She pushed herself upright, shifting into the corner of the sofa, wishing her cheeks would cool.

He watched her move. "You're not gross."

Hair fell across the side of her face and she didn't bother to push it away. "I can't believe you stayed all night."

"Yeah." His voice was careful. "That all right?"

She peeked up at him. He looked too good, his hair barely in disarray, a trace of stubble lining his chin.

She probably had mascara bleeding into her eyelids.

And he was still waiting for an answer.

Becca didn't have one to give him. It never mattered what anyone did. It only mattered what people *thought*. She had to clear her throat. "Does anyone know you're here?"

"I texted my mom to say I was staying at a friend's."

"But not—you didn't put it on Facebook or something—like, about spending the night with me?" Her breathing felt a little quick.

"No. I didn't." He paused. "I should have woken you up—I'm sorry—"

Becca shook her head forcefully. She was about to ruin this whole moment. She could feel it. "No. I'm being stupid. People just—get the wrong idea about me, and I don't like to give them more reasons to start something—"

"No one knows." Hunter shifted forward and touched her face, brushing his fingers along her chin. "It's all right."

His touch offered security, like the night he'd taught her self-defense techniques. She leaned into his hand.

"Look, we have to be at school in a half hour," he said. "Let me go home and change, and I'll swing back to give you a ride. Then you can tell anyone who asks that I gave you a lift because your car was totaled."

Would anyone really notice? She was being a freak. She knew it. But she nodded. "Thanks."

Becca walked him to the door. Now that he wasn't touching her, she wanted to ask him to stay. Her skin longed for his warmth, and she had to remind herself that they hadn't done anything more than kiss.

Hunter held the front door closed when her hand reached for the knob. "Wait."

He stood very close, and she held her breath, sure he was going to kiss her again. But he took her wrist, the one with the stones.

"You want them back?" she said softly.

"Not yet." He smiled. "But I'll trade you."

His fingers slid along her forearm, untying the dark silver hematite. He replaced it with a rich red stone and a pale yellow one. They sat heavy against her wrist, warm from his touch.

Becca ran her fingers over the slick surface of each. "What are these for?"

He stopped her fingers over the red stone. "Garnet, for confidence."

"Garnet?" Her eyes flicked up to his. "For real?"

"Yeah." A smile. "Don't lose it."

She touched the paler stone. It felt warmer than the others, almost searing her fingertips. She had to let it go. "And this one?"

"Citrine." Then he did lean forward and brush his lips against hers. "For courage."

His kiss seemed to breathe heat right into her body. She had to stop herself from grabbing his shirt and dragging him tight against her.

It was bad enough she was practically panting against the wall.

Hunter caught her hand and kissed her palm, laughing lightly. "I'll see you in twenty minutes."

He turned the knob, letting cool September humidity sneak into the house, carrying the scent of grass and pollen. Becca inhaled deeply, glad for the fresh air to clear her head.

Then he pulled the door wide.

And there on the porch, his hand poised to knock, stood Chris.

CHAPTER 27

Becca had no idea what to say.

Chris looked surprised for a bare instant—then his blue eyes were walled up and ice cold.

"So," he said. "Guess you've got the ride to school covered."

She opened her mouth to respond—but he was already turning, stepping off the porch, heading for his car.

His *running* car. With his brothers inside.

Crap.

And Hunter was going after him. "Hey."

Chris ignored him.

"Hey." Now Hunter's voice carried a thread of anger. "Chris."

There was no possible way this could go well.

"Stop. Wait." Becca leapt off the porch, feeling grit from the walkway scrape at her feet. She wasn't even sure which one of them she was addressing.

Hunter grabbed Chris's arm. "Hey, man, I'm *talking to you*—"

Chris rounded on him. "Let go of me."

Becca felt the air flicker, or move, or *something*, like the humidity was a mere prelude to a storm. The hairs on her arms stood on end and she shivered.

Hunter must have felt it, too. His stance shifted, as if he was bracing himself. "I want you to leave her alone."

"News flash: I *was* leaving. And I really don't give a shit what you want." He gave Hunter a solid shove, enough to dislodge the other boy's grip.

"Yeah?" Hunter shoved him back. "Need some convincing?"

"Hey! Stop." Her voice was squeaking, so Becca tried again. *"Stop it."*

It bought her a moment of hesitation—from Chris anyway. He drew back and gave Hunter a wicked smile—but Becca saw the way his hands curled into fists. He jerked his head her way. "You going to pee on her next? Mark your territory?"

"Nice," she snapped. "Look, guys, this is stupid—"

Hunter cut her off, his attention focused on Chris. "I don't know what your problem is—"

"You," said Chris, heat in his voice. He got up close to Hunter and shoved him again—just a little more roughly. "Right now *you're* my problem. You don't even know what you're *talking* about."

Hunter shoved him back, harder. "I know enough."

"Guys." Her heart pummeled her rib cage. "Stop."

Hunter didn't even glance at her. He spoke low, right into Chris's face, punctuating his words with a shove for every sentence. "I know Becca gets hurt every time she's near you. I know you put her in danger. And I know you're too selfish to give a crap what happens to her—"

Chris punched him.

Becca jumped. He might as well have hit *her*—shock knocked her back a few steps. He'd taken Hunter by surprise, too. The other boy almost went down.

He recovered pretty darn quick.

The twins were out of the car before she registered the sounds of the doors opening. She had half a second to worry whether Hunter could hold his own against three guys, and then Chris's brothers were pushing them apart.

Wind swirled through the space between them, lifting debris from the driveway and reminding her she only wore a tank top and yoga pants.

The instant that breeze touched her, she felt power riding the wind, like silk streamers from the tail of a kite, flicking against her skin before whipping free to look for more interesting targets. But once she realized the power had just as much substance as something solid, she discovered she could grab hold and follow it to its owner.

Nicholas.

He felt it, too. He'd been the one to block Hunter, but his head whipped around to look at her, as if she'd grabbed the edge of his coat and given a firm yank.

Was this how Chris told them apart? She'd never felt their abilities like this—maybe something had happened on the bridge to give them more potency. Chris had mentioned that strength came with numbers, that tense situations stole their control.

Chris still looked ready to fight, his shoulders high, his fists locked. She could hear his breathing from here. But Gabriel was blocking him, a hand on his shoulder, speaking low. Talking him down.

Then her heart slowed enough for her to catch what he was saying—or maybe the wind just changed.

". . . you want to beat the crap out of this guy, we'll do it. But really, man, for *what?* Chris, I warned you about this chick. We could probably come back any morning this week and find a different one. . . ."

Each word hit her like a fist. Her insides felt like dry ice, so frozen it was starting to burn.

Wind whipped across the driveway, harsh and fierce enough to scrape at her cheeks. There were no streamers now, just rage in the air.

"Get out," she said. She could barely hear herself over the wind. She was shivering and it was probably lucky her voice was steady. "All of you. Just get out."

Hunter took a step toward her. "Becca. Let me just—"

"No." She had enough anger to share with him. He'd picked this fight. "I'll get my own ride."

Then she leapt onto the porch, flung the marked door wide, and threw herself into the foyer.

And without a backwards glance, she slammed the door on the wind and the whole lot of them.

Becca rode the bus. She half expected Quinn to be there, but her friend must have gotten a ride from her mother.

Becca hadn't done this since sophomore year, and she hoped she wouldn't get another chance. The vehicle was crowded with freshman boys who must not have learned to shower in the morning yet. She hunched against a window with her English Lit book. She was supposed to have read two chapters of *Anna Karenina* the previous night, and she hadn't even cracked the spine.

You should have had Mom write you a note.

She should have. But her brain was shot.

To think she'd almost *liked* Gabriel. What a dick.

Then she remembered the way he'd tamed fire until Chris got her to safety.

The way he'd almost gotten himself *killed*.

This was too confusing.

Hunter was right: Trouble followed Chris around like he kept it on a leash. But that didn't mean Hunter had a right to chase the guy off for offering her a ride to school.

Becca was dreading English, wondering how she'd meet Chris's eyes after Gabriel's little monologue in the driveway. But he must have skipped—his seat stayed empty.

World History would mean Hunter and Chris in class together—one of whom was supposed to be her partner. Would Chris skip two classes in a row? She almost ditched, but Hunter caught up to her in the hallway.

There was a bruise on his cheek, faint but present. "I'm sorry," he said.

She shrugged her backpack higher on her shoulder and looked down the hall. "Does your face hurt?"

He hesitated, like it was a trick question. "No?"

"Too bad." She reached up to poke his bruise.

He was way too quick—he caught her wrist. "I am, Becca. I

shouldn't have picked a fight with that guy. Seeing him show up, with what you're going through—"

"Chris and his brothers saved my life." She pulled her hand free and turned away. "You have no idea what I'm going through."

He put an arm against the wall and blocked her way. "So tell me."

For a moment, it seemed his voice held a note of awareness, as if those three simple words meant more than they should have. She looked up to find his eyes close, intent on hers.

No, this was stupid. He was just being Hunter, as direct and challenging as ever.

She ducked under his arm. "We have class."

Becca readied herself for an apology to Chris. He had saved her life. He'd come to offer her a ride to school, not to fight with Hunter.

But Chris wasn't in World History, either.

When she opened her notebook, it fell to the last page where she'd written. Where she'd told Chris she was going to ask for another partner.

Becca swallowed and turned to a fresh page. Then she took two sets of notes, writing fast until her hand ached.

She booked it out of the classroom ahead of Hunter, hoping to find some familiar sanctuary with Quinn at lunch.

But Quinn wasn't at their usual table.

This sucked. Becca couldn't figure out who to apologize to and who to fight with, and the mental debate was exhausting. She had Chris's History notes in her bag, a flimsy excuse to drive over there after school. She got the distinct impression that her welcome at the Merrick house might have worn well past thin. Could she call him? And say what?

Gabriel played sports. Hadn't Chris said something about watching practices after school so he had a ride home? The last place she wanted to go was the soccer field, but maybe the players would be engrossed in drills and scrimmages or whatever, and she could just talk to Chris.

Quinn appeared beside her when she turned the corner behind the gym.

Becca jumped a mile. "Quinn! You scared the crap out of me."

"I called your name, like, three times."

Becca turned her head to look at Quinn. Her friend looked tired, her eyes shadowed and dark. She wore a long-sleeved crop top that showed her abs, with aged denim capris that sat at her hips. Quinn had dropped some weight somewhere along the line, but Becca couldn't decide if that was a good thing. With that weathered look on her face, Quinn seemed . . . worn.

"You all right?" Becca said.

"You care?"

Wow. Becca felt the end of her rope coming up quick. "Yeah, Quinn. I care. So either tell what's going on with you or don't, because I've got—"

"Forget it." Quinn turned away.

"Stop." Becca caught her arm.

They stared at each other for a long moment.

Becca decided she might as well start with Quinn. "I'm sorry. It's been a crappy week. I totaled the car last night, and then Hunter spent the night, and with my dad in town . . ."

Her voice trailed off, and Becca realized she was waiting for Quinn to interrupt her with an exclamation of surprise, or a gasp, or something more than just standing there staring.

"I heard you were in that accident," Quinn finally said.

"And you sound so concerned."

Quinn looked her up and down. "You're not hurt. You didn't even *call* me. Rafe's dad works at the hospital. I heard about it from *him*."

Becca let go of her arm. "I'm sorry." She paused. "Really, Quinn. I'm sorry." Then she realized what Quinn had said. "You were with Rafe last night? Are you guys getting serious?" She felt like Quinn had checked out of her life for a month.

"Yeah. Why, did you call dibs on all the guys in school or something?"

Becca jerked back. Her throat felt tight. "What does that mean?"

"What do you think it means?" Quinn's voice was fierce, her breathing quick. "You're supposed to be my best friend and I don't even know which guy you're dating! You're always with someone else, you don't talk to me anymore, you don't want me around—nobody wants me around—"

And suddenly Quinn was crying.

Becca lost a second to complete shock. Then her bag dropped to the ground and she threw her arms around her friend.

Quinn didn't fight her off—which was another shock in itself. Becca had never seen her friend cry. Not when her mom hit her, not when her dog died. Not when Rick Jakubowski took Quinn's virginity in ninth grade and then refused to acknowledge she existed.

Becca held her, murmuring stupid things that made no sense—not that it mattered, as hard as Quinn was sobbing against her shoulder.

Quinn swiped her eyes. "God. I must be PMS-ing. Let's pretend this didn't happen."

Becca hesitated. "You want to tell me what *did* happen?"

"They threw me off the dance team."

"Just now? But you're an incredible dancer! How could they—"

"They don't care about that, Bex." Quinn wiped her eyes again. "I'm too mouthy, and too fat, and too—"

"You are not fat!"

"Well, that's what Miss Harkins said. I don't have the right 'body type,' and my attitude needs work, and since I'm not willing to be kind, maybe I should look into other sports."

"What did you say?"

Quinn sniffed and shifted her bag higher on her shoulder. "That the school must have a double standard on body types since they let a woman with an ass like hers coach dance team."

Becca couldn't help it—she laughed. But Quinn cracked a smile, too.

Becca sobered quickly. "I'm really sorry, Quinn."

"Me too."

"Not just about the dance thing."

Quinn nodded. "I know."

Becca bit at her lip. Quinn loved dance—and it loved her

back. Becca's mom had once made a comment that she was glad Quinn had a physical outlet for all the anger she carried around, especially one that channeled it into something expressive.

"Stop looking at me like that," said Quinn.

"Sorry," said Becca. "Where were you going, anyway?"

Quinn made a face. "To watch soccer practice. I promised Rafe I would."

"He plays?"

"He gets splinters in his ass. The only reason he's on varsity is because he's a senior. Why were you going this way?"

Becca felt heat crawl up her cheeks. "To see Chris."

"Didn't you just say Hunter spent the night?"

Becca shrugged and looked off toward the fields again. "Yeah, well, it wasn't like that. At all."

Quinn was silent for a long moment. "So . . . you going to tell me about it or what?"

Their friendship teetered on those words. Becca could feel it. If she shrugged Quinn off now, their friendship might not recover.

"Come on," she said. "I'll tell you while we walk."

She told Quinn everything that had happened since they'd left school yesterday afternoon—everything except the Guide's involvement. It was surprisingly easy to stick to the mundane. She remembered Chris telling her how easy it was to cover up what they were.

"So Chris hit him?" said Quinn, when they were getting close to the bleachers. "Jesus, I love when guys fight."

"Yeah, it was great," Becca returned flatly. "I should have made popcorn."

"Seriously. When they're all slow and tentative and circling, and then ka-*pow*, they just explode with power. It's totally sexy."

Becca was trying to figure out if Chris was one of the guys on the bleachers. There were a couple cheerleaders doing cartwheels or something, but it didn't look organized; more like goofing off than actual drills. The soccer team wasn't practicing yet, but most of the guys were in the middle of the field. About ten people sat scattered on the section of bleachers behind the cheerleaders, enjoying the sunlight.

When they got close enough to make out features, she stopped short. They were approaching from the side, so they hadn't been spotted yet. Chris sat with one of the twins on the bleachers. They had textbooks open beside them and notebooks on their laps. It had to be Nick since the other had a foot up on the lowest rung and was lacing his cleats.

Quinn grabbed her arm and dragged Becca along. "Come on. If they're jerks, I'll punch them."

"Great," said Becca. "It'll be totally sexy."

CHAPTER 28

Gabriel seemed to be having trouble tying his cleats. It might have had something to do with the fact that he was trying to watch the cheerleaders.

"I still don't see what you're talking about," he said, and Becca could hear a bit of a taunt in his voice. "Show me again."

The girls giggled and did some weird cartwheel handspring combination that looked disorganized at best. They did some silly cheer right along with it, though the routine didn't seem to match. But all that activity made their skirts go up, and some guys high on the bleachers whistled.

That made the girls giggle harder. Becca didn't recognize either of them.

"Don't you see?" said one. "It's supposed to end with a handspring into a back tuck but it doesn't work right."

"Do it again," said Gabriel, a wolfish smile on his face. "Maybe I'll get it."

"Why don't you just tell them to take their clothes off?" said Quinn. "Save time."

Oh, good. Quinn was going to make this go smoothly.

Becca watched Gabriel notice her, but he didn't lose the smile. Maybe he didn't want to show his mean streak in front of potential conquests. "Just doing my part," he said.

"Yeah," said Quinn. "I'm sure you're all kinds of worried about 'your part.'"

Now Nick laughed. Chris hadn't said a word—hadn't even looked up. He seemed to be studying his Trig book extra hard. Becca's lips didn't want to work. It felt like she'd been chewing on sawdust.

One of the cheerleaders leaned on the other one's shoulder. It made them look like they were rehearsing for a *Maxim* photo shoot. "Ohmigod you're so helpful," the blonde said to Quinn in a flat voice. "Please. Keep being a bitch."

The other, a lanky brunette, just looked at Quinn. "You think you can do better?"

Quinn didn't say anything, just dropped her bags next to the bleachers and kicked off her flats. She backed up to give herself some room, then sprang forward into the routine the girls had just demonstrated. She added an extra handspring, and even did the call—though that carried a bit of mockery. Every beat matched perfectly, and she finished with a flourish.

Most of the people on the bleachers clapped. Quinn got more whistles than the real cheerleaders had. She blushed.

Becca grinned, forgetting her nerves for a moment. "I had no idea you could do that."

The blond cheerleader scowled, then flicked her hair and flounced off. "We're late," she called over her shoulder.

"How'd you do that?" said the brunette.

Quinn was reclaiming her things. She shrugged. "It's all in the counting. You guys didn't have enough beats."

"You cheer for the rec league or something?"

Quinn snorted. "No way."

The other girl was halfway across the field, calling her friend. The brunette glanced after her, then looked back at Quinn. "You should come try out next week. We're down two girls." She looked Quinn up and down, then started to turn to follow her friend. "We need more strong people who can do the power stuff like that."

Now Quinn was just staring at her.

"She'd love to," said Becca.

Quinn whipped her head around. "I do *not* want to be a cheerleader," she hissed.

"Look for the signs," the girl called. "Next Thursday!" Then she was off, jogging across the field, cheerleader skirt bouncing, a dark ponytail flying behind her.

Gabriel watched her go. "God, that Tamar is one hot piece of—"

"Easy," said Nick. Becca noticed he was still watching Quinn. "That was pretty good," he said.

"Thanks." Quinn climbed onto the bleachers and pulled out her own Trig book.

Gabriel stepped closer, watching her. "Didn't I see you sucking the face off Rafe Gutierrez last weekend?"

He was quickly killing any of Becca's residual feelings of gratitude.

"Jealous?" said Quinn.

"Maybe," said Nick.

Quinn was suddenly blushing again. "Well, I came to watch him practice."

"Good luck," said Gabriel. "I think Coach sent him to fill the water jugs."

Quinn shrugged. "He told me to bring my homework, so I figured as much."

"Why'd *you* come?"

Chris's voice. Becca snapped her head up. He was watching her, his eyes hard and daring.

When she didn't respond right away, his expression turned cold. "Boyfriend busy?"

"He's not my boyfriend," she snapped.

"Yeah," said Gabriel. "There's another term for that. Friends with benefits? Or do you just prefer fuck bud—"

Becca hit him. Hard. Right in the face.

As soon as she did it, she wanted to go find Hunter and give him a kiss or write him a check or promise him her firstborn child. Because it was a solid punch, with power behind it, and Hunter had taught her exactly how to do it.

Nick and Chris were on their feet, but they hadn't moved

from the bleachers. She'd struck Gabriel hard enough that he'd rocked back, and she realized she should be counting her lucky stars that he wasn't coming after her.

He touched a hand to his face, looking a bit stunned.

"Holy shit," said Quinn. "Would it be wrong if I applaud?"

Becca glared at Gabriel, enjoying the redness across his cheek. "You're an asshole," she said, feeling strong for the first time in a long while. "I came here to apologize to Chris. I came here to *thank you* for helping me last night. I didn't ask to be part of this. I helped your brother because he was getting hurt. I warned you guys at that party. I didn't sleep with Hunter."

Skepticism flickered in his eyes. Becca shoved him in the chest, hard enough to push Gabriel back a step.

"I *didn't*," she cried. "I was scared, and he came over. That's *all*."

"Whatever you say," he said. He glanced off across the field, as if he were merely enduring her theatrics.

"Look at me." Her eyes felt hot, but she ignored it. "I heard what you said to Chris. I heard your little *warning*. Do you have any idea what that feels like? To know everyone thinks you're something you're not?"

He didn't move, but now she had his attention. She had to get her breathing under control or she was going to go to pieces. Her cheeks felt hot, and she was deathly afraid she was about to cry.

"Everyone's willing to believe I'm screwing half the school, but no one wants to believe I'm not. I never slept with all those guys they say I did. Drew McKay was drunk, but I really liked him. I didn't even know what he—it was just—his friends were there, and they're, like, ten times stronger than I am, and—"

Then she was sobbing into her hands and this was the most humiliating day of her life.

No, the second most.

Arms wrapped around her. Quinn, holding her tight, murmuring the same reassuring crap Becca had been saying twenty minutes ago.

"Merrick!" The coach was calling from the center of the field. "Quit screwing around."

"Go on, dickhead," said Quinn.

Gabriel didn't say anything. Becca heard nothing but her own sobs, then a quick swish of cleats through grass.

She thought Gabriel was leaving, but Quinn muttered, "Oh, crap."

"Come on, man." Drew's voice. "What are you—wait. Becca?"

Becca lifted her head. Her face felt like a punching bag. She wished, wished, *wished* she hadn't used up that punch on Gabriel. Because now her rage was a puddle in the grass. And Drew was the one who really deserved it.

Gabriel still stood there, looking down at her. His eyes, that same blue as Chris's, were cold and unreadable.

Drew punched him in the arm. "Let's go, dude." Then he gave Becca that signature smile, the one that used to melt her insides but now mostly made her want to puke. "Wait—you're not breaking up with her, are you? You know, most guys don't date her, they just—"

Gabriel punched him.

Becca gasped. It was a good thing Quinn was holding on to her, because shock would have knocked her down.

Especially since Gabriel grabbed the front of Drew's jersey, hauled him forward, and slugged him again.

Drew went down. His nose was bleeding. He couldn't seem to get his joints to organize.

"Merrick!" The coach was running. Other players were running. Nick was off the bleachers and he'd grabbed his brother's arm.

But Gabriel stood back and didn't try to take another swing.

They were ordered off the field. All of them. The coach was so furious he was almost incoherent. He was hollering about detentions and suspensions and something about needing a goddamn cigarette.

Becca grabbed her things and fell into step beside Quinn.

She almost stopped short when Gabriel fell into step beside

her. His cheek was even redder now—he was definitely going to have a black eye.

"Sorry," he said. "I didn't know."

She shrugged. Quinn reached out and squeezed her hand.

"That guy's an asshole," he added.

"Yes," she agreed. "He is." She paused. "Thanks for hitting him."

He grinned and touched his face. "Next time I'll let you do it."

She smiled back—a little.

Then she remembered something Chris had told her. "Wait— I thought you wouldn't be able to play all year if you got in another fight."

Nick snorted behind them. Gabriel laughed and dropped an arm across her shoulders, almost giving her half a hug. "You're sweet. I'm not worried."

Becca left his arm there. It felt good—brotherly. Like when she'd played foreman in their driveway.

She looked up at him. "You're not?"

"Nah. Don't you remember? They all think I'm Nick."

CHAPTER 29

Chris sucked it up and went to class on Wednesday. He hauled ass to make it to the room before Becca, but now he was doodling in his notebook, fighting not to fidget. He sketched a rather impressive pyramid before deciding it made him look like a complete tool. So he flipped to a clean page.

The Guide seemed to be lying low since they'd chased him off at the bridge—or maybe he was plotting something bigger. Whichever, they'd had a peaceful night—or as peaceful as it could be with Michael and Gabriel walking a razor edge of tension all evening. Once darkness fell and his brothers settled, Chris had relished the silence, replaying every moment of that scene in front of the bleachers.

Becca had come walking across the field, looking like a loud noise would send her bolting for safety. But she'd kept her head up and her pace even, determined as ever.

No, not determined. *Brave.*

She'd punched Gabriel right in the face—something Chris wasn't sure he'd try himself. Even before that, she'd stood up to Tyler and Seth—had saved Chris without knowing the stakes. He couldn't remember two words he'd spoken to Becca before that mess in the parking lot. Now he couldn't make himself forget a single thing about her.

Seeing her tears on the field had almost been his undoing.

He'd wanted to hold her. No, he'd wanted to kill Drew and any-one else who'd laid a hand on her. That guy was lucky Gabriel got to him first.

But no, Chris had just sat there and watched. He could kick himself.

He should have talked to her, after. He should have walked her to her car. Called her last night to check on her.

What had she said about Hunter? *I was scared, and he came over.*

Would she have wanted Chris to call?

Any minute now she was going to come strolling in here with Hunter. She'd sit down, smelling like almonds and vanilla, and Chris would pretend he didn't notice. She'd think about World History.

He'd think about *her*.

God, he was going to drive himself crazy. He looked down at his notebook. He'd drawn a spiral, pressing so hard that the pen was going through the paper.

But wait—hadn't she asked for a new partner? So she wasn't going to sit next to him at all. Someone else would drop into the empty seat, and he'd obsess over Becca from across the room.

That would probably be better.

Chris felt the air move as someone stopped next to his desk. He swung his head around as Becca slid into the seat beside him.

"I thought you switched partners," he exclaimed, before real-izing he sounded a bit too frigging excited.

"Beamis wouldn't let me."

Oh. That explained it.

Chris flipped to another page in his notebook while she pulled her textbook from her bag. Had she walked in with Hunter? Chris hadn't been paying attention—and the new guy was already in his seat, staring at the board.

He had no idea what to say, so he pretended to listen as Mr. Beamis called the class to order.

"Here," Becca whispered, pushing a piece of paper his way.

Chris glanced down. The notebook paper was covered in her

handwriting, careful cursive that looked nothing like the big bubble letters of the girly-girl set. Had she written him a letter? His heart tripped before catching itself. Then he read the words.

Class notes.

Figures. This was probably a subtle reminder not to cut.

"Thanks," he murmured. "I'll copy them and get these back to you."

"They're yours," she said. "I took two sets so you wouldn't miss anything."

He swung his head around. She wasn't looking at him, but her cheeks were faintly pink.

"Thanks," he said again. He hesitated, then leaned the tiniest bit closer. Almonds, vanilla, torture. "You know, you didn't have to—"

"Mr. Merrick?"

Goddamn Beamis.

Chris flung himself back in his chair. "What?"

The teacher raised his eyebrows. "Every student in my class deserves a chance to learn. Do you understand me?"

"Sure." Chris didn't have a clue what he was talking about.

Beamis clearly wasn't convinced, either. "Are you harassing Miss Chandler?"

Harassing her? Was that what this guy thought? After that dick two rows over had been tossing "notes" onto Becca's desk? After what Drew and his friends had done? Beamis thought *Chris* was harassing her?

And now the whole class was staring at him. Half the school had probably heard what happened on the soccer field—or some approximation of it. He wondered just what stories were flying around.

And where he fit in.

"He's not," Becca said quickly. "He was just repeating a point I missed."

Beamis gave him another long look, then nodded and turned back to the board.

Chris didn't dare say anything else to her. He sighed and looked at his notebook.

His eyes kept straying to the page of notes she'd written. Becca tapped his arm and gestured to her notebook.

Sorry. I didn't mean to get you in trouble.

He shrugged, then reached up with his pen.

Not your fault.

Then Beamis turned around, addressing the class, and she didn't write anything else.

But the end of the period brought an activity, fifteen minutes for them to begin work on the semester project and design an outline.

Chris started a new page, fully expecting her to want to work exclusively on the project. But she put her hand over his to stop him from writing.

It just about stopped his heart, too. He couldn't look at her.

"What's up?" he said.

"I really did come to apologize yesterday," she said softly. "Hunter shouldn't have picked a fight with you. Especially after what you—what you *and* your brothers did."

He dragged his eyes up. "It's all right. Gabriel shouldn't have been such an ass."

She made a face. "I shouldn't have hit him." She flexed her fingers. "My hand still hurts."

Chris smiled. "Oh, no, I loved that part."

She didn't smile back, so he dropped his.

Awkward silence hung there long enough that he turned back to his notebook.

Then she said, "I wish I'd been the one to punch Drew."

"Yeah?" He looked over again, his voice angry. "Me too."

Her eyes widened and he wished he hadn't said anything. He almost started doodling again, just to give his hands something to do.

"You know," she said, "like four people have walked up to me in the hall to give me a high five. For hitting your brother."

Chris snorted. "You're probably living a dream."

Her voice got quiet again. "I think more people heard about that than the . . . the other stuff. But Vickers made me come see her during first period."

Chris looked up again. Ms. Vickers was the guidance counselor. "Yeah?"

"Yeah. But what's funny is that I don't think I need her help now. I finally feel like I can handle Drew, or pretty much anything, on my own. Does that make any sense?"

He held very still, as if sudden movement would make her realize she was confiding in the wrong guy. "Yeah, Becca. It does."

She hesitated, then gave him the smallest of smiles. "You called me Becca."

"Sorry." Then he mentally kicked himself. Why the hell was he apologizing for using her *actual* name?

"No—I was just getting used to Becky."

Oh.

He had to be reading this wrong. But she stared up at him until he almost couldn't stand it; he was going to have to touch her, to take her face in his hands and share that moment of breath before—

The bell rang. She snapped back, grabbing her notebook, shoving it into her bag.

He'd lost the moment. Beamis was talking; students were clambering for the doorway. Becca was gone before he could figure out what had just happened.

Chris fought his way through the cafeteria, throwing food on his tray without paying attention. Was she just being friendly, offering some kind of truce in the middle of all this crap about the Guide? Or was it something more? She hadn't looked at Hunter once the entire class; that much he was sure of. It didn't seem like they'd left together, either, but it was hard to tell in the stampede for the cafeteria.

She'd been pretty pissed at the dude yesterday morning, now that he thought about it.

What she'd said in class—it felt painfully personal. She wouldn't randomly spill that to a guy she hated. Definitely not to a guy whose presence she was just *enduring*.

A boy she liked?

Chris grabbed an apple by the register. He knew where she sat.

Maybe he'd sit down. Maybe they'd start over.

Money couldn't leave his hand fast enough, and he almost told the lady to keep the change. He practically shoved other kids out of the way, navigating the maze of people to get to the back of the cafeteria. Just like in a movie, the sea of students seemed to part for a moment.

There she was, spinning a bottle of water on the table in front of her. She was smiling, almost blushing like she'd been in class.

I was just getting used to Becky.

Chris grinned, and told himself he looked like an idiot.

He couldn't help it.

Then he got closer, and he realized her smile, her blush, wasn't about him at all.

It was for the guy sitting across from her. Hunter.

"So are the stories true?" asked Hunter.

Becca watched him slice into his grilled chicken. Quinn was taking a makeup exam, so they had the table to themselves. She still wasn't entirely sure about Hunter. Her mind was having a tough time reconciling his gentle patience with the way he'd gone after Chris in her driveway. It was like seeing a friendly old golden retriever turn vicious. All laid-back kindness, but make the wrong move and you learn those fangs aren't just for show.

Then again, Hunter had spent the night comforting her—and hadn't tried anything. He'd found her yesterday and apologized—then backed off to let her figure out where she stood.

That was a big part of the reason he was sitting here.

"Depends," Becca hedged. "What have you heard?"

"That you knocked two seniors on their asses on the soccer field, then flipped off the coach."

"Absolutely true," said Becca, deadpan. "I'm surprised you doubted a word."

Hunter leaned in, and his voice dropped. "Would you feel better if I told you the only thing I don't believe is the part about the coach?"

His tone was making heat crawl up her neck. She had to glance away. "Too bad. That's the only part that really happened."

He sat back, not convinced. "You'll tell me when you're ready."

"Don't get cocky. I might have to give you a firsthand demonstration."

Hunter laughed. "You're on. Friday night?"

She almost lost the smile. He'd sure turned that around. Was he asking her out? Or still teasing?

She had to hedge again. "You want to spend your weekend nursing a black eye?"

"Now who's cocky?" His eyebrows went up, but he was smiling. He dragged his fork through the rice on his plate. "Maybe we could save the ass-kicking for the end of the evening, though. Just to be safe."

"Just to be safe?" she mimicked. "What exactly are you planning?"

Some of his easy confidence slipped a bit. He glanced away before looking back to meet her eyes. "I was wondering if you'd like to go to Homecoming."

Her breath caught. She'd sure walked right into that one. Was Homecoming really this Friday? She'd never planned to go—even now she had no idea where she could come up with money for a dress. Maybe she could borrow Quinn's from last year.

If she said yes.

"No fighting with Chris," she said.

He grinned. "I thought you just said I'd be fighting with you."

"I'm not kidding."

He lost the smile. "I won't pick a fight with Chris. I promise."

She pointed her water bottle at him. "Or his brothers."

"You have my word."

"Then you're on," she said.

"For Homecoming or the ass kicking?"

She smiled. "Both."

Chapter 30

Becca's mom slid a bobby pin against Becca's head, securing another curl. "Would it be wrong," she whispered, "if I offered Quinn a cardigan?"

Becca rolled her eyes. "Mom."

"And maybe a pair of jeans?"

"*Mom.*" Becca glared at her in the bathroom mirror. She was sitting on the edge of the tub while her mother created a rather impressive updo. Quinn was painting her toenails in Becca's bedroom—right next door. "She'll *hear* you."

"That's what I'm hoping."

"It's not that short." But it was. Quinn's strapless baby-doll dress had multicolored rhinestones across the chest, giving everything a nice lift and leaving very—*very*—little to the imagination. The skirt flared beneath the bodice, a spray of tropical colors that made her look like a butterfly. The whole thing stopped about six inches above Quinn's knees.

Her mom slid another pin into place. "At least your dress is a little more elegant. I can't believe Quinn had this hanging in her closet and she bought that thing."

"Yeah, me either." Becca swallowed. Quinn only had this dress "hanging in her closet" because Becca had used her dad's emergency credit card to buy it—and she hadn't wanted her mom to know.

The dress was strapless, a pink chiffon gown with a corseted back, laced with a dark pink ribbon that bared a strip of skin down the center of her back. The skirt flared from her waist and fell just past her knees. She'd paired it with strappy silver heels to flash it up, but next to Quinn, she looked downright modest.

"I think that's it," her mom said. "What do you think?"

Becca stood and looked in the mirror. Her mom had pinned curls at the crown of her head, leaving tendrils to curl around her face and down her back. Quinn had done her makeup, all shimmering pinks and silvers, and the colors left her gray eyes bright and open. Innocent.

Looking at her own gray eyes made her think of Chris.

He'd been distant since Tuesday. Her father had painted over the pentagram again, and this time it had stayed gone. When she asked Chris about it, he'd looked at her hard and said, "So you don't need to worry about us anymore."

Becca wasn't sure how to take that. He ran so hot and cold. Showing up to offer her a ride to school—but making surly comments in her driveway. Defending her to Michael—then chasing her off their property. She couldn't figure him out.

So she'd shut up and focused on class.

She had no idea whether he'd be at the dance.

"Bex?" said her mom. "You all right?"

"Yeah." She shook herself. "It's beautiful, Mom. Thank you."

Quinn wolf whistled from the doorway. "I can guarantee you won't be wearing that all night."

"Quinn!" For god's sake, her mother was standing *right here*.

But her mom, at least, was used to Quinn's antics, and she just swept the remaining bobby pins into the box. "Come downstairs so I can take some pictures before I have to leave."

Her mom was working tonight, sparing Becca the awkward-ness of introducing Hunter—and forcing him to endure pictures and questions, while guaranteeing herself a bunch of crap to-morrow morning about his piercings.

They posed for the photos; then her mom was out the door, and it was just Becca and Quinn.

They sat on the couch, perched on the edge so they wouldn't wrinkle their dresses.

"I like that bracelet," said Quinn, reaching out a hand. "Very new age. Where'd you get it?"

Becca blushed. "Hunter. Sort of." She didn't think twine bracelets worked with the dress—but for some reason she couldn't make herself leave the stones sitting on her dresser, either. So she'd strung them on an old silver chain and looped it around her wrist a few times.

"He really likes you."

She stroked her fingers over those stones. "I really like him."

"But you're thinking about Chris Merrick?"

Becca stared at her.

Quinn shrugged a little. "I'm not an idiot, Bex. You wouldn't have dragged me across the field to apologize if you didn't have a thing for him."

"I do not have a *thing* for him."

"Please. There's some serious pining going on here."

Becca giggled. "I am not *pining*." Was she?

"Maybe we should do a side-by-side comparison," said Quinn. "Like one of those charts. Best ass. Nicest hands. Sexiest eyes. Oh, I know! Biggest—"

Becca hit her with a throw pillow.

Then the doorbell rang, and Rafe was standing in the foyer, his Hispanic coloring and dark suit making him look suave and debonair.

"Wow," he said, sounding a bit strangled as he took in Quinn's appearance. He pulled at his tie. "Your dress is—you look—"

"How about my face?" said Quinn, smacking him under the chin. "How's that look?"

He grinned and made a show of ogling her chest. "If you wanted an answer to that, you shouldn't have worn this dress."

If a boy had said it to her, Becca would have grabbed a sweater. Quinn just laughed. "Come on, Romeo, before Bex has to mop up your drool."

Quinn kissed her on the cheek and was out the door.

Becca smoothed her skirt and sat on the edge of the couch again. She kept thinking of Chris's comment in class. He'd hardly said a word since Wednesday, since she'd apologized. And told him that pentagram was gone.

So you don't need to worry about us anymore.

Light arced across the living room wall as a car pulled into the driveway. Hunter.

Becca tried to keep herself on the couch, but her heart leapt and shoved her toward the door. She flung the door open before he'd even made it up the steps.

God, he looked hot. If she was being honest with herself, she'd been a tiny bit afraid that he'd show up wearing one of those stupid tees with a shirt and tie printed on it. But he was wearing a black suit with a charcoal shirt left open at the neck, and no tie. It fit him well.

Really well.

Becca almost felt like she should go back in and change. He looked sleek and sexy and dangerous. She felt like she should be heading out to teach Sunday school.

He looked up in surprise; then his face broke into a smile. He came the rest of the way to the top of the stairs. "I hope you're not in that much of a rush to kick my ass."

She brought her hands up and balled them into fists. "Too bad," she teased, willing her heart to slow. "We're starting with violence."

"Yeah?" His expression shifted, his eyes bright and challenging. "Bring it."

So she swung at him.

He brought a hand up to deflect her hit, which she expected. But he used her momentum to trap her wrist and pin her arm behind her back.

None of it hurt. And it put her chest right up against his, his face right above hers.

The chiffon was thin. She felt the line of his body matching her own. He had to be able to feel her heartbeat.

He smiled. "Now what are you going to do?"

"Gouge your eyes out with my keys."

Hunter laughed. "I should have trapped both hands. I didn't realize you'd be such a lethal date."

"The night's still young."

"The pretty ones are always the most dangerous." He reached up with his free hand and brushed a tendril of hair off her forehead. "And you look very, very pretty."

That made her blush. He still hadn't let her go, and she found her body relaxing into his. She rested her free hand on his shoulder. "This is nothing. Wait 'til you see Quinn."

"So you'll let me keep my eyes a little while?"

"Maybe." She hoped she didn't sound too breathless. "If you promise to be good."

"I'll try." And he kissed her.

His mouth was soft, gentle. An innocent kiss. But the pretend fighting, the banter, the heat of his body—it lit her up like a live wire. Her lips parted and her hand tightened on his shoulder, sliding to his neck, pulling him closer.

But he broke away, turning her loose, holding nothing but her hand.

He tapped a finger on her lips. "You can't make me promise to be good, then do that. We'll never get to the dance."

She almost didn't care. She actually almost *said* that, but then her brain kicked into gear.

Hunter must have gotten the gist anyway, because he chuckled and kissed her palm. "Come on, beautiful."

Then he turned to move down the steps, and, attached to his hand, she followed right behind him.

Every year, the school tried really hard. But no matter what they did to it, the gym still looked like a gym, just with the halogen lights turned off and red and blue streamers everywhere. The acoustics sucked for a band, but the deejay seemed to have a handle on the sound system, because Becca could actually distinguish lyrics from the throbbing bass line.

Becca spotted Quinn right off, her friend's dance skills on full display. She and Rafe had carved out a space near the center of the dance floor, and the jewels on her dress caught the light and flared with color.

Becca leaned into Hunter and said, "See what I mean?"

"I don't know what you're talking about," he said. "That's totally subtle."

Rafe took Quinn's hand and spun her, and the dress flared, generating plenty of catcalls and a few insults.

"She's crazy," said Becca.

"She's just having fun. Come on." Hunter pulled her into the crowd of people.

Neither her dress nor her dance skills were enough to buy Becca the kind of room Quinn enjoyed. Kids pressed in around them, nameless faces she barely recognized under the strobe lights. Hunter didn't seem to mind, keeping her close for fast songs—and closer for slow ones. She had no idea if he was a good dancer. She just liked the feel of his body against hers.

Like that live wire feeling on the porch, she felt electric tonight, charged by the music or the energy or the emotion in the air. It reminded her of that moment when Nick sent wind whipping across her driveway, like something tangible flickering just out of her reach. All she had to do was grab hold.

"What's with you tonight?" said Quinn when they had a moment alone. The boys had gone to fetch sodas, and she and Quinn were giggling and swaying to some eighties hit by the side of the crowd.

"I don't know," said Becca. "What?"

"You're, like, glowing or something—wait. I know." Quinn reached out and took her chin, tilting her face up and down, then sideways, as if looking for something. "You're happy. I didn't recognize it."

Becca knocked her hand away. "You're crazy."

"Pine all you want for Chris, but New Kid actually put a smile on your face."

"Damn it, Quinn, I'm not *pining* for—"

"Oh. Okay. So it won't bother you if I tell you he's over there with Monica Lawrence?" Quinn pointed.

Becca whipped her head around before realizing it probably

wasn't a good idea. Quinn was right. There stood Chris by the edge of the indoor bleachers, his face half in shadow. He had a drink in one hand, and Monica had her entire body up against his.

He didn't exactly look like he was fighting her off.

"Is it me, or is she humping his leg?" said Quinn.

"Shut up," Becca muttered. Then Hunter was back, holding out a cup of soda. She drank the whole thing in almost one swallow.

Hunter watched this feat with a bemused expression on his face. "You know that's just Diet Coke, right?"

"Maybe I'm just warming up," she said.

And then she kissed him.

She caught him by surprise—but that didn't last long. His lips parted for hers, and her fingers tangled in his hair, holding him close. Hands caught her waist, strong and sure through the thin chiffon.

She could swear she saw starbursts, like that night on the bridge. Wind in her hair, fire on her lips, the ground beneath her feet, parquet over concrete stretching into the earth below. And water—water everywhere. The first flare of sweat on her skin, the taste of Hunter on her lips, the ice in the cup hanging from her fingers.

Ice. She felt that same cord of power she had felt with Nick's wind in the driveway.

Chris.

She jerked back from Hunter.

His breathing sounded a bit quick, his cheeks flushed. The entire front of her body felt warm.

Just how closely had she been pressed up against him?

"So, Bex," said Quinn, her voice kind of strangled, "most people wait until they're in a room—or at least in the *dark*—"

"I'm sorry," said Hunter. His eyes were wide.

He was sorry? She'd practically mauled him in front of the whole gym. At least most of the people around them seemed to be following their cue. Not that she wanted to watch half her classmates make out, but it was better than them watching *her*.

She remembered that connection she'd felt, the ice in her cup. Had Chris done something? Had his brothers?

Becca looked for him in that darkened corner. Would he be making out with Monica, striking her back for the little show she'd just put on with Hunter?

No, but Chris *was* leaning close, brushing hair away from Monica's ear to whisper something—then looking very deliberately in Becca's direction.

Monica giggled and clung to him. They walked away from the bleachers and disappeared into the crowd.

Becca swallowed.

This was stupid. She wasn't some wallflower to be mocked—she was here with Hunter.

Hunter, who was stroking a thumb across her cheek now, leaning in to brush his lips across hers very gently. "Don't do that again," he murmured, and she heard a smile in his voice.

"Why?" she whispered back, feeling her heart leaping around her chest. "Don't tell me you're scared of kissing me now."

He hesitated, then laughed against her lips. "Your kisses just might be addictive." Then he caught her hand and spun her into the music.

She wondered if someone *had* spiked the soda. Her body felt weightless yet strong. She kept up with Quinn, dancing with her friend when the boys ran out of stamina.

"Becca."

The voice spoke from over her shoulder, perfectly timed for that break between songs. She couldn't tell whether it was Hunter or Rafe since the crowd was so loud, but she was glad of the distraction. Her perfectly curled tendrils had dampened with sweat, and hair clung to her neck in places. She could use a soda.

So she turned, ready for just about anyone.

Except Drew McKay.

Drew's face was still bruised from the beating Gabriel had given him, a dark wash of shadow across one cheek and around one eye. He'd paid good money for that suit, but it seemed to hang from his frame awkwardly, as if he'd lost some weight or some muscle or just couldn't be bothered to button it right. He looked pathetic.

"Gee," she said loudly, over the music of the new song. "That black eye looks really painful."

He fidgeted for a second. "Becca, I need to talk to you."

"You need to leave her alone." Hunter must have come up behind her, and now she felt his hand on her shoulder.

She hadn't told him about Drew, but the rumor mill must have carried the story full circle. She was tempted to let Hunter chase him off. It would be easy.

But she'd already done this the "easy" way. And Hunter wasn't her keeper—he wasn't even her boyfriend yet. She suspected that the new attitude she was getting around school had more to do with Gabriel Merrick's reputation than her own. If she kept letting guys defend her, she'd never find the type of respect she desperately needed.

For her own good.

So she turned and looked up at Hunter. "I can handle this."

He stared back at her. She could tell he was remembering the altercation in her driveway, their discussion at lunch.

Then his eyes flicked to Drew, and she read the dislike there. Hunter dropped his hand. "All right."

"Besides," said Becca, turning back to Drew, "I'm not going to listen long unless he's going to start spouting an apology—"

"I am."

He didn't even look at her for those two words, and they sounded like they'd been choked out of him.

"Let's hear it," she called over the music.

Now he looked up, and she caught a hint of his familiar scowl. "Can we go outside or somewhere I don't have to yell? I don't really want to announce this to the whole school."

"Too bad," snapped Quinn. "I think we should do a public castration right here—"

"Quinn." Becca sighed.

"Hey," called a guy in the crowd, some senior that Becca didn't know. "Look. It's McRapist." Then he punched Drew in the shoulder, hard.

"Yeah," said another guy. "I liked the hottie's idea of a little public payback." Then he shoved Drew.

And suddenly more students were crowding them, full of cat-calls and anger.

Drew set his jaw and glared, but Becca saw him flinch.

And something about that spoke to her. She knew exactly what it felt like.

"Come on," she said to him. "You have five minutes." Then she looked back over her shoulder at Hunter, who already stood poised to follow. "Stay."

The night air had chilled a few degrees, full of dampness that promised rainfall wasn't far off. Dozens of kids were on the quad, so despite the darkness, she didn't feel alone with him. Still, Becca shivered and wished for a sweater.

Drew's hands were shoved into his pockets. He was walking along the face of the building, and she kept pace with him, glad to be moving.

He didn't look at her. "You know half the school thinks I'm a rapist."

"Huh," she said. "What's that like? For half the school to think something about you that isn't true?"

"Don't be like that, Becca."

Unbelievable. What an asshole. "This is one hell of an apology, Drew."

"Just what are you telling people?"

She rounded on him. "I'm not telling anyone *anything*," she snapped. "I'm not *like* you. I don't spread lies about people."

"Yeah, poor baby. You know what you did. And now you're walking around, acting like I didn't do *exactly* what you wanted."

That stung, like he'd struck her.

He started walking again, toward the dark corner by the edge of the building.

She paused before following him. There were still kids out here, a few standing under the trees smoking.

"Why'd you do it?" she demanded. "Do you know the last six weeks have been *hell* for me, Drew? Do you know people think I slept with half the school—"

"Maybe you did, Becca. Who knows?"

"I do." She pointed to her chest, feeling her eyes burn. "*I* know."

He glanced off into the darkness. "Whatever. Like it matters."

"It matters to *me*." Her voice broke. There had to be a reason why he'd done it. Had to be. Would he have spread such vicious lies for nothing more than a stupid whim? That was almost more crushing than everything else.

She swiped at her eyes and forced her voice to be strong. "It matters to me, Drew."

He didn't say anything. She heard the distant thrum of music from inside the gym, occasional bursts of sound as students came and went. Wind looped between the buildings to lift her hair and cool her neck.

Just when she was going to give up and go in, Drew spoke.

"I thought you were going to press charges."

It took a minute for this to sink in. Then she wanted to explode with fury. "But I didn't! I didn't want *anyone* to know! And then school started on Monday, and *everyone—everyone* knew. They knew about you and me, and all your friends. But they thought we'd—they thought—" She shoved him in the chest. "Why would you *do* that? Why, Drew?"

"Don't be stupid, Becca. I have a scholarship to Virginia Tech." His voice was cruel, his eyes hard in the night. "I wasn't going to let some silly girl who couldn't hold her liquor fuck that up."

Then she got it.

He'd thought she was going to report him. So he'd made her look like a tramp and got his friends to back it up. So if she ever tried to go to the cops, no one would believe her. He was Drew McKay, captain of the soccer team. Who was she?

Just Becca.

And all for some stupid scholarship.

"Now everyone thinks I raped you," he said, his voice vicious. "Coach kept me on the bench for the game. It's my senior year. Vickers is on my case. People are calling the house, leaving messages. Someone spray painted my *car*, Becca—"

"Sounds rough." She started to turn.

"Well, I've made a decision." He grabbed her arm.

She glared up at him, feeling his fingers pressing into the muscle. Other students remained nearby, and she made her voice strong and clear. "Let me go, Drew."

It worked. One of those figures by the tree straightened and headed their way. A cigarette flared red in an arc to the ground, where it died under a shoe. "Hey."

Drew's hand tightened on her bicep. "I think it's time to level the playing field."

"Let me go," she said again. "Right now."

Another student moved toward them.

Drew dragged her close, and for the first time, she felt fear slide around her chest and jerk tight.

"Isn't there some stupid saying?" he said. "Something like, 'If I'm going to do the time—' "

"Shut up!" She swung her free hand, driving her fingers at Drew's throat the way Hunter had shown her. She felt the swing all the way up her arm, strength and power conspiring to put him down.

But arms wrapped around her from behind, a hand sliding over her mouth, beefy hands trapping her arms. Someone large, strong. Way bigger than she was.

"Hey, Becca." Hot breath on her ear. She knew that voice.

Tommy Dunleavy.

She couldn't see the others yet, but now she knew. Those weren't just other students at the trees. Those were Drew's *friends*.

She screamed—or she tried to. That hand clamped down on her mouth, preventing any sound from getting out. She struggled, but he was too strong. They wrestled her around the corner of the building, where it was truly dark. The music from the dance was too loud. Even if she screamed here, no one would hear her.

Drew stroked a hand down her side, the feel of his hand hard through the thin material of the dress. She squealed and squirmed away from him.

"Yeah," he said. "If I'm going to do the time, I'm sure as hell going to enjoy the crime."

And then he grabbed hold of the front of her dress. And began to tear it free.

CHAPTER 31

Chris drained the soda from his cup and swirled the ice around the bottom. Monica was yammering about something to do with her nails or her dress or her friends, but he had a pretty low tolerance for stupidity, so he'd tuned her out fifteen minutes ago. The only reason she was hanging off his arm was because her dickhead boyfriend had stepped out for a smoke. Did she think Chris was so clueless he wouldn't *know* that?

He was only putting up with it because Monica made for a good cover.

Becca had seen him. She'd seen him and then she'd kissed Hunter.

Crystal clear.

He had enough to worry about. He shouldn't be watching Becca. He shouldn't give a crap.

He just couldn't help himself. He'd watched the little drama unfold with Drew.

Stalker, he'd told himself, but it didn't matter, because Becca had Hunter. He'd stop her from going with Drew. Or follow. He'd keep her safe.

Chris had waited, but no one followed. Becca had walked out of the gym with Drew while Hunter stood with Quinn and stared at the door.

What a jackass. When it was obvious Hunter wasn't going to do anything, Chris slammed his cup on the table and moved to follow.

Monica giggled and hung onto him. "Wait—you wanna go watch or something?"

God, it was like she didn't have an off switch. He wished there were some way to take out her batteries.

Then he realized what she'd said.

He stopped and looked down at her. "Watch what?"

She staggered a little and dug her nails into his jacket. She'd been drinking—a lot. "Ohmigod, I told Tommy we should get a video. Chandler thinks she's the shit all of a sudden, but everybody knows the truth about her—"

Chris shoved her away from him, making her sit down hard on the bleacher seat. "What are they doing, Monica?"

She giggled again. "It was Drew's idea, but it's gonna be *epic*—"

He grabbed her arm. "What are they *doing*?"

She hiccupped and looked at his hand. "Ow, Chris . . ."

God, what did it matter? They could be hurting her *right now*.

What if they'd gotten her into a car?

He turned on his heel and made for the door. What would Drew have said to get her outside? Why would she *trust* that asshole?

Then again, Becca had a core of kindness—no, of *empathy*—behind all those walls and defenses. Chris was living proof of that.

If that guy hurt her—if he *touched* her—Chris would kill him.

He felt the humidity in the air, even here in the gym. It wasn't anywhere near as good as rain or mist, but it was enough to let power flicker beneath his skin.

He and his brothers were already marked for death. What was the worst that could happen?

He wished he could spot the twins. They were out in the

crowd somewhere—the humidity told him that much. But it wasn't enough to send power through the room, to throw up a flag of warning.

He couldn't waste time looking. There were at least five hundred kids in the gym.

A hand closed on his arm. "I told you to leave her alone."

Hunter. They were closer to the door; Chris could feel a storm brewing outside. "Yeah, alone isn't what she needs right now."

"I think Becca can take care of herself."

"I bet she'll thank you for that." All he needed was someone to open the door. Just one little surge of water in the air. Maybe it was even starting to rain. He gave Hunter a little shove. "Get your goddamn hands off me."

Hunter held fast. Bastard was strong. "Or what?"

The door opened and some laughing girls poured through. It wasn't raining, but misting. Chris could see it. Better, he could *feel* it. He rallied the moisture in the air, calling it to him, training it on Hunter. Maybe it was his fury, maybe it was the tension of the last few weeks, but this power felt good. Strong. Focused. Like millions of tiny ice daggers, too small to see.

With this much clarity, Chris was almost afraid to turn it loose.

Something like shock flickered in Hunter's expression. "Water," he said.

Chris almost lost control right there. For all the moisture in the room, he suddenly had to wet his lips to speak. "What?"

Hunter was staring at him, his eyes too wide, his breathing too quick. "You're Water. But then—there's not only one." He didn't look frightened—he looked stunned. Like life had just yanked the rug out from under him.

Chris understood the feeling. "What the hell are you *talking about?*"

"Chris." Nick came up beside him—of course, he'd probably felt the power in the air. "What's going on?"

Hunter glanced up at him, and Chris watched something settle in the other boy's face. Not anger. More like . . . resolve.

"Now I get it," said Hunter. He let go of Chris's arm and made to move away.

"Wait a minute." Chris grabbed *him*.

And *wham*. All that power hit Chris right in the face, and knocked him back. It was like taking a snowball to the face. A frozen one. Backed by a baseball bat.

He shook his head to clear it, feeling like his brain was rattling around inside his skull. He wiped at his eyes and his fingers came away with ice crystals. He could barely feel his face.

But he could see. Hunter was gone.

Nick swore. "What the hell *was* that? Did you lose control—"

"No," said Chris. His thoughts felt pulled in too many directions. "He did that. He knows, Nick. What we are. He knows. He's one of us."

"We'll find him. I'll get Gabriel. You go—"

"No, you go." Chris staggered toward the door. He wished his head would settle. He probably looked drunk. "I need to find Becca."

Finally getting outside helped immensely. The mist could feel his fury and danced on his skin, begging for a target. He pulled as much power as he could from his element. If Hunter was out here, Chris would be ready this time.

He asked the rain for answers. Water didn't understand things like fear and intimidation.

Danger, he thought. *Find me danger.*

At first, nothing. The water agreed with his quest, but offered no direction. Then rain began to fall, solid drops.

This way.

Chris headed east, following the front of the building.

He couldn't let go of what had happened with Hunter. He knew. And he was *strong*—strong enough to turn Chris's power against him. Another water Elemental? Chris had never met one, but he'd always thought he'd recognize someone who shared his abilities. This felt subtly . . . different.

The Guide?

Chris almost stopped short and ran back to his brothers.

But Hunter had metaphysically punched him in the face and

run. The Guide had caused a multi-car pileup and taken out the bridge, then tried to kill them with lightning. The two didn't seem to match. And Hunter seemed like such a goody-goody; Chris couldn't see him putting other people in danger.

Jesus Christ, and where was Becca? He'd almost reached the playing fields, acres of grass and darkness. No lights penetrated this far beyond the school. If he wasn't careful, he'd be getting a face full of steel bleacher supports.

Lightning flashed somewhere in the distance, followed by the low roll of thunder. Chris walked to the middle of the first field and turned in a full circle. There was the school, the gym, the dark baseball fields to the west, the parking lot that you could probably see from space.

Rain hit his cheeks, every drop a message. *Danger. Danger. Danger.*

"I get it!" he said. *"Where?"*

And then he heard the scream.

Becca couldn't see anything. She had no idea how far they'd dragged her from the school; it felt like it took an hour but had probably been fewer than three minutes. She fought the way Hunter had showed her, all elbows and knees, aiming for weak points. But there were too many of them.

At least it felt like there were. It was too dark to count. All she knew was there were enough boys to carry her and keep her arms pinned.

They weren't so lucky with her legs. She finally got one of them in the crotch with her knee.

It seemed like a good idea. But then they dropped her.

Her back slammed into the ground and she forgot how to breathe for a moment. Grass poked through the material of her dress. *Wet* grass, damp from the slow drizzle of rain that was now collecting in her hair and sealing the chiffon to her body. Drew had started to tear at it, but his hands were clumsy and she'd gotten in a good yell during her struggles.

Now she was praying the corseted back would hold everything together.

She started to roll, choking on nothing, grabbing fistfuls of grass as if she could somehow drag herself away from them.

They shoved her onto her back. Pinned her wrists. She didn't even recognize all their voices.

Light. God, she'd give anything for some light. The darkness trapped her as effectively as their hands.

Lightning flashed, a flare of light in the distance that revealed nothing.

The last time, she'd been drunk. She'd gone along far too long, until she didn't know what she initiated and what they intended. The last time, she'd *wanted* to be there. They might have taken it too far—way too far—but she'd started it.

She'd put up with all the crap at school because she hadn't been able to figure out just how much was their fault—and how much was her own.

Now she knew. Now she wanted them to pay. To suffer.

Now she wanted to press charges, even if they stopped, got their hands off her legs, her arms, got their hands out of the top of her dress.

Would anyone believe her?

She bit the hand over her mouth. The guy swore and jerked his hand away.

She couldn't think too hard about where other hands were. She'd lose it, turn into a puddle right here in the grass.

"Touch me again," she snapped, baring her teeth at him, "and I'll bite your fingers off."

They laughed. The bastards. *They laughed*.

"I'll press charges," she swore. "You'll all go to prison. You know what they do to rapists in prison—"

"God, *shut her up*."

Seth Ramsey. She heard liquid slosh, the grunt of a guy taking a draw from a bottle.

"I'll tell everyone." Her voice sounded like a rush of air through her teeth. "They already think you did it—"

A body slid on top of hers, hot and heavy. Drew's wool pants scratched her bare legs. His hips squared over hers, and she regretted the chiffon. She could feel everything. *Everything*.

She couldn't breathe.

This was going to happen.

This was going to happen.

This was going to happen.

The clouds spun in the sky. Raindrops hit her cheeks and felt warm.

She saw stars. Grass dug through her hair to poke at her scalp.

"Hey, Becca." Drew's voice. She could smell the liquor on his breath. "Don't you want to be conscious for this?"

Then he shifted, rubbing himself against her.

Even with clothes on, the feeling of violation was raw. She tried to curl in on herself, but there was nowhere to go.

He dropped his weight on her, his hand finding her knee and beginning a path up her leg. His hands were so hot. Rough on the sensitive skin of her thigh. She jerked away from him, but it put him more intimately against her.

She fought. She cried. She couldn't help it.

He spat in her face. "God, you're such a fucking tease. You know you want it."

Some of his saliva got in her mouth. She coughed and spit, not wanting anything of his inside her. She thought she might vomit.

Maybe she'd choke and die.

"No, no, baby." His face must have been close. She couldn't see anything but the faint glitter in his eyes.

She clenched her own shut.

"You'll take anything I give you," he said.

Then he kissed her.

At first she choked on his tongue. Revulsion had her twisting her face, trying to escape the pressure of his mouth, but he caught her chin and held her there.

She wanted him to die.

She bit down. Blood filled her mouth.

He jerked back and screamed. Loudly.

More than her bite seemed to warrant.

Then he was rolling off her, and he seemed to be clutching at his chest. His screams were cut off, as if someone had pinched his lungs closed at the top.

"Help," he gasped.

The other guys weren't moving, but she could feel their confusion. Two still had her hands pinned, but others were standing.

"Dude," said one. Seth. He shifted from foot to foot. "Dude, you okay?"

Drew was writhing on the ground, hands clutched to his chest or his throat. She couldn't quite tell. It sounded like he said, "Someone help me," but his words were barely intelligible.

"He's having a heart attack," she said.

She had no idea whether that was true. She couldn't even make herself care if he died.

But she needed to get free.

It worked. They let her go to help their friend. She dug her toes into the wet ground and made to run.

Seth caught her arm and spun her around. "How do we know this isn't a trick?"

What an idiot. A trick? That Drew was in on?

She didn't ask him. She just used that spinning momentum to drive her elbow into his face.

Something cracked. She felt wetness on her arm. And he was yelling, just as loud as Drew.

Then he was on the ground, yelling, clutching his chest.

What the hell was going on? The rain started to pour, hard and driving and soaking her dress.

And freezing. Her teeth started to chatter.

"What the fuck did you do to them?" one of the guys was screaming at her. He grabbed her before she could see him coming, trapping her arms. "What did you—"

A fist came out of nowhere and punched him in the face. Her arms were free. She couldn't make out her savior, but two guys were grappling off to her left. Drew and Seth were still writhing on the ground.

The rain turned to sleet—unheard of in September. Each drop stung, a wallop of power against her skin.

Chris. Chris had come after her. She almost started to sob.

But this wasn't over yet. She wasn't close to safe. They were still outnumbered; Chris just had the element of surprise working for him.

She could help with that. "Get out of here!" she yelled. "I'm calling the cops! Get the hell out of here!"

Someone threw a punch, and she saw a shadow fall. She flinched, worried for Chris.

Then she heard his voice, low and lethal. "Get out of here before I kill you."

They did. Two ran off through the grass. Three dragged the other two, swearing while they went.

And then she was alone with Chris. For an instant, all she could hear was the freezing rain and the rush of her shaking breath.

"Becca." Chris moved closer, but he stopped a few feet in front of her. She heard the whisper of fabric as he shrugged out of his jacket. "Becca. Are you hurt?"

She shook her head, then realized he probably couldn't see it. "N-no."

He stepped close enough to swing his jacket around her shoulders, then stepped back. The lining was still warm from his body. She clutched at the material, pulling it close.

"Put your arms through the sleeves," he said, his voice low. "You'll be warmer."

She nodded and threaded her arms through the holes. The sleeves were long, leaving her hands covered. She felt like a little girl wearing Daddy's clothes.

The thought was so incongruous with what she'd just gone through she started crying.

"Becca." She heard the anguish in Chris's voice. He'd stepped closer, but he didn't touch her. "Becca, I'm so sorry."

She flung her arms around his neck, then pressed her face into his shoulder. It was probably wholly inappropriate, but she couldn't stand here and carry all this weight by herself.

He stiffened, and for a fraction of a second, she thought he might reject her.

But then his arms came around her back, and his head dropped until she could feel his breath against her hair.

She held him tight, so tight, but he didn't pull away.

CHAPTER 32

Chris stood in the rain and held her until she stopped shaking. Even then, she didn't let go, so he didn't, either.

Probably a good thing, since Drew and his friends wouldn't have made it back to the school if he'd been able to go after them.

"Did you make the rain warm?" she asked, her voice thick.

"Yeah." But he couldn't make the air warm, so he probably wasn't helping much.

A moment passed. "Thank you."

He nodded.

She drew back and looked up at him. "No—I mean *thank you*. For—for—"

"It's all right," he said. "Shh, Becca. It's all right."

Lightning flashed. Thunder growled in the sky, closer now.

It sounded like a warning. He was alone in this field, a sitting duck at a time he should be with his brothers. The rain was still singing along his skin, looking for adventure.

Danger, danger, danger.

Becca pressed her face against his shoulder again, and he knew he wasn't going anywhere.

"You keep saving me," she said.

"Yeah, well." He stroked the hair down her back. "I think we might be close to breaking even on that."

She laughed, just a little.

A siren sliced the night air, not too distant. Becca sobered. "What do you think happened to them?"

Chris had heard Drew's scream, had seen him writhing on the ground, clutching at his chest. Seth hadn't looked much better. Drugs? Too much beer? The cold? Chris had no idea, but maybe someone with some medical training had called an ambulance.

He hoped the medics took their time.

"Who cares?" he said. He should have kicked that stupid prick in the head while he was lying there. "We should walk back so we can tell someone—"

"No." Her fingers clutched at his shirt.

"Becca." He breathed her name against her hair. "Becca, we have to."

"Drew didn't rape me."

Chris touched her face. He didn't think there'd been time—but if he'd showed up five minutes later, she might be telling a completely different story. "Just because he stopped doesn't mean we shouldn't—"

"No, Chris. Before." Now she wasn't looking at him. She swiped rain from her cheeks and took a deep shuddering breath. "He never raped me."

Her voice sounded fragile, so he waited, letting the rain fall.

"I liked him," she said. "Really liked him. He did that stupid pre-season soccer camp in August—you know the one for the varsity players?"

Chris nodded. The only reason Gabriel hadn't done it was because summer was Michael's busiest time with the landscaping company—and they needed all the help they could get.

"I watched the whole thing," she said. Her voice sounded close to breaking. "I *hate* soccer, and I watched every practice, every stupid scrimmage, hanging around Drew like some vapid groupie. Right before school started, they had this party, and when he asked me, of course I went." She started to draw away, and Chris let her go.

She pushed wet hair off her face and looked up at him. "Pathetic, right?"

He shook his head. "You're not pathetic."

"Yeah. Well." She swiped at her eyes again. "I was. They were drinking, so I started drinking. I'm such an idiot—do you know I felt *special* that I was the only girl there? And when Drew started kissing me, I thought I was so, *so* lucky. I never wanted it to end."

The rain started to change, responding to Chris's temper.

Becca shivered and hunched down in his jacket. "So then he told me to kiss Tommy. He said it would be *hot*. And you know what, Chris? I *did it*. I did it because I liked Drew, and I wanted him to like me. Tommy stuck his hand up my shirt and I *let him do it*. And then Drew was unbuttoning my pants, and I kept *letting him*—" Her voice broke, and she started crying again, her hands clutched to her stomach.

Chris moved forward, to hold her, to stop her, to save her.

She jerked back from him. "Don't you see? I kept letting them do it, and when I wanted them to stop, it was just too late. They were all touching me, and I just couldn't make them stop, but I'd started—"

"Jesus, Becca." Chris grabbed her shoulders. "It was *not your fault*. Do you understand me? This was not. Your. Fault."

She wasn't even looking at him. "I don't even think they knew I was fighting them. There were just so many. I think I was hyperventilating. But Drew put his hands down my pants, and I threw up when he—when he touched me." She gave a choked sob. "I guess that killed the mood because they threw me out of the party."

Chris would kill them. The rain was turning to sleet again.

"It wasn't your fault," he said, pulling her forward. He put his hands on her face, making her look at him. "Becca, it wasn't your fault."

"I didn't tell anyone," she said. "Even Quinn doesn't know all of it. I just—school was starting, and I wanted to pretend it never happened. But then he told everyone—everyone—"

"I know," he whispered. "Becca."

She dropped her head against his shoulder. "I'm so stupid, Chris."

"You're not stupid. Look at me." When she didn't, he pushed her back so he could look at her. The darkness kept most of her face in shadow, but he could feel every drop of water on her skin. "Look at me."

"I am looking at you," she whispered.

He put his hands on her face, his thumbs tracing the contours of her cheekbones, feeling raindrops thrill under the weight of his palms. "You're the bravest girl I've ever met," he said. "I've thought that since the night you helped me."

"Brave," she scoffed, though there was a sob mixed in there. "I'm hiding in a *field*—"

"You're brave. I'm living proof. And you're smart. That day you showed up in our driveway? Michael handed you that clipboard to *screw with you*. He knew you had no idea what that stuff was. But you picked it up and ran with it. Do you know I heard him mock Nick about it?" He dropped his voice to a gruff imitation of his oldest brother. " 'Girl off the street loaded the truck in half the time you take.' "

Her mouth twitched. A smile? She started to push his hands away. "Chris—"

"And you're strong. Or did someone else break that guy's nose tonight?"

She went still. "I broke his nose?"

Chris really had no idea. But she was listening, so he went with it. "It should have been his neck."

Her voice got dark. "It should have been Drew's neck."

Chris smiled. There was his girl. "You're kind," he said. "You took those notes for me even though I'd been a total prick."

She made a face. He felt it. "You probably didn't even read them—"

"I read them. Every word." Okay, he *might* have skimmed some of it. It was World History, after all.

But now she was in the present, with him, not trapped in some horrible memory. He had her attention. He loved the feel of her face between his hands, could stand here with her in the rain all night.

"You're beautiful," he said softly. "Innocent."

The word made her flinch. "I'm not—"

"Yes," he said, feeling anger leak into his voice. "You are. Just because a few idiots treat you like . . . like *that*—doesn't mean you have any idea what it's *supposed* to be like."

She went still again.

He moved closer, bringing his face down to hers so he could speak low, through the rain. "You're not stupid, Becca. Not at all." He paused. "I am."

"Why?"

He felt her breath on his face when she spoke. Pure torture.

"Because," he said. "I can't stop thinking about you. I fell for you the night you drove me home. I just didn't do anything about it. And then you started dating some stupid tool who couldn't figure out that letting you go with Drew was a bad idea."

She stood frozen, her eyes barely gleaming in the shadowed field. "Chris—"

"It's okay," he said. It was better this way. He and his brothers probably weren't going to last the week. "I just wanted you to know that you're better than what you think you are. Don't let Drew define you, Becca."

Thunder cracked, wind streaking across the field. She jumped, and he caught her.

"Just a storm," he said, glad for the distraction. He didn't want to hear some gentle letdown—and that wasn't what his little speech had been about anyway.

The raindrops fell heavier. He'd been gone forever. His brothers were going to be flipping out. "We should walk back."

Silence hung between them for a moment. Then she nodded. "All right."

But when he turned to walk, she caught his hand and held it.

"If I tell the cops," she said, "will you go with me?"

"Yeah." Thunder cracked again, and her grip tightened. He glanced down at her. "You'll be all right, Becca."

She nodded.

The rain began to fall harder, heavy drops that rolled down

his cheeks. He was so focused on Becca that it took him a minute to realize each drop felt thick with power.

And it wasn't *his* power.

Lightning struck near the edge of the field, still a good distance off, but lightning on its own looked for something to strike. Lightning hitting the ground meant someone was giving it direction.

Chris straightened, thinking of Hunter's trick in the gym. He stared out into the darkness, willing the shadows to reveal more than just an absence of light. He hadn't wanted to hurry Becca, but now he did. He tugged at her hand. "Speaking of our local narc, just what do you know about him?"

"Hunter?" Her head lifted. She must have heard the note of danger in his voice. "Why? What happened?"

He opened his mouth to respond—but lightning struck the ground ten feet in front of them. Chris had never seen Gabriel call lightning of this force, a solid pillar of electricity bolting into the ground.

Becca had practically attached herself to his arm. Chris spun, looking for an attacker, dragging her with him.

He saw nothing.

Lightning hit closer, about eight feet to their left.

He swore, yanking her with him as he backpedaled across the field.

"Do something!" she cried. "Can't you build a wall of ice, or—"

"Are you kidding?" he said. "I'm not an X-Man! This is—"

Crack. Lightning bolt, right where they'd been standing. Becca screamed.

He needed Nick, so they could move the storm. Or Gabriel, to harness some of this lightning. The rain refused to listen to him, and by himself, he was at his weakest. Hell, he'd probably helped this guy by warming the rain, changing the air temperature enough to bring the storm this way.

He was going to die—and he'd be taking Becca down with him.

"Run," he said, trying to pry her hands off his arm. "Run for the school."

"Are you crazy—"

"Becca, run! He wants me, not you." He pulled his cell phone out of his pocket and thrust it into her hand. "Text Gabriel when you get to the school—tell him what's—"

Thunder cut him off. Lightning struck. She ran. Chris watched her streak across the field until the darkness swallowed her up.

And here he was, standing in the middle of an acre of grass.

He couldn't run to the school—this guy had already proven he wasn't afraid to take out innocent bystanders. Chris didn't want to think what would happen if a lightning strike of this magnitude hit the gym.

Then he realized he wasn't thinking in the right direction. Curtis Creek ran along the back of the school property, a forty-foot-wide stretch of water that wasn't much of a creek at all but more of a river.

He'd be safe in the water. If he could get to it.

Chris ran.

Ten seconds told him this was a bad idea. The grass grabbed his feet, tried to slow him down.

He begged the rain for strength, for power. Every step was a struggle.

Not to mention the lightning piercing the earth. He dodged hard, losing his footing more than once.

Was this field a mile long? God, he felt like he wore a target on his back.

The grass underfoot changed, becoming thicker, less manicured. He'd left the soccer fields, and soon he'd be crashing through a few dense copses of trees; then he'd find the creek beyond. He was running hard, despite his speed. If he wasn't careful, his foot would find a root—

Chris went sprawling. His head hit a tree.

It hurt. For a minute, Chris scrabbled at underbrush, trying to figure out which way to run. He was barely sure which way was *up*.

But the water knew he was coming, and he felt it calling him.

The trees must have been providing some kind of cover, because lightning hadn't struck since he'd fallen. He stayed low.

There was a twenty-foot stretch of grass between the trees and the creek. He could run it. Would he be a live target for lightning again?

Lightning hit a tree to his left. It didn't so much catch on fire as *explode*. Bark and limbs went flying into the air.

Yes. He'd be a target.

But now there were flaming bits of debris in the air, and smoke curled through the rain. This was probably the best cover he'd get.

He burst out of the trees, feeling flaming bark catch at his shirt and burn. It didn't matter. He'd be in the water in ten seconds. Nine. Eight.

He jumped a fallen branch. Seven. Six.

He could see the creek now, a dark roll of angry water, fed by the storm and his power. His enemy might be stronger here in the rain, but Chris knew instinctively, if he got in that water, he'd tip the scale of power in his favor.

Five. Four.

Three.

Screw it. Chris leapt into the air, arms outstretched. He could dive like an Olympic medalist. The water was there, below him, waiting.

Lightning cracked.

Chris felt his hands hit the water.

And then he didn't feel anything at all.

CHAPTER 33

Becca ran for the front of the school, stumbling in her heels, sure she'd be the center of attention with her torn and soaked dress, Chris's jacket hanging from her shoulders. But most of the kids from the dance were outside—and just as drenched as she was. Apparently, there'd been quite a show when Drew and his buddies showed up, demanding an ambulance.

No one gave her a second glance.

Becca shivered under the flagpole and used trembling fingers to search Chris's contacts for Nick and Gabriel.

Only Gabriel answered.

We'll take care of it.

"Becca!" Quinn appeared at her shoulder, her blond hair plastered to her chest. "Come on! We need to get out of the rain!"

Becca let Quinn drag her, but stopped when she realized she was being pushed into Rafe's car. The lightning had stopped—that had to be a good thing, right? "Wait," she cried. "I need—I can't—"

"Don't worry," said Quinn. "I told him we'd get you home."

Becca blinked at her. "Chris?"

Quinn frowned and shoved her the rest of the way into the car, sliding in behind her. The scent of sweat and summer rain was thick in the air. "No, Bex. Hunter. He was really upset," she said. "He got a call or something and had to go home."

That tore Becca's attention off the cell phone clutched in her hand. "He just *left?*" It made her remember Chris's comment. *You started dating some stupid tool who couldn't figure out letting you go with Drew was a bad idea.*

"He was flipping out. Something with his mom, maybe?" Quinn grimaced. "I'm sorry, Bex, there was just a lot going on. I was trying to look for you, and then the ambulances showed up—"

That was the best part of this evening. Now people were suspecting Drew and his friends had taken a hit of something and had a bad reaction. First a rapist, now a user.

She hoped they'd be expelled.

Becca flipped Chris's phone open. No new messages.

What had happened? The Guide, for sure. But Chris and the twins had driven him away from the bridge. Would they be able to do it again?

Her own phone beeped. She almost jumped a mile, but got it together to dig it out of her purse.

Despite the fact that she was holding Chris's phone in her lap, she had the uncanny hope that this would be a message from him.

No luck. But it was from Hunter.

Are you OK? So sorry to leave you.

She stroked her thumb over the display, deliberating how to respond. Then she tapped a quick reply.

What happened?

His response took forever, and when it came, it didn't say much:

Family stuff. Too much for txt. 2morrow.

Figured. She sighed. But Becca kept hearing Chris's question, right before the lightning started to strike.

Speaking of our local narc, just what do you know about him?

Did Chris think Hunter was somehow involved with what had happened?

She stared at his words on her phone, absently fingering the rocks on her wrist. New age nonsense? Or something as familiar to him as Chris's water or Nick's air?

She stared out at the night. Still no lightning. Just rain, whipped by wind to strike the car.

Quinn's voice interrupted her thoughts. "You all right, Bex?"

Was there an answer to that? Becca nodded, but didn't look at her. "Fine."

"You never told me what Drew said."

Becca gave a halfhearted laugh. "Too much. Not enough. I don't know."

Quinn didn't say anything, and Becca was suddenly aware of Rafe's eyes on her in the rearview mirror.

"What happened?" said Quinn, and her voice was low.

"He didn't want to apologize. He just wanted to finish what he started at that soccer party." Now she looked up, meeting Quinn's eyes. Her voice sounded flat, but it was better than the alternative. "It was a trick. He and his friends dragged me onto the soccer field."

Quinn shifted closer, taking her hand. "Oh, Bex . . ."

Becca shook her head, shocked to feel another tear roll down her cheek. She swiped it away. "It's okay. He didn't—Chris stopped them."

Quinn's eyes widened. "You mean—how they looked on the quad . . . Chris did that?"

Becca squared her shoulders. She remembered the feel of her elbow smashing Seth in the face, the taste of Drew's blood on her tongue. "And me."

Rafe whistled from the front seat. "You go, girl."

Quinn didn't spare him a glance. "Do you want me to stay with you tonight?"

"No, I'll be fine." Becca gave her friend a weak smile. "You kids have fun."

Her house felt emptier than usual. Quinn had almost demanded to stay—and Becca had almost let her. She just couldn't bear the thought of reliving it all for Quinn, who would surely want details.

Becca sat at the kitchen table and stared at Chris's cell phone, checking it every fifteen seconds.

Nothing.

She scrolled through his contacts again, letting her thumb stop on *Michael*.

Would Chris want her to call him? He and the twins had been pretty emphatic that they didn't want him involved. And Gabriel had said they'd take care of it—if they wanted Michael, they would have called him.

Right?

She opened the front door. The chill in the air seeped right through her skin and into her bones. The rain had stopped entirely, and a few stars peeked between broken clouds.

The storm was over.

She just didn't know whether that was a good thing or a bad thing.

Becca took a hot shower and dressed in flannel pajamas, curling beneath her comforter to combat her shivering. She checked the phone again. Nothing.

Then she lay in the dark and stared at the ceiling, remembering the feel of Drew's body trapping her own.

The moment in the field had only lasted a minute, but here in the dark, it seemed to last an hour. Two. She watched the clock count the minutes. Just the thought of Drew was enough to trap her.

She couldn't breathe.

But then she remembered the sleet on her face, slicing through her panic.

You're brave. And you're strong. Or did someone else break Seth's nose tonight?

A tiny smile found her lips.

Then it was gone. "Chris," she whispered.

She pulled his phone off the nightstand and checked the messages again.

None.

She switched his phone to vibrate and hugged it to her chest, staring at the ceiling until sleep crept out of nowhere.

Chris woke up.

And that right there was a frigging miracle.

He was lying on something cold and rough, like concrete. It hurt to move, so he didn't try. Pounding filled his head and made him stay still for a long minute. For a panicked moment he thought something was wrong with his eyes—he couldn't see anything.

Then he realized there was no light.

The air felt stale, too. No ventilation.

And not a drop of water anywhere near. He felt like he'd lost one of his senses.

He slid his fingers along the ground. Definitely concrete, and cold.

Then he heard something shift against the ground, that soft rasp of grit against fabric. Then a hissed breath.

He rolled to a crouch. Every muscle protested, but adrenaline helped. "Who's there?"

The noise stopped. Chris put a hand against the ground and fought to hear. Something, anything.

Then a voice, rough and dry, barely more than a whisper. "Chris?"

"Nick?" Chris crawled forward a few feet, moving in the direction of the voice. For the first time, he had no sense of his brother—he didn't even know if he was guessing the right twin. "Keep talking so I can find you. Are you hurt?"

A choked sound that might have been a laugh. "You remember when we were kids and Gabriel begged me to make a tornado because he wanted to ride one?"

"Yeah?" he said, just to keep Nick talking.

"That idea is overrated."

Chris followed his voice. Straight ahead, a bit to the left. Maybe ten feet? He had no idea. Chris went slow, crawling, sliding his hands along the ground, not wanting to find a trap. His body didn't like all this movement, but he told his body to get over it. His head wasn't as easily convinced.

His hand hit something solid, and further examination discovered a steel pole. Chris was glad he hadn't tried to bolt across the floor. He edged around it and kept going. "What does that mean?"

"It means I think my leg is broken." Nick's breath caught and trembled, then steadied. "Maybe other stuff, too. My hands are tied. I don't think—I can't feel my fingers—"

"Hold on. I'm almost there." Though Chris didn't have a damn clue what he could do for Nick. Untie him, at least.

Unless he was chained.

Don't panic. He kept crawling. "What happened to Gabriel?"

It was the wrong question. Nick's breathing accelerated. "I don't know. We got caught—the storm—I don't know—"

"Easy." Chris kept his voice steady. Nick was usually the one to keep the rest of them calm. "If he's not here, he probably got away."

The words hung there in the darkness. Nick didn't say anything.

Chris kept moving.

"You're close," said Nick. "I can hear you."

"Good." So Chris rushed.

Stupid. His hand came down on something solid, with a slight give. Fabric over skin. Plus something with an edge that scraped against the side of his hand.

Then Nick was yelling and Chris flung himself back.

Nothing was worse than listening to his brother scream in the darkness. Chris slapped his hands over his ears, then felt like a total wuss.

He jerked his hands down. "I'm sorry." God, it sounded like he was about to start crying. "Nick—I'm sorry—"

"Chris." Nick's screams had given way to ragged breathing.

"Yeah." Chris kept his hands tight against his stomach. What had he felt? Had that been bone? Couldn't you bleed out from a compound fracture?

"Don't do that again." Nick was sweating now—Chris could feel that. Every drop whispered pain.

Sweating meant shock, right? Or something else?

He should have paid more attention in freshman Health.

"Jesus, Nick—I'm sorry—I didn't—" He didn't what? He didn't mean to poke his brother's broken leg?

"Stop apologizing." Nick's voice sounded breathy. "Look, I think my phone might still be in my pocket."

A phone! But Chris couldn't force his hand to reach out. "Do you want me to untie you first, or—"

"I'm lying on my hands." Nick gave a rough laugh. "And I don't think moving would be a good idea."

Chris would give anything for a bare hint of light. "Okay. We'll call Mike or Gabriel, and they'll have us out of here in, like, five minutes—"

"Oh yeah? Where's *here*?"

That threw him. Chris didn't have an answer. He didn't even know how long he'd been unconscious.

He didn't even know if it was day or night.

"Stop thinking," said Nick. His voice was losing the thready current of shock, and now carried a tremor of pain. He sounded like he was clenching his teeth. "Just find it."

Chris steeled his nerves. This time he traced the seam of the pants with the barest edge of his fingertips. The fabric was bunched and torn in places. Chris tried not to think of what that might mean.

At least Nick was conscious. Good, right? He should probably keep him talking.

"Gabriel's going to be pissed."

It took Nick a second to answer. "Why?"

"He'll have to break his leg so people won't be able to tell you apart."

Nick snorted. A laugh. Good!

Then he said, "This room is airtight, Chris."

"How much air do we have?"

"A day, maybe."

Chris might have panicked about that, but then his hand found the gap of fabric that had to mean a pocket. Thank god they'd been at the dance and his brother was wearing dress pants. He couldn't imagine fighting a phone out of a pair of jeans.

He flipped the device open. The blue display cast a sphere of light into the darkness, not stretching much farther than three feet. The glow caught Nick's face and made his eyes dark and hollow. His shirt was unbuttoned at the neck, his tie gone. Bruises ran down the side of his face, and it looked like blood was caked in his hair.

"Chris," said Nick.

Chris shook himself. He dialed Michael's number and hit Send. Thank god they had a phone. Some guy in a tech room somewhere would be able to trace the signal, and they'd send, like, a bazillion cops, and—

The phone beeped. No signal.

Chris swore.

The phone went dark. He punched a button to make it light up again.

"I knew it," said Nick, his voice resigned. "I knew he wouldn't be stupid enough to leave it on me."

"At least we can see—"

"See what, Chris? Our prison?"

"Each other." Chris had never heard his brother sound so bleak. He stared at him, hitting a button on the phone again when it went dark. "I'm going to walk around the edge in a minute, see if I can get a signal. But first I want to see your leg."

He braced himself for something bad. He'd never been a squeamish guy, but he'd never seen a bone come through skin before, either. It got worse when he realized Nick was holding his breath in grim fascination, too. He gritted his teeth and turned the phone.

No bones.

Instead, a splint. Old school and rustic, made of thin strips of wood, cotton bandages, and duct tape.

Chris had no idea what that meant. No frigging way Nick had done that himself.

"He did that?" he said. "The Guide? Why?"

"Who knows," said Nick. His voice was still strained. "I'd rather have a Percocet. See if there's a way out of here."

Now that he had the cell phone light to work by, Chris walked the length of the room. The light didn't penetrate far, and by the time he made it to a wall, his brother was left in total darkness.

"You all right?" he called.

"Just keep talking."

Of course then Chris couldn't think of what to say. He just started narrating. "The walls are stainless steel, the floor concrete. Stainless steel shelves line the wall at one end." Chris had yet to find a door.

"Are there vents on the ceiling?"

Chris pointed the phone up. "Yeah. But I don't think the air is on."

"We're lucky it's not."

Chris pointed the phone at him, but still couldn't see him. "You know where we are?"

"Not *where*. We could be anywhere."

Great.

"Use your brain, Chris." Nick paused. "Airtight, not a drop of water in sight. It's the perfect room to hold us. No wonder we can't get a signal."

Chris touched a hand to the wall, letting his fingers streak down the stainless steel.

Then he had it. "A freezer. Like a walk-in kind."

"Yeah. And you know what sucks about these? One door. Easy to lock from the outside."

"No way out."

"Yeah," said Nick. "Trapped."

CHAPTER 34

Becca woke to the smell of breakfast cooking.

That was so foreign it dragged her out of bed. She checked Chris's phone.

No messages. None on her phone, either.

Her mom was bustling around the kitchen, frying bacon and pouring pancakes. Becca glanced at the clock over the microwave. It was barely after seven.

"Mom?" she said, rubbing her eyes. "What are you doing?"

Her mom hardly glanced up as she turned the bacon. "I'll give you three guesses."

"But—why aren't you still at work—"

"Well, it was a quiet night, so I left at six. Want some coffee? I thought I'd make us breakfast while I still had the work adrenaline thing going."

Becca dropped into the kitchen chair. "In a minute."

Her mom gave her a knowing smile. "Rough night?"

Probably easier to let her mom think she'd knocked back a few beers with Quinn and was sitting here hungover. "Too rough."

Becca stared at Chris's phone, willing a text to come in.

It wasn't very obedient.

She couldn't take it anymore. She flipped open the phone and scrolled through Chris's contacts until she stopped on *Michael*.

Did Chris make it home OK?

The response took fewer than thirty seconds.

Who is this?

Of course he wouldn't know. She mentally kicked herself and sent back her name. This time his response took a moment longer.

Was Chris with you last night?

She wrote back,

I haven't seen him since the storm.

Then she waited, but Michael didn't respond. She sent a few more texts asking about Chris, all of which went unanswered.

Her mom set a cup of coffee on the table beside her. "Who are you texting?"

"Some guy."

"Some guy?" Her mom sounded too interested. "Want to tell me about this 'some guy'?"

"Not like that." Maybe she could borrow her mother's car after she went to bed for the day.

Her mom started putting bacon on a plate, then layered the pancakes on a large platter. Becca wasn't surprised to find food coloring smiley faces on hers. She didn't know who was going to eat all this food.

Someone knocked on the door.

Becca's heart leapt into her throat. Chris? Hunter?

Her mom frowned and put the mixing bowl in the sink. "Who knocks on the door at seven-thirty on a Saturday?"

Becca shoved out of her chair and nearly ran down the hallway to the foyer.

"Slow down, Becca," said her mother. "Are you expecting someone?"

Becca ignored her and threw open the door.

Then she stopped short. "Michael."

His jeans and boots were filthy and caked with mud, along with some darker spots that looked like dried blood. Something big had bitten his right forearm and hadn't wanted to let go. Scrapes encircled his wrist and traced the tendons along the back of his hand. A nasty cut started over one eye and led into his hairline, backed by a harsh bruise.

"What happened?" she whispered.

His eyes were wary and guarded and almost feral, and Becca watched him glance from her to her mother and back. "I think I need you to tell me that."

"Becca," said her mother. "Do you know this boy?"

Her brain stumbled over the word *boy*, but Becca nodded. "Yeah. Yes. I do." She struggled to find a way to explain Michael— and how he looked. "He's—well—"

"Come inside." Her mom pulled the door wider. "Let's go in the kitchen."

"No," said Michael. "I can't stay here. I just need—"

"You just need to get in here and sit down." Her mom gave him a once-over. "How long ago did this happen?"

"Look," he growled. "I'm fine—"

"Get in here." Her mom stood back and pointed to the kitchen. "I'm not sending a kid back on the road looking like you do." Her mom was in full ER nurse mode—using the voice she typically saved for drug addicts and unruly street kids with war wounds.

"I'm not a kid," he snapped. Becca winced.

But her mother stepped forward and put a hand on his shoulder. "Come on. At least have a cup of coffee and an aspirin."

Maybe it was touching him that did it. Michael seemed to deflate a bit, and Becca could feel his hesitation in the air.

"Come on," her mom said again. "I think I left the stove on anyway."

Then she was bustling back down the hall, and Michael was stepping across the threshold. He bent to work his boot laces.

There was another scrape on his side, another line of blood. She winced and wondered if she should offer to help him.

He glanced up. "Why do you have Chris's phone?"

"He gave it to me. At the dance." She paused, feeling her throat tighten. "You haven't seen him?"

Michael stepped out of his boots and straightened. It stole an inch from his height, and seeing him standing there in his socks made him just a little less intimidating.

"No." His voice was a bit softer, a bit less gruff. "I haven't seen any of them."

She stared up at him, holding his eyes. In that moment, she figured out what was behind all that anger and aggression: fear. Vulnerability. Her mom had called him a kid on the porch, and for the first time, Becca realized he wasn't *that* much older than she was.

Michael must have seen her expression soften, because he walled that emotion back up and looked away. "This is stupid." He reached for his boots. "I should be looking—"

"Hey." She caught his forearm. Michael was the only person who might be able to help. "Come sit down. Maybe we can figure it out."

"How do you take your coffee?" her mother called.

Michael glanced down the hallway, then back at Becca.

"I won't think you're any less of a jerk if you act like a normal human being and have a cup of coffee," Becca said. "I promise."

He sighed. "Black," he called.

Figured.

In the kitchen, her mother directed him to stand at the sink. "Let water run over those bites," she said. "Puncture wounds like that can be a problem. What, did you have a run-in with a dog?"

"Something like that." He did as her mother had directed, but Becca saw him glance her way.

"She's a nurse," Becca said. "You're probably lucky Mom's not wrestling you into the ER."

"We'll see what those look like when they're cleaned up," her mother said. "Then we'll talk about wrestling. Becca, can you help me get a few things from the powder room?"

Becca frowned and followed her into the hallway. Her mom kept some of her medical stuff under the sink in the front bathroom, but it was just bandage tape and squares of gauze, nothing that required "help." Becca probably could have gotten everything in one hand.

But her mom pointed at the commode. "Sit."

Her voice was terse. Becca sat. "Mom, what's—"

"I knew something was going on with you, Becca, and I thought you would tell me eventually." Her mom flung open the cabinet below the sink.

How could she ever explain this? Becca swallowed. "Look, it's complicated—"

"Oh, I know it's complicated." Her mom shoved a box of gauze into her hands, followed by a tube of Neosporin. "I didn't think you'd *hide* things from me. Not something like this."

Becca swallowed. "Mom, I just—I'm still figuring it out, and—"

"Well, I've figured it out," her mother said. "That boy is *way* too old for you, Becca. Do you understand me?"

Wait a minute.

"Mom!" Becca stared at her. "You think—you think I'm dating *Michael*?"

Her mom stared back at her, obviously thrown. "You're not?"

This would be hilarious if her mom didn't look so serious.

"Oh my god," cried Becca. "Are you *kidding?* Michael is the *last* person I would ever—oh my *god*. I wouldn't go out with him if someone *paid* me. Ugh, that's just—"

"You know I can hear you, right?" called Michael.

Becca flushed. "I'm friends with his younger brother," she whispered. "His *much* younger brother. Chris Merrick. He's in my class." She hesitated, wondering how much to tell her mother. "Chris and his brothers didn't come home from the dance last night. Michael's trying to find out where they went."

Her mother pulled the last of her supplies out of the cabinet. "Where are his parents?"

"They're dead." When her mom looked up in surprise, Becca nodded. "Michael's like their legal guardian or something."

That seemed to renew her mother's mission to help him. Back in the kitchen, she started cleaning up Michael's scrapes, ordering him to sit at the kitchen table, then ordering Becca to get him a plate of pancakes.

Michael glanced at the plate she slid in front of him. "I'm really not—"

"Eat," her mother said. "You look like you've been up all night. Becca said your brothers never made it home after the dance?"

He glanced at Becca. She shrugged.

"Yeah," he said. "The twins have stayed out all night before—but Chris isn't—he's not—"

His voice faltered. Becca reached out and put her hand over his. He pulled it away and stared at the table. His jaw looked set.

Becca's mom watched this whole interaction and rubbed Neosporin into the claw marks on his forearm. "Must be tough, looking after three teenage boys. How long have you been on your own?"

"Five years."

"You work?"

Michael nodded. "My dad had a landscaping company."

"How nice. I love gardening."

Becca recognized this voice. It was her mom's let-me-distract-you tone. But maybe her mother sensed Michael's mood, because she glanced up. "I'm sure your brothers will turn up. Boys do tend to get into a lot of scrapes. We had a couple teenagers from that dance in the ER last night, but no car accidents, no John Does, even."

Becca perked up. "Who came in?" she asked, though she had a pretty good idea.

"You know I can't tell you that. No one by the name of Merrick." Her mom moved to the sink to wet a paper towel. "Looked like a drug overdose, anyway. They were in bad shape." She came back to the table and started to blot at the cut over Michael's eye. He winced.

"Eat," she said. "You'll hurt my feelings."

He picked up his fork and cut a piece of pancake. "Smiley faces?" he said, spearing some with his fork.

"Mom gets into her cooking," said Becca.

Michael must have liked the pancakes. He cut another piece. "I forgot what that was like."

"Cooking?" she said.

He didn't look up. "Having a mother."

His words hung in the silence for a moment. He was such a jerk that Becca had never considered what it must be like to be Michael, to graduate from high school and instead of heading off to college, have to stay home, take over his father's business, and finish raising his three brothers.

"Did you go back to the school?" her mother said. "See if their car is still there?"

"It is." He glanced at Becca. "When did you last see Chris?"

"Late," she said. "But he was on the soccer field." She gave a meaningful glance at her mother.

If Michael saw it, he didn't acknowledge it. "I'll go back. Look around."

"I'll come with you," said Becca.

Michael jerked his head up in surprise—then his eyes narrowed in suspicion. "Why?"

"Because I care," she snapped.

"It's not a bad idea," her mom said. "Bex could show you where she saw them last. You'll probably find them sleeping off a hangover under the bleachers."

"Probably," echoed Becca. "Let me go get dressed."

She felt Michael watching her, but she couldn't look back. She remembered those bolts of lightning on the field, the way the power had flared in the air and brushed against her skin. She remembered the smell of fear and rain and scorched earth.

If they found anyone on the field, they definitely wouldn't be hungover.

They'd be dead.

CHAPTER 35

Becca pulled on jeans, a tee shirt, and a long-sleeved hoodie to combat the chill in the air. She worried about how the drive would go, considering her history with Michael. Once they were on the road, she realized she shouldn't have bothered.

He didn't say a word.

Halfway to school, she couldn't take it anymore. She'd rather listen to him snipe at her than suffer this silence she could only fill with worry.

"How did you know where I live?" she asked.

Michael glanced over at her. His window was down, his arm on the ledge. The wind pulled strands of hair from his ponytail, and he needed a shave.

"You made a path," he said.

She rolled that around in her head for a second. "Are you deliberately being cryptic?"

"No." He looked at her as if she was deliberately being stupid. "Chris told you what we are, right?"

"I think I got the CliffsNotes version."

He turned back to the road. "You've been to the house several times. Once you lay a path, the ground starts to remember you. If you'd only been to the house once, I wouldn't have been able to do it."

"So I guess you can't bitch about me showing up unannounced anymore."

"I guess I can't," he conceded.

"You going to tell me what really happened to you?"

He was silent so long she wasn't sure he was going to answer. But then he said, "I'm not sure. Someone came after us. I felt the power in the woods behind the house."

"When?"

"Just before midnight maybe? I didn't check my watch. I was able to run him off, so I thought it was Tyler or one of his buddies, and then the guys never came home. . . ." He shrugged and let his voice trail off, but she heard everything he wasn't saying.

Before midnight. That was later than when the Guide had attacked them on the field.

But also after Hunter left the school for an "emergency." Becca couldn't get Chris's question out of her head.

Just what do you know about him anyway?

The school was deserted, but some of the Homecoming decorations were still stuck to the glass doors of the gymnasium, red and blue decals that had started to peel after the storm last night. Cigarette butts littered the ground around the flagpole.

"Can you do that tracking thing to find them?" she asked.

Michael shook his head. "I already tried. There were too many people here."

"Come on," she said. "I last saw Chris on the soccer field."

He followed her, striding silently by her side. True to form, he didn't say a word. He just stopped about thirty feet from the bleachers, dropping to a knee to touch his hand to the ground. "This is where you last saw Chris?"

"Ah . . . yeah."

He glanced up. "What were you doing out here?"

"Nothing. Just talking."

"I don't buy that for a minute."

She flushed and hugged her arms against her body. "We did. I don't care if you believe me or—"

"Fine. Then it must have been one hell of a conversation." Michael gestured. "Come here. Touch the ground."

She squatted and pressed her fingertips through the grass and into the dirt. At first she felt nothing but mud, cold and gritty, sliding below her fingers.

Then awareness crawled up her arm.

Her brain couldn't quite comprehend what she felt. Not words—more like things that *wanted* to be words. Like a foreign language she'd studied years ago and could barely remember. She could almost piece it together, but the concepts kept evading her, turning from wisps of thought into coils of something darker.

Whatever it was, the longer she kept her fingers planted in the earth, the less she liked it.

She yanked her fingers back, feeling her breath quicken. Her heart was already racing in her chest. "What just happened?"

"You see why I'm not buying the 'we just talked' crap."

"Chris saved me," she said, talking quickly because the words wanted to escape her lips. "Some guys—they were—they were—"

"I get it." His voice was even. "There's blood here."

"There was a fight. Just boys from school. Chris—we ran them off. But something happened. Lightning started chasing us across the field or—I don't know." Again, she didn't have the right words. "But when it started, he gave me his cell phone and told me to get his brothers."

"Jesus, Becca." Michael set his jaw and looked off across the field, then back at her. "*I'm* his brother, too."

She flushed as guilt smacked her in the face. "I know. I'm sorry."

Michael punched the ground, and the field between them cracked and split like a windshield hit by a rock. She scrambled back a few feet, but he was looking out at the trees now. "I could have helped them. I could have—" He punched the ground again. "*Where are they?*"

"I should have called you last night," she said, hearing pain behind the fury in his voice. "I just—he told me to text the twins, and they were able to chase off the Guide at the bridge, so I thought—"

"Stop." His eyes locked on hers. "Run that by me again."

"Last Monday, when the Guide destroyed the bridge—" She stared at him for a long minute. "They never told you."

"No," he said, his tone resigned. "But you can."

So she talked, going back to the morning she'd found the first pentagram on her door. She gave him every detail about the Guide she could remember, right up to the bolts of lightning last night, to the way the rain had turned to daggers on her cheeks. Then she had to back up and tell him about the night at the party, the way Chris had dragged her into the water, the way Tyler came after them with a gun.

She didn't falter until she noticed the ground knitting itself together, mending the break between them.

"That's all you know?" said Michael. His tone implied it wasn't very helpful.

"Yeah. That's all."

"Was there gunfire last night?"

She thought back, to the chaos on the field. "No. I don't think so—but the thunder was loud."

Michael looked out across the field again. "Tyler came after you with a gun because it's one of the few surefire ways to kill us." He shook his head. "I can't believe they wouldn't tell me."

She could.

She was beginning to sweat beneath her dark hoodie. She pulled it off and knotted the sleeves around her waist, glad she'd worn a tank top underneath.

Michael glanced at the sky. "I'm going to walk the rest of the field."

He walked, and she followed, stopping at points where lightning had scorched the earth. She wished she could do what he did, that the ground could whisper secrets to her and create a path for her to follow.

She swiped a hand across her forehead. Crazy hot for September. It had been sixty the day before.

Then she felt the heat trickle along her skin, as if the sunlight had fingers. The hair on her arms stood up. She held her forearm in front of her eyes. "Michael? Do you feel that?"

"Yeah." He turned in a slow circle as if expecting to find someone. The field was empty. He frowned at her. "You do, too?"

Did she? She rubbed her arms to get rid of the sensation—but it didn't help. "Maybe. I don't know."

That morning at her house when the brothers had fought with Hunter, she'd felt Nick's power like the tail of a kite, a tangible thing she could grab hold of. This felt like nothing so substantial—it lacked direction and force.

"Can you follow it?" she asked.

Michael took a step forward, his hand held out. "It's vague. Weak. It might not be anything."

But he walked anyway, and she followed him. Sweat developed between Becca's shoulder blades, running a line down the center of her back. Michael had been stopping at the scorch marks, but now he kept walking, moving more quickly as they neared the edge of the athletic field and the woods that led to the creek. It felt stronger here, a definite wash of power in the sunlight.

Michael didn't hesitate, he strode into the underbrush as if a clear path was carved there. Becca saw nothing move, but she could swear that plants shifted out of the way of his boots, leaving her to scramble after him in the tangles of vines and thorns. The heat made her feel like they were fighting through the rain forest.

Just as she was about to snap at him to slow down or make the foliage move for her, too, he stopped short. So short, she nearly ran right into him.

Then she brought her gaze up from the solid line of his back, to see what had made him stop.

"Gabriel," he said, his voice full of something like wonder—and relief.

Gabriel sat against a tree. His eyes had been closed, but they cracked open when Michael said his name. He still wore dark-colored slacks from Homecoming, but they were damp and filthy. He'd lost his dress shirt somewhere along the line, but he still had a white tee shirt, also wet and clinging to his chest. Water dripped out of his hair, tracing lines though the dirt on his face. He looked like he'd crawled through a pile of leaves soaking wet. He didn't move.

All the heat in the air seemed to be pulling toward his body.

"Are you all right?" asked Michael.

Gabriel shook his head. "I lost them." Then he put his hands against the ground to struggle to his feet.

Michael rushed forward to help him.

Gabriel shoved him away, a motion full of so much fury that he knocked himself back to the ground. *"Get off me."*

The rage in his voice forced Becca back a step. The heat in the woods seemed to flare, singing her skin.

"Yeah, yeah." Michael caught him under the arms and pulled him the rest of the way to a standing position. "You're so tough."

"Shut up." Gabriel fought him, wrenching free of Michael's grip to shove him away again. "Shut the *fuck up*." He punched Michael in the chest with both fists. "I *hate* you."

Michael fell back, but his arms were tight, his hands clenched at his sides.

Becca skittered back, out of the way. She could barely breathe. The heat in the woods was almost unbearable.

"I fucking hate you," Gabriel said again, his voice fierce. "First Mom and Dad—now Nick—now Chris—" His voice broke, and he struck Michael in the chest again. "You killed that girl. We should have let them take you—we should have let them—"

God, Becca could feel his anguish through the heat, tightening her chest.

Michael was moving forward, reaching for his brother. "Gabriel—"

"Don't touch me." Gabriel hit him again, his voice thick.

Michael caught his wrists and held them.

Gabriel fought him, wrenching his hands free to strike at his brother, over and over again, driving Michael back through the underbrush. She could hear every hit, could feel him pulling power from the heat in the air to add force to the blows.

"I hate you," he said with every strike, his voice breaking. "I *hate* you."

The violence stole what was left of her breath. She stared, digging her nails into the tree she'd grabbed for support.

Then Michael caught Gabriel by the back of the neck, and she knew Michael was going to knock him out, or throw him down, or retaliate somehow. The fury in the air was electrifying, crackling along her skin, begging for release.

But Michael pulled him close and held him there, too close for Gabriel to get a good swing.

"I'm sorry," he said, his voice soft, rough, almost lost in the air. "Let me help you."

Gabriel went still. His breathing was ragged. There were tears on his cheeks.

Then he was struggling. "Fuck you."

Michael tightened his grip. "I'm sorry." His face was close to his younger brother's. "I'm sorry."

"Whatever." Gabriel sniffed and gritted his teeth and looked past him. "I don't care. You don't care."

"Goddamn it, Gabriel!" Michael shook him. "*I loved them, too.*"

"So *what?* Mom and Dad would have wanted to fight—they would have kept us safe—they would have—"

"I'm trying!" Michael drew a breath, and his voice sounded strained. "Okay? I'm trying."

Gabriel said nothing. The air hummed with power and emotion, and Becca clutched tight to her tree, afraid to move, to upset the balance.

Then Gabriel's shoulders drooped. "It was my fault." He spoke low, almost too quiet to hear. "It was my fault they broke the deal."

"They were looking for a reason to break the deal."

"They sent a Guide. We didn't tell you—"

"It's okay. Tell me now."

"He had Chris, and Nick and I thought—we thought we

could take him." He gave a soft laugh, a broken sound with no humor behind it. "We were wrong. Nick had the wind, but the Guide took control of it. Then Nick was hurt—"

He stopped, his eyes fixed on the ground. His silence said enough.

"You got away?" said Michael.

Gabriel nodded. "Barely. I hid." He sounded ashamed.

"Where?"

Gabriel's eyes flicked up, and for the first time, Becca saw the spark of his usual defiance. "The last place he'd look for me."

"In the water," she said.

Gabriel lifted his head and looked at her, then shrugged off Michael's hands.

He'd clearly forgotten she was there—if he'd ever noticed at all.

Then he ran a hand through his wet hair, pushing it off his forehead. "Yeah. In the water. Almost all night."

"All night?" said Michael, his eyebrows raised.

Gabriel pulled at his wet clothes. "Yeah. All night."

"Do you have any idea where he took them?" asked Michael. "No."

Michael sighed. "Well, let's go back to the house. The Guide came looking for me last night, too; maybe he'll show up again."

Now it was Gabriel's turn to raise his eyebrows. "You got away by yourself?"

"Maybe you're not the only tough guy around here."

Gabriel stared at him for half a second, as if trying to decide whether Michael was making a joke—or picking a fight. He didn't say anything, just turned to walk.

As they started off across the field, Becca couldn't help wondering about a Guide who could take out Chris and the twins—especially after the demonstration she'd seen at the bridge—but not Michael.

Tough guy or not, the facts weren't matching up.

CHAPTER 36

Becca walked between the brothers. She hadn't picked the arrangement, but it made her feel like a needed barrier. Gabriel was still pulling heat from the sky, and it was like walking next to a sunbeam.

Her phone chimed, and she fished it out of her pocket. Sunlight glinted across the face.

Her mom, asking if everything was all right. She tapped out a quick response. Hunter's rock bracelet bounced against her wrist now that the chain wasn't trapped under her sleeve.

Gabriel glanced down at what she was doing. "Who are you texting?"

His voice still echoed with the pain and uncertainty she'd heard in the woods. She wanted to give him a hug, but Gabriel didn't seem like the kind of guy who'd take it well.

"My mother," she said. "Checking up."

"Your mom's nice," said Michael. He glanced down, too.

Then he caught her wrist and hauled her to a stop. "Where did you get these?"

He was looking at the bracelet, holding her wrist up so the stones caught the light.

"From a friend," she said, snatching her hand back. "Why?"

"Oh, just a *friend?*" he said. "You mean you're walking

around with these on your wrist and you don't know what they *are?*"

"They're rocks," said Gabriel. "Leave her alone."

"They're not just rocks." Michael glared at her. "Are you playing me? Was this a trap to find Gabriel—"

"No!" she cried. "What the hell is wrong with you?"

"I'm so stupid," he said. "The way you felt the sunlight, the way you knew we'd find—"

"What are you *talking about?*"

"These." Michael grabbed her wrist again. "These rocks. They're full of power. Who are you, Becca? What do you—"

"They're not mine!" She was ready to tear them off her arm. "They're not!"

Michael's face was right in front of her. "Then whose are they?"

She took a deep breath. "Hunter's."

"That punk kid?" said Gabriel. "The one who got into it with Chris last night?"

"Yeah." She glanced between him and Michael. "He said they were his mom's. He said they were for silly things, like . . . like . . . confidence, or clarity of thought." Then she realized what Gabriel had said. "Wait. He got into it with Chris?"

"Yeah. Nicky, too. I don't know what happened, because all hell broke loose, but he said they had a run-in."

"What were they fighting about?"

Gabriel snorted and gave her a look. "Guess."

"These rocks are for a lot more than confidence or clarity of thought," said Michael. "Take them off."

"This is stupid. A lot of people wear crystals. What, are you going to do some magic—"

"Just shut up and take them off. If you've got nothing to do with this, then *he* does."

Michael looked like he was going to rip them off her wrist if she didn't concede. She was ready to dig in and fight—but she kept hearing Chris's words on the soccer field the night before.

Just how much do you know about our local narc?

Hunter had never been anything but kind to her. If anything, he was overprotective. Maybe protection just ran in his family, with his police officer uncle and special forces father. Hunter coming to town at the same time as the Guide was nothing but coincidence. An accident.

I don't believe in accidents.

His father had been killed in a thunderstorm and a rock slide. Was that a coincidence? An accident?

Becca unchained the rocks and held them out to Michael.

He pulled the chain free, letting them drop into his palm. Quartz and amethyst, from the night she'd choked down too much tequila. Citrine and garnet, from the morning Hunter had picked a fight with Chris.

Michael studied all four, then picked up the clear quartz. "What did he tell you this one was for?"

She tried to remember. "Ah, to make the rest of them work better, I think."

"More likely to keep track of the rest of them." He held it up and crushed it in his palm.

"Are you *crazy?*" she sputtered. "That wasn't even—"

"He was tracking you, Becca." Dust trailed out of Michael's hand and into the grass below. "Give it five minutes. I bet he'll call—"

Her phone chimed.

Michael smiled, but it was grim. "See?"

She scowled at him, but her heart was making a racket against her ribs. "It's probably just my mother writing back."

But it wasn't. It was Hunter.

Are you OK?

She stared at the phone, nibbling at her lip.

Gabriel grabbed it out of her hands and looked at the display. "I should have kicked that kid's ass in your driveway."

"It doesn't mean anything. That could be a coincidence. He could—"

Her phone chimed again. She reached to grab it from Gabriel, but he backpedaled, obviously typing something back.

"This is stupid," she snapped. "Give me that."

He stopped and handed it to her. Hunter had sent another inquiry, but Gabriel had already responded. She looked at what he'd sent.

Help. Chris's brothers won't let me go.

She glared at him. "Did you spend too much time in the water? Why would you type that? He doesn't even know where I am. What if he calls my mother, or—"

"Or what if he's the Guide?" said Gabriel, his voice dark. "And he killed Chris and Nick?"

His words were a fist to the gut. "Gabriel—Hunter isn't a killer."

"I guess we'll find out."

Becca didn't like the look in his eyes—it reminded her too much of Chris, when he'd talked about how easy it was to kill someone and make it look accidental.

The hair on her arms was standing up again. "I want to go home," she said.

"Why?" said Michael. "We already told him we won't let you go."

Now she didn't like the look in *his* eyes. She took a step back.

But Gabriel put a hand on her arm. "Just wait. Ten minutes. Please."

She thought of his pain in the woods, so clear now in his expression.

Ten minutes. Ten minutes to prove them wrong, so they could follow real leads, figure out where Chris and Nick were.

Ten minutes to wonder why Hunter would track her, why he'd fill her ears with nonsense about colors and stones and Krav Maga if he was really just here to kill Chris and his brothers.

Ten minutes to figure out what was an accident, and what was very intentional.

It didn't take ten minutes.

Hunter showed up in five.

He strode across the athletic fields, Casper trotting through the grass beside him. Hunter moved like a panther, all loose joints and casual aggression wrapped up in jeans and a long-sleeved tee shirt. Even from thirty feet away, she could see him sizing up the situation, taking in her relaxed posture, the tense brothers by her side.

Hunter stopped before coming much closer, his eyes narrowed.

"You look all right," he said to her.

"I've been better," she said.

"If this guy's the Guide," said Gabriel, low, soft, more for Michael's ears than her own, "he hides it pretty damn well."

She could feel the brothers drawing power. The ground thrummed under her feet. The sunlight grew fingers that clawed along her skin. She had to breathe through it before it choked her.

But even with Hunter standing there, proving Michael's claims, she didn't believe he was the Guide.

So she left the brothers and walked across the grass toward him.

Hunter held up a hand when she'd made it halfway. "Are you with them?"

She didn't stop walking—Hunter didn't frighten her. "I'm not with anybody. And I don't think I'm the one who needs to answer questions."

He was pale. Sweating a bit, but steady. He glanced from her to the brothers and back. "Becca, if you're not with them, then you need to get out of here."

"Why, so you can kill them?"

"Becca. Go."

"Did you track me?" she demanded. "All that crap about confidence and courage and making me sober. Total crap, right? Are you an Earth like Michael?"

"No." He glanced behind her, and his posture tightened. Casper growled. "Becca, *go*."

She didn't turn to look. She knew who was behind her. "Did you track me, Hunter?"

He winced. "Yes."

"Why?"

"Because I thought you were one of them." He said the words in a rush. "Becca, you need to *go*."

Then she felt the power through the ground, the burn of sunlight against her skin.

Michael spoke from behind her. "Why does she need to go anywhere?"

"It can't be him," said Gabriel. "I don't feel it."

Becca's feet felt rooted to the ground, locked in place in the athletic field, a hundred times stronger than the night she'd tried to escape Chris's house. Her breath caught.

"I feel it," said Michael. "He was at the house last night."

"You got lucky," said Hunter, his voice sharper than she'd ever heard. "It won't happen again."

Casper was snarling beside him, but apparently he couldn't move, either.

"Lucky?" said Michael. He wasn't rooted at all. He stepped up beside her, looking down at Hunter, just out of arm's reach. "Just how lucky do you feel right now, kid?"

"Pretty lucky," said Hunter.

And then he pulled out the gun.

CHAPTER 37

"Holy shit," Becca whispered. Hunter had the gun pointed straight at Michael's face.

Michael was so still beside her, she wasn't sure he was breathing.

She wasn't sure *she* was.

"No powers," Hunter said. "I can pull this trigger faster than you can call elements."

"Want to bet?" said Gabriel. She heard the flick of a lighter.

Hunter cocked the gun. "Try me."

"Gabriel," said Michael, his voice sharp.

"It *is* you," said Becca, her voice shaking. That gun was way too frigging close to her face. "You're the Guide."

"No," said Hunter. His eyes didn't leave his target. "My father was."

His father was? But his father had died *months* ago. "Hunter," she whispered. "Think about this. Just—"

"Think about it? All I've *done* is think about it." His hand was steady, the gun not wavering. But she heard something in his voice, a tremor in the words, maybe. He kept his eyes on Michael. "I read my dad's notes. He wasn't coming here to kill you. He should have been. You sure didn't have a problem killing *him*."

Becca had to stop looking at his finger on the trigger. "Please, Hunter. Put the gun down."

He didn't move. He didn't even blink.

"I don't know what you're talking about," said Michael, his voice careful.

"You've killed people," said Hunter. "A girl, right? Seth Ramsey's parents?"

Michael hesitated—then nodded.

Becca swallowed.

Hunter drew a breath, and this time she heard it shake. "You knew my father was coming for you."

Michael shook his head. "No. I didn't. I don't know who your father—"

"You knew!" Hunter's voice cracked. "You had to know!"

Casper barked.

Becca flinched.

"Easy," breathed Michael. "I swear to you—"

"Shut up," said Hunter. "You got away with three murders. You're not getting away with five."

"I didn't know," said Michael. "I swear to you, I didn't know."

"His father was killed in a rock slide," Becca said, the words falling out of her mouth in a rush. "His father and his uncle. Hunter was in the car—"

"Becca!" Hunter's voice made her jump.

"You want to talk dead parents?" said Gabriel. "Get in line."

"Shut up," said Hunter.

"You shut up. A rock slide? Some fucking power your father had, he couldn't even—"

Hunter put the barrel of the gun against Gabriel's forehead. "You. Shut. Up."

Gabriel shut up.

"Listen to me," said Michael, his voice low and rapid and almost shaking. "I didn't mean for that girl to die. We were at the quarry and the rocks gave. I knew it was happening. I stopped it before anyone else got hurt. But I was angry. Her brother and his friends were chasing us, so I hesitated, just for an instant. I just wanted to slow them down." He drew a tremulous breath full of emotion. "I didn't want to hurt her. I never meant to hurt her. I regret it every day."

Hunter didn't move.

"Seth Ramsey's parents came after me," said Michael. "After all of us. We went to Seth's house and tried to work it out. But they wanted a fight. My parents weren't ready. My brothers and I, we didn't know what we were doing. We were so young. We just wanted them to stop fighting. There was a fire. It just—it was so fast." His voice broke. "Not everyone got out."

Becca hadn't heard this part of the story from Chris. Gabriel had been furious at Michael in the woods. She wondered how much of that fury was directed at himself, for starting the fire that had killed his parents.

"Save it," said Gabriel, his eyes intent on Hunter. "He won't pull the trigger."

A muscle in Hunter's jaw twitched.

"I didn't know about your father," said Michael. "I swear."

"Hunter," she whispered, wary of spooking him. "Sometimes accidents really do happen."

For an instant, she felt hesitation in the air. She honestly thought he'd lower the gun.

Then he swung the barrel around to center on Michael. "I don't believe in accidents."

"Why?" she said. "Because otherwise it's your fault?"

Hunter flinched—then caught himself.

"You didn't make your dad come back for you," she said. "You didn't. It was just—freakish timing, or fate, or—"

"Stop." Hunter had to draw a long, shaky breath. "Becca."

"This wasn't your fault," she said. "I know what it feels like to blame yourself—"

"You don't," he said, and his voice almost broke again. "Not like this. You don't."

"I do," said Gabriel.

"I do," said Michael.

Hunter didn't move, but Becca could feel his uncertainty. His breath was shaking.

"You don't want to do this," she said. "Hunter, you're not a killer."

"He is," he said, his eyes hardening. The barrel touched Michael's forehead.

"*You're* not," she said, feeling her voice rise in pitch.

"This is bullshit," said Gabriel.

"Damn it, Gabriel," said Michael, his voice breathy.

"It is," Gabriel said. "You didn't kill that girl. You didn't start that rock slide. You don't even know if you *could* have saved her. You're not a superhero. You were seventeen years old, and you probably should have gotten a medal for saving the kids who did make it out of that quarry. Seth and Tyler and the others tried to drown you and Chris—Mom and Dad were right to go after their parents. They wanted to kill us that night—it got out of control. All of us—we were *out of control.*"

Hunter didn't move, but he was listening. Becca could feel it.

Gabriel took a step closer. "But this—" He paused, looking at Hunter, his expression disgusted. "*This* is bullshit. Michael is a huge pain in the ass, but he's the closest thing to a parent I have left. He didn't want us to go after Seth and Tyler the night they tore up Chris. He refuses to let us use our powers, then bitches about homework and forgets to sleep. He works twenty-four seven. He barely has time to make dinner, much less set a trap for someone. Self-defense, yeah, I'd buy it. But cold-blooded killer? No way."

Gabriel took another step, until he was almost in Hunter's face. "You pull the trigger? *That,* kid, is all on you."

Hunter swallowed.

"Give me the gun." Michael put a hand out, his voice soft.

Tension rode on the sunlight as she listened to Hunter's breathing shake.

"It's okay," said Michael. "You don't want to do this."

Inch by inch, Hunter lowered the gun into Michael's palm, finally letting go.

Michael didn't move. "You all right?"

Hunter nodded.

"Good." Michael wrapped his hand around the hilt.

Then he lifted it, cocked the hammer, and put the barrel against Hunter's forehead. "Now where the fuck are my brothers?"

A door slammed, and Chris jumped.

He'd fallen asleep. Stupid.

Nick's hand was wrapped around his, a lifeline in the darkness. "What was that?"

Chris shook his head, then realized his brother wouldn't see it. "I don't know." He cast his senses into the air, but the only moisture in the room was attached to their skin, focused on things like pain and worry.

"Food," said Nick. "I smell it."

"Should we trust it?"

"There might be water."

There wouldn't be. Chris would have felt it from here. But he couldn't squash the hope in Nick's voice. "I'll check."

A paper bag sat on the ground near the door. The cell phone light revealed a McDonald's logo.

"Fast food," he said. "And milk shakes. Hilarious."

"I could eat," said Nick.

Chris carried the bags over.

"I'll try not to fall asleep again," said Chris. "I missed a chance."

"We don't even know if it was him. Besides, how long could it take him to shove a bag through the door?"

"Still."

They ate in silence for a minute. The food was still hot— meaning they weren't out in the middle of nowhere.

The room was soundproof, though, or pretty far from anyone who could hear him. Chris had spent a good amount of time banging on the walls and shouting until Nick told him to stop using up all the air.

"Why do you think he brought food?" said Nick after a while.

"I don't know," said Chris. He stared out at the darkness and wondered if Becca had made it off the field. He'd dreamed of water, the way rain traced lines down her face during the storm.

"Do you think Gabriel and Michael are looking for us?"

"Probably." Chris didn't mention the alternative.

He didn't say this, either: He hoped his brothers weren't looking at all. He hoped they stayed away. He hoped they ran.

Because now he understood the power he'd felt on that field. If his brothers came looking, they'd just end up in the same situation.

Trapped.

Or dead.

CHAPTER 38

Becca was having a hard time figuring out whose side to be on.

Hunter had his hands up, but his eyes were furious.

Michael pressed the steel barrel against Hunter's forehead, making him bow back a little. "Where are they?"

Hunter glared at him and didn't say anything. Casper was snarling beside his master, obviously still trapped in the grass.

Michael grabbed the front of Hunter's shirt and shook him. "*Where are they?*"

"Stop it!" she cried. "Michael—"

"He knows," Michael growled.

"I don't," said Hunter, his voice dark. "I don't have any idea."

"Hey, Law-and-Order," said Gabriel. "Let him go."

Michael didn't move. "Why?"

"He's not the Guide. He's not strong enough. I was on the bridge. I was on the field last night. That guy—it's not a teenager. And he wouldn't be bowing to a gun."

"He knows something." Michael adjusted his grip on the weapon.

And then Hunter moved.

Becca couldn't even follow it all. An arm here, a fist there. Michael was suddenly on the ground, disarmed.

The gun was back in Hunter's hand, pointed at Michael. His feet hadn't shifted. "You want to keep playing?"

Michael gaped up at him, looking more stunned than hurt.

Gabriel was staring at Hunter. "Dude. I'm going to need to see that again."

Hunter didn't put the gun away. "Something tells me you'll get another chance."

He'd trapped his emotion somehow, and now had full control of himself. His easy confidence spoke to her, reminded her that Hunter was a friend—or had pretended to be.

"Was it all a lie?" she said. "From the start?"

He didn't glance up, but his voice was soft. "I never lied to you, Becca. Even at first, when I thought—" He shook his head slightly. "I never lied."

"How about now?" said Becca. "Do you know where they are?"

"I have no idea where they are."

"He's *lying*," snapped Michael.

"Why would I lie?" Hunter shot back.

"There has to be another Guide," she said. She remembered Tyler's threats, when she'd first met him. "When your father didn't show up, Tyler and Seth called for another. Would you recognize him? Could you help us—"

"Why would I help *them*?" said Hunter, keeping his gun trained on Michael.

"You think you're safe?" said Gabriel. "You're not a real Guide. What if he comes after you next? You know he'll stay in town until he finds all the Elementals, finds out who's a threat. Rogue kid with a gun? Might make the list."

"Yeah," said Becca. "What if someone paints a pentagram on *your* door?"

Their words seemed to hit Hunter like stray bullets, drawing his attention away from Michael.

"What about your grandparents?" Becca paused. "What about your mom?"

Hunter flicked his eyes her way. "Are you threatening me?"

Her heart was threatening to escape her chest. "Yeah. I am. How's it feel?"

He shook his head. "I've never threatened you, Becca. I never wanted to hurt you."

She didn't believe that for a minute. All the times he could have told her—confided in her. He'd put a tracking stone on her wrist the first night they'd gone out. He probably followed her to Chris's house. He'd probably known what had happened on the bridge. All that anger about Chris—he didn't give a crap about her safety.

"Yeah," she scoffed. "You're such a good guy. What were you going to do next? Shoot Gabriel? Shoot me?"

"Becca." He gave her a wounded look. "You don't under-stand—"

"I understand that's a *gun*. Didn't you sit on my couch and tell me people carry guns when they want to *kill people*? Didn't you warn me away from Chris because he was nothing but trou-ble? Chris *is* a good guy." Her voice was close to breaking, but she saved it. "Chris helped me last night. He saved me on the beach. Now some guy has kidnapped him or killed him or—" Now her voice did break, and she had to take a heaving breath. "I know you miss your father, Hunter. They miss theirs, too. Nothing will bring your father back. But you could help. You could—"

"I won't help them."

"Would you help *me*?" She wasn't above begging. She didn't even have to fake the hitch in her voice. She moved closer, until she was right beside him. "Hunter? Would you help me?"

That got his attention. "Becca, if he's already taken them, there's nothing—"

"But you're strong! They're strong! You could help."

"Becca, I can't."

She reached out a hand and put it on his arm, gently, so as not to spook him. "There's been too much violence, Hunter. The Merrick brothers have been tormented since they moved here. They shouldn't be killed because a bunch of bullies are scared of them."

He didn't say anything.

"You saw what Tyler and Seth did to Chris," she said. "You saw how they came after the Merricks at the party. They are *not* good guys."

Hunter was shaking his head. "Becca, I can't—"

"Did you know Seth and Drew tried to rape me in the middle of this field last night?"

His head jerked up.

"Yeah. They did." Wow, her voice was actually steady. Strong. "That apology? Crap. They grabbed me and dragged me to the middle of the field and tried to rip my dress off and—"

She stopped. Hunter actually looked stricken.

"They did," she said, more quietly. "And Chris saved me, while you were off trying to kill Michael. That's the only reason he was on this field last night, and the only reason the Guide got to him while he was alone. So don't tell me you can't get involved."

"Becca," he whispered. "I'm sorry. I had no—"

"Don't be sorry!" She wanted to punch him, but he still had his hands wrapped around a gun. "Sorry doesn't mean anything, Hunter. *Do something.* Help me."

He wasn't looking at Michael anymore, but at her. His expression was a mix of pity and regret, anger and sadness and rage barely contained behind flushed cheeks and rapid breathing.

She stared back at him. "At least put up the gun."

Hunter glanced at Michael. "Not until he lets go of my feet."

"Gun first," said Michael.

"I'm not falling for that again," said Hunter.

"Then give it to me," said Becca.

Hunter raised his eyebrows.

Then he sighed, turned the gun sideways, and released the hammer. She swallowed and held her hand out, but he only gave her half a smile.

Then he lifted the edge of his shirt and slid it into a holster at the small of his back.

Now that the gun wasn't pointed at him, Michael climbed to

his feet—slowly. He was watching Casper, who was still growling at him.

"So now you'll help," Michael said.

"I'll help Becca," Hunter said. He paused and looked out at the field. "Though I don't know what I can do. I haven't seen another Guide in town. I'm assuming you've tried to track—"

"Yeah," said Michael.

"Maybe we could create a diversion," said Gabriel.

They all looked at him.

"You know," he said. "Make something explode, or call up a storm—" He stopped short, as if remembering his brothers weren't with them. "Or an earthquake, or something to draw out the Guide."

"If we go to the center of town," said Michael, "an earthquake would definitely get his attention—"

"Or," said Becca, "maybe we could try something completely mundane."

Now they all looked at her.

She pointed at Casper. "He's a police dog, isn't he? Can he track a scent?"

"Sure." Hunter frowned. "But we'd need something of the Guide's to track."

"Maybe not." She fished the second cell phone from her pocket and held it out. "How about something of Chris's?"

Becca trudged beside Hunter, following the plume of Casper's tail as he bounded ahead of them through the underbrush.

"We've already come this way," she said, just to break the silence.

"Looks like an army came through here," Hunter answered, though she had no idea how he could tell the difference. Just looked like a bunch of brush and branches to her. "Maybe Casper can pick up a second trail."

She didn't understand how he could be acting so normally, as if he dealt with things like guns and violence and missing Elementals on a daily basis.

Then again, maybe he did.

"So are you going to tell me?" she said.

"Tell you what?"

Was he deliberately being infuriating? "You said you're not an Earth," she said. "So which one are you?"

He laughed and gave her a sidelong glance. "Come on, Becca."

"Come on *what?*" she said. "Just—no more games. No more lies. Just tell me."

Hunter stopped and turned to look down at her. A line appeared between his eyebrows. "You're serious."

"Yeah."

"But—" He frowned. "The way people hassle you at school. You work with dogs. I mean—your mom's a *nurse,* for god's sake. And then, you said Drew tried—on the field last night." He ran a hand through his hair. "I never thought what it would be like for a girl, but—"

God, she wanted to punch him! "*What the hell are you talking about?*"

"He's a Fifth," said Michael, stepping up beside her.

"Yeah." Hunter glanced at him, then back at her. That line still hung between his brows. "Like you."

She shook her head, wishing people would stop assuming she was with the Merricks. "I'm not one of them. Tyler only *thought* that because I saved Chris that night."

"You are, Becca," he said. "You have to be. I can tell—"

"Hunter, I'm not."

"You are."

She glanced at Michael and Gabriel, hoping they'd look as skeptical as she felt, but they didn't.

They looked intrigued.

This was ridiculous. They were wasting time. She looked back at Hunter. "Fine. Prove it."

"People hassle you, right? Too much." He tapped his chest. "It's because our element is all about the spirit. Life. People are drawn to that—"

She scoffed and turned away. "People aren't *drawn* to me, Hunter."

"Hey." His voice sharpened. "Just because they aren't *nice* doesn't mean they aren't drawn to you."

She froze and looked over her shoulder at him, remembering how he said he'd been hassled—to the point that his father had to teach him to physically defend himself.

"Lots of people are bullied," she said. "Every day. It doesn't mean they have superpowers."

He walked back to her. "Not superpowers," he said softly. "Maybe—maybe just a stronger connection to this element."

"You felt the power in the sunlight," said Michael.

Gabriel was nodding, too. "That night in Chris's bedroom. The fire reached for you—"

"That doesn't *mean* anything," she said. "Nick was making the fire flicker."

But her conviction was wavering. She kept thinking about the way she'd felt the connection to Nick's power, that morning in her driveway.

"I knew it right away," said Hunter. "That night at the party, the way you wanted to help that stupid girl puking in the bushes, or how you wanted to warn Chris about Tyler, or—"

"Maybe I'm just a nice person!" she cried.

Hunter looked startled. "You can't be both?"

She faltered. This was too much. She couldn't debate it now. They needed to be looking for Chris and Nick—not arguing over something impossible.

"You saved Chris," said Michael. "You fought Tyler and Seth for him."

"But—" She hesitated, unsure whether to give his theory any credence. "I never had some weird event when I hit puberty. I never started setting fires or causing earthquakes or—"

"How about something humanitarian?" said Hunter. "Think back to middle school. Did you volunteer at your mom's hospital, or in a nursing home, or anything like that?"

"I'm not that nice a person," she said, making a face. But then she paused, remembering how she used to walk the woods, looking for hurt animals to save.

"You've thought of something," said Hunter.

"It's nothing. I used to rescue animals. It made my mother crazy. It was just a phase."

"Aha." Hunter stepped closer, then spoke low, just for her. "Remember when you kissed me on the dance floor?"

She flushed, then nodded.

"Remember," he said quietly, "how you felt the power in the room? The connection to the crowd?"

She did. The fire on her lips, the sweat on her body—she remembered it all.

Becca stared up at him.

He must have seen something like acceptance in her eyes. "You believe me. You might not want to admit it yet, but you do."

"But my parents aren't like you," she sputtered. "They're not—"

"Your mom's a nurse," said Michael. "What's your dad do?"

She bit at her lip, remembering Chris's comment about *Fifths* hitting the genetic lottery. "He works with wildlife—"

Casper barked, somewhere in the woods up ahead.

"Come on," said Hunter. He took off at a run. They followed.

The dog had stopped at the edge of the woods, just before a long stretch of grass that ran beside the creek. Charred branches littered the ground and burns scored the grass.

"Lightning," said Gabriel, his voice grave. He looked up at the cloudless sky, then back at the ground. "A lot of it."

"Chris was running for the water," said Michael.

Casper barked again, spinning in circles.

"He didn't make it," said Hunter. "Come on. I think Casper's found a new scent to follow."

The dog led them to the road, to the far side of the bridge that had been destroyed. The county had put up concrete barriers and those ROAD CLOSED signs, and some random construction equipment was parked along the side of the road.

"This is where we saw the Guide last Tuesday," she said. She was starting to get a little breathless from trailing Casper, though the guys weren't having any trouble. "How far have we gone? Like three miles?"

Gabriel gave her a look. "Like *one*."

So she needed more cardio.

"That night of the bridge collapse," said Hunter. "That's the first time you saw him? Was he on foot?"

"Yes," said Gabriel.

"No car?"

Gabriel shook his head. "We chased him off, but he ran for the woods." He pointed east, toward the tree line on the other side of the road. "We were able to pull a hell of a lot of power from the storm. I thought it was the adrenaline, but I couldn't generate anywhere near as much last night."

"No kidding," said Hunter. He gave her a grim smile. "Becca wasn't with you."

Her breath caught, and she wanted to protest.

But she remembered feeling the power that night, too. The strength in the storm, the way the wind and rain had kissed her skin and called for vengeance. "Holy crap," she whispered.

Hunter nodded, but he looked out at the trees. "What's beyond those woods? More residential properties?"

"No," said Michael. "Commercial. A couple strip malls, fast food, a car dealership, that kind of stuff."

Hunter frowned. "Maybe it's a dead end, then. Maybe he kept a car there."

But Casper found a trail right away, leading out of the woods. They stopped behind a McDonald's, hidden in the shade of the trees. A hundred feet ahead sat a four-lane road, busy with late morning traffic. The drive-thru was packed.

Hunter had a tight grip on Casper's collar, though the dog was obviously onto a scent. "You guys should wait here."

"Why?" said Michael. "So you can warn him?"

"No." Hunter glanced at him, and it wasn't a friendly look. "Because Casper's found a trail. A strong one. The Guide might be nearby."

"Good," said Gabriel, and now Becca heard the fury in his voice. "Let's go."

"Yeah," said Hunter. "But he's *looking for you*. I can check it out, see what we find, then—"

"I don't care," said Michael. "I don't trust you."

Hunter narrowed his eyes. "Look, man, I don't *have* to help you."

Becca put a hand on Hunter's arm and looked at Michael. No way she was letting stupid male posturing screw this up. "Do you trust *me?*"

Michael's expression hardened, just for a moment. Then she watched something soften in his eyes. He nodded. "Yeah. I do."

"Come on," she said to Hunter. "Let's check it out." Without waiting for him to agree, she started forward, half sliding down the grassy hill into the McDonald's parking lot.

Casper bounded past her, then Hunter appeared at her side. "Take it slow," he said. His voice turned wry. "You had a pentagram on your door, too."

She swung her head around, unsure what emotions were rattling around in her head. "You knew. All that time, you knew."

He shrugged, and she didn't know if that was indifference or embarrassment. "Not all that time. At first I was only sure about you. It wasn't until that morning in your driveway that I really started to suspect the Merricks." He paused. "I also thought you were with them."

"So all that—when you wouldn't kiss me in the parking lot." She swallowed. "You thought I was in on some plot to kill your father?"

"No." His voice was sharp again, and he caught her hand and pulled her into a jog as Casper rounded a corner into the strip mall parking lot. "I knew you couldn't have done it. I figured that out right away. But I thought maybe the Merricks were using you. And you trusted me. You were an easy link to follow."

"God." She shook her head. "And I thought all those rocks were *so* special. I'm such an idiot—"

"They are," he said. "They are." He pulled her to a stop, looking down at her in the middle of the blacktop. The breeze lifted hair from her neck, wrapping around her body and urging her close to him.

"Just the quartz tracked you," he said. "Everything else did exactly what I said it did." He paused. "Do *you* trust me, Becca?"

She licked her lips, uncertain. He'd lied about so much. Was he lying now?

Casper barked again, halfway across the parking lot. He was heading for the grocery store area, where dozens of cars were parked in a big colorful mass, drawing sunlight like gems.

"Shit," said Hunter. He took off after his dog.

She took off after him.

Casper was dodging between cars, leaping onto hoods and down, probably reliving his good ol' days as a police dog.

"Casper!" Hunter called. *"Hier! Fuss!"*

Casper didn't *hier*. Or *fuss*.

He dove down another row, and Hunter and Becca almost caught up to him. The dog stopped on the far side of a green pickup truck, and she heard a man yelling. It sounded like groceries hit the pavement.

Becca had almost forgotten who they were tracking. She'd succumbed to the more immediate worry that Casper was going after someone who had a bag full of hot dogs or something. So though her brain registered the logo on the side of the truck, though her mind registered the familiarity of the voice, she didn't put two and two together until she skidded around the side of the bumper.

And there was Casper, snarling viciously at his prey, the man Hunter had ordered him to track.

Becca's father.

CHAPTER 39

Chris had found a crack in the concrete floor. He was spitting at it.

"This is kind of a stretch," said Nick.

Chris spit again, running his finger along the four-inch crack, making sure he wouldn't lose it in the darkness, coaxing his saliva into the opening. "What else do we have to do?"

"That crack would have to go all the way through the concrete. Like, through the foundation. And Michael would have to be within . . . what, fifty feet? A hundred?"

"Again, what else do we have to do?"

Silence for a while, during which Chris silently agreed with Nick. His spit was evaporating before it could travel too far. He didn't have enough power to force it more quickly.

"Pee on it," said Nick.

Always practical. He could probably feel Chris's frustration.

Chris had thought of that anyway. "I'm worried if I stand up, I'll lose the crack."

He kept thinking of the power on the bridge, how he'd drawn such strength from the water. He'd saved Becca's life. She hadn't been breathing. He'd never felt such a strong connection to his element.

Why couldn't he do that now?

There'd been the car accident. The fire. Becca had been trapped. He'd pounded on her window, desperate.

He had no shortage of desperation now.

He'd been standing in water. Was that it? He'd been standing in water that night he called the wave on Sillery Bay, at Drew's party.

No, but the bridge power was even stronger. He'd been so desperate to get her out of that car, he'd punched right through her window. Blood had gone everywhere, diluted from the rain.

That night Becca saved him, his face had been a mess. She'd poured water down the side of his face, over the cuts on his temple.

Blood. He needed blood. His blood, mixed with the water.

If he thought about this too long, he'd chicken out.

He put his teeth against his wrist. And bit down.

Goddamn, it hurt. He hadn't even broken the skin, and he was already sweating.

"Nick," he said. "I think I'm going to need you to bite my arm."

"I think I'm going to need you to run that by me again."

"Shut up! I need to bleed. I think if I can get blood in the crack, it will make a difference."

Nick was silent for a long moment. Then he cleared his throat. "You can't just stab yourself with the prong on your belt buckle?"

"That's better?"

"From my angle, yes. It's better." He paused. "Scrape it against the concrete for a few minutes. You can probably get a pretty sharp point."

It worked. Too well. Chris barely felt the prong slice across his wrist before blood was running down his hand and across his fingers.

But the blood found the crack. It went all the way through. Chris could feel it.

And then his blood found the earth.

* * *

Becca couldn't make it add up in her head. This had to be a mistake. Her dad had to have some raw meat in his bag, or Casper must have picked up on something else, or maybe the Guide had parked here yesterday.

At least Casper had him distracted. Her father hadn't even noticed her.

Hunter had hold of her wrist, and he was trying to drag her back, away, around the front of the truck.

"Wait," she said, struggling, still trying to piece this all together. "That's—that's my—"

"Becca?" Her father sounded confused—and he sure didn't look like some terrifying Elemental Guide, the way he was backed up against his truck. He glanced between her and the dog growling at his knees.

"Dad," she said, choking on the word.

Well, that made Hunter stop pulling at her arm. "Holy crap," he said. "It's your *father?*"

Her dad seemed to notice him. "Is this your dog?" He glanced back at Becca. "What are you doing here?"

"Dad," she said, feeling her heart pound. Like on the soccer field, the air felt alive with sunshine. She could reach out and touch it. "This is a mistake. We're just—this is a mistake."

"It's not," said Hunter, his voice low. "Becca—it's not a mistake."

Her father still looked confused. "What's not a mistake?"

She'd been so ready to find a James Bond type, someone sleek and muscled, someone with terrifying charisma and the type of power that could cause car accidents and destroy bridges. Someone with the will to kill teenagers. Her father had showed her how to set the wing of a baby bird. He protected wild animals. He'd comforted her after the car crash.

How could he be the same person who had attacked them at the bridge?

How could he have terrorized the brothers to such an extent that Gabriel would spend the night hiding in the creek?

She still couldn't speak.

But the longer she stood here, the more her shock started to turn to fury.

She'd been on that bridge. *She'd* been on that soccer field.

"Could you call off your dog?" her father said to Hunter. "I don't know what you kids are doing, but—"

"Casper," said Hunter. *"Platz."*

The dog dropped to his haunches—but he stayed right in front of her father.

"It's you," she said flatly. "I guess we can forget the crabbing violations. I don't know why I'm surprised. What's one more lie?"

He frowned. "Becca, I'm not sure—"

"You're the Guide."

She'd hoped the accusation would hit him between the eyes, but he didn't even flinch. He lost the frown, and his eyes hardened. He didn't look away, didn't move. "Becca, you don't know what you're talking about."

"Did you take out the bridge behind the school?"

He didn't answer.

Her voice was rising. "Did you attack us on the soccer field?"

"Becca, you don't—"

She stepped closer to him, wanting to hit him. Her voice came out as a whisper. "Did you kill my friends?"

"They're not your friends," he said. "Becca, they're dangerous—"

"You're dangerous," she hissed. "They are my friends! You have to—"

"Becca." Her father's voice sliced right through hers, and he stepped toward her. "We are in the middle of a grocery store parking lot." A hand reached out as if to grab her.

Hunter seized her wrist and dragged her behind him. "Keep your hands off her."

Her father glared at him, but then glanced around the parking lot. They'd already earned a few looks from other patrons. "Becca," he said quietly. "We can talk about this somewhere else."

"Unless this somewhere else is where you're holding Chris and Nick, we're going to talk about it right here."

Her father took a step forward—making Hunter take a step back. She was right up against him now, her hands against his lower back, her hands brushing the holster.

I don't believe in accidents.

She hadn't even thought it through before her hands were on the gun.

And then she was pointing it at her father.

He went white. At least she had that satisfaction. "Becca—this is crazy. You have no idea what you're doing."

A woman screamed, somewhere nearby. A guy was yelling for someone to call 911.

Holy crap. She was pointing a gun at her father.

A father who'd tried to kill her. More than once.

"Becca," whispered Hunter. He took a long, slow breath. "Give me the gun."

"Talk!" she cried. "Where are they? Did you kill them? Did you—"

"I didn't kill them," her father said. "Becca, if you know I'm the Guide, then you know there are things we can get away with. Shooting someone in public is not one of them."

"Do you hate me?" she said. Her voice cracked at the end.

"What?" He shook his head. "Becca—no—"

"Do you?" she cried. "You left me. *You left me.* And now you're back, and you've tried to kill me twice—"

"I have not tried to kill you. I'm trying to keep the Merrick brothers away from you. When I left, I did it to protect you. Do you understand me? I'm trying to *protect you.*"

"Bullshit." She wished she knew how to cock the gun, just for effect. But she was worried she'd shoot him by accident.

She heard sirens.

Holy. Crap.

Her breath was shaking. "Talk fast."

"No one knew about you," he said. "Your mother isn't one of us, and I wanted to keep you out of it. I wasn't even sure you'd come into your abilities. But when you were eleven, a girl died, and the Merrick brothers were involved. A Guide was called." He was looking at her significantly. "Me, Becca. They wanted me to take care of it."

The gun was heavy. She felt her arms starting to waver. "I still don't understand."

"We lived in the same town! You went to school with one of them. When I went to the house—well, their mother was very convincing." His tone was grim. "She knew about you, Becca. For the first time, someone had leverage against me."

"Skip to the part where you left," she snapped.

"Damn it, Becca! That's *why* I left. She swore to leave you alone if I did—and she kept that promise. I couldn't take the chance of someone else finding out. I didn't want this for you. The pain of having to destroy others, the regret—" His eyes flicked up, to Hunter, hardening for an instant. "I didn't want you to be another teenager trained to kill. But then I got called for the family again—only to find out their parents had died in a fire. Now another Guide has been killed—apparently they're terrorizing the other families in town—"

The sirens were getting closer. She was so mad she almost couldn't see straight. "The *Merricks* are terrorizing the other families? Didn't you ever think to check your facts? You've been gone for years. You shouldn't be here now. You're helping nothing." Her voice broke again, and she started to lower the gun. "You're hurting everyone, just like before."

"Becca." His voice softened. "Becca, please."

She started to waver. She had no idea what was true anymore.

She tightened her grip on the gun. It suddenly felt like it was falling, slipping out of her hands.

No, that was her. Falling because of the earthquake.

CHAPTER 40

"Holy shit! It worked!" Chris had his hands pressed to the concrete. The floor had started to move.

A lot.

"It worked!" he said again, bracing his hands against the floor. He recognized his brother's power. He knew it. He *knew it*.

"Yeah," Nick said, and it sounded like he was speaking through clenched teeth. "This feels great."

The floor shook harder. Nick swore, and his voice vibrated with the rocking of the earth. "I'm g-going to k-kill Michael."

Steel started to whine and creak from pressure, and Chris heard bolts pop somewhere across the room. Metal sheeting ripped from a wall or the ceiling and rattled onto the concrete floor, a deafening sound.

Chris had a moment of panic. Were they underground? Was this a basement?

"Air!" cried Nick. "New air. Check the door."

Chris scrambled across the floor, terrified that any moment a sheet of metal was going to come crashing down on his head, and he'd be as incapacitated as Nick. The trembling floor kept throwing him off, and it took him too long to find it.

But when he did, it was open. He had to fight with the hinges to convince it to let him through, but suddenly he was outside the freezer, in a small corridor. They were in a basement. A flight of stairs sat just to his left.

Stairs. How was he going to get Nick out of here?

"Go," Nick yelled. "He has to be close. Don't try to drag me. I can't—"

Crash. More metal sheeting.

"Nick!" Chris yelled. "Nick, are you all—"

"Go, Chris. I'm fine." His voice sounded weak. "Just hurry."

Chris hurried.

Hunter had her hand and they were running.

Or he was running. Becca kept falling. Cars were veering all over the place on the main road, and they narrowly missed getting creamed in the parking lot. She lost track of her father entirely.

Casper, however, was easy to keep track of, loping beside them despite the shaking earth.

Hunter must have reclaimed his gun. She had no idea what had happened to it.

"Where are we going?" she said, clutching his arm to keep her feet.

"Michael's making the earthquake," he said.

"So?"

Hunter glanced at her. "That means something's happened."

Michael and Gabriel weren't where they'd left them, but it wasn't hard to follow the power radiating from the ground.

The epicenter was five stores down from the McDonald's, behind an abandoned restaurant. The exterior walls were old wood, practically crumbling from the effort of keeping the place upright during the earthquake. Michael stood in the middle of the cracked parking lot, his hands on the pavement, pouring power into the ground.

"What happened?" she yelled. "Michael, what are you doing?"

"I felt Chris," he said, and she could hear his panic even over the cacophony caused by the earthquake. "They're here. They're close. I just don't know—"

She caught his arm—and it took more effort than it should have. "Michael. Stop."

He lifted his hands from the ground. The earth rumbled to a stop.

They heard nothing for a long moment.

Then pounding from inside the restaurant. Gabriel made it to the locked doors first, fighting with the rusted handle.

Then Michael, his hands beside his brother's, rammed the door with his shoulder. Becca felt him pouring strength into it, but those old doors were built to last.

So she added her strength.

Hunter added his.

And together, they pushed it through.

CHAPTER 41

This time, Chris and Nick ended up in the Emergency Room. Becca didn't get to go with them. Too many people—too complicated. They were already trying to come up with a good story, something about getting drunk on a dare, and sneaking into the restaurant and—well, she couldn't keep up with it all.

Hunter drove her home.

"Are you worried about your dad?" he asked quietly when he parked in front of her house.

She was. But she didn't want to talk about him. "I'm more worried the cops are going to come after me."

"For the gun thing?" Hunter shook his head. "With the earthquake mess, I'll bet no one remembers it happened."

She stared at the front door of her house. "I will," she said. "I could have shot my father."

"No, you couldn't," said Hunter.

He was probably right, but she turned to look at him anyway. "You didn't think I could do it?"

He smiled, a little sadly, a little knowingly. "Becca, I've never doubted your resolve." Then he leaned in, his voice a bit wry. "But your finger was never on the trigger."

He walked her to her door, but that was it. She slid her key into the lock, and he turned to go.

"Hunter."

He stopped, but he wasn't looking at her. "Yeah?"

She didn't think she could ever trust him again—but she had to know. "You and me," she said. "How much was real?"

He turned. "Time will tell."

Then he was in his jeep, and then he was gone.

Chris sprawled in the desk chair in Nick's room. The moon hung low outside the window, a cloudless night. No chance of rain on the horizon. Eighteen stitches formed a crooked line along Chris's forearm, and he wondered if he could keep the cut out of water long enough for a scar to form.

Nick was flat on his back in bed, fighting to stay awake through the painkillers they'd given him at the hospital.

Gabriel was helping the effort by sitting on the end of the bed and heckling them both.

"So, Chris," he said, "you couldn't make a smaller cut?"

Nick's eyes were closed, but he smiled. "Chris asked me to bite him first."

Gabriel gave him a disgusted look. "You are one sick bastard."

"I was desperate." Chris smiled, too, but then he dropped it. "Desperate people do crazy things."

They fell silent for a long moment. Chris wondered if Nick had fallen asleep.

Chris wouldn't be far behind. His eyelids felt heavy, but Gabriel would never let him live it down if he went to bed before ten.

Gabriel spoke into the silence, his voice weighted and quick, as if the words had to rush past his lips. "I'm sorry I couldn't save you."

"You idiot," said Nick, his voice amused. "You did save us."

"No," said Gabriel. "Before. And I provoked them into calling the Guides—"

"This wasn't your fault," said Nick. His eyes opened to look at his twin. "Not even a little."

"I'm glad you provoked them," said Chris, feeling heat in his voice. "I'd do it again."

"Hey." Michael appeared in the doorway and leaned in. "This started way before that mess with the truck and the fertilizer, okay? None of you started it. *None of you.* If anyone did, it was Mom and Dad, when they made the deal in the first place."

The sudden silence smacked Chris in the face. He just stared at Michael standing there in the doorway. So did his brothers.

It must have taken Michael by surprise, too. He looked slightly abashed. His hands dropped from the molding and he drew back. "Not too late, okay? You all need to get some sleep."

Gabriel inhaled quickly, and Chris braced himself for words with an edge, some comment that would ramp up the tension in the house again.

But Gabriel just nodded. "All right."

Then Michael glanced at each of them, and without another word, started to move down the hallway. Chris met Gabriel's eyes across the room and held them.

"Hey," called Chris. "Michael."

Michael came back to the doorway, his expression wary, as if he thought their acquiescence a moment ago had been too good to be true. "Yeah?"

Chris straightened in the chair, surprised to find himself uncertain now. "We're just talking about stuff. Want to come in?"

"Yeah, come in," agreed Gabriel. He looked up at their oldest brother, not an ounce of mockery or derision in his expression now. "Join us."

By Sunday, Becca still hadn't heard from her father.

But late in the afternoon, Chris came to see her.

Remembering the last time he'd come for a visit, she peered around him at her driveway, finding nothing but weakening sunlight sliding across the pavement. The SUV sat there, but it looked empty.

"No brothers?" she said.

He smiled, but it was cautious. "No brothers."

"Want to sit on the porch?" she said. "My mom's sleeping, so . . . if you want to talk . . ."

"Sure."

So they sat on the porch swing, barely rocking at all.

"How's Nick?" she asked. "I bet he's bummed about the cast."

Chris shrugged as if pleased she'd introduced a safe topic. "Actually, no cast. He just has to wear one of those Velcro things. Even that, probably only a week."

"I thought you said he had a compound fracture!"

He grinned. "Yeah, well, air is everywhere, Becca. He'll heal pretty quick now that we're out of that room." Then he lost the smile. "How are you?"

Her turn to shrug. "I haven't heard from my father, if that's what you're asking."

"It's not." He leaned close, his voice low, intense. "You, Becca. How are *you*?"

She shifted on the bench and looked out at the yard. "Confused."

"Yeah?" Chris reached out a hand and brushed a piece of hair from her face, tucking it behind her ear.

His touch was gentle but electric, and it made her breath catch. But that was all he did before settling against the backrest. Maybe it was a casual thing. She shouldn't read meaning into it, the way she had with Hunter.

"I don't know why my father would keep this from me," she said.

"From what Hunter told me, he had his reasons."

She sat up straight. "You talked to Hunter?"

He nodded.

"Did anyone throw a punch?"

He raised an eyebrow. "Not the way you mean. But Gabriel asked him about that self-defense stuff."

"So you're all friends now?"

"Not by a long shot." He shook his head. "Michael says Hunter's lonely. I actually think he feels bad for the kid."

"You know Hunter held a gun to his head. He came here to kill him."

Chris shrugged. "Guys bond over weird stuff, I guess." He

leaned in again and sighed. "Jesus, Becca, it's impossible to get you to talk about yourself. I didn't even mean the Elemental stuff. Are you *okay?*"

She stared across into his blue eyes, just now wide with emotion.

And then she realized he was talking about what had happened at Homecoming.

"Yeah," she said, and she hated that her voice was rough. "I wasn't going to say anything. It was—you stopped them." Her shoulders felt tight, braced against the wood of the swing. "I didn't think it would do any good. I figured everyone would be talking about me again, and I just—I didn't want to go through that." She gave a little laugh, and was surprised when a tear rolled off her cheek to land on her finger.

"Becca," Chris whispered. "You can't—"

"No, I changed my mind." She looked up at him through her lashes. "I will now. I kept wondering what good it would do for me to report them, for me to tell people what they'd done. Why put *myself* through it? But then I started thinking about your parents, about Tyler and Seth and all those other dickheads. I thought of all the deals, and the secrets, and the lies people told in the name of *protection.*"

He was staring at her, and she had to take a breath. "What if your parents had just stood up to Tyler and Seth's folks from the start, and said, 'Call the Guides, our kids have done nothing wrong. Can you say the same?' "

He flinched a little, and she immediately regretted her words.

But then he nodded. "You're right." He paused, and his voice was thick. "I wish they had."

She stared at him, remembering the potency of Gabriel's emotion in the woods. She'd wanted to hug Gabriel then, but she wasn't sure how he'd take it.

Now she threw her arms around Chris's neck, pressing her face to his shoulder. "Chris. I'm sorry."

He held her, his arms secure around her back. She felt his breath against her hair, quick for a moment, then easing.

They were rocking gently now, and it felt nice. She didn't let him go.

Chris stroked the hair away from her face again, lightly, gently, his fingers a bare touch on her cheekbone. "You turned the conversation away from yourself again."

"I don't want to talk about those guys. I've wasted enough time on them, and I'll spend enough time talking about them tomorrow."

He nodded, and she relaxed into his shoulder.

Then she lifted her head, finding his face close, his eyes shadowed and intent.

"What?" he said.

"Will you still go with me?"

"Yes." He placed a hand against her cheek. "I promise."

"Thanks, Chris." She paused. "You're a good friend."

They almost-rocked for a little while, and she enjoyed the late September wind tickling across her cheeks.

Then Chris shifted her a little. "What about you and Hunter?"

She sighed. "I don't know. He lied to me about so much—he won't even tell me what *was* real—"

"So you're not dating anymore?"

"No." She lifted her head again, hearing disgust in her voice. "I don't even know if we were dating to begin with. I mean, he—"

But she couldn't finish that sentence.

Because Chris had her face in his hands, and he'd brought his lips to hers.

BEYOND
THE
STORY

Many crystals and stones are known for their mystical properties. As a Fifth, Hunter has a special connection to certain ones, and he wears the following stones at all times.

Loaned to Becca

Amethyst—Purple. Contains healing properties for mind and body; also provides a calming influence. Strong connection to Spirit.

Citrine—Yellow. Banishes negative energy and enhances natural courage. Promotes open-minded acceptance. Strong connection to Air.

Garnet—Red. Enhances confidence, also provides a certain degree of protection from outside influences and negative Elemental power. Strong connection to Fire.

Hematite—Black. Improves clarity of thought and reduces anxiety. Strong connection to Water.

Quartz—White. Amplifies the effects of other stones; also used for tracking. Helps focus Elemental power. Strong connection to Spirit.

Kept by Hunter

Jade—Green. Repels enemies and negativity; also symbolizes serenity. Strong connection to Earth.

Lapis—Blue. Enhances charisma and confidence, strengthening relations with others. Strong connection to Air.

Tiger's Eye—Multicolored browns. Enhances inner strength. Strong connection to Fire.

Turquoise—Blue-green. Protection from negative forces and enemies. Strong connection to Earth.

Bloodstone—Green with red flecks. Feeds stamina and strength. Strong connection to Fire.

Coral—White. Inspires prudence and wisdom. Strong connection to Water.

Opal—Bluish white. Enhances emotion, both negative and positive. Strong connection to Spirit.

ELEMENTAL:
Where it all begins . . .

CHAPTER 1

The thrill of having a summer job wore off about fifteen minutes after Emily Morgan started working. She'd had two customers all day. The sports complex was such a joke. No wonder she hadn't had any competition for this job.

It wasn't even a *sports* complex, not really. Mini-golf that no one wanted to play when it was a hundred degrees outside. Batting cages that no one would use until school started up in the fall. She probably wouldn't see another soul until after five, when the white-collar dads showed up to use the driving range in a last-ditch effort to avoid going home to screaming kids.

Even then, in this heat, she'd be lucky if there were many.

Ugh, her hair was already plastered to her neck. Days like these, she wished she had enough power to do more than stir up a gentle breeze.

Then she choked off that thought.

She knew what happened to kids with *power*.

Besides, sitting here wasn't *so* bad. She worked the shop alone, so she could blast the entire sound tracks to *Rent* and *Les Mis* and sing along, and no one would give a crap. She didn't have to watch her brother Tyler light insects on fire with a magnifying glass and a sunbeam, like he'd done last summer. She didn't have to listen to her parents argue.

She could count the days until she turned eighteen.

Until she could get away from her family.

The shop door creaked and rattled, sticking in the humidity. Emily straightened, excited for a customer, for someone—*anyone*—to break up this cruel monotony.

Anyone but Michael Merrick.

For a second, she entertained the thought of diving behind the counter.

Real mature, Em.

But her hands were slick against the glass casing.

It wasn't that he *looked* all that intimidating. He'd be starting his senior year this fall, just like she would, but sometime over the last six months he'd grown to the tall side of average. He worked for his parents' landscaping company, she knew, and it couldn't have been light work—his arms showed some clear definition, his shoulders stretching the green tee shirt he wore.

He was filthy, too. Dirt streaked across his chest and clung to the sweat on his neck. His jeans had seen better days, and his work boots would probably track dirt across the floor. Even his hair, dark and wild and a length somewhere between sexy and I-don't-give-a-crap, was more unkempt than usual.

Emily didn't care about any of that.

She had her eyes on the baseball bat in his hands.

He'd gotten into it with Tyler last weekend, had sent her brother home with a black eye and a bloody nose, leaving their parents to argue for an hour about how they were going to handle the *Merrick problem*.

Emily slid her hand along the counter, toward where they kept the putt-putt clubs for little kids.

"I don't want any trouble," she said, her voice solid but too quick. Her fingers wrapped around the handle of a club.

Michael's eyes narrowed. "I don't either."

Then she realized he hadn't moved from the doorway, that he was still standing there staring at her, his hand on the knob.

He glanced past her, at the corners of the shop, as if reassuring himself that they were alone. She had no idea what that meant. She watched him take in her stance, the way she'd half pulled the putt-putt club free.

He followed her gaze to the bat resting against his shoulder.

His expression hardened, and he shoved the door closed. He was halfway across the floor before she realized he'd moved, and she yanked the club free, ready to swing if he gave her an excuse.

Then he was within reach, and she registered the bat leaving his shoulder, and, god, her parents were right—

He was going to swing—

He was going to kill her—

His hand shot out and caught the steel bar.

Emily stood there gasping. She'd done it—she'd swung for his head. The end of the putter hung about five inches from his face.

And his bat was leaning against the counter.

Harmless.

She couldn't move. He didn't let go of the club, either, using his free hand to dig into the pocket of his jeans. A five-dollar bill dropped onto the glass counter between them.

"So can I get five tokens or what?"

Tokens. For the batting cages.

Of *course*.

Emily couldn't catch her breath—and that *never* happened. Her panic had kicked the air into a flurry of little whirlwinds in the space between them, teasing her cheeks and lifting his hair.

She could catch his scent, though, sweet and summery, mulch and potting soil, honeysuckle and cut grass. A warm fragrance, not something that belonged on someone she was supposed to hate.

He was staring at her, and he had a death grip on the club. She could feel his strength through the slim bar. "Well?"

"Yeah." She coughed and cleared her throat, using her own free hand to punch at the cash register. "Sure."

It took effort to look away from the dark brown of his eyes. Wasn't there some kind of rule about not looking away from an enemy? She fished the tokens out of the drawer, almost dropping them all over the floor. Somehow, she got them onto the glass counter and slid them toward him.

Then they stood there comically, connected by the slim rod of the club.

She wanted to let go—but she didn't.

Especially now that she'd tried to hit him, when he'd never made a move to lay a hand on her.

She swallowed, thinking of Tyler's bruised face after he'd gone a few rounds with Michael Merrick.

He leaned in. "I come here every Wednesday and Friday."

Emily nodded.

"You going to try to kill me every time?"

She shook her head quickly.

He let go of the club. She sheepishly lowered it, but didn't put it back in the bucket with the others.

Michael swiped the tokens from the counter and jammed them into his pocket. He swung the bat onto his shoulder again.

Emily opened her mouth—for what, she wasn't sure.

But then he was through the door, pulling it shut behind him without a glance back.

The ball came flying out of the machine, and Michael swung the bat hard, feeling it all the way through his shoulders.

Crack. The ball went sailing into the net.

One place. That's all he wanted—one place where he wouldn't get hassled.

And now he was screwed.

What the hell was Tyler's sister doing here, anyway? She wasn't a jock chick. From what he knew of her, she should probably be flirting over the counter at Starbucks or something, not babysitting a half-dead sports center.

Summer should have meant a break from this crap. Ever since they'd moved here in sixth grade, school had been a prison he got to escape at three o'clock every day.

Only to be hauled back in the next morning.

Just like a real prison, not everyone sucked. There were the people who didn't know he existed. The people who knew but didn't care. The latter made up the bulk of the student body.

But then there was the group that knew everything about him. The group that wanted him dead.

The Elementals.

Like he'd picked this. Like he'd woken up one morning and said, *I'd love to be tied to an element. I'd love to have so much power it scares me.*

I'd love to be marked for death because of something I can't control.

Another ball.

Crack.

This wasn't the only place with batting cages, but it was the cheapest. One sat closer to home, with fake turf in the cages and everything, but here his feet were in the dirt, pulling strength from the ground below.

If he took his shoes off and swung barefoot, he could draw enough power from the earth to blow the ball straight through the net.

Oh, who was he kidding? He could practically do that *now,* steel-toed work boots and all.

That was part of the problem. He was a *pure* Elemental. Power spoke to him straight from the earth. The others in town had power, sure, but nothing like his. He could theoretically level half the town if he lost his temper.

Which was why they wanted him dead.

Another ball.

Crack.

At least his parents had worked out a deal: He'd stay out of trouble, and the other families wouldn't report his existence.

There'd been money involved, sure. He had no idea how much. But sometimes he couldn't believe his entire being rested on a signed check and a frigging *handshake.*

It didn't help that the other kids in town—the kids who *knew*—seemed determined to make him reveal himself.

The hair on the back of his neck pricked, and Michael punched the button to stop the pitches, whirling with bat in hand.

He wouldn't put it past Emily to call her brother and his friends.

No one stood in the dust between the batting cages and the office. Dad's work truck was still the only vehicle in the parking lot.

Michael swiped the sweat off his forehead and turned to slap the button again. Another ball came flying.

Crack.

He'd have to think twice before bringing Chris or the twins here again. It was one thing to walk into enemy territory alone, and entirely another to drag his little brothers.

And, damn it, this shouldn't have *been* enemy territory!

Crack.

God, it felt good to hit something.

Well, he wasn't giving it up. This was *his* thing. If Emily wanted to take a swing at his head with a putter twice a week, she could give it her best shot. What did she think he was going to do, instigate an earthquake from the batting cages? Make too much grass grow on the driving range?

That prickle crawled along his neck again. Michael spun.

Emily stood there, ten feet behind the chain link, her arms folded tight against her chest. Tendrils of white-blond hair had escaped her ponytail to cling to her neck in the humidity.

Michael could practically hear his father's daily warning in his head: *Don't start something. Just leave them alone.*

How was he supposed to leave them alone if they kept coming after him?

He automatically checked behind her. Still no cars in the parking lot.

"Back to take another swing?" he said.

She scowled, but didn't look away. "No." She hesitated. "I just . . . I wanted to—"

A ball rammed the fence beside his shoulder, rattling the entire structure. Michael swore, and Emily jumped. He turned to slap the button again.

When he turned back, she'd come closer, until only three feet of dirt and a chain-link cage separated them.

"I need this job," she said, her voice full of false bravado. Like she'd had to dare herself to walk out here.

"Maybe you shouldn't try to kill your customers, then."

She licked her lips and fidgeted. "I didn't . . . I thought you were going to—"

"Yeah, I know what you thought I was going to do." He adjusted the grip on his bat and turned back to face the machine. No matter how careful he was, all they could see was his potential for damage.

Like he would have *needed* a bat. Didn't she understand that?

He hit the button. A ball came flying. He swung.

Crack.

"Well," she said from behind him, "I saw what you did to Tyler last week."

What *he'd* done. That was rich. "Yeah, poor Tyler."

"He said you jumped him after school."

Michael couldn't even turn around. Fury kept him rooted until the next ball shot out of the machine. He swung hard. This one hit the nets and strained the ropes.

Of course Tyler would make him out to be the bad guy.

He tossed a glance over his shoulder. "I'm sure you got the whole story."

She hesitated. "If you're just coming here to hassle me, I'll tell my parents."

From any other girl, it would have been an empty threat. The kind of threat you stopped hearing in third grade.

From her, it meant something. Emily Morgan's parents could cause serious problems for his family.

Michael gritted his teeth and made his voice even. "I'm not doing anything to hassle you."

Ball. *Crack*. He brushed the sweat out of his eyes.

She was still standing there. He could *feel* it.

"Here," she said.

He didn't turn. "What?"

She was close enough now that the earth whispered to him about her presence. "I'll get today," she said. "For trying to kill you and all." Then the fence jingled, as if she was fiddling with it.

Another ball was coming, so he couldn't look. He swung and sent it flying.

She'd get today? What did that mean?

He turned to ask her, but she was already slipping through the tinted door into the office.

But strung through the fence was his crumpled five-dollar bill.

CHAPTER 2

Emily pushed rice and chicken around her plate and wished she hadn't mentioned Michael Merrick to her parents. Because now they had a new topic to argue about.

As if they needed one.

"You're going to quit that job," said her father.

"I *need* my job," she said.

"Oh, you do not," said her mother. "What could you possibly *need* a job for? We give you everything you need."

In a way, they did. She had her car, a hand-me-down sedan she'd gotten when she turned sixteen and her father decided he wanted something new. Her parents covered insurance. She always said she'd pay for her own gas—but they'd given her a gas card for her seventeenth birthday.

But she doubted they'd pay for a security deposit on a new apartment in New York City after senior year. Having a stash of cash meant freedom to do what she wanted to do.

"He didn't bother me," she said. "I think he was just as surprised to see me—"

"The last thing the Merricks need is leverage," said her father, gesturing with his fork. "This deal was a bad idea from the beginning, before we knew how powerful that boy would get."

Emily sighed. "I'm not leverage."

"You could be," said her mother. "I'm not having you come home looking like Tyler."

Emily peeked through her bangs across the table at her brother. He wasn't eating, either—his fingers were too busy flying across the face of his phone, his own mode of ignoring their parents. He was two years younger, but already stood about four inches taller than she did. He'd spent freshman year growing into his features, and now, for the first time, he looked older. The bruising on his cheek had turned yellow and purple, sharp and striking against his pale skin and white-blond hair. She studied the injury, remembering Michael's sarcasm from the batting cage.

Poor Tyler. I'm sure you got the whole story.

"Take a picture," Tyler muttered without looking up. "It'll last longer."

"Original." Along with the height, he'd grown into a crappy attitude, too. "Who are you texting?"

"None of your business."

She didn't really care, but it was easier to bicker with Tyler than to fight with her parents. "Sounds like a girl."

He shot her a glare over the phone. "Well, you sound like a—"

"Tyler." Their mother's voice sliced through his coming insult. "No electronics during dinner."

He made a disgusted sound and put the phone in his lap.

But Emily knew he'd be back at it as soon as their folks were distracted again.

"What did he say to you?" said her father.

"Nothing." She pushed the food around her plate again. She hadn't mentioned her own actions with the putter—and didn't plan on telling them now. "He just came in to use the batting cages. It was fine."

"Convenient," snapped her father. "Your first day of work, you're alone, he comes in there—"

"He said he goes there all the time!"

Her parents went still. It was the wrong thing to say.

"I don't want you going back there," said her mother, her voice hushed.

"It's *fine*—"

"The hell it is," said her father. "I've been talking to Josh Drake. He thinks we should just take care of the problem ourselves."

Tyler rolled his eyes. "Seth's dad says that every time he cracks open a beer."

Though he was a few years younger, Seth Drake was Tyler's best friend. He was an Earth Elemental like his dad—and like Michael Merrick—but the Drake abilities stopped at pulling strength from the ground they stood on. Emily had no idea where Michael's abilities stopped.

And that was part of the problem.

"I think we might all be overreacting," said Emily. "He didn't start anything—"

"Overreacting?" Tyler threw his fork down against his plate. "You saw what that asshole did to me."

"Tyler!" said their mother. "I won't have that language at the table."

Emily stared at him. "And what exactly happened again?"

He stared back at her for a beat. "I told you," he said evenly. "He jumped me and Seth."

"That's it," said her father. "I'm calling over there."

"To Seth's?" said Tyler.

"No. To the Merricks."

Michael heard the garage phone ring while he was out back, playing catch with his youngest brother. He was tired from work and the batting cages, but he'd found the twins pinning Chris in the hallway, trying to spit into his mouth.

Michael never cared if Gabriel and Nick beat the crap out of each other, but he hated when they ganged up on Chris.

So now they were killing time out back until the twins found some other trouble to get into.

Someone else must have grabbed the phone, because the ringer cut off quickly. Michael hadn't even bothered moving. He couldn't remember the last time someone had called the house to talk to *him*.

"You're so lucky," said Chris, pelting the ball back to him.

It went wide. Michael stretched to reach it, and the ball smacked into his mitt. *"Lucky?"*

"Yeah. You get to go to work with Dad all day. I'm stuck here."

Michael threw the ball back. This was the first summer Chris and the twins had been deemed old enough to stay home alone while their parents worked. "Do they pull that crap all day long?"

"Nah." Chris caught the ball and shrugged. "It's just boring."

Boring. A code word for lonely. Michael remembered being too young to drive, before he knew about his abilities, when summertime seemed to stretch out with infinite possibilities—and ended up basically being three months of house arrest. He regretted not stopping at home to bring Chris along to the batting cages—but then he considered Emily and the putter and thanked god he hadn't bothered. That was a story he didn't need Chris dragging home to their parents.

"I'll talk to Dad," he said. "Maybe you can come along for some of the smaller jobs."

"Really?" Chris flung the ball back. "That would be awesome! I'll go every day! We could—"

"Easy." Michael smiled. Chris *had* to be lonely if he was willing to spend his summer pushing a mower and laying mulch. "I said I'd *ask*."

Then he wondered if something more than boredom was motivating his little brother. He remembered himself at Chris's age, how his element had begun calling to him, how he'd wanted to be outside all the time. Neither Chris nor the twins had shown any inclinations yet—but maybe it was right around the corner.

The thought was both exciting and terrifying.

And the worst part was that a selfish little piece of Michael wished one of his brothers would turn out to be as powerful as he was—just so he didn't have to carry this burden alone.

As soon as he had the thought, he squashed it.

The back door slid open and their mother stuck her head out. "Michael?"

Chris had flung the ball hard, so Michael didn't look over. "Yeah?"

"Can you come in here for a moment?"

She was using her Serious Voice, and since she was pretty laid-back, it made Michael look over. "What's up?"

"Your father and I want to talk to you."

Five minutes later, Michael was fuming at the kitchen table. He wanted to put a fist right through the wood surface. "But I didn't *do* anything. I didn't even know she worked there."

His father sat across the table, his expression implacable. "It doesn't matter. You should have left. You know we're in a precarious position here—"

"That's not my fault!" Michael shoved his chair back from the table and half stood. "I didn't want this stupid deal to begin with—"

"Keep your voice down." Dad looked ready to come across the table himself. "I'm not having this argument with you again. This deal sets a precedent for your brothers. We have a family to consider—"

"You think I don't *know* that?" God, didn't his parents have any idea what his life was like? Couldn't they see just how much he gave up, just because of their agreement?

His mother reached out and put a hand over his. Her voice was gentle, her eyes compassionate—a direct contradiction to his father's. "We're not angry with you."

Michael jerked his hand away. His breathing felt too quick. Had Emily said he'd done something? Knowing that family, she'd probably said he stole her five dollars.

One place. That's all he wanted. One place to call his own, to do something that had nothing to do with elements or deals. One place where he could forget all this.

And now it was gone.

His throat felt tight. "I hate this."

"I don't care if you hate it." His father waited until Michael looked back at him. "You're not to go near that family again. Do you understand me?"

"Me! What about them?" He was almost shouting now, and he didn't care. "You know what Tyler did to—"

"*Not again.* If you see them, you go somewhere else."

Michael gritted his teeth and looked at the back door just so he wouldn't have to look at his parents. "I want to leave."

His father made a disgusted noise. "We're not talking about this again. If we move to a new community, there's no guarantee we could keep your abilities hidden—"

"Not all of us," Michael snapped. He pointed to his chest. "Just *me*."

"Go ahead," said his father, his tone equally sharp. "They'd report you before dark. Rogue Elemental on the run? You'd be lucky to make it 'til sunrise."

"John," said his mother. "That's enough."

"He's bluffing."

Michael leaned down and put his hands against the table. "Try me."

His father stared back. "This isn't a game."

"Trust me. I'm not having any fun."

His father's voice lowered and lost some of the anger. "I'm not kidding, Michael. Running away from this won't work. It's a death wish."

Michael flung his chair in against the table. "Maybe I should just take my chances."

He stormed across the kitchen, sure his father was going to call him back, to lecture more, to issue ultimatums and threats until Michael caved and promised to try harder.

How do you try harder at something that consumes every waking thought?

But his father didn't say anything. Michael kept going.

Only to find his three brothers waiting, wide-eyed, just outside the kitchen doorway, their expressions some mix of betrayal and anger and confusion.

Great.

"You're leaving?" said Nick.

"Look. Guys . . ." Michael sighed and ran a hand through his hair. "I didn't mean right this second—"

"So you are," said Chris. "You're leaving."

Gabriel had backed up against the wall, and his arms were folded across his chest. "What's going to happen to the rest of us?"

"Are they going to kill you?" said Chris, his voice hollow.

"Tyler won't stop," said Nick. "Just because you're gone, the rest of them will still—"

"Boys."

Michael felt their mother come up behind him, felt her slim hand on his shoulder. "No one is leaving," she said. "People say things in anger all the time. Michael didn't mean it."

Three sets of eyes locked on his.

"Tell them," she said.

Michael looked at his three brothers. He could read the new emotion there: desperation. They wanted him to deny it.

He wanted to.

He just didn't want to lie.

So he shrugged off his mother's hand and went for his bedroom.

And he didn't come out all night.

CHAPTER 3

Emily stared at the door to the shop. Sweat was trickling down her back despite the blasting air-conditioning.

I come on Wednesdays and Fridays.

Maybe he wouldn't show. Her father sure hadn't been subtle when he'd called the Merricks. But maybe that would work against her. Just like the other day. Michael had seemed just as surprised to see her—and then she'd gone and provoked him. Sure, her parents had a deal with his, but it felt flimsy. Kind of like those treaties with countries who kept nuclear warheads.

We promise not to use them unless you piss us off.

Maybe she should keep a putter on the counter.

Maybe she shouldn't have told her parents.

But at least they hadn't made her quit.

The clock struck four, the time he'd shown up on Wednesday. No Michael.

At four-thirty, the door swung open, but it was only a young mother with children coming to use the putt-putt course.

She had to do something to settle her nerves. She plugged her iPod into the sound system and scrolled through for her favorite musical.

The hands of the clock were creeping toward five, when her shift ended. Maybe her father's phone call had worked. Besides, this wasn't the only place around town with batting cages.

But then the doorknob creaked.

Her hand closed around the handle of a putter. If she screamed, would the woman with the preschoolers hear her?

The door swung open. Michael stood there.

But he didn't come through the doorway. Just like the other day, she watched him sweep the corners with his eyes.

What was he *looking* for?

His gaze settled on the putter on the glass counter, then lifted to meet hers. "I was kind of kidding about you trying to kill me every time."

She flushed and slid it into the holder.

He came all the way into the shop and put a five-dollar bill on the counter. "Can I get five tokens, or do you need to check with Daddy first?"

Her blush deepened. For some insane reason, she felt like she should apologize—when he was the one who should be avoiding her.

She fished the tokens from the drawer and slapped them onto the glass counter. She mustered the courage to meet his eyes, to let him know she wouldn't let him screw with her. She tried to make her voice hard—and it ended up making her sound like a bitch. "Is that all?"

His eyes flashed with derision. "So brave."

What a jerk. Her eyes narrowed. "I'm not the one tempting fate by coming here."

He shoved the tokens into his pocket, and for the first time, he sounded resigned instead of antagonistic. "Aren't you?"

Then he was through the door, and she was left there with the music in the air.

Emily almost went after him.

Are you crazy?

She didn't understand how, with everything he was, he could stand there and make *her* feel like the bad guy. Of course she'd told her parents—he should be counting his lucky stars that her father hadn't driven over there.

But even that thought made her blush. She was damn near eighteen years old.

He was right—she had gone crying to her parents.

She glanced at the clock. Her shift ended in four minutes.

At the stroke of five, she shoved through the back door of the office, stepping into the dense humidity. The air slid against her skin and welcomed her into the sunshine.

The batting cages were down the hill and beyond the putt-putt course. She could hear the crack of the bat from here, and once she passed the mini-golf windmill, she saw Michael in the fastball cage.

She stopped before he could notice her. A red tee shirt clung to his shoulders, reminding her of those matadors who swung a red cape to taunt a bull to fight to the death.

Reckless. That's what this was.

Michael swung the bat, sending the ball into the nets. Even from here, Emily felt the speed of the ball flying through the air, knew exactly how much force it would take to make it change course.

She remembered the strength in his grip when he'd caught the golf club.

Just when she'd convinced herself to turn back, he glanced over his shoulder and saw her.

She wondered if the earth had told him she was standing there—and wondered if that counted as using his powers. Was it really any different from her sensing the trajectory of the ball ten seconds ago?

He turned around long enough to hit the next ball, then glanced back again. "What, do I get a running start?"

"What are you talking about?"

"Didn't you call out the cavalry?" He turned back without waiting for an answer.

"No." Her cheeks felt hot. "I didn't."

Another ball came flying, and Michael swung hard. The impact resonated like a gunshot.

She'd never been into sports, but hitting something with that much force—it looked amazingly cathartic.

"Look," she said. "I need this job. It's important."

He didn't turn. "So?"

"My father is going to make me quit if he finds out you came back."

Another ball, but this one glanced off his bat and went wide. Michael swore and swiped a forearm across his forehead. "I don't see why that's my problem."

A threat sat on the tip of her tongue, but she couldn't say it. She moved closer, glad for the chain link between them. "Please. I'm just trying to talk to you."

He didn't say anything, just waited for the next ball and swung.

This was a mistake. She shouldn't be out here anyway. What did she expect, that he'd leave after she asked nicely? What if someone drove by and saw her talking to him?

"Forget it." Her feet slammed the packed earth as she walked away.

Another ball. The air moved with his swing. *Crack*.

But then she heard his voice from behind her. "Wait."

Emily stopped halfway to the office, but she didn't turn around.

"*My* father," Michael called, "said he'd take my keys for the rest of the summer if he caught me coming back here."

Crack.

She came back to the fence. "Really?"

"Yeah. Really." He ducked his head to wipe his forehead on his sleeve.

"But you came back anyway."

The pitching machine died, and Michael finally turned, stepping up to the fence. "So did you."

She'd never stood this close to him before, to where she could see the flecks of gold in his brown eyes, could count each individual strand of hair that the sun had lightened. He still smelled like summer, cut grass and sunscreen with a hint of something woodsy.

The chain-link fence between them somehow made this more intimate instead of less.

Don't be stupid. Even serial killers can be hot.

She had to clear her throat and force her eyes away. "Like I said. I need this job."

He gave a somewhat humorless laugh and looked past her, at the parking lot. "I won't tell if you won't."

His voice was vaguely mocking. That was sarcasm, not a real offer.

But she kept thinking about the weeks she'd spent looking for employment. She kept thinking of the train ticket to New York City—that would cost a week's pay, to say nothing of rent and expenses once she got there.

So she swallowed. "Okay. You've got a deal."

A deal. Michael snorted. He'd let his guard down for thirty seconds, and it was a mistake.

"You're crazy," he said.

"No," she said. "I'm serious. You can play with the batting cages, and I can—"

"I can *play* with the batting cages?" he said, incredulous. "Just what the hell do you think I'm doing here?"

She looked taken aback. "I mean—you are *playing*—"

"Forget it." Michael grabbed for the latch on the gate. He still had four tokens left, but they'd keep until next Wednesday. What had he been thinking, talking to her like she was just some ordinary girl?

It was the *please* that got him. He couldn't remember the last time any of them had said *please* about anything.

Really, he couldn't remember the last time any of them had talked to him civilly.

Michael was halfway to the parking lot when he realized she was following him.

He stopped short and turned to face her. "Damn it, *what?* You got what you wanted, okay? I'm leaving."

She drew back, her hands up, as if he'd drawn a gun or something. "That's not . . . I wasn't . . . that's not what I want."

"Oh yeah? Then why'd you cry to your father about me?"

Her cheeks were faintly pink, her breathing rapid. The blond hair and fair complexion made her brother look like a freak, but it suited her. He'd say she looked like a china doll, but then she'd swung a putter at his head on Wednesday. A contradiction in terms: strong and fragile, all at the same time. Like she might cry, but she'd slug him first.

It made him want to apologize.

To *her,* of all people! He turned and started walking again.

Loose rocks ground against the pavement as she jogged to catch up to him.

Michael whirled before she could say anything. "I don't know what you're playing, but it's not going to work. You think you can provoke me into losing control? You think I'm going to give you a reason to call the Guides? This was *my* place, get it? *Mine*. It's a batting cage. I'm not hurting anyone." He took a step closer to her. "So just *leave me the hell alone.*"

And with that, the pavement cracked and split between them.

Emily jumped back, but Michael caught it before his power caused too much damage. Just a twelve-foot crack in the parking lot, only an inch wide. Anything could have caused it, really. Rain. Weeds. Anything.

But Michael knew he'd done it. Worse, *she* knew he'd done it.

She was staring at him now, wide-eyed, her breathing quicker than before.

Run.

Pride wouldn't let him do that. But he turned on his heel and made for the truck, and it took every ounce of self-control to keep from tearing out of the parking lot.

CHAPTER 4

Emily was pushing her dinner around her plate again.

Tyler was texting again.

Her parents were bickering again.

She kept thinking of Michael in the batting cage, the fury that carried through every swing. The conviction in his voice as he'd confronted her in the parking lot.

I'm not hurting anyone.

And then that twelve-foot crack had split the pavement.

But worse, she kept thinking of the color of his eyes in the sunlight. The moment of intimacy when all that stood between them was a few links of steel.

In a way, he reminded her of wildcats at the zoo. Mountain lions, maybe, or panthers. All sleek and dangerous, but so beautiful you'd reach out and touch if you could.

"Emily?"

She snapped her head up. Her father was staring at her, and it sounded like he'd called her name more than once. "I'm sorry. What?"

"I asked if you had any more trouble at the sports complex."

Here was her chance. She could tell them what Michael had done. Her father would call the Guides, and they'd eradicate the problem.

But she'd provoked him.

This was my place. Mine.

If she'd poked a mountain lion with a stick and it bit her hand off, would that be her fault or the lion's? Guilt had a hold of her gut and refused to let go. She speared a few noodles with her fork so she wouldn't have to look at her father. "No. No trouble."

"Good," said Tyler, without looking up from his phone. "Seth and I were going to stake the place out if he kept pulling that shit."

"Seth!" snapped their mother.

"He's got a point," said her father. "Josh Drake and I talked about doing the same thing."

"A stakeout," said Emily. "Really."

Her father's eyes were like ice. "It's for your safety. I don't like you going back there until this is resolved."

She glared back at him. "I think you resolved it with your phone call."

He didn't back down from her tone. "It won't be *resolved* until that boy is dead."

Emily's fork scraped across the plate. "So your plan is . . . what? To sit outside the office and wait for him to show up and use his powers?"

"There are ways to make him break the deal."

At that, Tyler looked up. He met their father's eyes across the table.

And smiled.

Michael spent Friday night in his room, lying on his bed, staring at the ceiling.

Waiting.

When Emily reported him, how long would it take for the Guides to come after him? Would they kill him right away, or would they take him somewhere else?

Michael hoped they'd take him somewhere else. He kept thinking of his brothers, how every time they looked at him now, he knew they were just waiting for him to drop some bomb about running away.

That was nothing compared to watching an execution.

A soft knock rapped at his door just after nine. Had to be his mother; no one else in the house would knock softly.

He wanted to pretend to be asleep, but no way would she buy it this early.

"Yeah?" he called.

She cracked the door and leaned in. "Sure you're not hungry?"

He was, but he couldn't sit in the kitchen, look his parents in the eye, and pretend everything was fine. Even now, he couldn't face his mother. Not knowing what he'd done.

He shook his head and kept his eyes on the ceiling.

"Well"—she eased into the room—"I made you a little something, just in case." A plate slid onto his bedside table.

He glanced over and immediately felt like an ass. She'd made him a turkey sandwich. A good one, too, with extra slices of lunch meat and cheese piled high with tomato and lettuce. He could smell the deli mustard. Three oatmeal-raisin cookies sat on the plate as well.

She had to have made them just for him. No one else in the house liked oatmeal-raisin.

His throat felt tight. God, he'd been so stupid.

Maybe he should run now, before he brought them all down with him. He should have run last night.

It took him a second to find his voice. He still couldn't look her in the eye. "Thanks."

"Can I sit down?"

He nodded and shifted until he was sitting up against the wall. She sat beside his knees, and the side of the bed barely dented with her weight. He remembered being young, before his brothers had come along, how she'd sit with him in the dark at bedtime and ask about his day. That time grew shorter when she had twins to take care of—and shorter still when Chris arrived—but she hadn't stopped until *he'd* outgrown it. It always made him feel special.

Now he knew just how much being *special* sucked.

He couldn't even remember the last time she'd been in here.

He picked up the sandwich and took a bite, just to avoid the need to say anything.

It didn't stop her from talking, though. "Do you want to tell me what happened today?"

He almost choked on the bread. "Nothing."

"You don't hole up in your room for nothing."

"I'm just tired."

She was quiet for a moment. "I know you think you're alone, Michael, but you're not. Your father and I love you. Your brothers love you—"

He snorted. "Don't be so sure about that. I caught the twins trying to write on my face with a Sharpie at three a.m. the other day."

She smiled, but her eyes were still serious. "I'm just trying to tell you we're here for you. No matter what."

"I know, Mom."

She touched his face. "You sure?"

He nodded. He was sure—and that was the problem. They shouldn't *have* to be here for him. The thought of his family getting caught in the cross fire for something he'd done, for something he *was* . . . Michael almost couldn't take it.

And that was the only reason he was here instead of running. When Emily reported him, when the Guides came for him, he was ready to surrender.

As long as they left his family alone.

CHAPTER 5

By Monday afternoon, Emily had completely reorganized the designer golf balls in the display case, making a rather impressive tower of alternating colors, if she did say so herself. She was blasting the *Wicked* sound track today, louder than usual so she could belt along with Idina Menzel.

This kind of heat always made business slow, but today was ridiculous. Maybe people were finally done with the weather, and everyone had gone to the beach.

When "Defying Gravity" came on, she cranked it a few notches higher, then stepped out onto the floor to rearrange the rack of golf shirts by size and style.

Just as she got to the chorus, a man cleared his throat behind her.

Emily jumped and shrieked and nearly knocked all the shirts off the rack. Her face went from cool to blazing in half a second.

She steadied the rack and called over her shoulder, loudly enough to be heard over the music. "I'm so sorry—"

Then she stopped short. Michael Merrick stood there.

She stared at him, unable to move.

He made a circular motion with his hand. "Could you turn this down?"

"Oh . . . sure." She dashed for the stereo behind the counter and yanked her iPod cord free. The music died instantly.

When she straightened, Michael was at the counter. She could barely catch her breath.

"Don't get me wrong," he said flatly. "I like Broadway musicals as much as the next guy."

Her cheeks felt hotter—if that was possible. "Sorry. It's been dead. I mean . . ." She hesitated. "You need tokens?"

"I have some from the other day."

"Oh. Okay."

But he was still standing there, staring down at her. It took some effort to meet his eyes, but at least she could read the emotion there: surprise, and intrigue, and confusion.

"About Friday," he said.

She wet her lips. "Friday?"

"I stayed up all night." A self-deprecating shrug. "Most of the weekend, really."

She frowned. "Okay . . . ?"

"I was waiting." He rested his forearms against the glass, and his voice dropped a notch. "I thought you'd turn me in."

"For the parking lot?" She shrugged and picked at the disclaimers taped to the glass counter. "It's not a big deal—"

"It is to me."

Emily stopped fidgeting and looked at him.

"So," he said, his voice softer and almost gentle, "thanks."

She had no idea what to say to that.

And he didn't wait. He picked up his bat and turned for the back door to the shop, stepping out into the humidity without a backwards glance.

Emily cheated the time clock out of fifteen minutes and strode down the hill to the batting cages. Michael was still there, in a royal blue tee shirt today, using the fastest machine they had.

She didn't even hesitate this time, just walked up to the cage and hooked her fingers through the fence.

"It's Monday," she said.

He didn't look. "No kidding."

Crack.

"You said you only come on Wednesdays and Fridays."

He glanced over his shoulder. "Maybe I didn't want to miss the show."

His voice wasn't quite friendly—but it sure wasn't hostile. She blushed again and wished her skin weren't so fair. Maybe he'd attribute it to the heat.

Then he turned back to swing for the next ball.

There was something addictive about the sound of the machine, the regular crack of the bat, the motion of his body as he swung to hit.

Before she knew it, four pitches had gone by, and she realized she looked like a freak stalker.

She had to say something. "That looks so . . . therapeutic."

"Want a turn?"

"What—No!" God, she'd been standing here staring. She couldn't even remember why she'd come down to the batting cage. "Sorry. I'll just . . . I'll . . ."

"I'm sorry about Friday." Michael fed the machine a new token. "Not just for the parking lot." He tossed a glance over his shoulder. "For being a dick."

She should turn and walk away. She didn't want to. "It's all right."

He paused to swing. The crack of the bat stole her breath.

Another glance. He tapped the bat against the dirt. "Sure you don't want a turn?"

Emily shook her head quickly. "I've never played baseball. I'm not sure the fast-pitch machine is the best place to start."

He snorted. A laugh? She couldn't tell. She felt like they'd completely ventured off the map of what felt sure and certain.

Then he said, "So why do you need this job so badly?"

"I want to move to New York City."

The words were out before she could stop them. But he'd surprised her with his gratitude, followed by this apology. And for some reason, it was easier to have a conversation while his back was turned and his attention was focused elsewhere.

"New York?" *Crack*. The ball strained at the nets before dropping to the earth.

She swallowed. "Yeah. I have a friend who graduated two years ago who's an understudy on Broadway. She says she'll help me get a job."

"You want to be on Broadway?" The surprise in his voice was almost tangible.

She bristled, ready for the mockery she'd gotten from her father when she'd mentioned this last year. There was a reason she made the appropriate noises about researching colleges but kept her true plans a secret. "Yeah, so?"

He didn't say anything, the bat poised over his shoulder.

"I mean, it's not like a guarantee or anything," she said, folding her arms across her chest. "I'll probably end up waiting tables and calling my parents to borrow cash after six months."

A ball flew at him. *Crack*.

"Nah. I could see it. You kept up with that *Wicked* song."

Her jaw almost hit the ground. "You recognized the music?" And was that a . . . compliment?

He shrugged. "My dad got our mom tickets for her birthday last spring. We all had to go. Some crap about needing more culture."

His dad got tickets to *Wicked* for their mom? She couldn't remember the last time her father had given a present to her mom—much less included her and Tyler in on it.

"I think living in a city would make me stir-crazy," said Michael.

She thought of his parents' landscaping business and wondered if a guy like Michael would actually suffer in a city. "I guess we're not fated to be together, then."

She'd meant for it to come out flippant, full of sarcasm, but the words fell flat and honest. He looked over his shoulder. "I guess not."

The machine buzzed, signaling the last pitch. Michael hit hard, sending the ball into flight before it hit the nets and dropped dead.

She expected him to feed it another token, but he stepped over to the fence and hooked his hand on a link exactly five inches to the left of hers.

Again, he was too close. Her heart kicked. She stared up at him and stopped breathing.

"Want to learn?" he said.

"Learn?" Her voice was squeaking.

He tapped the fence with the end of the bat. "How to hit."

She couldn't. She'd already spent too much time talking to him. This had *danger* written all over it.

But some part of her heart had already told her brain's insistent thoughts to shove it.

Because she was already saying yes.

His brain kept asking him what the hell he was doing, but Michael ignored the doubts and led Emily to the slowest cage. All afternoon, her presence had been little flickers against his skin, not entirely unpleasant. From the moment he'd caught her in the office, blushing and stammering and fighting to turn down her music, he'd been fighting the urge to reach out and touch her, to see if those little flickers were a promise of something more.

She hadn't reported him. That had to mean something.

Right?

Especially now, when she stood with him in the eight-foot-square cage, listening to him talk about things like stance and hand position and letting the ball come to her.

God, he needed to shut up. He felt giddy and nervous and it was a miracle he could even form a coherent sentence. He held out the bat. "Here. Let's just try."

She made no move to take it. "I'm probably going to give myself a concussion."

"Come on. My brother could hit off this machine when he was eight."

She made a face. "Now I feel better." But she took the bat and attempted to hold it the way he'd shown her.

She looked ridiculous and adorable and he tried not to laugh.

Just as quickly, he choked it off.

What was he *thinking*?

Sharp words sat on his tongue, ready to drive her away. He could stop this now. They could go back to being mortal enemies. She'd let one mistake slide. That wasn't the same as helping him. Or even *accepting* him.

She looked over at him, and he was sure she could read the doubts on his face.

Just like he could read the doubts on hers.

Michael jammed his hands into his pockets, feeling his shoulders tighten.

Before he could say anything, she said, "I look like an idiot, don't I?"

He let out a breath. "Nah." Then he paused and almost smiled. "Well. Maybe."

"Tell me what to do so I don't take a ball to the frontal lobe."

So he demonstrated again, and she took the stance again, and when she said she was ready, he fed a token to the machine.

At the first ball, she didn't even try to swing. She flung herself back and almost dropped the bat. "Holy *crap*, that's fast!"

He caught her shoulders before she could plow into him, intending to set her straight, the way he would one of his brothers.

She froze, just for an instant, but it was enough. He yanked his hands down.

She didn't say anything, so he backed away to lean against the chain link, putting clear distance between them. "You want me to go get a putter?" he said. "You have no trouble swinging those."

That earned him a rueful glance over her shoulder.

But then her expression softened. "You can show me." She paused. "It's okay."

He hesitated, just long enough for him to hear the machine revving up for the next pitch. So he stepped forward, caught her shoulders again, and pushed her into place. Then, without thinking about it too carefully, he put his arms over hers, his hands on the bat, and guided her into the swing.

"Don't run from it," he said. "Stand strong."

She got a piece of this one, and you would have thought she'd scored the winning home run at the World Series. Bat in the air, jumping up and down, silly smile on her face.

"I hit it! I hit it!"

It made him smile. This was vastly more satisfying than showing Chris how to hit a curve ball. "Okay, try not to make it a foul ball next time."

She made a face. "Killjoy." She tapped the bat against the ground and got back into position. Like a frigging major league player.

He laughed.

And then he shut up real quick when she threw another glance over her shoulder. "You going to show me again or what?"

CHAPTER 6

Michael crossed the parking lot with a spring in his step. He told himself to knock it off, that one batting lesson didn't mean *anything*.

Especially not with Emily Morgan.

But he kept thinking of the feel of her hands under his, of the way her shoulders fit perfectly within the circle of his arms, of the smell of her skin.

He found himself wondering what other things would feel like. Holding her hand. Touching her hair.

Kissing her?

Stop it. You're an idiot.

But the curve of her neck had been right there. She hadn't flinched from his touch. Really, if you took away the baseball bat, the way he'd been holding her had been pretty damn intimate.

When he inhaled, he could *almost* still smell her.

Stop it!

He'd already told her too much. How baseball let him clear his mind and focus on something not related to his element. How he worried every day would end with a loss of control—like Friday.

How badly he wanted to leave town.

He could have kicked himself for revealing that one.

But then she'd talked about her parents' fighting. How sometimes she didn't care about making it in New York; it was just a new place, a new beginning.

She told him how she was sick of every day being focused on hate.

And for the first time, he let himself start to wonder if this deal *could* work out.

She'd left ten minutes ago, after he'd told her to go so they wouldn't be seen walking out together. He'd killed ten minutes burning through his last token, remembering the feel of her body with every swing he took.

Dad's truck sat alone at the back of the parking lot, dark in the shade of an old elm tree. Michael had the keys in his hand and a bemused smile he couldn't get off his face.

He didn't even hear the attackers until his head was slamming into the concrete.

They were all on him at once. He couldn't even get a handle on how many guys had tackled him. One had come from the bed of the truck. They had the chain Dad kept back there to tie down loose loads, and they had it against his throat, pinning him to the parking lot. Someone else trapped an arm, kneeling on his wrist, grinding his skin into the pavement.

And then, just as he registered the blond hair, someone punched him in the face. A good, solid punch, with power behind it.

He saw stars for a second, long enough for them to pin his other arm. He struggled, but he had no leverage.

"Hey, asshole."

Tyler. He'd swung the first punch—and he did it again.

Michael coughed against the chain on his throat. He gritted his teeth. He could pull power from the earth and throw them off, but he doubted they'd give him a free pass like Emily had.

Keep it together.

God, he'd been stupid. Every time he came here, he checked the store, and every time he left, he checked the truck. Every time, ready for an ambush.

Until today.

Tyler hit him again. Michael tasted blood.

Keep. It. Together.

"Do it," said Tyler. "You know you want to."

Someone kicked him in the side, and Michael redoubled his struggles. They were too heavy. He couldn't get loose.

They kicked him again.

Power rushed through the ground, coming to his aid without his asking. He forced it back. He could take a few punches.

Tyler laughed and spit in his face. "Good thing Emily told us where to find you. I didn't think we'd have this much fun all summer."

Michael froze. Tonight at the batting cages—had she been *stalling* him?

You going to show me again or what?

He coughed. "Go to hell, Tyler."

"Funny you should mention hell." Tyler held up a butane lighter. "Since I brought the fire."

Then he clicked the trigger. Flame burst from the end.

Michael tried to recoil. He only succeeded in slamming his head against the concrete again. He was straining against the chain so hard that he almost couldn't breathe.

Flame lit Tyler's features. He brought the lighter close to Michael's face, until the heat was painful.

Michael strained away. He had no idea if Tyler would really burn him, but flame against his skin would definitely push his control past the brink.

"Do it," said Tyler. He leaned closer, until Michael wanted to clench his eyes shut. *"Do it."*

Michael prayed for another customer to arrive. But he knew how dead this place was.

Tyler put the flame against the chain. It seared right through the metal. "First we're going to burn you, and then we're going to burn your little brothers."

The pavement cracked and split. Michael surged against their hands. He slammed someone into the concrete before he could stop himself. The chain went flying.

But then he heard someone yelling. The guys. They were scattering, stumbling away from him, tripping on the loose pavement.

No, not stumbling away from him. Away from the girl with the steel bar in her hands.

Emily, with a putter.

"Dad is going to *kill* you," said Tyler. "What the hell are you doing?"

"Michael," she called. "Can you drive?"

It took Michael a second to get it together, but then he realized his keys were on the pavement, where he'd dropped them by the door. His joints didn't want to work, but he was able to get the keys into his palm. "Yeah." Stars still danced in his vision. "I think."

And then he *must* have been losing time, because he was starting the ignition of the truck, and Emily was in the passenger seat beside him.

He took a deep breath, and it seemed they were pulling onto Mountain Road, leaving the sports center behind.

He rubbed at his eye, surprised when his hand came away with blood. "I should have said no," he said.

She gave him a concerned glance. "What?"

He winced, and suddenly there were two roads in front of him. "I shouldn't be driving."

She unclicked her seat belt and knelt up on the passenger seat, leaning across to brace a hand on his shoulder.

It was almost enough to make him hit the guardrail. "What are you doing?"

"Keep your eyes on the road."

"Did you set me up?"

"Shhh. Drive." She leaned in close and blew on his neck.

No, *that* was almost enough to make him hit the guardrail. He pushed her away. "Stop. Tell me the truth. Did you—"

"No. I didn't. Let me help you." She shoved his hand out of the way and knelt up again.

Her breath on his skin felt awful and amazing at the same time. He fought not to make a sound.

"I'm sorry," she whispered. "I wish I had more power."

"No," he ground out. "You don't."

"I saw their car," she said. "Around the corner. Tyler and my dad have been talking about staking out the sports center all week—"

"Thanks for the heads-up."

"I never thought they'd really do it."

He gave a humorless laugh. "Of course not."

She fell silent for a while, and all he heard was her breath whispering along his skin. Too much had happened in a short span of time. Part of him wanted to push her away again, but a bigger part wanted to pull her closer and beg her to say she was on his side, that she'd had no part in this.

Finally, he couldn't take the silence anymore, and he needed a destination. He couldn't go home, not with her in the truck, and he sure as hell wasn't driving to her house. "Where am I driving?"

"Go to the quarry."

His head had cleared enough for him to look away from the road. "The quarry?"

"There's lots of exposed rock. That'll help you, right?"

"Yeah, but there will be other people there." Given this heat, probably half the senior class would have snuck in to go swimming.

"Don't worry. I know a hidden path down to the water. We can stay out of sight."

"Why are you helping me?"

She didn't say anything for a long moment. When she spoke, her voice was soft. "For years, I've been hearing how dangerous you are. How we shouldn't have made this deal, because you're out of control, that you're mean, that you'll hurt us if we get close to you."

Michael snorted. "I've been hearing the same thing."

"But you're not! All week, you've been nothing but nice—"

"I wouldn't go that far."

"—when I keep hearing my father talk about how they should

just take care of the problem themselves. And then Tyler does this . . . this horrible thing, when you didn't even provoke it. I don't think you're dangerous at all."

Michael didn't say anything. They came to the turnoff for the one-lane road that ran behind the quarry, and he hit the turn signal.

"Even tonight," she said. "You didn't kill them, and I know you could have. On Friday, you could have hurt me, and you didn't. I've heard the way you talk about your brothers. I know you care about your family. I told you already—I'm sick of living with all this *hate*. But I've been blaming you, when I should have been blaming *them*."

He pulled the truck onto the gravel shoulder when there was space and killed the engine.

Suddenly, the car was only full of the sound of their breathing.

"Please," she said. "Say something."

He looked over at her. "I wanted to kill them."

Her breath hitched, but he wasn't done.

"All of them," he said. "Including your brother."

"But you didn't."

He held her eyes. "If he'd kept up with that lighter, I might have."

She swallowed, but nodded.

She looked so tiny in the front seat of his father's work truck. Michael couldn't believe she'd faced down her brother and his friends with a putter. "Are you still afraid of me?"

She shook her head.

"Good." And he leaned over and kissed her.

CHAPTER 7

Emily sat with Michael near the water's edge, at the far side of the quarry, hidden among the clumps of trees. He'd been right: Despite the creeping darkness, a dozen kids were swimming at the other side, where the cliffs weren't as steep and the depths were free of debris.

Here, though, the trees were silent and the water still, and it was easy to pretend the mess they'd left had never happened.

Especially with Michael's fingers wound through hers, the taste of him still on her lips.

"Are you still hurting?" she said.

"I'm all right." He turned to look at her, and the fading sunlight caught his eyes. "I was worried they'd follow us."

Emily shook her head. "I don't think so. I slashed Tyler's tires."

Michael's eyes widened, and then he laughed. "You're definitely not predictable." A pause. "In a lot of ways."

"It took me a minute, or I'd have been back sooner." She reached up to touch his chin, where the skin was darker and a bit blistered. "I'm sorry Tyler did this."

He caught her hand and brushed a kiss across her knuckles. "He's *definitely* predictable."

She reveled in the feel of his breath against her skin. Every time he touched her, his gentleness took her by surprise.

"Will you tell me what really happened last week?" she asked. "With Tyler?"

Michael looked back out at the water. "It's not important."

"It is to me."

He sighed. "The twins were cutting through the woods to walk home. Tyler and Seth roughed them up."

She frowned. "So you went after Tyler to get back at him?"

"I never *went after* Tyler." His sudden fury was palpable. "Believe me, I'd leave you all alone if—" He stopped short. "Forget it."

"Tell me."

"In the woods, Nick got away. He ran all the way home and got me. By the time we made it back to them, they'd ganged up on Gabriel. Tyler and Seth ran when I got there."

Emily frowned. "But Tyler had a black eye—"

"Yeah. You know who gave it to him? Gabriel." He shook his head. "Of course he'd say it was me. Can't be running around telling people he got decked by a twelve-year-old."

She wasn't surprised to hear her brother was a liar *and* a bully. "I'm sorry."

"You didn't start this fight, Emily." He looked down at their joined hands. "Even this . . . it won't work."

But he didn't let go.

"We could try," she whispered.

He stared back at her. "Emily . . ."

"We could stand up to them. I could tell the others about you, that you're not—"

"Wait. Shhh." He put a hand to her lips, his attention focused up the hill.

She whispered around his hand. "What?"

His eyes snapped back to hers. "They did follow us. They must have had another car. Is there a different way back up the hill?"

Then she heard branches breaking, boys calling to each other in the darkness. Fear punched her in the stomach, hard.

Michael squeezed her hand. "Come on. Is there another way?"

She shook her head quickly. "No—we beat down this path last summer."

"We know you're down there!" Tyler's voice. "We saw the truck."

She could almost feel his presence through the air—he was close.

"Through the water," said Michael. "We can swim across the quarry."

"You go," she said. "I'll stall them—"

He swore. "You are out of your mind. I'm not leaving you to face them." Then, before she could answer, he was dragging her down the hill, to the edge of the rocks, until the water was glittering below them.

"So we run?" she said.

"Yes. For now." He glanced back at the darkened woods. "The underbrush will slow them down."

"When we get to the other side—" she started.

"We'll figure it out."

"Together," she said.

He nodded. "Together."

Then he took her hand, and they jumped into the water below.

CHAPTER 1

Gabriel Merrick stared at the dead leaf in his palm and willed it to burn.

It refused.

He had a lighter in his pocket, but that always felt like cheating. Clouds blocked the morning sunlight; no help there. He *should* be able to call flame to something this dry. The damn thing had been stuck in the corner of his window screen, had probably been there since last winter. But the leaf only seemed interested in flaking onto his Trigonometry textbook.

He was seriously ready to take the lighter to *that*.

A knock sounded on his bedroom wall.

"Black," he called. Nicky always slept later, always knocked on his wall to ask what color he was wearing. If he didn't, they ended up dressing alike.

Gabriel looked back at the leaf—and it was just that, a dead leaf. No hint of power. Behind the drywall, electricity sang to him. In the lamp on his desk, he could sense the burning filament. Even the weak threads of sunlight that managed to burn through the clouds left some trace of his element. If the power was there, Gabriel could speak to it, ask it to bend to his will.

If the power wasn't, he had nothing.

His door swung open. Nick stood there in a green hoodie and a pair of gray track pants. A girl on the cheer squad had once asked Gabriel if having a twin was like looking in a mirror all the time. He'd asked her if being a cheerleader was like being an idiot all the time—but really, it was a good question. He and Nick shared the same dark hair, the same blue eyes, the same few freckles across their cheekbones.

Right now, Nick leaned on a crutch, a walking cast peeking from the hem of the pants, evidence of the only thing they didn't share: a broken leg.

Gabriel glanced away from that. "Hey."

"What are you doing?"

Gabriel flicked the leaf in the wastebasket beneath his desk. "Nothing. You ready for school?"

"Is that your Trig book?"

"Yeah. For a minute, I thought I'd told you the wrong assignment."

A complete and total lie. Gabriel always attempted his math homework—and then he handed it over for Nick to do it *right*. Math had turned into a foreign language somewhere around fifth grade. Then, Gabriel had struggled through, managing Cs when his twin brought home As. But after their parents died when the twins were in seventh grade, he'd come close to failing. Nick started covering for him, and he'd been doing it ever since.

Not like it was a big challenge. Math came to Nick like breathing. He was in second-year Calculus, earning college credit. Gabriel was stuck in Trigonometry with juniors.

He was pretty frigging sick of it.

Gabriel flipped the book closed and shoved it into his backpack. His eyes fell on that walking cast again. Nick had cut the seam of his pants to make them fit. "You're not going to make me carry your crap all day, are you?"

His voice came out sharp, nowhere near the light ribbing he'd intended.

Nick took it in stride, as usual. "Not if you're going to cry about it." He turned for the steps, his voice rising to a mocking falsetto. "I'm the school sports hero, but I can't possibly carry a few extra books—"

"Keep it up," Gabriel called, slinging the backpack over his shoulder to follow his brother. "I'll push you down the stairs."

But he hesitated in the doorway, listening to Nick's hitching steps as he descended the staircase, the creak of the banister as it supported his weight.

Gabriel knew he should help. Christ, he should probably be taking the place of that crutch. That's what *Nick* would do for *him*.

But he couldn't force himself through the doorway.

That broken leg was his fault. Gabriel hadn't been strong enough to protect his brother from the Guide that night. He'd let Nick call storms that were too strong, begged him for more power. The fall had practically shattered his leg—if they weren't full Elementals, he probably would have needed surgery.

Even then, Gabriel couldn't keep him safe. The Guide had kidnapped Nick, held him prisoner.

Nick didn't seem to mind. He picked up the slack, just like always. *Life's good, move on, no use complaining.*

Just like with math, Nick was used to his twin being a failure.

Gabriel pulled onto Becca Chandler's street and glanced in the rearview at his younger brother. Chris was chewing on his thumbnail, leaning against the window.

"Nervous?" said Gabriel.

Chris looked away from the window and glared at him. "No."

Nick turned in his seat. "Make sure you open the door for her. Girls eat that crap up."

"Nah," said Gabriel. "Play it cool. Make her work for it—"

"For god's sake," Chris snapped. "She just broke up with Hunter, like, *yesterday,* so it's not like that. Okay?"

Jesus. Someone was worked up. Gabriel glanced back again. "But she asked you for a ride."

Chris looked back out the window. "I offered."

Nick turned his head to look at his twin. "Very nervous," he whispered.

Gabriel smiled and turned into Becca's driveway. "Very."

"Would you two *shut up?*"

Becca was waiting on the front steps, her arms around her knees and her hands drawn up into the sleeves of a fleece pullover, her dark hair hanging long and shining down her back.

"She looks upset," said Nick.

She did, her eyes dark and shadowed, her shoulders hunched. Or maybe she was just cold. Gabriel wasn't one for figuring out emotion.

Her face brightened when she saw them, and she sprinted for the car almost before Chris had time to jump out and hold the door for her.

She stopped short in front of him, spots of pink on her cheeks. "Hey," she said, tucking her hair behind her ear.

"Hey," Chris said back, his voice soft and low.

Then they just stood there breathing at each other.

Gabriel hit the horn.

They jumped apart—but Chris punched him in the shoulder when he climbed back into the car.

Becca ignored him and buckled her seat belt. "I'm glad you're all here."

Her voice was full of anxiety. So Nick had been right.

Chris shifted to look at her. "You all right?"

She shook her head. "My dad just called. He wants to see me. Tonight."

No one said anything for a moment, leaving her words floating out there in the warm confines of the car.

Her dad was an Elemental Guide, sent to kill the brothers because of the powers they'd grown into. He'd been the one to kidnap Nick and Chris after Homecoming, and he'd almost succeeded in destroying them all—including Becca.

When they escaped and didn't hear anything for two days, they'd all started to think he'd run off again, the way he had when Becca was eleven.

Chris took a breath, and his voice was careful. "Do you want to meet him?"

Gabriel glanced at her in the rearview mirror. She was practically hunched against the door, staring out the window. "I want him to get the hell *out of here*."

Chris was still watching her. "He is your father." He paused. "You sure?"

"He might have made a 'contribution,' but that man is *not* my father."

"I want to see him," said Gabriel. His shoulders already felt tight.

She hesitated. "Wait. You'd . . . go with me?"

"Yeah. I owe him a little payback."

"*We,*" said Nick. There was heat in his voice, too.

"Did he say why he wanted to meet?" asked Chris.

"He said he wants to help us. That they'll send another Guide if he doesn't report back that you were . . . um . . ."

"Killed." Gabriel hit the turn signal at the end of her road.

She swallowed. "Yeah. Hey, make a left. We need to pick up Quinn."

Gabriel glanced at her again. He wasn't a big fan of Becca's mouthy best friend, especially when there was so much left to talk about. "Quinn? She can't get a ride from Gutierrez?"

Becca shrugged. "They're having issues. Something about him misunderstanding that they didn't have an *open* relationship."

"Anyone else?" said Gabriel. "Should I pick up Hunter, too?"

Becca faltered and glanced at Chris. "I'm sorry—I should have asked—"

"It's fine," he said, his eyes on his brother. "I'm sure he's not intentionally being a dick."

Gabriel ignored him. "What time tonight? Did he say where?"

She blinked, and it must have taken her a second to come full circle and realize he was back to talking about her father. "Annapolis Mall. Eight o'clock. Make a right at the stop sign. She's down at the end of the block."

"We'll come," said Chris. "Find out what he wants."

"If we let him talk that long," said Gabriel.

VISIT

www.ElementalsBooks.co.uk

FOR MORE INFORMATION
ABOUT BRIGID KEMMERER'S
THE ELEMENTAL SERIES